THE YIELDING

THE YIELDING

Age of Faith: Book Two

TAMARA LEIGH
USA Today Best-Selling Author

ISBN: 194232605X
ISBN 13: 9781942326052

Splitting Harriet, 06/15 (ebook), 2007
(print): RandomHouse/Multnomah
Faking Grace, 2015 (ebook), 2008 (print edition): RandomHouse/Multnomah

Southern Discomfort: A Contemporary Romance Series
Leaving Carolina: **Book One,** 11/15 (ebook),
2009 (print): RandomHouse/Multnomah
Nowhere, Carolina, 2010 (print): RandomHouse/Multnomah
Restless in Carolina, 2011 (print): RandomHouse/Multnomah

OUT-OF-PRINT GENERAL MARKET TITLES
Warrior Bride, 1994: Bantam Books
*Virgin Bride, 1994: Bantam Books
Pagan Bride, 1995: Bantam Books
Saxon Bride, 1995: Bantam Books
Misbegotten, 1996: HarperCollins
Unforgotten, 1997: HarperCollins
Blackheart, 2001: Dorchester Leisure

*Virgin Bride is the sequel to *Warrior Bride*
Pagan Pride and *Saxon Bride* are stand-alone novels

www.tamaraleigh.com

1

Stern Castle, England, February 1157

BY TRICKERY THEY were had.

Beatrix looked from her mother who gripped the missive with trembling hands to her sister who stared at the king's man with trembling mouth.

"Surely there is some mistake," Beatrix's mother protested.

The king's man widened his stance, causing the dog sniffing at his boots to sidle away. "No mistake, Lady Isobel. We are to escort one of your daughters to Broehne Castle upon the barony of Abingdale where she will wed Baron Lavonne."

Past a throat so constricted it hurt, Beatrix dragged a sustaining breath. She knew what this was—King Henry's attempt to end the feuding between the Wulfriths and the Lavonnes. And she knew why. Though the two families had once been allies, the relationship had become strained following the accident that forced the old baron to pass his title and lands into the hands of his inept eldest son, Geoffrey. When Beatrix's oldest brother had defiantly wed Lady Annyn Bretanne, whose betrothal the future King Henry had given to Geoffrey, it had gone from bad to worse. And worse yet when Geoffrey's assault on Annyn resulted in the loss of his own life. Thus, for the past three years, the Wulfrith lands had been plagued with raids and pillagings devised by Geoffrey's embittered father and younger brother as retribution for what they deemed an unjust death. And this was the solution—that the Wulfriths yield up a sister in place of Annyn. How King Henry must gloat to thus repay Garr Wulfrith for his defiance!

The king's man cleared his throat. "'Tis for you to determine which of your daughters will join with Christian Lavonne, my lady." He glanced at Gaenor, dismissed her with a lift of his eyebrows, and settled an appreciative smile on Beatrix.

She curled her hands into fists at his blatant disregard for Gaenor's feelings.

"My youngest has chosen the Church," Lady Isobel said, stepping to the edge of the dais.

The man inclined his head. "Aye, but she has yet to make her profession."

Though Beatrix felt her mother's disquiet deepen, Lady Isobel's voice was deceptively level when next she spoke. "It is decided."

After a long moment, the man sighed and once more looked to the oldest of the sisters. "Then 'tis Lady Gaenor we shall have the privilege of escorting to Broehne Castle."

Guilt flushed Beatrix. True, eldest daughters usually wed first, but she ached for Gaenor who had no say in whether or not she was the sacrifice King Henry demanded of the Wulfriths. And what a sacrifice!

Beatrix's anger deepened at the thought of what Gaenor would endure wed to Geoffrey Lavonne's brother, a man surely as cruel and vindictive as his infirm father.

"We shall avail ourselves of your hospitality this eve," the king's man said, "and depart at first light."

Beatrix could stand it no longer. With a snap of her skirts, she stepped from the dais. "'Twas planned! King Henry summoned my brother to London that our sister might be stolen away and wed to that...miscreant!"

"Beatrix!" her mother hissed.

Years ago, Beatrix would have heeded her—indeed, would not so much as thought to challenge a man—but that was before Lady Annyn won Garr's heart. Since, Beatrix had learned by her sister-in-law's example that women did, indeed, have the right to question wrong.

Imagining what Annyn would do if not that she was laid abed abovestairs, Beatrix halted before the king's man. Too late realizing she should have remained on the dais that had placed her nearer his height, she strained her neck to look up at him. "Is it not true that King Henry planned this, Sir Knight?"

He narrowed his lids, causing the torchlight reflected in his eyes to dim. "I cannot speak to the king's intentions, my lady. I but carry out his orders, and this order is that I deliver one of Baron Wulfrith's sisters to Baron Lavonne for the purpose of marriage."

Beatrix looked to the man's entourage. It was comprised of a dozen men, half of whom were said to belong to Christian Lavonne. As with each time she turned her eyes in their direction, her attention was drawn to a young, fair-haired knight whose gaze bore into hers with unsettling intensity. Though he was pleasing of face, something dark dwelt in his pale eyes.

"We shall require food and drink," the king's man said, "and pallets upon which to pass the eve in your hall."

Lady Isobel nodded. "Of course."

Beatrix swung around. "But, Mother, surely you will not allow—"

"Enough, Daughter! Our guests require hospitality, and we shall accord it as your brother would have us do."

Beatrix drew a deep breath. "As you say." She looked to Gaenor who had fixed her gaze on the rushes strewn before the dais. Feeling her sister's churning and seeing it in the hands she balled in her skirts, Beatrix stepped toward her.

"While I see to our guests' needs," Lady Isobel said, "accompany your sister abovestairs and assist with her packing."

Beatrix would have protested again, but the glimmer in her mother's eyes told that she had a plan. King Henry would soon learn it was no easy feat to steal a daughter from this woman, even though it was by marriage only that she laid claim to the Wulfrith name.

Beatrix ascended the dais and laid a hand on her sister's arm. "Come. There is much to do ere morn."

Gaenor allowed herself to be guided across the hall that, if not for the arrival of the king's men, would now be settled by the castle folk who made their beds here.

As the sisters neared the stairs, Beatrix peered over her shoulder at where her mother directed the servants to erect the trestle tables that had been put away following the evening meal. Praying Lady Isobel's plan did not run aground, Beatrix started to look forward. As she did so, her eyes once more met those of the fair-haired knight.

He smiled—if that crooked, leering twist of the lips could be called such.

So affected was Beatrix by what it told of his impure thoughts that she stumbled on the first stair. If not for her grip on her sister's arm, she would have dropped to her knees. However, Gaenor seemed too deep inside her thoughts to notice the few moments she supported her sister's weight.

Once out of sight of the hall, Beatrix stepped in front of Gaenor. "Do not fear—"

"Do not?" Gaenor stood taller and thrust her shoulders back. "'Tis easily said by one who has naught to fear herself. Look at you—you who are of pleasing face and height and form, you who would be better wed to a man than I. And yet, never will you be chained to a man's whim. Nor his cruelty."

Beatrix was acquainted with Gaenor's feelings about her ungainly height, which had caused several suitors to look elsewhere, but never had she shown such resentment. But then, never had she been forced into marriage with a Lavonne.

Beatrix gently squeezed her sister's arm. "Do not despair. Mother and Annyn will know what to do."

Though Gaenor tensed further as if she might reject the attempt to console her, a moment later her shoulders eased. "Let us pray so."

Aye, pray—at which Beatrix had become proficient these past years since the commencement of her training for the Church. When the abbey that her brother raised five leagues from Stern Castle was complete a year hence, she would go there. And perhaps one day she would be named its abbess as was her mother's desire. *If I am worthy.*

Beatrix leaned forward and touched her forehead to her sister's, possible only because Gaenor stood a step down. "We ought to visit the chapel."

Gaenor's lids narrowed and mouth tightened, evidencing how ill at ease with Church and God she was, but she nodded. "Mother would approve."

Most highly. In fact, if they lingered long enough, Lady Isobel would surely join them there. Yearning to place Gaenor's troubles at the Lord's feet, Beatrix entwined her fingers with her sister's and drew her up the stairs. They entered the candle-lit chapel, traversed the aisle, and knelt side by side before the altar.

Dear Lord, Beatrix beseeched behind steepled hands, *deliver Gaenor from King Henry's plotting and Baron Lavonne's hatred.* She glanced at her sister who stared sightlessly at the altar. *Use me as You will.*

"Sir Durand and Sir Ewen await you in the wood at the barren rock," Lady Isobel said as she drew the mantle's hood over Gaenor's head. "Stay low as you cross the meadow lest the king's men have set a watch."

Gaenor nodded and Isobel looked to her younger daughter who had already pulled her hood over her head to ward off the chill of night that painted their breath upon the air. Though Isobel had argued against Beatrix accompanying her sister to Wulfen Castle where Isobel's second son would shelter her until Garr received word of the king's plans, Beatrix had insisted and Gaenor had pleaded. In the end, Garr's wife, Annyn, had convinced Isobel it was best that Beatrix also flee lest the king's man attempt to deliver her to Christian Lavonne instead. As for Isobel, she would remain at Stern Castle with Annyn who had recently delivered her second child and was slow to recover from birthing so large a son. God willing, the king's men would not dare lay hands on either of them.

"We should go," Beatrix urged, her teeth beginning to chatter.

Lady Isobel stretched to her toes and kissed her oldest daughter's cheek. "Godspeed, my dove," she whispered and turned to Beatrix. However, her youngest child had already stepped through the hidden doorway set in the castle's outer wall.

As Isobel watched her daughters merge with the dark night, all she could think was that she should have called Beatrix back, that she should have pressed her lips to the impetuous one's cheek, that she should have wished her "Godspeed."

2

"WE HAVE PAUSED long enough." Sir Durand rose from the log he had rolled to the stream's bank and offered a hand to his charge.

Shielding her eyes against the brilliance of the newly risen sun, Beatrix tilted her head back. As with each time she looked near upon the knight, she regretted the admiration with which he regarded her. Convent-bound though she was, she was not so unlearned in the ways of men and women to be ignorant of his feelings for her, but she knew it was best not to acknowledge them. After all, the only bridal garments she would ever wear were those reserved for a bride of Christ. Which was just as she wished it.

"My lady?"

She placed her gloved fingers in Sir Durand's and let him draw her to her feet. When he was slow to release her, she pulled free and eased back a step.

Sir Ewen snorted.

Beatrix looked to the mounted knight who grinned as if he enjoyed Sir Durand's fascination with their lord's sister. Mounted beside him was Gaenor, the soft smile hanging about her own mouth transforming her features. Though tall for a woman and somewhat plain of face, she had but to turn up her lips and call her dimples into being to become what she declared she could never be—lovely. Unfortunately, smiling was something she mostly reserved for their three-year-old niece and newborn nephew.

"Mount up," Sir Ewen called.

Pulling her mantle close to ease the chill that seemed to have settled into her bones throughout the night-long ride, Beatrix stepped to where Sir Durand had taken the reins of her brown palfrey. Once more, he touched her hand to assist her into the saddle, and once more Sir Ewen snorted.

Beatrix scowled. "Have you something lodged in your nose, Sir Ewen?"

"Nay, but I believe my friend has something lodged in his eye."

His heart? She looked to Sir Durand and gained a glimpse of the high color that swept his face before he pivoted, strode to his mount, and swung into the saddle.

Feeling for him, Beatrix narrowed her gaze on Sir Ewen. "Do you wish to lead, or shall I?"

He jerked his chin toward the other knight. "Methinks Sir Durand has already determined to do so himself."

True enough, the humiliated knight had set off ahead of Gaenor.

With Sir Durand in the lead, Sir Ewen bringing up the rear, and Gaenor and Beatrix in between, they began the second half of the journey that would see them at Wulfen Castle before nightfall.

To counter the chill buffeting her face and wending the weave of her clothing, Beatrix bent low over her horse, huffed warm breath up her face and down her chest, and silently urged the sun to more quickly temper winter's grip—a difficult task considering the grueling pace with which their mounts parted the air and the spray of frost their hooves loosed from the brittle grass.

After what seemed hours, the sun climbed high enough to return feeling to Beatrix's fingers and toes. Savoring the warmth in the small of her back, she sighed, winced as her cramped muscles resisted their unfolding, and eased herself upright. Ahead, Gaenor and Sir Durand had also straightened in their saddles.

Beatrix glanced over her shoulder, and the half smile Sir Ewen slanted at her confirmed that the hardest part of the journey was past. Though Wulfen Castle still lay many leagues ahead, it was increasingly unlikely any would prevent them from reaching it. This night, Gaenor would be safe within its walls and Christian Lavonne would have to look elsewhere for a bride.

"Thank you, Lord," Beatrix whispered and drew a deep breath that smelled of pine and loam and the leaves of Autumn past. And, doubtless, beyond the din of their ride arose the song of birds that braved England's inhospitable weather and the chitter and chatter of small woodland creatures. Now if only Gaenor would open her own heart to the beauty and benevolence that the Lord——

A shout shook Beatrix out of her musing. Searching for the source, she landed on Sir Durand where he rode at the fore and saw he pointed west.

"Please, nay," she whispered and looked around.

A dozen riders. Though yet distant, one would have to be a fool to believe they were anything other than the predator to the prey.

"To the wood!" Sir Ewen bellowed.

Trading speed for the wood that, blessedly, boasted an abundance of evergreens capable of providing cover, they veered right and slowed only enough to accommodate the trees and undergrowth.

Dear Lord, Beatrix prayed as they passed single file among the trees, *deliver us.*

"My lady!" Sir Ewen warned.

Beatrix opened her eyes in time to duck a low-hanging branch that would have unhorsed her. Resolved to praying with her eyes open, certain God would not fault her, she glanced over her shoulder. Heartened by the sole presence of Sir Ewen, she urged her palfrey after Gaenor and Sir Durand as they increased their speed and veered toward a rise.

Thank you, Lord, for shielding us from our pursuers——

Distant bellows broke through Beatrix's prayer, and she snapped her chin around. Though their pursuers had yet to reappear, it could not be long now.

"Deliver Gaenor, Lord," she whispered as her sister and Sir Durand disappeared over the rise. "I ask it in Your name."

"They are near upon us!" Sir Ewen shouted.

As Beatrix picked out the blur of riders beyond him, a whimper cleared her throat. Given a few moments more, she and Sir Ewen would also have been over the rise and out of sight. Of course, given the speed at which the king's men covered ground and the facility with which they handled their mounts amid the wood—skills Beatrix and Gaenor could not possibly match—it would not have been long before they once more had their prey in sight.

In the next instant, realization landed like a slap, and Beatrix caught her breath. She had become a liability to Gaenor, but that could be undone, providing Sir Ewen followed her lead.

She jerked the reins and turned her palfrey aside. Blessedly, the Wulfrith knight came after her—as did the king's men.

Pressing her mount harder than she had ever done, she fought her fear with the reminder that each thundering hoof beat increased the distance between the king's men and her sister. Barring a miracle, she and Sir Ewen would be overtaken, but Gaenor and Sir Durand would further distance themselves and, God willing, escape.

"Just try and force wedding vows from my lips, you vile red-bearded beast of a king," Beatrix muttered. "Soon you will learn my blood is as Wulfrith as any of my brothers'." And for just this one excitingly fearful day that was unlike any day she had ever lived, she believed it.

Shouts and the whinny of horses once more drawing her regard, she peered beyond Sir Ewen where he continued to protect her back and saw the king's men rein in their horses. Why? They had been so near they were not even minutes from overtaking her.

A moment later, two of their pursuers broke from the others and resumed the chase while the greater number rode opposite. Obviously, the difference between the figures of the two sisters had become clear the nearer they drew. Thus, the king's men now directed their greater effort toward bringing Gaenor to ground. Might Sir Durand have gained a large enough lead to hide her?

Beatrix bowed her head and squeezed her eyes closed. "Pray, let it be so."

"Do not slow!" Sir Ewen called, the desperation in his voice evidencing their pursuers were gaining on them. Because of her.

She set her teeth, leaned low over her palfrey, and urged the animal to greater speed.

Still, the din of pursuit did not lessen as they sought paths between the trees and over muddy ground that sorely tested the footing of their mounts.

"Go right!" Sir Ewen shouted.

She obeyed and, moments later, burst onto a clearing, the center of which was divided by a rocky ravine.

The Wulfrith knight drew alongside her. "Ride, my lady," he commanded, eyes wide and fiery. "Do not look back!"

She did look back and saw him turn his horse, draw his sword, and charge the riders. However, only one crossed swords with him while the other turned his mount aside and lunged past to intercept Beatrix.

She looked forward again. "Faster!" she rasped, vigorously applying heels to her mount. "Pray, find wings!"

Too soon the knight drew alongside. It was his eyes that first made him known to her, those pale orbs out of which darkness shone. Next, his mouth with its leering smile that bespoke such ill it made her skin feel as if she were already a corpse to the vermin that would one day visit her earthen bed.

When the knight reached for her, she lashed out with hooked fingers, but he evaded the rake of her nails by sweeping his arm high and and slamming it into hers.

Pain coursed Beatrix's forearm, and she snatched it to her side even as the impact knocked her opposite and presented her with a view of the blurred ground that yawned wide to receive her.

Something struck her back, clawed at her side, and wrenched her from the saddle. For a dizzying moment, she dangled between the horses, and then she was thrust hard onto the fore of another saddle.

"You are had, Lady Beatrix!" The knight gave a triumphant laugh and turned his mount.

He had saved her, but for what? If not for the ring of swords and shouts of anger from Sir Ewen and his opponent where they clashed astride their horses, Beatrix would have resumed her struggle. Instead, she prayed her brother's knight would prevail as the huffing horse carried her and her captor toward the ravine alongside which the two men fought.

"Your man is just this side of dead," said the dark-souled knight, his moist breath in her ear making her cringe even as anger shot through her.

She jerked her head around and met his gaze amid the fair hair fallen over his brow. Though she thought herself prepared for the darkness in his eyes, up close it was more fearsome, and she knew what it said of him even before he slid a hand up her waist and groped her chest.

"Nay!" She strained away.

He chortled and redirected his hand to her thigh.

She opened her mouth to scream, but a terrible shout silenced her.

"Ah, nay," she breathed and sought out Sir Ewen.

He sat unmoving in the saddle, face downcast as he stared at the blade piercing his center, then he looked up, met Beatrix's gaze across the distance, and toppled to the ground.

"Lord!" Beatrix cried, unable to believe God had not brought her protector through this trial as he had done the aged knight who gazed down at Sir Ewen from atop his destrier. Unlike the one who held her, the man's face reflected regret. But regret would not breathe life back into Sir Ewen who had risked all to see her safely away from these men.

"Release me!" Beatrix jabbed her elbows into the man at her back and twisted side to side to loosen his hold. "Let me go to him!"

The young knight dragged her so hard against him she feared a rib had cracked.

"Release the lady, Sir Simon," the aged knight ordered.

Her captor's mouth touched her ear. "Be you assured, we are not done."

When he dropped his arm from her, Beatrix scrambled off the horse. She lurched forward past the aged knight and dropped to her knees alongside Sir Ewen.

His eyes were closed, but as she leaned over him, his lids flickered and opened. "I have failed you, my lady," he rasped. "I have failed Baron Wulfrith."

She cupped his face in her hands. "Nay, you have not, honorable knight."

The corners of his slack mouth strained upward. "Sir Durand... holds you in high affection. I would not have you lost to him."

She shook her head. "Even were I lost, I am not his to be found."

He drew a suffering breath. "So your mother requires."

Denial rose to her lips, but she did not speak it, for it was cruel to argue with a dying man.

"My lady..." He raised his head slightly and peered down his body. "The Wulfrith dagger. Take it. Use it, if you must."

Beatrix followed his gaze, and the sight of his torn center nearly made her gag. Quickly, she refocused her attention on the belt from which his empty scabbard hung. Alongside it was the dagger awarded to all knights who trained under the Wulfriths, its pommel set with jewels to form the cross of crucifixion.

Dear Lord, where are you?

"Take it, my lady!"

Skirts shielding Sir Ewen from the knights, she touched the hilt. Though her sister-in-law, Annyn, had trained at weapons and could swing a sword and wield a dagger as well as many a knight, the closest Beatrix had come to such was the meat dagger she used at meal.

"Now, my lady, ere they draw near."

She unsheathed the dagger, lifted the hem of her skirts, and slid the weapon in the top of her hose—somehow without mishap since the blade was well-honed.

Sir Ewen sighed and dropped his head to the ground. "God keep you, my lady." A moment later, he stared at the heavens.

Beatrix's tears fell. *Dear Lord, open your gates to this man. Forgive him his transgressions.*

"I leave the lady in your care, Sir Simon," the aged knight's rusty voice ground the remainder of her prayer to dust.

She hastened to her feet, swung around, and sought his gaze where he remained astride ten feet away. "You are leaving?"

"I must rejoin the search for your sister, my lady." He jerked his chin at his companion who had guided his horse alongside his. "Sir Simon will serve as your escort."

"Nay, I beseech you, do not leave me with this man."

"Worry not, my lady, you will be safe." He turned his gaze hard upon the young knight. "Is that not right, Sir Simon?"

It was a warning, Beatrix realized, but would it be heeded?

"Of course, Sir Hector."

The aged knight considered him, then said, "Rejoin us as soon as possible."

Beatrix took a step toward Sir Hector. "Sir—"

He spurred his destrier away, leaving her alone with a man who had touched her as a man should not. Though the chill February morning had warmed considerably as it moved toward the nooning hour, she shivered.

Sir Simon smiled, showing white, uncrowded teeth that might as well have been stained and overlapped for all the ill in his face. Ill that Sir Hector had chosen to overlook in his eagerness to rejoin the chase.

"It seems you are to suffer my company a bit longer, Lady Beatrix. But it cannot be all bad, eh?"

Do not cower. Annyn would not. "Provided I not also suffer your touch," she snapped.

He narrowed his lids at her.

Though she longed to flee, there was no hope of escape. She had Sir Ewen's dagger but could not use it. Of course, Annyn could.

But I am not Annyn. As much as she admired her sister-in-law, it was not in her to draw blood, even in defense of her person. But this man could not know that, could he?

When he urged his destrier forward, Beatrix swept up her skirts and drew the dagger from her hose. "Come no nearer!"

He pulled the reins. However, he must have seen in her face that her words bore no weight, for he laughed. "Best you hand that over ere you harm yourself, my lady."

She retreated a step and came up against Sir Ewen's still form.

"Give over, Lady Beatrix." Brow folded with amusement, Sir Simon beckoned.

She glanced over her shoulder and her eyes landed on Sir Ewen's destrier where it grazed alongside the ravine. Could she reach it? Make it astride? It was her only chance.

She lunged to the side and, wishing for legs as long as Gaenor's, ran as she could not remember ever running. Somehow, she reached the destrier ahead of Sir Simon, but as she grabbed the pommel to swing into the saddle, the knight drove his mount alongside the other horse.

Trapped between the two, chest pressed hard into the side of Sir Ewen's destrier, Beatrix swept her dagger-wielding hand back in a blind attempt to fend off her assailant, but all she caught was air. However, Sir Simon succeeded where she failed, capturing her wrist and rendering the dagger useless.

As Sir Ewen's destrier snorted and trotted away, Beatrix turned from the ravine to face her captor. What she saw in his face made her shudder. Though she had not considered him handsome, his countenance had been pleasing enough. No longer.

"Give over, witch!" he growled.

Despite the pressure on her wrist, she maintained her grip on the dagger and strained backward.

With a yank that nearly wrenched her arm from its socket, he once more dragged her up onto his saddle, turned her sideways, and clamped an arm around her waist. "What will you do now there is no one to defend your virtue?" he taunted, digging fingers into the flesh of her wrist.

Still she held to the Wulfrith dagger. "Release me, cur!"

"Ah, but then I would be negligent in my duty to serve as your escort—among other things."

"I vow——" She gasped as the increased pressure on her wrist made pain shoot up her arm. "I vow the king's man and Baron Lavonne will hear tale of how you *escort* your charges—how they are made to suffer your vile attentions."

He chuckled. "You think me blind to the way you looked at me at Stern Castle, Lady Beatrix? I know the thoughts that coursed your mind—what you want from me."

"All I want from you is your absence!"

"How you do lie." He lowered his head, and his mouth would have claimed hers had she not jerked her head aside.

In the next instant, she realized that though his hold on her rendered the dagger impotent, he had made no such provision for her other hand. She bunched it into a fist and slammed it into his chin.

It could not have pained him as much as it did her, but he cursed and dragged her so hard against him her breath fled. "If that is as you wish it, my lady!" His kiss—if it could be called that—ground her lips against her teeth and filled her mouth with the taste of blood. Still she did not give up the dagger. She would rather die.

When he ran his mouth down her neck, inhaling deep as if to feed his senses, she recalled that her sister-in-law had said the only thing necessary to render a man impotent was to catch him unawares. Annyn had referred to the vulnerability of the groin, which had made Beatrix and Gaenor giggle, but it was no longer a matter at which to laugh, especially as Beatrix's proximity to her assailant denied her that vulnerability. But perhaps there was another way to catch him unawares.

She closed her eyes and went limp. It took longer than expected for him to realize something had changed, but when he did, he lifted his head and she felt his gaze hard upon her face. A moment later, he eased his hold on her.

Beatrix jerked her dagger-wielding hand free, swung her left elbow high, and drove it into his throat.

Eyes wide with disbelief, he made a terrible sucking sound, but even as he strained breath into his lungs, he reached for the dagger she held aloft.

Use it! a part of her cried, while the other recoiled at the act of drawing blood.

Sir Simon stole the argument from her, wrenching her forearm down with such force the dagger's pommel struck his horse's neck.

The destrier gave a high-pitched neigh, lunged sideways, and reared.

And there was the ravine, its harsh, jagged edges seeming to rise toward Beatrix.

But she was the one in motion. Overwhelmed by the sensation of falling and the dread anticipation of the rocks below, she screamed and registered an answering shout and felt hands that never should have touched her—hands that should have let her go. Air rushed past and, when it was exhausted, all that remained were the rocks to break her fall. To break her.

Gaenor wailed and would not have ceased had Sir Durand not clamped a hand over her mouth. Staring at the terrible sight in the ravine below, she sobbed against his palm.

The knight was silent where his destrier pressed alongside her palfrey and, past her pain, she slowly became aware of his own. Dragging a deep, shuddering breath, she looked around.

Sir Durand made no attempt to avert his moist gaze, the only movement about him the convulsive bob of his throat.

Gaenor pried his hand from her mouth. "We must go to her. Perhaps she is—"

"'Tis not possible. She could not have survived such a fall."

"But—"

"Look! Even from here you can see blood."

She did not want to look again, but she did. Below the wooded hill upon which they had paused was a clearing where three horses grazed and a knight—surely Sir Ewen—had fallen to the sword. In the center of that clearing, as though its heart had been torn from it, was a ravine. Partway down its craggy length, the unmistakable figure of Beatrix was crumpled on a ledge. And sprawled across her was the one responsible for this heinous crime—a man sent by the king to deliver a bride to the detestable Christian Lavonne.

"She is lost to us," Sir Durand said softly.

Gaenor longed to shout that Beatrix could have survived, that the blood belonged to the unmoving knight, but his fall had been broken by her sister's delicate figure. It had to be Beatrix's blood.

"We must go, my lady."

Tears spilling, Gaenor shook her head. "We cannot leave her."

"If the king's men capture you, her sacrifice will be for naught."

"Sacrifice," Gaenor whispered. And knew it was so. When she had realized her sister and Sir Ewen were no longer at their backs, something had told her it was of Beatrix's doing. Beatrix who was always thinking ahead of her feet. Who would not hesitate to place herself at risk to save her sister. Who believed in God as Gaenor did not pretend to do. Aye, Gaenor knew He existed, but He did not answer prayers nor place hedges of protection around those who truly followed Him—as deaf to Beatrix upon her rocky grave as He so often was to Gaenor.

"My lady?"

She nodded. "Let us be away from here—as far as you can take me."

She would rather die than surrender it. Was that what had happened? *Had* she died?

She flexed her fingers and felt the gems through the leather of her glove. The dagger was still to hand, so she must yet live. She tried to draw a deep breath, but it felt as if a great weight pressed upon her.

Taking a shallow sip of cool air, she eased her lids open and winced at the pain that raked fingernails across the inside of her skull.

She squeezed her eyes closed, but there was no escape from the ache that spread and intensified until it felt as if it knew and hated every ounce of her being.

What happened? Where am I? Why so much pain?

Darkness once more beckoning, she slid toward it. However, a vague memory dragged across her thoughts and, though she longed to let it pass, she pulled it back and saw a man's leering face and eyes that were at once pale and dark. Then there was the dagger she yet gripped. He had tried to wrest it from her.

Why? And who was he?

She forced her lids up and blinked until the blur came into focus. To her left, rising steeply overhead, a wall of rock was interspersed with dry winter grass.

Did I fall? This the reason my head aches and legs will not move?

She eased her head up. Grinding her teeth against the pain caused by the movement, she peered down her body.

Blood soaked her mantle where a man lay across her.

She cried out and wrenched sideways, and the man rolled off her. Closing her throat against sobs that threatened to shake her apart, she dropped to her back again and peered across her shoulder at the one who had come to rest on his side facing her. His chest bled crimson, meaning the blood upon her must belong to him. But why? Because of the dagger she would rather die than release? She raised her hand and whimpered at the sight of blood coloring the blade. Had she—?

Nay, she would not have.

She dropped her hand back to her side. It had to have been an accident. Had it happened before they had fallen down into this place? After? As she searched for an explanation, time crawled over and around her, leaving behind a trail so gray and damp and coldly silent that she longed to scream.

She struggled to sitting, pressed a hand to the left side of her head, and touched a tender swelling. When she drew her hand away, blood smeared her gloved fingers. Her blood. She wiped it on her skirts and once more took in the blood that covered her mantle. His blood.

Breathing hard, she clawed at the ties of her mantle, released them, and threw the garment off. But still there was blood, the crimson having soaked through to her cream linen gown.

As sobs broke from her, she dragged her legs beneath her—legs capable of movement now that she was free of the dead man's weight. Continuing to hold to the dagger, she crawled toward the ravine wall. Once there, she pressed her aching back to it, drew her legs up, and buried her face against her knees.

How long she remained thus, wafting in and out of consciousness, she did not know, but the sun still warmed the winter sky when voices sounded overhead.

Friend or foe? And how was she to know the difference when she could not recall how she had come to be here?

She startled when the door to a memory swung open—two knights, faces familiar though she could put no name to them. And her sister. "Gaenor," she whispered. "Aye, that is her name."

Dear God, what is wrong with me?

As the voices drew near, she pressed herself tighter against the wall and convulsively gripped the dagger she must not release lest death find her defenseless.

Small rocks and clumps of dirt rained down and, though she knew someone scaled the ravine wall, she did not move.

As consciousness once more dimmed, she heard a gruff voice shout, "He is dead, Sir Kearse, but the lady lives."

Only as long as I do not let go of the dagger.

A darkness darker than night swelled over her and drew her back to its breast, but still she held to the hilt.

"Will she live?"

Michael D'Arci, physician to Aldous Lavonne who had years earlier relinquished his title to his sons, first Geoffrey, then Christian, looked over his shoulder. "Do you wish her to live, my lord?"

Towering before the door, Christian seemed to struggle—as did Michael, who now shared a brother's death in common with his embittered lord. He ground his teeth at the memory of Simon D'Arci laid out in the hall below, his gut torn open by the dagger the baron's men had pried from the Wulfrith woman's hand when they had found her over Simon's body. And that was another thing the D'Arcis and Lavonnes had in common. The Wulfriths were responsible for both deaths. Of course, Simon's might have been prevented had Sir Hector not left him alone with Lady Beatrix.

Remembering the silent knight who had said little during Christian Lavonne's questioning, Michael clenched his hands. Despite an unwillingness to talk, there had been regret in Sir Hector's eyes which, strangely, receded each time he had looked at where Simon lay.

Michael returned his attention to the unconscious lady he would have refused to tend had his lord not ordered it—she of flaxen hair, angelic face, and petite form that none would believe capable of murder. But that was Simon's blood on her bodice. Simon's blood on the Wulfrith dagger that the baron had shown him. How the lady and Simon had ended up in the ravine, none knew, nor did Michael care. What mattered was that Beatrix Wulfrith had killed his brother.

Baron Lavonne heaved a sigh. "I would have her live."

Regardless if it meant Michael would burn in hell, it was not the choice he would have made. But though he would walk away and leave her to die, as would likely be her lot if he left her untended, he would do his lord's bidding.

He met the baron's gaze. "She should not have survived a fall such as your men described." Surely they had exaggerated, for only a miracle would have preserved her life. "Hence, though I vow I will tend her as best I can, I make no guarantee that she will live."

Christian Lavonne turned to depart but paused at the door. "As I would not have the Wulfriths descend upon Castle Broehne, none are to know she lives until I determine her fate."

"What of the king's men?"

The baron smiled—a rarity. "'Twas my men who found her and your brother, and well they know I would not wish any interference in this matter."

Then he would not inform King Henry that the lady had been delivered to Castle Broehne—an omission that could prove detrimental when the truth was learned as it must surely be.

"Despair not," the baron said as he opened the door. "If the lady lives, justice will be yours."

They were not idle words. Christian Lavonne was the lord his brother had never aspired to be, having earned the respect of his people who knew exactly what was expected of them and who had prospered in the absence of the rapacious Geoffrey Lavonne.

Michael inclined his head. "Thank you, my lord."

Christian Lavonne ducked to avoid the lintel and stepped into the corridor.

As the door closed, Michael considered Beatrix of the Wulfriths. The sight of her bloodied bodice gave him pause and made his stomach roil. Drawing a deep breath, he told himself she was undeserving of modesty and removed her belt. Once more, he paused, this time over the psalter on her belt. It was a sign of godliness that a lady carried such evidence of her faith, but for this woman it was mere pretense. Like so many, Michael included, God was revered only in the presence of others—a show of faith and little else. To truly live a Christian life took too much effort, sacrifice, and repentance of those things most pleasurable, such as the needs of the flesh, to which he was particularly susceptible. Though not to the extent some believed.

He tossed the belt aside and pulled at the gown's side laces. Upon removal of the garment, he saw that neither had the chemise beneath been spared Simon's blood.

When his brother's murderer finally lay bare beneath a sheet, he turned her onto her side, pulled his physician's bag near, and began cutting away the hair that would allow him to stitch up the wound above her ear. Though he knew her injury had to be a result of the fall, he did not allow himself to delve deeper. Regardless of what had happened to her, there was nothing to excuse her of Simon's death. Simon who had only been doing his king and overlord's bidding. Simon who would not know another sunrise or sunset. Simon whose murderer would be brought to justice. One way or another.

3

THE LIGHT WAS distant, a pinprick in the darkness, but she was certain that if she felt her way forward, she could reach it.

Hands before her, she trudged onward. Though the light grew larger, it remained elusive. Why it was so important that she reach it, she did not understand. She simply knew she must not take the easier path back into darkness even though it offered relief from her pain.

When she finally stepped into the light, the brilliance made her throw up a hand to shield her eyes. It was then she realized she had lost the dagger.

Aware of a voice somewhere beyond her, she tried to peer between her fingers. As the ceiling overhead wavered, she heard a door open and close, then all fell silent.

Beatrix lowered her hand and slid her narrowed gaze to the wall opposite. The door was there, and the longer she stared at it, the more it came into focus until she could pick out the grains of the planks from which it was fashioned.

No sooner had she begun to breathe easier than the door swung inward and a man appeared, one of such great height he had to dip his head to enter—taller even than the Wulfrith males and, thereby, Gaenor.

For a moment, Beatrix forgot about the man in the doorway. Where was Gaenor? Why this fear that all was not well? What was this place? What was she doing abed with sunlight filtering through oilcloth-covered windows? And who was this man who came uninvited into her chamber? She returned her gaze to him and saw he had closed the door.

"Lady Beatrix." His voice was cold enough to chill the warm air wafting from the brazier. "You are returned to us."

Us? As she pulled her hands up the sheet, she caught her breath at the realization she was bare beneath.

The big man halted alongside the bed. "We had begun to abandon hope you would awaken." From his tone, it seemed it would not have troubled him much. As she had never known anyone to hate her, she could not be certain that was what he exuded, but what else might it be?

She parted her lips to speak, but her mouth was so dry it was impossible to form words. He must have seen her struggle, for he stepped away and returned with a goblet.

Holding the sheet to her chest, Beatrix pushed onto her elbows and reached with the other hand to accept the vessel. Their fingers brushed as he passed it, and a glance at his face told he was repulsed by the contact.

Lord, what have I done to warrant such loathing?

The sweet wine that coursed over her tongue and down her parched throat nearly made her choke. Fearing it would earn her further scorn, she sipped more slowly. When she had drained the goblet, the man took it from her.

"Do you know where you are, Lady Beatrix?" He set the vessel on the table beside the bed.

She collapsed back on the pillow and shook her head.

"Castle Broehne."

The name sounded familiar.

"I am Christian Lavonne, baron of Abingdale." He watched for a reaction.

And she gave it to him, though she could not say exactly what caused her to startle. She knew the name and that it boded ill, but that was all.

"What happened?" she croaked, surprised at the effort required to form so few words.

"You do not recall?"

Why did she not? Why were the doors of her mind closed?

"The physician told that your mind might not be right after the head injury you sustained."

This the reason for the throb radiating from the left side of her skull? She slid a hand through her hair and touched the threads that closed her broken flesh.

He narrowed his lids. "But methinks it more likely pretense you work. Eh, my lady?"

"Pre...tense? Why would I...?" *Lord, what binds my tongue? I am capable of better than this!*

"Why?" the baron repeated. "Murder, mayhap?"

"I do not understand."

His nostrils flared. "I speak of the murder of Sir Simon D'Arci."

Another name she knew, but—

"Ah, you remember now."

Pale eyes, yet dark. A cruel smile.

"Be you assured, my lady, though you are a Wulfrith, you will go to trial for murder."

But she had killed no one. "You are...wrong. I—"

He moved so suddenly she jerked. Two strides carried him to the end of the bed where he tossed back the lid of a clothes chest and withdrew a mantle and gown. When he turned the latter to reveal blood across the bodice, she remembered a ravine, a man across her chest, crimson soaked through her clothing, blood on the blade.

"The...Wulfrith dagger." She looked to her frightfully empty hand. Though she did not remember her fingers being turned from around the hilt, someone had taken it. And now she would die.

"The Wulfrith dagger," the baron scorned. "A fine piece of proof that will assure retribution is finally dealt a Wulfrith. That is, unless you can offer a better explanation for how it came to be planted in Sir Simon's chest."

Beatrix felt as if she were drowning, surfacing only often enough to suffer a slow, painful death. With a sigh that sounded nearer a sob, she turned her face away and stared at the brazier across the chamber.

After a long silence, the baron said, "Michael D'Arci will be both surprised and displeased to learn you have finally awakened. Though he tended you, I do not doubt he hoped his physician's skill would fail him."

Then he believed Simon D'Arci's relation had coaxed her out of darkness? It was so preposterous she could have laughed, for it was God who had returned her to the light, though for what purpose she could not fathom, especially now that her mind was so far removed from her tongue.

Keeping her head turned away, she asked, "How long have I been…" The word she sought mocked from afar.

"Unconscious?"

Threatened by tears of frustration, she nodded.

"Seven days, my lady."

A sennight. It was hardly surprising that D'Arci had not expected her to live. Seven days without sustenance—a slow wasting away.

She heard the baron move around the bed but kept her gaze on the brazier.

"I shall send word to D'Arci that you have awakened."

Then he was no longer here. Of course, he had expected her to die.

"I am sure he will wish to see for himself that the woman who murdered his brother is returned to health."

Though Beatrix longed to argue her innocence, she not only lacked the words but also memory of the events that had caused the man to be impaled upon the Wulfrith dagger.

The baron lingered as if he expected a response, but she closed her eyes in the hope he would leave her alone to muddle through her confused mind. Shortly, the door closed. But for all her straining, her memories remained ghostly images without substance. Nothing to save her from judgment by the enemy she had somehow gained.

"Lord," she whispered, and the mere utterance of her savior's name was as a balm. There was something—someone—who could save her. Someone who had not deserted her as her memories had done.

She closed her eyes. "I place my life in your hands, Lord Jesus. Your will be done."

4

SHE HAD KILLED a man. Or so it was said.

During the ten days since her awakening, Beatrix had tried every locked door within her memory. Some creaked open wide enough to allow her to peer inside such that she now remembered her flight from Stern Castle with Gaenor, Sir Ewen's death, and Sir Simon's face when he sought to violate her. Though she remembered little beyond the hands he had laid to her, she was fairly certain he had not stolen her virtue. But there was that gap between her flight from Sir Ewen's side to the fall.

Suddenly light of head, she lowered to the chest at the foot of the bed and breathed deep until the feeling passed. Then, as she had done time and again, she struggled to fill the gap preceding her return to consciousness in the ravine when she had rolled the knight off her. But once again, the memory she needed to defend against the charge of murder was denied her. However, that was not all she needed. She required words to tell what had happened, words that too often teased her tongue, the absence of which made her seem a simpleton.

Four days past, when she had first recalled Sir Simon's attempt to ravish her, she had begged an audience with Baron Lavonne. He made her wait two days and, when he finally appeared, it had been for naught. Like a moth straining to light, she had tried to voice the terrible memory, but the head injury had bound her tongue and incurred the baron's impatience. That second visit to her chamber was his last.

Thus, she would soon be brought before the sheriff, but even if she could tell what had happened, there seemed no outcome other than death—unless her family delivered her. Each day she set herself before the window to watch for them, certain they would come, but they did not. Why? The castle was not barricaded, the folk allowed to move freely within and without the walls. Surely she would not stand alone before the sheriff and her accusers?

She touched a finger to her lips in anticipation of what she would say, but even when she thought the words through before speaking, her tongue and lips faltered as if she were empty of mind. She was not. Of course, one would not know it to be near when she opened her mouth.

She felt the place where her hair had been cut away to stitch up her scalp. Though she might never again be as she was, she was alive thanks to the elusive Sir Michael D'Arci who had yet to appear though he had surely been apprised of her recovery.

Dreading his arrival that the curt chamber maid who attended her had told would be this day, Beatrix stood and once more crossed to the window. Shivering in the cool air that her removal of the oilcloth allowed within, she watched the lowering sun draw shadows across the castle walls. As always, her gaze was tempted to the wood and, leaning forward, she stared at the bordering trees and wished she could reach them. Of course, what then? She might once have been capable of finding her way back to Stern, but now…

She lowered her gaze to the inner bailey. It bustled with those whose work for their lord was done for the day. Now they could return home, break hunger, and bed down for the morrow when they would again rise to serve their lord.

As if the thought made the baron appear, his immense figure emerged from the stables. He was not alone. Beside him strode a man of obvious rank. Michael D'Arci? It had to be. And now he would ensure justice was done. His justice.

Beatrix considered the dark-haired man. As he and the baron neared the donjon steps, the latter said something. Though his words aspired to

Beatrix's window high above, they arrived in unintelligible pieces. But there was no mistaking her name that fell from his lips, nor that it caused the dark-haired man to stiffen and look around.

His revealed face made Beatrix's breath stick. Even at a distance, she knew his countenance, for it was that of Sir Simon—albeit crowned by black hair rather than blond.

She clenched her hands at the realization that soon she would stand before one whose resemblance to that miscreant would surely cause her words to fail. Though he was not as big a man as Baron Lavonne, from the dark upon his face, he might as well be a giant.

He looked up, and though Beatrix knew she could not be seen among the shadows, she took a step back. The frown that crossed his face darkened it further. And as surely as she breathed, she knew he knew it was upon her chamber he looked.

She turned, retrieved her psalter from the bedside table, and pressed it to her chest. Such relief she had felt upon discovering it the day of her awakening. Telling herself God's word would sustain her, she opened the psalter and settled down to await Sir Simon's vengeful kin.

Hours passed, her supper was delivered, more hours passed, and still he did not come.

When her lids grew heavy, she slid beneath the bed covers. "Lord," she whispered, "you allowed me to survive a f-fall I should not have, but surely not for this. Pray, re-reveal to me what you would have me to do."

'Tis said you are a devil, Michael.

Not in all things, but some—namely, women. But he had good reason. And now, more so.

Michael returned to his memory of the lonely youth who had followed him to the roof of their father's donjon years earlier. He saw the night breeze lift Simon's fair hair and sweep it across his troubled face.

Would that I could be like you, Michael.

Had he known what it was like to be Michael D'Arci, a man unwelcome at most nobles' tables, he would not have wished it so.

Drawing breath past the bitterness, Michael opened his fists and began beating a rhythm on the window sill. He loathed waiting on any-thing or anyone, especially a murderess whose face ought to be set upon an angel.

No fair maid will ever want me.

And for that, Simon ought to have been grateful. Still, Michael had been pained by his brother's plight, especially when he saw moonlight sparkling in the boy's tears. Tears for fear he might never know a woman.

Michael looked to the postered bed where Beatrix Wulfrith's still figure was played by the light of a dimming torch. Though her face was turned to the wall, denying him full view of her beauty, the slender curve of her neck was visible, as was the turn of an ear and the slope of a cheekbone swept by hair of palest gold. Deceptive beauty. No woman was to be underestimated, not even his stepmother who had been as a mother to him.

I would be a man and mother would have me remain a boy, Simon's voice found him again.

The boy's mother had loved him too well, refusing to see past her own heart to what was best for her son.

Trying to put away the memory of Simon's bent head, slumped shoulders, and the sobs jerking the youth's thin body, Michael returned his focus to the bed, something of a feat considering the amount of wine he had earlier consumed. Too much, as evidenced by his presence in the lady's chamber when he had vowed he would wait until the morrow. But she had only been two doors down from the chamber he was given, and he had been unable to sleep. To resist the impulse to seek her out, he had donned his mantle and walked the outer walls for an hour, but when he returned to the donjon and drew near her door…

Would she awaken? It was as he wished, for he had waited too long to delve the guilty eyes of his brother's murderer. If not for the delay in delivering him tidings of her recovery, she would have been brought before the sheriff by now, but it had taken a sennight for Christian Lavonne's men to locate Michael in London where he had gone to assist with an outbreak of smallpox. However, Simon would have his justice as Christian had promised—and so, too, would the old baron, Aldous.

Recalling the two hours spent in the company of Christian's father, tending the man's aches and pains that should have ended his suffering long ago, Michael shook his head. For years he had urged Aldous to not dwell on Geoffrey's death, to accept it and continue as best he could in his ravaged body, but it was as if the old man's life hinged upon working revenge on the Wulfriths.

With Simon's death, Michael now understood Aldous's pain. Indeed, this day the old baron had wagged a horribly bent finger at his physician and goaded him for finally knowing such terrible loss. The bile in Michael's belly had stirred so violently he had been grateful when Christian appeared. Christian who allowed his father his acts of revenge but had not refused to take a Wulfrith bride despite Aldous cursing him for acceding to King Henry's plan. Christian who was now the baron but had once been a man of God. Christian who was in many ways still a man of God but hid the threads of his former life behind an austere front. And among those threads was the notion of forgiveness.

Remembering the supper and conversation he had shared with his lord, Michael tensed. Though Christian had promised justice, any mention of it this eve had caused the man to fall silent or speak elsewhere. Michael feared he wavered and suspected it was not only due to the tidings that King Henry still expected a union between the Wulfriths and Lavonnes but Christian's training in the ways of the Church. Regardless, the baron would wed Gaenor Wulfrith as agreed. Of course, first she must be coaxed out of hiding.

Though it was believed she was at Wulfen Castle, the Wulfrith stronghold dedicated to training young men into worthy knights, it could not be confirmed due to the impregnability of the castle. But eventually the Wulfriths would have to yield her up, for King Henry would not long suffer their defiance. It was likely he did so now only because it was believed his edict had resulted in the death of Lady Beatrix. Though the Wulfriths were as much vassals to the king as any other baron, they were allies worthy of respect that King Henry afforded few. But if that respect precluded the dispensing of justice—

Nay, his brother would have justice!

You are the only one who has a care for me, Simon's voice once more resounded through him.

Often it had seemed he *was* the only one who cared. Unfortunately, too much time had passed between his visits home for him to do more than play at training his half-brother into a man. It had boded ill for Simon whose mother found excuse after excuse to avoid sending him to a neighboring barony for his knighthood training. Thus, when she was forced to relent, Simon had struggled to keep pace with what was expected of one his age. However, after a long, arduous journey toward knighthood, he had attained it, unaware that his accomplishment would soon be stolen from him. By this woman.

Michael increased the thrum of his fingers. Reckless and willful his brother might have been, but he could not have warranted such a death. Might the lady seek absolution from her crime? Might she say the murder was the result of a bent mind, as it was not uncommon for those of the nobility to claim in order to escape punishment? Might she put forth that her head injury prevented her from properly defending herself at trial? The latter would likely serve her better, as there was proof she had suffered such a blow. Indeed, according to Baron Lavonne, her speech was affected, though he submitted it might be more pretense than impediment. What if she *were* absolved?

Michael seethed over the still figure beneath the covers. As his movement about the chamber and thrumming upon the sill had not moved her, mayhap he ought to shake her awake. But that would mean laying hands on her, and he did not trust himself. How was it she slept so soundly, without the slightest twitch or murmur? It was as if she feigned sleep.

That last thought settling amid the haze of too much drink, Michael stilled and considered it more closely. Indeed...

Beatrix stared at the wall and strained to catch the sound of movement. Though the man's fingers had ceased their thrumming, and there was only the soft pop and hiss of embers that were all that remained of the brazier's fire, she knew Sir Simon's kin was there as he had been for the past quarter hour. Once more reminded that she was alone with the brother of a man who had tried to ravish her, and that he was likely no different, she suppressed a shudder. Why had he come in the middling of night? And what was she to do?

He strode so suddenly around the end of the bed that there was no time for her to close her eyes. Wearing a mantle as red as new-spilled blood, a tunic as black as a moonless night, he slowly smiled.

"Lady Beatrix awakens." He angled his head, causing his dark hair to skim his shoulder. "Or mayhap she has been awake some time now."

Waiting for him to leave, devising a way to deter him if he tried to do to her what his brother had done. But the only thing near enough with which to defend herself was the pewter goblet on the bedside table.

"I am Michael D'Arci of Castle Soaring. You know the name, my lady?"

Too well as well he knew.

"Have you no tongue?"

Aye, but the bridge between it and her mind was in poor disrepair. If a reply was forthcoming, it would surely come too late.

He pressed hands to the mattress, leaned forward, and narrowed his lids over pale gray eyes so like his brother's and yet somehow different. "Mayhap you are simply frightened?"

As he wished her to be.

"Or perhaps you are as witless as I have been told."

Anger built the bridge to her tongue. "I am not witless!"

"Ah, she speaks. What else does she do?" He bent so near she could almost taste the wine on his breath. Though he did not appear unsteady, she sensed he had imbibed heavily, a dangerous thing for an angry man to do—especially dangerous for her.

His eyebrows rose. "She assists her sister in escaping the king's edict"—

Had Gaenor escaped? Though Beatrix had asked after her sister when Lavonne last visited her chamber, the man who was to have been Gaenor's husband had not answered.

—"puts daggers to men as easily as to a trencher of meat, and survives a fall that should have seen her dead."

A tremble, as much born of anger as fear, moved through Beatrix. Struggling to keep her breath even, she reminded herself of the goblet. If he tried to defile her, she would bring it down upon his head. *If* she could get it to hand. *If* she could harm another.

"You wish to know the reason I tended your injury?" Michael D'Arci continued. "Why I did not allow you to die as is your due?"

She did not need to be told. Her words might be slow to form, but she knew he sought revenge.

"Justice," he said.

Revenge by a lesser name was still revenge, especially where unwarranted.

"Though you may be clever, I vow you will be judged and found wanting."

In the past, she had been called clever. Would she ever be again— lacking D'Arci's taint of sarcasm?

When she gave no reply, he said, "Could you, you would kill again, hmm?"

Again, her tongue loosened. "Most assuredly I would defend my person against any who seeks to violate me." Was that her voice? Strong and even without break or searching? Whence did it come?

"You speak of ravishment?" D'Arci bit.

Though she longed to look away, she kept her gaze on his face, noting his full mouth, straight nose, broad cheekbones, and heavily lashed gray eyes—so like his brother's she strained to hold back the panic that would have her scurry for cover.

Of a sudden, he cursed, his unholy use of the Lord's name making her flinch. "Is that what you will tell the sheriff? That you murdered my brother because he ravished you?"

Beatrix blinked. Though ravishment had surely been Simon D'Arci's intent, it seemed the Wulfrith dagger had stopped him. Determined to correct Michael D'Arci—to assure him she was fairly certain his brother had failed to commit the heinous act—she searched for words. However, his darkening face once more caused her tongue to tangle. Could the devil assume human form, he would surely be pleased to do so in the image of Michael D'Arci.

But for all of her fear, hope slipped in. Of that day at the ravine, he surely knew only what Baron Lavonne had shared. What if she told him the truth, even if most of the truth she could only surmise?

"I did not..." She swallowed. "I tell you true, I..."

"Did not murder him?"

"I could never murder. I but d-d-defen—"

"Defended yourself?"

How she detested his impatience! "'Twas surely hap—"

"Happenstance?"

That word she had not lacked. "Aye, happenstance."

"You do not know for certain?"

"I do. I just cannot...remember it all."

"What fool do you think me, Lady Beatrix?" he growled.

"I am not a m-murderer."

"You expect me to believe the young man I knew well was a ravisher, and you whom I know not at all are no murderer? I should have let you bleed to death."

Anger streaked Beatrix's breast, and her next words sprang free as if she were quick of tongue. "Your brother would have!"

D'Arci drew a sharp breath, then splayed a hand across her throat. "You lie, witch, and I shall see you dead for it."

Though certain he meant to strangle her, his fingers did not tighten. Still, fear denied her breath. Was he playing with her? First torment, then death?

She glanced at the goblet. Providing she did not alert him, she could reach it. Providing he had imbibed as much wine as his breath told, she could escape him.

He slid his hand further up her neck. "When you stand before the sheriff"—

She was not to die this night?

—"I will savor your fear."

She swallowed hard against his palm and reached. "Nay, you will not," she said and swept the goblet to hand.

As he jerked his chin around, she slammed the vessel against his temple. For a breathless moment, he was still, and then he collapsed atop her.

Staring at his head on her chest and the trickle of blood coursing his brow, she quaked in remembrance of his brother who had similarly fallen across her.

Had she killed Michael D'Arci?

Nay, he breathed, but that did not mean she had not damaged him terribly. She, better than most, knew what could result from a blow to the head. Recalling her return to consciousness in the ravine when she had seen crimson on her gloved fingers, she began to shake. That day, her young life had come as near to ending as one could come without actually dying.

She squeezed her eyes closed, but when she opened them, the crimson remained. This time it bled from Michael D'Arci.

Knowing he might soon regain consciousness, she wriggled out from beneath him and dropped to her knees alongside the bed. Now how was she to escape?

Think. Think hard, Beatrice. She shook her head. *Then pray hard, for you cannot do this without help.*

Though she knew she risked much, she delayed her escape to call upon the Lord. And when she said, "Amen," she knew what must be done. As her only covering was the chemise the chamber maid had delivered the day Beatrix awakened at Broehne Castle, and the baron had taken her bloodied gown and mantle for evidence, she would have to impose on Michael D'Arci.

She slid a hand under him and released the brooch that clasped the red mantle at his throat. Blessedly, the lining was black, which would allow her to merge with the night. She turned the inside of the garment out and dragged it over her shoulders. As she secured it with the brooch, she saw the dagger and purse on D'Arci's belt. Beseeching God's forgiveness, she appropriated both and retrieved her psalter. Not until she reached the door did she realize she lacked footwear, but there was nothing for it as D'Arci's bulky boots would only hinder her.

She eased the door open and peered into the dim corridor. Unlike the first sennight since her awakening, there was no guard present. Obviously, Baron Lavonne had grown confident she would not—or could not—escape. Now if she could make it through the hall, into the bailey, and out the postern gate.

Though she had known the latter would prove difficult, if not impossible, since so much of a castle's defenses depended on the gate being well disguised, she quickly located it and slipped through.

Not until she was outside the castle walls, driving one leg in front of the other beneath a cold sliver moon, was the hue raised. Entering the wood she had so longed for, she paused and pressed a hand to her throbbing head.

Which way? She peered through the darkness and, clutching her psalter in an attempt to pry free the icy fingers of fear, made her decision. The only way that mattered was away from Broehne, though not so far she could not watch for her family who would surely come for her.

A good plan, for Lavonne and D'Arci would never expect her to remain on the barony of Abingdale.

5

Purley Abbey, April 1157

BENEATH THEIR NOSES. For more than a month she had sheltered among the ruins of Purley Abbey less than three leagues south of Broehne Castle, but for all those who passed by, none knew of her presence. Even the ones who sheltered among the crumbling walls during the thunderous spring rains gained no glimpse of her.

Beatrix raised her face to the sunlight that flooded the roofless presbytery, a place that had some hundred years past housed the high altar. As its roof was absent, few ventured near, and then only the occasional scavenger hoping to uncover a relic.

When trespassed upon, she retreated to the crypt beneath the presbytery that had been used for the safe-keeping of such relics. Fortunately, none hazarded past the false crypt that had been constructed fifty feet in front of the true crypt. The ceiling of the former having collapsed, it yawned wide and empty, offering seekers little more than a nasty tumble. As for the true crypt, were its location discovered, one would be disappointed by its spoils. But it was everything to Beatrix, its vaulted ceiling having sheltered her while she waited. And waited.

When would her brothers come? She could not remain at Purley past autumn when the chill winter so recently left behind set in again and the fear of being discovered once more denied her a warming fire. If no one came for her, she would have to seek Stern Castle on her own.

As always, the thought of making her way across unfamiliar land among unknown people was daunting. Noble or common, no woman was safe traveling alone, especially one who had difficulty expressing herself. She would be prey to many, one of whom might be Michael D'Arci.

Lifting an arm from the mantle she had taken from him, Beatrix fingered the scar beneath her hair that D'Arci's stitches had made. D'Arci who had saved her life that he might see it taken.

The vibration started at Beatrix's toes, swept to her heels, and shuddered up her calves. Though she knew the riders were too distant and would not likely glance at the abbey ruins amid the dense undergrowth, she slipped behind the presbytery wall.

Seeking reassurance, she glanced over her shoulder beyond the false crypt to the grassy, stone-strewn floor where the high altar had once been raised. The narrow breach in the ceiling of the true crypt lay ten feet in back of the crumbling pillars. In less than a five count she could be down it. A two count later, the false floor she had constructed of branches, leaves, and grass would be positioned over the breach. None who ventured to the easternmost boundary of the abbey would know she hid fifteen feet below.

Beatrix peered around the wall as the vibrations increased and riders appeared. Unfortunately, since they passed at great speed and were too distant, she could not ascertain whether her brothers were among them. But it had to be urgency that drove them so hard and fast.

She knew what she had to do—as she had done thrice before. Beneath cover of her stolen mantle, she would steal into Broehne Castle. Though it was a terrible risk, it would be more terrible if her family came and she could not be found.

Closing her mind to the fear that tried to dissuade her from straying from the abbey, she stepped from the wall. She halted. Was she forgetting something? She squeezed her eyes closed, but though she searched, nothing revealed itself.

With calloused hands, she wrenched the hood of the mantle over her head. And caught the scent of the man to whom it belonged.

Of my imagining. No scent of him could remain, especially after all the rain the garment has endured.

Determining that first she would go to the nearby village she occasionally braved in hopes of hearing of her family, she drew the mantle closed and glanced down to confirm that no red was visible. In doing so, she noted that the uppers of the boots she had bought from a village boy had further separated from their soles. God willing, she would not need them much longer.

Fear curdled the meager contents of Beatrix's belly as she peered up from beneath her hood at the castle she had fled a month past. The talk of the villagers having yielded nothing of value, she had continued on to Broehne.

As she followed behind a wagon that rumbled over the drawbridge, she prayed no one would stop her, that it would be assumed she was with the villager who delivered milk and cheese to the baron's kitchens. There were others who came, whether to grind grain at the lord's mill or give service to their lord, but there was less chance of being stopped providing she stayed near the wagon. And so it was, though the momentary pause beneath the portcullis made her heart gallop.

Continuing to trail the wagon, she strained to catch the talk around her, but too many spoke at once, their voices entangling such that she caught only single words above the crunch of wagon wheels.

The inner bailey, she told herself. It would not be as riotous there, though certainly more dangerous. Passing into it, she squinted at the great donjon and was touched with faintness beget not only of fear, but too little sustenance. Though she filled her aching belly with various vegetation and had become proficient at spearing fish from the stream, failing that, she snatched simple viands from the villagers. However, it was never enough, and often she went hungry.

As she sent up a prayer that she would not collapse, her belly grunted again. What she wouldn't give for a swallow of milk, a bite of bread—

"You there!" a woman called.

Beatrix looked to the servant who came off the steps before the donjon and was relieved to discover it was another she addressed.

"Bring the wagon 'round to the kitchen," the servant directed the villager.

Beatrix drew a deep breath. She had not come this far to fall into Baron Lavonne's hands. She would learn what there was to know and be gone.

As the servant led the way for the villager, Beatrix skirted those who came between her and the wagon. Hanging back, she allowed the wagon to disappear around the side of the donjon before following lest the villager or servant became suspicious. At the gated entrance to the kitchen through which the wagon passed, she slipped alongside the wall and behind a tree.

"Our lord be well?" the villager asked among huffs as he unloaded milk and cheese.

"Well enough," the woman said without strain, evidencing she offered no assistance.

For some minutes, the two chatted about little of import, but just when Beatrix despaired of ever gaining tidings of her family, the villager said, "Any word of our lord's betrothed?"

Beatrix caught her breath.

"Naught. At least, naught that he allows these poor ears to hear."

Surely that was good. Though Beatrix had weeks earlier learned from talk in the village that Gaenor had never arrived at Broehne Castle, that was all she knew.

"Methinks he ought to choose another bride," the man said with a grunt.

"Aye, but 'twould seem he wants this one."

He *wanted* Gaenor? But was it not the king who had ordered the marriage?

"A Wulfrith, eh? He has his reasons, I am sure."

"That he does."

Revenge.

The woman sighed. "Of course, since the murder of Sir Simon, the baron's father is more opposed than ever to such a union. Woe to the lady, Beatrix, if ever she is found. And woe to her sister if she yet weds her family's enemy. Though old Aldous may spend his wasting life abed, still he can work ill where he wills."

What would Christian Lavonne and his father do to Gaenor if she fell into their hands? Deciding she had heard enough, Beatrix crept from behind the tree.

"We will require twice as much cheese on the morrow," the servant said.

"Guests?"

Beatrix paused to learn who had passed near Purley Abbey.

"Baron Cuthbert brought a fair-sized entourage with him."

With a sigh, Beatrix slipped away. When she reached the gatehouse, she gained the side of a corpulent woman who lugged a sack of milled flour. Keeping her chin down, she stayed with the woman halfway across the drawbridge, then surged ahead and nearly collided with a horse and rider.

It was the horse that caused fear to leap through her—some vague memory having roused an aversion to the animals she had once loved. As she murmured an apology to the rider whose leg she brushed against, a familiar scent teased her, but she had no time for it. She needed her sanctuary. Now.

Michael turned in the saddle and frowned at the slight, mantled figure hastening opposite. It was not a chill day. In fact, he had removed his own mantle after departing Castle Soaring hours past.

Remembering the welcoming arms of the wench he had left behind, he silently cursed the order that he present himself at Broehne Castle. Though Aldous Lavonne likely sought Michael's services as a physician, he and his son surely wished to know the result of the continuing search for Beatrix Wulfrith.

Michael gripped the reins tighter. A month had passed and still there was no word of the woman's whereabouts. All that was known for certain was that she had not returned to her family, for they believed her dead, as told by the sister who was said to have seen a bloodied Beatrix in the ravine. And Baron Lavonne had made no attempt to correct them. Thus, despite the absence of her body, which a delegation sent by the king's men had determined must have fallen prey to scavengers, the Wulfriths mourned their lost sister. Eventually, though, they would come in search of answers—would surely have done so before now had the eldest brother not been compelled to accompany the king to Wales. Doubtless, King Henry believed it would allow Garr Wulfrith time to cool his anger. The younger brothers could growl, snap, and claw all they liked, but lacking the bite of their older brother, there was little they could do. For now.

And that gave Michael time to hunt down Beatrix Wulfrith. Though he knew it was possible she had, indeed, become fodder for animals of one sort or another, something told him she had either begged sanctuary at an abbey or gone to ground. Despite her head injury, the wisp of a woman was cunning.

Recalling her accusation against Simon, he rumbled low in his throat. Wherever she was—he fingered the small scar caused by the goblet she had brought down on his head—he would find her.

"My lord!" One of three accompanying knights drew alongside. "Something is amiss?"

Michael looked away from the mantled figure, but not before a flash of red caught his eye. He frowned at the aging Sir Canute. "Naught is amiss—"

He jerked his head around and stared at the lower edge of the black mantle worn by the one who had blundered into his path. Had he imagined red? Surely she would not have returned to Broehne...

He reined his destrier around. "Tell Baron Lavonne I shall attend his father shortly."

The knight's face, resembling the bark of a gnarled tree, furrowed deeper. "You know the old man's temper, Michael."

Canute's concern, ever fatherly though they were of no relation, gave Michael pause. Now that Michael was keeper of Soaring, his old friend rarely addressed him by his Christian name. Only in privacy and matters of urgency did he lapse into the familiarity that Michael missed of their days as knights errant.

Michael eased his heels from his mount's sides, leaned toward the man, and gripped his shoulder. "You worry too much for me, old friend. Pray, ease your mind. I shall return anon."

"I ought to go with you."

"Anon," Michael repeated. As he guided his mount over the draw-bridge, he told himself it was a fool's quest. But it was the nearest he had come these past weeks. Aldous Lavonne could wait.

Beatrix tossed the hood back, lifted her face, and smiled at the distant clouds through which golden light filtered. "Again, You deliver me."

She hastened down the nave and skirted the false crypt. Before the remains of the high altar, she loosened the mantle and let it fall from her shoulders. Grateful for its absence that had flushed her with warmth, she glanced at the inner crimson and conjured a vision of the man to whom the garment belonged. Soon she need not worry about him, for on the return journey she had decided she would not wait for winter to journey to Stern Castle. She would give her family another sennight, and if they did not come, she would brave the wood and roads. It was a fearsome thing, but she wearied of the helplessness of waiting on something that might never appear—of hiding like a coward.

Smoothing the woolen tunic "borrowed" from the pack of a knight who had paused at Purley Abbey, she lowered to her knees.

The Pater Noster, she decided and squeezed her eyes closed to remember words that had once been as if written on her lips.

"Our Father in heaven...hallowed..." Though she faltered through the words, they were all there, unlike the memories that yet eluded. And that was something over which to rejoice.

"Lead us not into temptation," she finished, "but deliver us from the evil one."

"Do you truly believe He hears the prayers of a murderess?"

Heart staggering, Beatrix opened her eyes wide and struggled to make sense of the voice that should not be in this place. At last, she recalled the scent that had whispered through her on the drawbridge. It was Michael D'Arci she had brushed against. And something about their brief encounter had made him follow the hooded figure that hurried past him.

Slowly, Beatrix rose. Keeping her back to him, searching beyond the altar for an escape, her gaze stuttered over the breach in the ceiling of the true crypt. She gasped at the realization that *this* was what had eluded her before she had earlier departed the abbey. The false floor that she always took care to place over the breach lay where she had dropped it upon climbing from the crypt this morn.

Fool! But even had she covered the crypt, her hiding place was of no use now. Or was it? She slid her gaze to the ambulatory where once monks had walked and beyond that to the remains of a lesser chapel. D'Arci would follow. Unfortunately, if he had others with him, her plotting would see no light. But if he had come alone...

Though her conscience recoiled, she reminded herself he was no different from his brother. No consideration had he shown her and none must she show him.

"Lady Beatrix once more lacks for words?"

Deliver us from the evil one.

She turned and saw D'Arci stood thirty feet back. Shoulder braced against a column that had once supported a roof, arms folded over a broad chest, he projected the air of one who had won a deciding game. And even at this distance, there was no mistaking the victory in his pale, gray eyes.

Why did he have to look so much like his brother? If not that he was a handful of years older and his dark hair sharply contrasted with Sir Simon's blond, it would be the same man. However, she had not thought Sir Simon handsome. And Michael D'Arci was, though his eyes hated and his mouth twisted a smile that caused her fear to run faster. Though she told herself she cared not that he appeared to have suffered no lasting ill from the blow she had dealt him, she was relieved.

"I knew it was possible you had taken sanctuary at an abbey"—he swept his gaze around the ruins—"but this I did not expect."

As she had known, just as she had known he would not overlook the abbeys in his search for her. Thus, she had not sought sanctuary for fear that a goodly purse of coin might buy it away. Better faith in herself than faith in corrupt men.

D'Arci straightened. "I say again, do you think God hears the prayers of a murderess?"

She looked to the left and right of him. He appeared to have come alone.

He took a step toward her, causing sunlight to streak his sword hilt.

"God hears the prayers of all," she slipped the words past her lips before fear could smite them.

"Even those of my brother?"

In another life, she would have laughed, but there was nothing humorous about the panic rising in her breast and spreading thought to thought. She clenched her hands. If she could only be more angry than fearful, she might clear this impassable bridge.

Calling on her memory of that night at Broehne Castle when D'Arci had implied she was witless, she said, "Have you another brother, Lord D'Arci? For surely..." Her throat constricted. "...you do not speak of the same who made to..." Her voice trailed off and lids fluttered as she struggled to piece the fragmented word together. "...who made to violate me."

She envied the anger that leapt from his face. Were hers so large, nothing would stopper her mind or tongue.

"Will you come to me," he growled, "or I to you?"

Where was his horse? In the wood? Aye, it would not do to announce himself sooner and be denied her torment.

She took a step back. "I am no fool, Lord——" She cast about for his name, but it had gone into hiding. Embarrassment warmed her. Perhaps she *was* a fool.

"Aye, you are a fool, Lady Beatrix," he concurred and strode forward.

For a moment, she could not move, but then survival roused her and she turned and ran. Praying her feet would fall such that she spanned the crypt without drawing attention to the narrow breach, praying D'Arci—aye, that was his name—would not clear it, she landed her foot on the other side.

Though she winced in anticipation of his fall through the crypt, no sound rent the air. Or mayhap her blood rushed too loud to hear? Reaching the lesser chapel, she glanced over her shoulder.

D'Arci followed, though without urgency. But then, what had he to run for when he believed her only escape was past him? She swung around to face him and suppressed the impulse to look to the breach. Three more steps and——

"'Tis done," he bit.

Now only one...

His foot landed at the center of the breach and, with a shout, he plunged through the ceiling. There was a thud and a resounding crack. Something had broken. His neck?

A moment later, the abbey ruins resounded with blasphemies.

Not his neck, then. Though she longed to flee, she forced herself forward and dropped to her knees alongside the breach. As the sun was nearly gone past the afternoon, the crypt was slow to divulge its secret, but when her eyes adjusted, she saw the dark figure fifteen feet below.

Continuing to curse, D'Arci sat up and reached for something.

The rope! She scrambled for the end that ran up out of the crypt, caught it, and lunged backward.

"Hell's fire!"

Wincing at his profanity as the rope cleared the crypt's opening, she imagined the walls wept at being so desecrated.

"God's rood!"

That he should curse was sacrilege enough, but in God's abode...

Michael D'Arci was a blackguard through and through, his mouth so utterly fouled he could not possibly hope for heaven. But then, he *was* his brother's brother.

Beatrix scrambled to the edge of the crypt. "You are in the...House of the Lord."

His eyes glittered up at her. "It looks more the devil's lair to me."

She startled at what he named the sanctuary that was all the comfort she had known this past month.

"My leg is broken!"

Wishing compassion did not grip her so, she peered closer and picked out the peculiar bend of his left leg.

"Witch! By my own hand I shall light the fire that spews you to hell!"

His threat freeing her from her misplaced concern, she pushed to her feet. "You will light no...fire," she called down. "As you say, 'tis done."

His shouts pounded her back as she crossed to where she had dropped his red mantle and swept it up. This day she would begin her journey to Stern Castle, for she did not doubt D'Arci would soon follow.

Unless he dies down there.

Her feet faltered as compassion reached for her again. Surely someone would miss him. Someone in passing would hear his shouts.

And if no one does?

"I care not!" She stretched her legs farther. All that mattered was that she leave, and the sooner she was gone from here, the better her chances. In fact, given a horse—

Somewhere in the wood was D'Arci's destrier. However, the thought of mounting the great animal made her shudder and opened wide a memory of urging her palfrey to greater speed, an arm slamming around her waist, pale eyes, and cruel laughter.

She remembered Sir Simon overtaking her and pulling her onto his mount, but surely that had not beget this fear of horses. There had to be more, but though she strained to recapture what it was, the door remained closed. Regardless, that day had been the beginning of her end. So much she had lost that might never be hers again.

Tears wet her eyes. Though the simple act of expression continued to trip her tongue, albeit not as greatly as during her imprisonment at Broehne Castle, inside she was nearly the same. Inside she knew the intricacies of numbers and letters. Yet to hear her stumbling words and searching silence, one named her witless.

"Dear God," she whispered, "I tire of being a fool. Pray, heal my mind and deliver me home that I might find myself again."

She pressed onward, determined to find D'Arci's horse and leave its master behind.

6

A pox upon the witch!

Michael shook with an anger that was becoming increasingly familiar where Beatrix Wulfrith was concerned—first, when news was brought of his brother's murder, next when she claimed Simon had ravished her, then when he regained consciousness at Broehne Castle. Now he suffered a broken leg and a dark pit into which he had allowed himself to be led. And he had named *her* a fool!

As scalding pain shot knee to thigh and spread hip to hip, he ground his jaws so hard he thought he heard a tooth crack. "'Tis not done!"

Anger shook him harder, though he knew it was more than that. It was shock such as he had seen during the wars between King Stephen and Duke Henry when they had battled for the throne of England. Though Michael's days had been spent fighting for Henry's cause, often his nights were devoted to tending the wounded and dying. Time and again he treated broken limbs and the resultant pooling of blood beneath the skin as his stepmother had taught him to do. Thus, he had seen what often followed shock, but—curse all!—*he* would not lose consciousness.

Knowing he must act immediately if he was to walk again without hitch or hobble, he stretched his useless leg out before him and felt his hands down his calf. The leg was broken below the knee. That it was slowly numbing likely meant the bone ends pressed on an artery.

He grasped his calf and, with a shout that echoed around the crypt, forced the bones together. Perspiration coursing his brow, perception flickering, he drew slow, deep breaths until the darkness receded.

As he would need a splint to prevent further damage from the jagged bones, he swept his gaze around the dim, but the only thing available to him was his sword and its hard leather scabbard. Though it was a disgrace that a man's blade be reduced to a splint, he pressed the flat of it to the outside of the leg, the scabbard to the inside, and bound the two with strips torn from his mantle.

"Devil take!" He fell onto his back and stared through the breach at the clouds gathering over late afternoon. He cursed himself for not accepting Canute's offer to accompany him, cursed himself again for not sooner seeing the rope. He *would* lay hands to Beatrix Wulfrith. And the next time she would not escape.

Wincing as D'Arci's pained shout sounded around the wood, wishing her conscience was as lost to her as words, Beatrix stared at the golden destrier where it grazed near the stream. Or perhaps it was not conscience that refused to let her flee.

She looked back the way she had come, then right the way she ought to go. Perhaps fear of the horse held her here. But if that were so, she could simply walk away. God-given conscience, then. Still, she fought it, telling herself He would not wish her to risk her life.

She glanced at the darkening sky. Would the rain bring any travelers to shelter at Purley? It had not during the last rainfall, and previous to that it had brought brigands who had trod the false floor beneath which she lay. If one of ill repute answered D'Arci's call, it could mean his death, but if she remained, of what use was she to him?

She dropped to her knees, bowed her head, and prayed for guidance. Unfortunately, the guidance that fell heavy upon her was not the guidance she wished.

"'Twill mean my death," she whispered into the Lord's ear, but still she could not leave D'Arci.

She straightened. What was she to do? Just as she could not send for help, neither could she go into the crypt to tend her enemy. He was too much alive for that, though for how much longer?

Her writhing thoughts nearly made her cry. Wishing she could smooth them flat and look upon them without rent or wrinkle, she pressed the heels of her palms against her eyes in hopes the darkness would free her from distractions.

Food and drink. That she could provide D'Arci. She lowered her hands and looked to the man's destrier that eyed her as it chewed a mouthful of grass. Struck by its beauty, a thrill of old rippled through her.

If she sent the animal from the wood, might it lead D'Arci's men back here? If so, the sooner she could begin her journey to Stern—providing she stayed alert and ready to flee. Even so, D'Arci would surely be fast to her path.

She groaned, causing the destrier to turn one ear forward and the other back.

First the leather packs tied to the saddle, Beatrix decided. As she stepped forward, the horse snorted and jerked its head.

Though perspiration crept her neck, Beatrix continued forward. As she neared, she saw D'Arci had not tethered his mount, apparently confident it would await his return.

At ten feet, the destrier tossed its head. Great eyes staring, it followed her approach.

Beatrix swallowed. All she wanted were the packs and the skin that hung from one—hopefully full of wine that D'Arci could use to cleanse any open wound. A broken leg, he had told, which could mean the bone had come through the flesh. She prayed not—

Dear God, why must I care? Wishing He did not reside so full within her, she took the last steps to the destrier and only realized how near she was when she stood before it. Ears twitching, it continued to regard her.

"Be still, steed. I vow I shall not mount you." Feeling as if about to reach a hand to a flame, she took a step toward the packs.

The destrier snorted and tossed its head again, causing its white mane to ripple like silk.

"Upon my word, I shall not try to…gain your back."

He sidled and shook his head.

The protest striking her as exceedingly human, she smiled. "You do not believe me?"

Again, it shook its head.

A bubble of laughter parted Beatrix's lips and, for a moment, made her fear someone was in the wood with her. When was the last time she had laughed? It had been far too long.

She snapped a handful of grass from the earth. "I tell you, true, I shall not." Wishing her hand did not quake so, she proffered the grass.

The destrier leaned forward, noisily inhaled the scent, and plucked the offering from her hand.

Beatrix reached for more grass and felt a muzzle against the sleeve of her mantle—D'Arci's mantle. Did the animal smell his master on her as she so often did? Hoping it would make the beast more agreeable, she turned a palm up and jerked when the destrier swept its head to it. Would he allow her to trespass?

"Your packs only," she murmured. "Your master is in need."

When the destrier swung its head away, Beatrix stepped nearer and laid a hand to its shoulder. Another step and she was alongside. She reached to the first pack and loosened its saddle ties. It came free, and with it the wineskin.

The destrier looked around. Fortunately, both ears were forward, indicating it had passed from uncertainty to curiosity.

It was hard to resist the urge to make do with just the one pack, but Beatrix reached for the second. Shortly, it also lay over her arm. She stepped back. "Now be gone."

The destrier shifted its weight.

"Be gone, I say!" She slapped its hindquarter and the animal trotted away.

Hoping it would return to Broehne Castle and lead Christian Lavonne's men to the abbey ruins, Beatrix ran. As she approached the true crypt, she searched out the rope. It was where she had left it. Though no further sounds issued from below, D'Arci was down there.

Upon gaining the breach, she dropped the packs to the ground, dropped to her knees, and peered into the dim. Why did he not call out? Even if he had not heard her approach, surely the thump of his packs announced her presence. Unless he had lost consciousness.

Past his pain, Michael stared at the woman above. Why had she returned? To murder him as she had murdered his brother? He flinched as the muscles around the broken bone spasmed. She was mistaken if she believed he would be the easy prey Simon had proven. He had fought too long and survived too much—first, as a young knight whose lord had turned on him, then when he had assumed the life of a knight errant and fought for Duke Henry. Of course, the witch *had* bested him twice now. But that would not happen again.

"I wonder, Lady Beatrix, who is more the fool?"

She gasped.

Had she thought him dead? Such disappointment.

After a long moment, she said, "That would be you, Lord D'Arci." Her voice was as crisp as a barely ripe apple.

His spasming muscles nearly dragged a groan from him. If he *was* the fool, it would not always be so. "For what have you returned?"

She drew back. Then to taunt him was all she wanted? New rage hurtled though him, but what sounded like rummaging turned it aside.

Shortly, a bundle fell through the breach and landed beside him. Disbelief shot through him. His destrier would not have allowed her so near—unless Sartan was dead.

"Where is my horse?" he shouted as the wine skin also landed.

"Returned to...Broehne Castle, I expect."

There she was wrong.

The other pack fell, the clatter announcing it contained his physician's tools. Too, there would be bread and dried meat providing she had not taken them for herself.

She reappeared. "You have food, drink, and..." Her mouth worked and brow pleated.

"Medicinals," he ground.

She stood. "I shall find you something with which to...splint your leg."

Then, amid the shadows in which he rested, she could not make out the sword and scabbard with which he had bound the bones. But why did she do this? Surely she boasted no conscience, and she would be ten-fold the fool if she thought to turn him from seeking justice.

The sound of her footsteps evidencing she went toward the small chapel to which she had fled in leading him to the breach, he grunted as another spasm shook him. Unfortunately, those to follow would come harder before the muscles eased. He pushed onto an elbow, the resulting pain causing moisture to run into his eyes.

Forcing deep breaths, he opened the pack containing the foodstuffs and his physician's tools. The first vial that came to hand was not what he was looking for—he knew it by the shape and weight—but the third...

Aye. However, as he started to unstopper it, realization struck. The preparation of bitter mandrake might render him deeply asleep, thus making him three times a fool to Beatrix Wulfrith. He clenched the vial as another spasm thrust up his leg and radiated through his spine. He would simply have to suffer.

When droplets of water landed on the back of his hand, he glared up at the billowing clouds that portended a downpour.

"A scourge upon you," he muttered as he thrust the vial to the bottom of the pack. Without the succor of mandrake, he would have to drag himself back from the opening if he was to avoid becoming drenched. And the pain would be nearly intolerable.

The rain beginning to fall harder and seep through his mantle, he pulled the packs onto his lap and levered onto his outstretched arms. As he dragged his injured leg across the floor, biting down on the need to shout out his torment, the dark of the crypt swallowed him. Finally, some twenty feet distant from the opening, he backed up to a column.

Tunic clinging to his perspiring chest, he squeezed his eyes closed. By the morrow, the worst would be over. The muscles would be quieted and the bone set to undertake the long process of healing—providing he had not erred, which was possible in acting physician to one's self.

"Lord D'Arci?"

He looked to the opening that poured rain into the crypt. At this distance, he could see nothing of Beatrix Wulfrith.

Let her wonder where I have gone, he told himself. After all, questions often led to seeking.

The silence of rain enlarged, but just as he concluded she had withdrawn, something fell through the breach and sent a hollow clatter around the crypt.

"Splints for your leg," she called and pulled something over the hole that turned back the rain and cast darkness all around.

Michael stared into nothingness and considered the wooden splints. Though their use would return his sword to hand, he would leave them where fallen. Another question for Beatrix Wulfrith.

Remembering that which he had carried since he had tended her head injury—which had urged him on when it seemed she would never be found—he opened the purse on his belt. From beneath the coins, he extracted the tress of flaxen hair he had cut away to stitch up her head and rubbed it between thumb and forefinger.

"Seek me, witch. Seek me soon."

With night had come the sound of distant riders, but none had paused at Purley. Were they searching for D'Arci? Having been too fearful to allow herself more than snatches of sleep throughout the long dark, a fatigued Beatrix wove a path from the small chapel out into a morning that sparkled as if God had cast diamonds upon it.

For the moment forgetting her worries, she breathed that wonderful mix of rain, foliage, and earth, then sent up a prayer of thanks that she had been given another day. If not for the breach...

She looked to it and struggled as she had done when met with silence on the day past. How did D'Arci fare?

Fear had shot through her when she had peered into the crypt on the day past and found him absent, but she had calmed herself with the reminder there was only one way out and he must not be too badly injured if he was able to pull himself clear of the rain. Fortunately, the new day ought to throw enough light into the crypt to calm her conscience.

Lowering to her knees before the breach, she lifted the false floor. It fell back, its meeting with the moist ground causing mist to fly upon the air and fleck her tunic. She leaned forward.

Sunlight illuminated the stone floor of the crypt, as well as the wooden splints where she had dropped them on the day past.

Dear God, even I know broken limbs are best repaired immediately. She caught her breath. Michael D'Arci had dragged himself back from the breach, but that did not mean he was hale.

Where was he? Though sunlight lit the area beyond that which shafted the floor, it did so hesitantly. Beatrix squinted and swept her gaze to the shadows. He had to be among them. As the old passage into the crypt was choked with the debris of its collapse, he could not have gotten out. But where—?

There. She strained to pick out the still shadow and decided it was D'Arci propped against a column. With uncertain relief, she said, "Good morn, Lord D'Arci."

No answer. No movement. And yet...Did she only imagine his hating gaze?

"Lord D'Arci?"

What if he is dead? her conscience demanded.

What if 'tis deceit he works? she countered.

What if he yet lives, but this moment is dying?

I do not care.

You lie.

She looked to the rope, then over her shoulder at the fallen column to which she had anchored the opposite end. Its path, crypt to column, was concealed beneath dirt and stone to assure no one discovered her sanctuary. But D'Arci had, to his detriment. To *her* detriment, she must use the rope again.

She tried to convince herself it was a risk she need not take, but he had not splinted his leg. Though she had named him a fool, Michael D'Arci was not. Never would he sacrifice the ability to walk on the chance his unsplinted leg would bring her within reach.

She removed the mantle, gathered the rope, and dropped it into the breach. With one last look to assure D'Arci had not come out of the shadows, she lowered herself into the crypt. As she worked her calloused hands down the rope, she remembered how difficult a feat it had been when she had first taken refuge here. However, once she had gotten beyond the blisters and bleeding, it had become easier. It also helped that she did not weigh much.

She returned her attention to the shadow of D'Arci. Still no movement. Upon meeting the ground, she said, "Lord D'Arci?"

No response, as if his dark figure was but written in ink.

She pulled the dagger—D'Arci's—from her boot and retrieved the splints. "How do you fare?"

If he were halfway hale, he had to have heard her. Was he dire ill? Worse?

Clutching the splints, she advanced and was grateful when her eyes adjusted to the dim beyond the breach and picked out his pale tunic. Try though she did to catch the glitter of eyes that would show him capable of responding, she could not, but at ten feet, the sword alongside his leg took form, as did bands of pale cloth that crossed his lower leg and turned around what looked to be a scabbard. Then by his sword he was splinted—

She nearly ran, but foolishness prevailed at the thought he might yet be ailing.

Or lying in wait.

"Lord D'Arci, I..."

Words, Beatrix! First think them through.

"Is there...something you require?" She almost wished he were unconscious that she might be spared the humiliation of the stumbling speech that bothered her most in his presence. Was it because his learned mind grasped the knowledge of healing that should have been hers? In the long, cool days of abbey life she would have grown and studied herbs, concocted preparations and medicinals, tended the ill and prayed for their relief. If she did not regain her facility with speech and thought, what was left to her? How she loathed the prison walls her mind could not scale!

She took another step forward, and it was then she caught the narrow gleam of D'Arci's eyes. She dropped the splints and spun around.

"I had hoped you would draw nearer," his voice resounded around the crypt.

Beatrix turned. "I am not the fool you...think I am."

"This time you are not, but there shall be other times."

Why could she not abandon him? He sounded well, and surely someone would come. Perhaps if she left the rope down the breach he could pull himself out. But with his injury, did he possess enough strength? And what if he further injured himself?

Once more berating her conscience, she stepped into the shaft of light that shone through the breach and returned the dagger to her boot.

"Why have you not fled?" he called.

She gripped the rope. "Even you, Lord D'Arci, do not...deserve to die."

"I shall take comfort in that, Lady Beatrix." Were his voice of barb, she would be torn asunder. "A pity you did not show my brother the same consideration."

She pulled her denial back, for of what use was it? "A hundred times I would do again what I did," she said, anger ordering her words such that they flowed without falter.

"That I believe."

"You should." Regardless of the outcome, she would guard her virtue and life as she had done with his brother, though exactly how she had defended herself she still could not recall. "Now, have you need of anything?"

"The use of my leg and a hangman's noose."

That dampened her anger. "The one you shall have, but not the… other. As soon as someone happens upon you, I shall be gone."

"To Stern?"

Immediately, she rebuked herself for her surprise. Of course he knew her destination.

"Water," D'Arci said.

Beatrix frowned.

"I am in need of water," he snapped.

"The…well is foul. Will you take drink from the stream?" At this distance it ran cleaner than at the upper end where it passed near the village. One unaccustomed to the dross could suffer cramping and nausea as Beatrix had first done.

"'Twill suffice."

"Toss your…wineskin that I might bring it."

"I know not what has become of it."

Trickery? She glanced into the shadows where she had made her bed this past month. All she possessed was there—not only the skin used to gather water but, more importantly, her psalter.

Once more pulling her dagger, she stepped toward the pallet. Though D'Arci did not move, his pale eyes amid the shadows followed her.

Holding his gaze, she bent and felt for the skin. It came to hand, as did her psalter. The latter providing comfort she had missed on the night past, she pushed it and the skin beneath her belt and hastened to the rope.

Anything to return her to the crypt, Michael mused as he watched her slide *his* dagger into her boot. Anything to draw the flaxen-haired witch near.

As she climbed hand over hand, he was struck by the strength required to do so. True, she was light of weight—much lighter than when she had been at Broehne Castle—but one's upper body must still be in good form to pull along the lower.

When would she return? He glanced at the skin at his side. The wine would quench his thirst far better than the tainted water for which he had sent her. And when she delivered that, he would send her for something else if he could not tempt her near. He need only be patient. Unfortunately, he bored quickly, preferring all and everyone to move with utmost speed and resenting time wasted on waiting.

With a soft grunt, Lady Beatrix transferred her hands to the edge of the breach and levered herself out of the crypt.

Michael stared at the swaying rope that promised escape. Hearing her retreating footfalls, he began to smile. However, as he started to move from the column, she returned and reeled the rope out.

Curse her! He clenched his hands to counter the burn that shot up his leg. Though the long night had reduced the pain to a dull throb, even slight movement set him afire.

He reached for the nearest pack, removed the box of flint and tinder, and opened it to find only a half dozen pieces of tinder. Hoping fuel was to be had somewhere in the pit, as smoke might bring his or Baron Lavonne's men sooner, he removed the flint. On the first strike, the tinder caught and jumped light around the walls.

"God's eyes!" He clenched his hands into fists. Stone was everywhere, most conspicuously the open stairway that had long ago granted passage to this hidden room. As the steps had collapsed and broken away from the wall, there was a distance of at least eight feet from the top of the debris to the door set in the ceiling. Even if he dragged his broken leg up the strewn stairway and made it upright, his reach would fall short of the door.

The last of the tinder's flame nearing his fingertips, he continued to peer around the crypt, taking in the pallet from which the lady had retrieved the skin, next the discarded splints. The latter would not provide enough wood to sustain a flame for long.

He blew out the tinder, drew the wine skin from his belt, and took a long swallow. It was time to return his sword to hand.

He eased forward, each jolt to the leg causing him to gnash his teeth, but at last he reached the splints. Careful to keep his leg positioned so it would not require resetting, he made the exchange.

Sword once more honorable, he considered the pallet—that woman's sorry bed this past month that evidenced she was reduced to the squalor of the meanest villein. Still, she possessed determination, meaning no matter how blue her eyes, no matter how they illuminated her face, he must not forget it.

Deciding that even if the pallet proved infested, it was preferable to reclining against the column, he rolled onto his uninjured knee, pressed his palms to the stone floor, and slowly straightened despite his leg's vehement protest.

Curse Lady Beatrix for this laming! Curse her for the lie—aye, most of all the lie told of Simon!

With each halting step, he swore against her until he finally reached the dimly lit pallet. He put a foot to it, turned his back to the wall, and eased himself down the rough-hewn stone.

A scent struck him. Woodruff and...fennel? He drew another breath. Aye, and other scents so faint their names could not be called to remembrance. Though Lady Beatrix made her bed in a crumbling crypt, it seemed she was not reduced to squalor—at least, not entirely.

Michael pressed a hand to the woolen blanket that encased the stuff of her pallet. The sweet scent wafted stronger, though not in any way offensive. He nearly smiled.

Wondering what, besides a skin and psalter, the lady kept, he lifted a corner of the pallet and searched a hand beneath. A purse clattered its contents as he drew it forth—*his* purse—then came a coil of rope.

He looked to the packs he had left near the column. When she returned, he would ask her to deliver them to him. And perhaps this time she would draw too near.

"You wish to know of your family?"

Arresting her retreat, Beatrix stared at the rope she had come down a minute earlier.

"'Twas for tidings of them that you risked Broehne Castle, was it not?"

She looked over her shoulder at where he sat on her pallet. It bothered her that he had claimed that which she had every night lain upon. Then there was the matter of the wooden splints that had returned his sword to him.

"Was it not?" he pressed.

Not what? She looked to where she had tossed the skin of water alongside his uninjured leg. Of what did he—? Ah, her family.

"I l-learned all I must needs know." A lie, but surely he would demand a price for the telling of whatever he knew—*if* he knew anything.

"What did you learn?"

She started toward the rope.

"You know the reason they have not come for you, do you not?"

She swung back around. "What do you know of it?" She was but ten feet distant from him when she realized she advanced on him, just as he wished her to do. She hastened to the rope.

"I am in need of my packs," he snapped.

Heart bumping against her ribs, she looked from D'Arci on her pallet to the packs. If she retrieved them, it would put her distant from the rope, but would it give him enough time to come between her and escape? He *had* gotten himself across the crypt.

If not for the dagger, she would have refused him. She pulled it and, holding him with her gaze, hurried to the column. D'Arci did not move when she stepped toward him and tossed the packs at his feet. Keeping the dagger before her, she backed away.

"Too, I am in need of sustenance."

"There are…foodstuffs in your pack."

"No more."

She did not care for this game. "I do not believe you."

"Come near and I shall show you."

She shook her head. "At the noo——" The remainder of the word slipped away, and she felt her lids flutter as she struggled to recapture it.

"The nooning hour?" D'Arci supplied, derision in his tone.

Grasping anger to right her words, Beatrix said, "At *middle day*, I shall bring you f-fish." *Lord, if only I could harness my anger better!*

"Then my jailer intends to cook for me?"

"I do not. When your belly aches to pain, Lord D——" Gone again!

"D'Arci."

Frustration stung her eyes. Why did she persist in conversing with him?

"When it aches to pain, what?" he pressed.

Thankfully, his condescension caused her anger to course. "Then you shall eat it as I do. Uncooked."

That quieted him long enough for her to make it to the rope where she was struck by a feeling she would never be free of Michael D'Arci. Wherever she went, he would follow, and one day she would fall to him. Aching to clasp the psalter she had left aboveground, she climbed the rope.

7

THREE DAYS IN this stinking pit. Three days waiting to catch her unawares. But she never came near enough. This day would be different.

Drumming his fingers on the flint box, Michael looked to his lower leg. It was too soon to know how he would pass the remainder of his life, as a cripple or with two legs firm beneath him, but the pain had lessened and the spasming was nearing its end. Of course, what he intended might jeopardize—

Curse the leg! If it needed to be set again, so be it. He glanced at the collapsed stairway that was of no use to him. However, the coil of rope found beneath Beatrix Wulfrith's pallet was of certain use.

Where was she? It was past the nooning hour and she had not appeared. Had she gone for more fish? He grimaced at the ripening scent that transcended the other foul odors marking his stay in the crypt. On the day past, she had come with fish wrapped in cloth and tossed it to him. He had tried to coax her nearer, but to no avail. Thus, he had asked her to refill the skin, the water of which he had emptied on the stone floor. It was late afternoon before she returned, and then again she had not spoken a word, even when she saw the fish was untouched.

Twinged with regret at having shown contempt for her faltering speech, Michael frowned. For this—the shame that had shown upon her face—she held her words that might otherwise have brought her within reach. But his regret went deeper. It made him feel cruel to seek her unease by such means. Though impatience had made him speak for her, anger at his situation set the tone with which he had done so. Aye, cruel.

He stopped on that. As *she* surely did not war over the cruelty dealt his brother, why did he? The woman had bled out Simon's life then told he had ravished her!

Struck by memories of the boy left behind seven years past, Michael closed his eyes. Twice, sometimes thrice a year, he had returned to the barony given over to their eldest brother, Joseph. Each time, the impetuous Simon had begged at Michael's heels, seeking attention no others provided.

Michael had given what he could, training his half brother at arms, challenging him at chess, talking with him late into the night—excepting the last time that Michael had returned before joining Duke Henry's army. Simon had been absent, belatedly sent to the north to begin his squire's training. Though it was needed for him to transition from boy to man, Michael had missed the brash youth, as had Simon's fragile mother. She had wept on Michael's shoulder at having lost the argument with Joseph to keep her only child with her.

Not until Duke Henry gained the throne of England years later had Michael seen Simon again. When Christian Lavonne had awarded Castle Soaring to Michael—not only out of gratitude for Michael saving his arm from amputation, but out of need for a physician for his infirm father—Michael had sent for his brother. Eager as ever, Simon had appeared within a fortnight. Though Michael had intended to enlist him as a household knight, Aldous Lavonne encouraged his son to take him into his own household. Grudgingly, Michael agreed, knowing it would provide better opportunities for Simon, never guessing it would mean his death when he was sent to fetch the baron's unwilling bride.

Michael drew a breath of dank air. Cruel mockery was the least Beatrix Wulfrith deserved. Where was she?

Would they never come? They searched for D'Arci, that she knew from talk of the villagers she had slipped amongst this morn, but none found their way to Purley.

Leave. Someone will come.

Beatrix sighed and once more swept her gaze over the ruins. All appeared as it had when she had left. The rope alongside the breach was barely visible, coiled as it was beneath dirt and leaves, and the only movement was of birds and a trio of squirrels scurrying among the ruins.

She stepped from behind the tree and grimaced as her boots sucked mud up over the toes. Not that they were any worse than the rest of her, the journey to the village having flecked her toe to hip. Mayhap this afternoon she would bathe in the chill stream.

As she started across the nave, she dropped the hood of the mantle and pushed the garment off her shoulders so it hung down her back. It was not so much a warm day that made her seek relief from the heat, but exertion from having run all the way to the abbey.

She lowered to her haunches before the true crypt and touched the pouch at her belt. Berries of deepest pink, the name of which fled her, swelled the cloth and seeped their juice through the loose weave. Outside the village, she had paused to indulge in the sweet, slightly sour fruits. Though she told herself D'Arci would reject them as he had the fish, she had nothing else to offer. Was it poisoning he feared? If so, why did he drink the water? Or did he?

She leaned forward. The high sun shone through the breach, and when she peered nearer, she saw D'Arci was on her pallet. Watching and waiting.

She let the rope down and began her descent. When her feet met the floor, she stepped forward and only then realized she had not removed the mantle. As it was gotten by ill means, she was loath to wear it in D'Arci's presence, but there was nothing for it now.

Her eyes adjusted as she neared him and nose twitched at the ripening scent made worse by fish turning foul. Though she could not help but resent the waste of food that would have eased the ache of her own belly, she removed the pouch from her belt. Twelve feet distant from D'Arci, she halted.

"'Twas the red that revealed you." He jutted his chin. "My mantle."

So he had glimpsed the crimson when she had passed him at the castle—that bit of color her undoing. For the fool her tongue made of her, she resisted his attempt to converse and tossed the pouch to him. He caught it but granted it no more than a glance.

"Stay," he called as she retreated. "I would speak with you."

Nay, he would taunt her.

"You do not wish to know about your family? The reason they have not come for you?"

She struggled against snapping at the bait. And failed. "The reason?"

His hand tested the weight of the pouch. "Surely it must pain you to know they have left you at the mercy of Baron Lavonne."

Though she knew she ought to climb the rope as fast as her hands could reach, she took a step toward him, and another, all the while practicing the delivery of what she would say. "Why have they not come?"

"'Tis apparent, is it not, that by murder you have stained the Wulfrith name?"

She knew his words for what they were, for never would her family believe such ill of her. "That is as large a lie as the lie that I...killed your brother."

His brow lowered. "Then 'twas not you with Simon in the ravine?"

"'Twas me, but—"

"Not your dagger that rent his flesh?"

"It was, but—"

"And you would do it again, did you not say?"

"I did, but—"

"Pray, of what lie do you speak, Lady Beatrix?"

The anger of which she had lamented the absence, once more spoke through her and she stepped nearer. "I did not—"

"But you did! Simon is dead."

And no matter what she said, he would not believe her. Realizing how near she had drawn, she halted. "You know naught of me. Naught of what happened. Naught—"

Glimpsing the rope D'Arci held, she jumped back, but the loop on the floor, into the center of which she had stepped, struck her ankles and cinched tight as a hangman's noose.

With a cry, she landed hard on her backside. As she was dragged toward the pallet and the man whose eyes gleamed triumphant, she scrabbled for something to catch hold of, but there was no purchase over the stone floor. The dagger the only thing left to her, she wrenched it from her boot.

D'Arci pulled on the rope one last time and sprang. A pained grunt tearing from him, he fell on her and caught her wrists together before she could wield the dagger.

"I know naught of you?" He thrust his face near hers. "Naught but that anger is more your enemy than your friend, Lady Beatrix."

Friend to her tongue, enemy to good sense. Aching for her foolishness, she strained at her wrists.

"*Now* 'tis done." His warm breath fanned her face.

She searched a knee toward his man's place, but when he pinned her harder, causing his splints to gouge her calf, she was reminded of his injury—the only weakness available to her. If she could only...

Her anger flickered. She could not. As he said, it *was* done. This day, this very hour could prove her last. Unable to bear the light in his pale eyes, she turned her face opposite.

"Release the dagger."

Though she knew he would take it from her, she gripped it harder.

He levered up and pried at her fingers.

Certain he would snap her bones, she steeled herself for the pain, but there was only the discomfort of her resistance, and then he had the dagger.

She nearly wept. Would he disembowel her? Were he his brother, such a fate would surely be hers—after the ravishing.

He tossed the dagger aside. "I am done being your fool, Beatrix Wulfrith."

She looked around. Amid dark whiskers that had known no razor these past days, his teeth were clamped and perspiration beaded his brow. Doubtless, he had suffered further injury to his leg.

"As tempting as it is to see justice done now," he said, "you shall be punished before all as is Simon's due."

Emotion surged anew. "Already, your brother has his due. And you would have had I a-abandoned you down here as I should have done."

"More the fool you," he rasped.

Remembering the last time she had been so near a D'Arci, she closed her eyes. Aye, more the fool, and now he could not only do to her what she had denied his brother, but see her dead as Simon D'Arci had not. For all she had endured, she had gained but a month of reprieve.

"We are leaving this place," he said, a tremble passing from him to her.

She frowned. How did he intend to do that? Though she did not doubt his arms would carry him up the rope, his horse was surely gone. And there was the matter of inducing her to follow him up the rope. Of course, he might simply bind and drag her up after him.

When moisture fell to her cheek, she lifted her lids and was surprised by the dark gaze above her—until she realized it was nearly all pupil, the pale gray having narrowed such that it was barely visible. She looked to his brow and followed the lingering course of perspiration that was diverted by a faint ridge.

She peered closer. Evidence of her escape from Broehne? Aye, it was where she had struck him.

Another drop fell, dashing his salted taste upon her lips.

"By the saints!" He rolled onto his back.

It was a long moment before Beatrix realized he had released her, but before she could scramble away, he said, "Do you move, I vow to be fast upon you. And mayhap I shall not wait for the sheriff to render justice."

She did not doubt him. She looked at where he lay alongside her. He was flushed, his breath panting from him.

Though she told herself she should not care, that she should say nothing and await whatever advantage might be had, her heart rebelled against his suffering. "You have...injured yourself further?"

He levered onto his elbows, searched down his leg, and pushed to sitting. "You are a curse, Lady Beatrix!" Shaking, his fingers as deft as wooden pegs, he began to work the knot from the uppermost binding of his splinted leg.

Beatrix sat up. "Mayhap I—"

"Lie back!"

"But—"

"Do you wish me upon you again?" He wiped at the moisture running into his eyes. "Would you truly tempt me so?"

Was it ravishment of which he spoke? Death? Now that she saw the extent of his pain, she did not think it was the former. Too, there was something about him that did not mesh with Sir Simon—

Nay, he was no different. The circumstances were merely changed.

She returned to her back. What a fool she was when his ill fortune might mean *her* good fortune. Mayhap she was witless, but if so, the accident was not responsible. Her belief in God made her weak in a world where the strong made meals of their lessers. It seemed the only way to survive was to deny this heart turned to God. And that she could not do.

Mouth compressed, D'Arci bent over his leg. With the splints fallen away, he had pushed the hose down his muscled calf to reveal an unsightly bruise amid dark hair. Though it was difficult to see all of his leg, stretched on her back as she was, it did not appear misshapen as it had when he had fallen into the crypt. However, even a slight misalignment could cause the bones to mend such that he forever walked with a hitch.

With something between a shout and a grunt, D'Arci forced the bones together.

Beatrix turned her face opposite and stared at the rope that had carried her down into the crypt. If she could take D'Arci unawares, she might just reach it.

He shouted and added a curse to the tortured sound.

She winced at the blasphemy, and though she determined to not look upon him again, her chin came around as if pulled by an unseen hand.

Pain was grooved alongside D'Arci's mouth, nose, and eyes, and his skin had paled. He had never looked so vulnerable.

With her left foot, she tested the rope about her ankles. It gave some, D'Arci having loosened his hold to reset his leg. This was her only chance, then.

When he reached for the uppermost binding, she jerked her feet apart, rolled to the side, and rose onto her hands and knees. As she got a foot beneath her, a feral growl resounded around the crypt and the mantle clasped at her throat dug into her flesh. With a wrench, D'Arci pulled her feet out from under her.

"Curse your trickery!" the blackguard snarled as he hauled her back to the pallet. Hands biting into her shoulders, he tossed her onto her back.

The mantle about her throat easing, Beatrix sucked air.

"Curse your lying eyes and tongue!" His eyes sparkled amid the dark hair fallen over his brow.

Beatrix reached with hooked fingers, but he jerked his head back, caught one of her hands, and shoved it to her side. Pinning it with his body alongside hers, he seized the other.

Now would he kill her, making good the threat to not wait on justice? She twisted her lower body, kicked, and connected with one of the splints.

He bellowed, flooding her with regret though she told herself it was but a small measure of what was due him. Still, she once more fell prey to hesitation, and it cost her all.

D'Arci pinned her legs with his right, then fell on her. She could hardly breathe for the weight of him, and though she strained and writhed, he would not be moved.

The hair at his brow dampened by his effort, he stared at her across the inches separating their faces. "Termagant! I will see you to hell for this."

Anger once more guiding Beatrix's tongue, she snapped, "Then you and your beloved brother shall be reunited."

A gleam entered his eyes, nearly sharp enough to run her through.

Fervently missing the Beatrix of old whose visits were too brief, she held his gaze.

His eyes were the first to waver, then she felt the tension ease from his muscles. "Soon," he murmured and lowered his head alongside hers.

Beatrix caught her breath as his own filled her ear, shuddered at the peculiar sensation that played along her spine, and nearly whimpered when it came again with his next breath. Had he lost consciousness?

Every breath hard won beneath the crush of him, she slowly pulled an arm up her side and touched a hand to his shoulder.

"You test my patience," he hissed.

Grateful he did not lift his head to witness her sudden tears, she said, "I can hardly breathe."

"That is something to which you ought to become accustomed."

And so she would when a noose tightened around her neck. *Dear Lord, surely this is not your plan?*

Despair settling in her breast, she turned her head opposite. Unless God intended to spring a miracle on her, her bid for life was lost.

8

HE LIKED THE feel of her, though not the smell. He slid a hand up her ribs and settled it to the undercurve of a breast, only to grimace at the absence of perfume that would do well to cover her scent. What had he been thinking? Or had he been? Mayhap he ought to have more closely watched the fill of his tankard. Too, why was she still in his bed?

She murmured something.

Stirred by her husky whisper, he told himself there was no reason why he should not take advantage of her stay and slid a hand to her thigh—only to still upon discovering she was clothed. He was not such a pig he did not first see a woman out of her garments. But then, he was also clothed.

He opened an eye and peered into the darkness. Though he slept with the shutters wide open, barely a glimmer of moonlight fell upon his chamber.

He drew a long breath and grimaced at the depth of odor that assailed him, and in the next instant jerked at the realization of where he was and who he sprawled upon. Not drink, but pain. Not his chamber, but this detestable pit. Not a willing wench, but Simon's murderer. Not with two legs firm beneath him, but one.

He lifted his head and looked around the crypt. Gradually, his eyes took in the slender moonlight shining through the breach. It must be at least middle night, meaning he had slept long and deep to have not awakened sooner.

Just barely, he discerned the outline of Lady Beatrix. Not that he needed to see her face, for it instantly rose to mind. Her wan appearance had caused regret to tug at him when he had first confronted her amid the abbey ruins. Though at Broehne he had thought her face that of an angel, this past month of scavenging had turned it hollow and fatigued—still lovely, but no angel.

Beneath his hand on her thigh, he thought she trembled, and when he pulled it away, the release of her breath told him she was also awake. Did she fear he meant to ravish her? A woman he would sooner see dead? The thought made him recoil. Or should have.

"If you do more than breathe, I vow you shall know my wrath in full," he said, then carefully shifted his weight off her.

She lay still, the only movement about her the fear she exhaled on her breath.

Were she any other woman, he would explain why he had laid a hand to her that she would know he was not one to force his attentions on a woman. But what did it matter what she believed of him, she who had thrice seen him injured? Indeed, now that he was past the surprise of discovering she was not a wench who had come into his bed, his ire billowed. Because of her, he'd had to reset his leg. True, the bones had shifted only slightly, but even that could lame him for the remainder of his days.

Filling his lungs full, he suppressed a groan. Though Lady Beatrix would fair well from a bath, the smell was also of him. Even worse was the odor of fish rising above the stink of four days spent in the crypt.

Determinedly, he turned his thoughts to the darkness stretching before him, during which Beatrix Wulfrith would surely seek another opportunity to escape him.

As it would not do for him to cover her again, she would have to be bound. He sat up and, jaws clenched, searched a hand over the pallet and found the rope that had delivered his prey to him.

"Your hands," he ordered.

Though she remained unmoving, he sensed the pulse of her fear.

Why he thought he had to soothe her, he did not know, but he said, "Upon my vow, I shall not ravish you. Indeed, bedding you is most distant from my mind. Now reach your hands to me that we might rest well the remainder of the night."

Beatrix stared at the shadow over her. Did he speak true? If so, why had he touched her? His weight through the oppressive afternoon and into the night had rendered sleep nearly impossible and, when finally she had slumbered, it was only to be roused by his hand upon her. Now he wished to bind her?

Slowly, she turned onto her side to face him. "I give you my word," she whispered twice-practiced words, "and I beseech God in...this place to take heed: if you do not bind me, I shall not try to escape."

"The word of a murderess?" he scratched out in the dirt of contempt.

She sighed and pressed her wrists together. "Aye, 'twould be asking much."

As he bound her, his blunt fingers against her palms and wrists made her shudder such that, when he finally released her, she nearly went limp with relief.

"The blood should still flow," he said.

It was true. Though he had allowed no slippage of the rope, neither was it so tight her hands would lose feeling.

With a tug of the end rope, D'Arci asked, "Do I need to bind your feet as well?"

Beatrix swallowed. "I can go nowhere without my h-hands."

"Indeed." He lay back and drew the rope taut.

She stared at D'Arci's dark figure. Could it be he was not the same as his brother? Or was it his injury that deterred him?

Her belly grumbled. As she had last eaten a dozen or more hours past, and then only berries, she was hungry.

D'Arci levered up. "Sit."

She pressed her bound hands to the floor and rose. "What is it?"

She heard the sound of his rummaging, then he pressed something between her palms. "Satisfy your hunger."

She lifted it and sniffed—dried beef, though that second day he had said he had finished the foodstuffs in his pack. "You lied."

"With good reason."

"All lie with good..." She closed her eyes and, behind her lids, worked through the words before speaking them. "All lie with good reason. Their own, of course."

"You are right."

The tear of his teeth telling that he had settled to eating, she took a bite. The meat was so tough it made her teeth ache, but she could not remember any foodstuff tasting so fine. It took a dozen bites and ceaseless chewing to get through the piece, but she savored every moment.

"More?" D'Arci asked.

Why so generous? For fear she might expire ere he had his justice? "Please."

He passed her a chunk of stale bread.

"Drink?" he asked when she had swallowed the last bite.

She opened her bound hands and accepted the skin. Before the liquid touched her lips, she knew what it was. No matter how tainted, water did not scent the air so. It was the skin he had said he no longer possessed. And it was half full.

"Another lie," she breathed. "With good reason, I am sure."

"My own, of course."

As she put the spout to her lips, she was struck by the thought that his mouth had last been there. Swallowing the rush of wine, she thrust the skin at him. "Thank you."

His hand curved around hers, slid up, and pulled the skin free.

Beatrix heard him swallow, and something shuddered through her at the realization his mouth was now where hers had been. And it was not fear with which she was afflicted. If she was honest as she had ever endeavored to be, this feeling was carnal.

Dear God, mayhap I am witless.

She squeezed her arms against her sides and silently repented the temptation of D'Arci. What was it? The dark? The brief contact with his flesh? His faceless voice resounding through her? The danger of him?

She did not know, for she had no experience with men. Before Sir Simon had forced his unwanted attentions on her, the closest she had drawn near a man was as her father's daughter and brothers' sister. And she must not forget Sir Durand who had looked at her as if she was not promised to the Church.

Had her next thought not been so bitter, Beatrix might have laughed. Even if she escaped D'Arci's justice, the Church would not likely want her now, and neither would any man. Thus, she was adrift, or had been before falling fool to Michael D'Arci. Soon she would be aloft. Unless her family—

She caught her breath. Now that she was had, would D'Arci speak the truth? "My family. Why have they not come? And do not tell me it is...shame that keeps them away. Never will I b-believe it."

He was silent so long, she thought he did not intend to answer, but then he said, "You are dead to them, Lady Beatrix."

"They believe I died?"

"From the fall. Your sister and her escort told that they saw you and my brother in the ravine. Certes, they believed Simon's blood was yours."

She was relieved but also pained by the terrible hurt her supposed death had caused her family. "And Baron Lavonne chose not to correct them," she said.

"As the king's men concluded the absence of your body was the result of scavenging animals, the baron determined to use it to his advantage lest the Wulfriths descended and tried to deny my brother justice."

"But when I am brought to trial—"

"Then they will know—when it is too late for them to steal you away."

Which she did not want, Beatrix realized. Her family would surely find some way to hide her given the opportunity. However, not only would they suffer for their defiance of the law, but for the remainder of her days she would be confined and named a murderer. She could not live like that. She would rather die.

Lifting her hands to her neck, she felt her breath quiver through her throat.

"You are afraid?"

He wished her to be, didn't he? Wished her to tremble that her tongue might be further bound. She drew a sharp breath. "Am I as afraid of death as you are of not walking again as a man? Aye, but it shall pass, whether by noose or absolution."

Were his anger capable of taking form, its blow would have left her bloodied. "Absolution?"

She had not considered it before, but even if absolution could save her life, she would never admit to having killed Sir Simon and claiming she had done it as the result of a bent mind. But what harm to allow D'Arci to believe it?

After a single rehearsal of the words, she said, "If I plead madness, 'tis possible I shall be a-absolved of your brother's death."

He came across the dark so suddenly his warm breath swept the hair off her brow. "'Twill not save you!"

It took all of her will not to scramble backward. Fortunately, as she was as dark to D'Arci as he was to her, he could not see her fear. "The law makes..." What? If only he were not so near.

"What?" he snarled.

She slid her tongue over her dry lips. "It makes exceptions for those who are...ill of mind. They cannot be held responsible for their..."

"Sins?"

The heat of his anger met the flush of her embarrassment. "If that is what you would name it."

His hand fell to her forearm. "You murdered, and for that you will not be absolved. I will not allow it."

She jerked at her arm, but he held tight. Emotion soaring past her disjointed tongue, she said, "Until you are more than a vassal to Christian Lavonne, it matters not what you would or would not allow."

"Does it not? I could kill you this moment, the same as you did my brother."

"I did not kill him!"

"'Twas *your* dagger stuck in his breast, his blood on *your* breast."

She remembered—her gown rushed with red, blood on the Wulfrith dagger. Some of the anger ran out of her. "'Tis so, but his death was not...murder."

D'Arci's hand convulsed on her arm. "What was it?"

She startled. Was he willing to hear the truth—at least, what truth she knew of what had happened? There were so many gaps. So many wide, open spaces at which she could only guess.

"I wait, Lady Beatrix, but not much longer."

"His death was...unfortunate."

"Unfortunate!"

"Unintentional," she hastened.

"*Your* dagger. *His* blood. What is unintentional about that?"

"You were not there!"

"Then put me there."

She lowered her gaze to the darkness between them. "Why?"

Aye, why? Michael dropped his hand from her. He required no explanation of what had happened between her and Simon, and yet he wanted to hear what she had to tell. He needed to hear it, though only that he might know what her plea would be when she stood before the sheriff seeking absolution. But that was not entirely true. *Curse all!*

He looked to her pale hair that was all that was visible of her. "'Tis said you were found over my brother holding the dagger that killed him, and Baron Lavonne told that when you awakened, you offered no defense for Simon's death."

"Of course I did not."

"Why?"

"Because I could not. My tongue would not…uncurl. My lips would not…tell how your brother tried to rav—"

"Enough!" After Edithe, it had taken years to ease the belief that all women lied, but it came hard again with this woman's talk of ravishment. "I did not ask for lies."

Michael could not be certain, but he thought a sob escaped her. It pulled at him as women's tears were wont to do, and he hated himself for the weakness sown of his fondness for those born of Eve. Despite all, including Edithe, he liked women.

"They are not lies," Beatrix Wulfrith said and, with a slackening of rope, reached forward and touched his forearm. "I speak true. You did not know your…brother as you believe. Whoever dwells in your memory is not the same as the one who—"

He thrust her hands off him, disgusted that he should feel for her when her tears were deserved and as false as Edithe's had been. "We are done speaking, Lady Beatrix."

"You asked that I tell—"

"I asked for the truth!"

"I see. Your truth, not mine. And certainly not your brother's."

Her resignation pricked and, for a moment, made him wish to hear her tale. But she lied. Remembering their earlier conversation, he smiled grimly. "Did you not tell that all lie with good reason? Life or death— good reason, would you not say?"

"What I would tell is no lie."

Michael growled. "Let pass another word from your lying lips and I will gag you."

"I tell you—"

"Do not test me!" *Holy rood!* Another word he had said and then allowed her three. But if she spoke again…"Lie back, Lady Beatrix."

Her shallow breath weighted the air, though not as heavily as her unspoken words. As he opened his mouth to issue the order again, she complied.

Michael stared at the pale light of her hair and realized she had turned her back to him. It was well she had. Gritting his teeth against the jar of his leg, he settled on the pallet and twisted the end rope around his fist. If she moved, he would know.

He looked to the breach and wished the sky were above him that he could number the hours before dawn. But, eventually, morning would come and see them from here. Regardless of what Beatrix Wulfrith believed, he had only to call to bring his destrier from the wood.

"Your brother must have changed greatly," she murmured, once more defying him.

And once more, he let it pass without making good his threat. Though he had not known his half-brother frontwards and backwards, having been too often apart from him, the young man had shown no bent toward the ill of which she accused him. Impetuous, aye, but there was no crime in that. The only crime was that which could be put upon his murderer. And he should not doubt that person was Beatrix Wulfrith. However, there was doubt—slight, but present like the first weed lifting its ugly head above a garden's bounty. If he did not pull out every last root, it would strangle all that was good. That he could not allow. No absolution.

Unless Christian Lavonne deigns otherwise.

The thought slipped in, prodded forth by Beatrix's assertion that, as a mere vassal, Michael had no control over her fate. But even if Christian wavered, still there was his revenge-driven father, Aldous, who could be counted on to stand fast.

Though with each passing day Christian grew stronger in his role as baron, he continued to allow his father far more say over the barony than he should. Thus, whether with Christian's knowledge or guile, Aldous could still effect change. But for how much longer? The matter of Beatrix Wulfrith carried far more weight than a petty raid. Indeed, if Christian *did* wed her sister, Beatrix's fate would likely affect the remainder of the baron's life. It was not to be taken lightly.

9

THE MEMORY HOVERED in the distance, and from out of his troubled dream he reached to it.

"'Tis said you ravished a lady."

Simon's words pierced the crisp morning air and nearly broke Michael's stride. Affecting indifference though every muscle tensed, he said, "Is it?"

The boy who struggled toward manhood shrugged and shifted his bow. "Aye, though Mother says 'tis untrue, as does Father." He peered sidelong at his brother. "Is it?"

The brilliant autumn leaves beneath Michael's feet turning suddenly drab, their crackle reduced to a rustle, he said, "What do you think?"

Another shrug. "You take what you want."

Anger, of a shade nearly as dark as the day Edithe had worked her ruin on him, shot through Michael. But he contained it with the reminder that Simon could not know what ground he tread. "I take what I want, but only if it is due me."

Simon quickened his step as Michael's longer stride once more drew space between them. "Then you say you did not lie with her?"

Merciful Lord! Were it any other he would put a sharp end to this discussion. "I did not say that."

Simon halted and, when Michael did not, ran forward and turned into his brother's path. "Then?"

Aye, any other, Michael begrudged, but not this tousle-headed youth with a mischievous glint in his eyes. He stopped short, catching back turbulent emotions that might turn the glint in Simon's eyes to tears. "I took what she long offered. That is all."

Though there was no deer in sight, he reached behind, pulled an arrow from his quiver, and fit it to the string. "We are to deliver venison for the evening meal." He stepped past Simon but came back around. "Beware of women, Brother, lest one be your downfall."

Simon smiled a crooked smile. "I shall, Michael. No woman will ever do to me what she did to you."

"I pray not."

Beatrix thought it was a dream turned bad, but the light beyond her lids and the calloused palm clapped over her mouth told otherwise. Dragging air through her nose, she opened her eyes on dread morning. And Michael D'Arci whose fierce countenance was before her and whose chest once more pinned her.

Heart taking up the pound of a smithy to forge fear from the blood rushing through her veins, she wondered what she had done. Muttered in her sleep?

"Speak not a word," he rasped.

She tried to shake her head, but he increased the pressure on her mouth.

"Naught here!" a graveled voice sounded overhead.

Was it a passing traveler? Baron Lavonne's men? And why did D'Arci insist on silence when he ought to raise the hue? Did he fear brigands who would sooner slit his throat than offer aid?

She stared into his whiskered face that, in the light of first morn, appeared more bearded with the passing of another night. Strangely, he did not as closely resemble Sir Simon as she had first believed. Because of the whiskers?

She met his gaze. Despite the urgency there, he looked as if he had slept little.

"The baron will not be pleased," another voice sounded.

Not brigands, then. Now D'Arci would call out. However, his lips stayed firm as he returned her gaze. Why? One shout and he could be away from here and shortly abed with his injury well-tended.

The jangle of reins met the clop of hooves over the stone walkway, followed by muffled thunder that told the men rode into the wood.

D'Arci removed his hand. "Absolution," he muttered, then rolled off her.

"I do not understand."

"Aye, you do." Turning his attention to the splints, he tightened the bindings.

"They came for you, yet you did not call out. Why?"

He reached for his packs. "As I said—absolution."

A door opened in her sleep-muddled mind. As she had forewarned, he feared she would seek and be granted absolution. And regardless what risk it posed to him, he would not be denied revenge.

She started to lift a hand to her throat again but stopped. As the fearful gesture would not be lost on him, she turned onto her side, sat up, and pulled the mantle around her to ward off the morning chill.

"Eat." D'Arci thrust something at her.

More dried beef. Though she longed to refuse, she turned her joined hands and plucked it from him.

They ate in silence, and though she felt his gaze, she kept her eyes averted. What did he see when he looked at her? She cringed in remembrance of her reflection the last time she had gone to the stream: curves nearly lost to hunger, bones that jutted, skin freckled and darkened by too much sun. Surely, a more unbecoming woman did not exist. Even if D'Arci were not injured, she would likely have nothing to fear from him as she had feared of his brother.

He offered her the skin.

Continuing to withhold her gaze, she accepted it and sipped.

"Take another swallow," he said when she reached it to him. "You are more in need than I."

Though she knew she should not fuss, especially as the wine warmed as the mantle could not, she asked, "How do you know that?"

"Surely you do not forget that you were beneath me much of the night?" His voice mocked intimacy. "I certainly do not. Thus, I can say that there remained little of the woman I bared at Broehne."

Heat tumbled across Beatrix's cheeks. She did *not* forget the press of his body and certainly not the horror felt upon regaining consciousness at Broehne to discover herself unclothed.

D'Arci smiled tightly. "I know all of you—from your narrow thighs, to your bony hips, to your jutting ribs. You were hardly a comfortable bed." He nodded for her to take another drink.

A flush of anger pulled Beatrix up from embarrassment. Beneath his weight, she *had* suffered more than he. And she would have said so if not that she knew it would serve nothing. She gripped the neck of the skin and let the wine coat her tongue and slide down her throat.

"Aye, you are too thin," D'Arci said, sweeping his gaze over her.

She lowered the skin. "The easier to…hang."

A muscle in his jaw jerked. "I had not considered that."

From some dark corner of her memory, Beatrix pulled together her departed father's words and struggled to order them so her tongue would not stumble. "One should never overlook the ad-ad—"

"Advantage?"

She kept her chin aloft. "The advantage of lesser things."

"Indeed." He stuck out his hand.

She considered the long, blunt fingers that knew more of her than any man had known, including his brother. At least, she was fairly certain Sir Simon had not known her beyond the hands he had laid to her. She passed the skin to Michael D'Arci.

"And you need a bath," he said, then put his mouth around the spout, took a long draw, and lowered the skin. "Of what advantage is that?"

His question might have made her laugh were the situation not so dire. "Of what advantage that I remain unclean?" She shrugged. "None for you, Lord D'Arci."

"But for you?"

"Ah." She smiled, though it was a bitter thing. "The lack of temptation for a woman who possesses little…attraction. Had I been in such a state when I met your brother, he surely would not have——"

"Cease!" His pupils smote the color from his eyes.

Beatrix glared at him. "Methinks you ought not to ask questions to which you fear the answer."

To her surprise, D'Arci looked away and dropped the flap on a pack. "We are leaving." He settled both packs over a shoulder, gripped the end rope, and raised himself to a knee.

As he pushed upright, Beatrix considered his injured leg, the splints of which extended past the sole of his boot. Still, he gave it little weight. Did it pain him? More, would he walk again without falter?

"Come," he said.

And if she did not?

"I shall drag you if needs be."

Of course he would. But though *this* she could not fight, perhaps there would be something else she could do. After all, how far on foot could they go with his injury?

She pressed her bound hands to the floor and pushed up.

Moving slowly, D'Arci led her to the breach. "You shall follow me up."

"I cannot climb with bound hands."

He pushed her mantle aside, wended the end rope around her waist, and pushed and pulled it through a series of knots.

Watching him, Beatrix was once more struck that, even with a face scrubbed by whiskers and hair tousled from sleep, he was handsome. And tall—at least, beside her. She felt almost a child with her head tipped to gaze full into his face. Had she really thought he looked like Simon?

"'Twould benefit you not to defy me, Lady Beatrix," he warned.

"Do you not mean it would benefit you?"

"The justice I seek is assured."

"But my fate is not?" This time she did laugh. "I shudder to think I might go to the noose b-bruised and beaten. Save your...threats for one of better destiny, blackguard." Were the Beatrix of old capable of being clasped to her, Beatrix would have so welcomed her back. True, the words did not come without bump or botch, but they came.

D'Arci pulled her hands up, loosed the rope, and secured the end to his belt. Then he gripped the length of rope that hung through the breach and began his ascent. His arms were strong, easily carrying him up into the morning light, and it was not long before he peered down at her.

Despite numerous ascents, Beatrix lacked the ease with which he had climbed out. However, it wasn't long before sunlight shone upon her face.

D'Arci curled a hand around her upper arm, assisted her the last few feet, and straightened. Beatrix settled on the edge of the breach and watched him untie the rope from his belt. The light of day showed that his whiskers were as dark as his hair, though interspersed with bits of gray, and at the corners of his eyes were fine lines as of one who often squints against the sun's glare.

As he turned the rope around his fist, he trapped her with his pale gray gaze.

She felt a peculiar tug at her center and looked away. "Shall I make to the wood and...scavenge fallen branches to fashion crutches for the journey?" she asked.

"One should not walk when one can ride," he said and issued a shrill whistle.

Did he truly believe his destrier awaited him? Four days now, and since retrieving the packs she had seen nothing of the beast. He had to have gone—

She heard hooves. Shortly, D'Arci's destrier entered the nave, tossed its head, and whinnied.

"Sartan!" Its master called.

The beast skirted the false crypt, causing Beatrix's heart to lurch. She gained her feet and, as the destrier neared, took a step back, and another. Fortunately, she was not tethered so near D'Arci that she could not distance herself some. Unfortunately, he wrenched her back. "Be still, lest you discover how sore tested I am."

He did not know her fear, and she nearly she told him of it, but it would change nothing. Unless he intended her to walk alongside his mount—and with his injury he would not squander the time—she would be going astride.

D'Arci clapped a hand to the animal's great jaw. "For your patience, old friend, you shall be rewarded."

The destrier lowered its massive head, thrust its muzzle into D'Arci's open hand, and blew.

"At Soaring," D'Arci assured him.

Then he intended to take her to his home. As he had refused the opportunity to be delivered to Lavonne, it did not surprise her. But once there, what? And how would he hide her presence from his liege? Unless she was not to be present...

She eyed the rope. Mayhap she was nearer a noose than believed.

With a stiff-legged hitch, D'Arci stepped aside. "I believe you are acquainted with Lady Beatrix," he said to his horse as he drew the first pack from his shoulder. "Though why you yielded my packs to her, I do not understand." He secured them behind the saddle and turned to Beatrix. "Relieve yourself."

She gasped.

"Make haste, as we shall not pause ere we reach Soaring."

Though they would likely arrive at the castle before nightfall, even if the journey were a sennight long, she would not tend her needs in this man's presence. "I shall not. 'Tis...unseemly!"

"I will keep my back to you."

"Nay, I will wait."

"Only a fool would believe that possible. And I tell you, I shall not wait myself."

Then he meant to…? She swallowed and nodded toward the remains of a wall. "Do you let out the rope, we shall both have privacy. Upon my word, I shall not…escape."

He raised an eyebrow.

Beatrix put up both of hers. "'Tis all I have to give."

"'Tis not enough."

She grasped the rope. "Then you question your ability to tie a knot that holds?"

Her arrow struck, causing color to seep beneath his sun-warmed skin and Beatrix to marvel at her tongue that so freely delivered words to her lips.

"My knots hold." He nodded toward the wall. "Keep the rope taut, else I will drag you back regardless of your modesty."

She turned and D'Arci fed out the rope until she was around the wall. Careful to keep it taut, she quickly dispensed with the task, but for all the cover afforded her, her cheeks warmed.

"'Tis no more than he does," she whispered and pulled the mantle close about her. As she started to step from the wall, the rubble at her feet drew her gaze and she bent, scooped up two stones, and dropped one in each boot. Perhaps there would be an opportunity to use them, though if she could actually do so she did not know.

No sooner did she straighten than the rope snapped up the slack and she was pulled from behind the wall.

"Heed well my warnings, Lady Beatrix." D'Arci reeled her toward him. "They are not idle."

Embracing the anger that allowed her words to fly true, she said, "As I know well, *my lord,* for I yet suffer the gag with which you bound me to silence last eve."

Curse her! Michael braced his good leg beneath him. *And curse her smug mouth that bows just enough to turn her disheveled countenance beguiling!* What a fool he was to have not gagged her. What a fool to toss about idle warnings, then boast of them. It was not like him at all.

When she was within reach, he turned Sartan to mount him from the right side. The destrier would not like it, for the horse had only ever been mounted on the left, but Michael's injured leg would bear no weight in the stirrup.

"All is well." Michael patted the horse's neck.

Skin twitching, Sartan looked over his shoulder.

Michael gripped the pommel tight lest the horse sidle away. Though his splinted leg would have to bear his weight for a moment only, he ground his teeth against the anticipated pain. And pain there was, shooting toe to spine when he shoved his right foot into the stirrup.

As Sartan sidestepped, Michael swung his splinted leg over the opposite side and settled in the saddle. He looked to Beatrix whose eyes were wide in her flaxen-framed face, fear palpable. And Michael was not the only one to feel that fear.

Sartan shook his massive head and whinnied.

What frightened her, she who had come nearer yet to retrieve his packs? Michael clapped a reassuring hand to the destrier's neck, then reached to Beatrix. "Come."

"'Twould be best if I w-walked."

Then he had made such a fool of himself she believed him yet one. "Hours by horse, Lady Beatrix, a full day and night on foot." He shook his head. "I shall abide no defiance."

Gripping the rope, she met his gaze. "'Tis not defiance that makes me...refuse. I am..." Her tongue swept her upper lip. "I am frightened of horses."

"Did you not retrieve my packs from this same beast?"

"That was different."

"How say you?"

"You needed your...medicinals."

Reminded that she had delivered them, braving this fear of which she spoke, *and* that she had stayed when she might now be on the road to Stern, Michael was pricked with uncertainty.

Enough! To attempt to make sense of her would only prove him senseless. "Aye, I needed them, and now I need you to mount."

"Mayhap——"

"If needs be, I shall drag you astride." He stuck out his hand.

She reached to him only to snatch her arm back. "My psalter!" She turned toward the small chapel.

Was that where she had made her bed before he had captured her on the day past? Michael caught her arm and yanked her around. "You shall not need it."

"Pray, grant me this——"

"No amount of prayer or gilded word can change what will be, Lady Beatrix. Simon *will* have his justice."

Her lips parted, but no further argument was forthcoming. Eyes dimming, she slid a hand into his and stepped her foot atop his in the stirrup.

When Sartan sidled and snorted again, Beatrix jerked free.

Ignoring the protest of his injury, Michael leaned sideways, gripped her beneath the arms, and lifted her. He turned her sidesaddle and settled her between his thighs where she went so still that her shallow breath was all that moved about her.

She truly was frightened, he conceded as he stared at her pale profile. What had happened?

She clasped her hands in her lap, drew a deep breath, and shuddered.

What was she remembering? "I assure you, 'twill not happen again, Lady Beatrix." *Curses!* Had he truly offered her reassurance?

She looked sidelong at him. "Why do you care, Lord D'Arci?"

He nearly flinched. "I do not." He lifted a palm up. "Now give to me."

"I know not——"

"You would have me search you again?"

Understanding opened her lids wide and transcended the fear crowding her blue gaze.

"I shall do it," Michael warned.

"Hold," she said and slid a hand into her right boot. A moment later, she dropped a stone in his palm.

He closed his fingers around the jagged edges intended for him. "What else have you?"

"'Tis all."

He pitched the rock behind, caught back her mantle, and thrust a hand inside. As she tried to close her body to his searching, he pushed onward. Every curve he swept, and though he did not allow himself to linger, he was surprised by the familiarity beneath his fingers. True, his hands had been upon her when he searched her on the day past, but that did not account for this awareness of her.

Finding no evidence that she had secured any other weapon, he started to withdraw. But only a fool would leave it be. As he slid a hand into her right boot from which she had removed the stone, she stiffened, but the covering was empty save for her leg. Then her left boot...

Her breath caught as he splayed fingers down her calf and pulled the second stone from atop her ankle.

"For me?" he derided.

Her chin rose. "Had I quill and ink, I would write your n-name upon it."

Better her anger than the fear shown in mounting Sartan, Michael reflected only to question himself. It was the latter in which he ought to revel. Simon was *dead*.

Michael tossed the rock away, freed the rope from Beatrix's waist, and thrust it into a pack behind. Then he caught up the reins and put his right heel to Sartan.

The destrier burst forward, forcing Beatrix back against Michael. Every place they touched, from her shoulders to her back to the outside of her thigh riding the inside of his, she trembled.

Though Michael told himself he was pleased with her fear, part of him quelled. It seemed a woman's tears were not his only weakness.

10

BEATRIX EYED THE nooning sky that swept clouds toward them—bloated masses eager to turn day into night. Regardless of how hard D'Arci pressed, they could not possibly make Castle Soaring before the sky spilled its burden.

She pressed her shoulders back to ease the tension caused by the horse beneath her, the land running past, and D'Arci—most of all, D'Arci. Though she tried to ignore the blackguard's thighs against hers and his arm around her waist, there was no escaping his presence, especially when his warm breath wended her cheek and the scent of him met her indrawn breath. Never had she been so aware of a man, and it shamed her, especially since he was her enemy. Yet more evidence she was witless?

When a gust of cool air displaced the warm and rain began to fall, Beatrix closed her eyes and tilted her face up. Having grown uncomfortably warm this past hour, she welcomed the fat, cool drops on her face and hands. Still, she knew the relief would be short-lived and she would soon huddle into her mantle to fight off the chill of drenched garments.

When lightning jagged the sky, igniting the backs of her lids, and the rain went from soft to stinging, she opened her eyes.

"Cover yourself!" D'Arci shouted.

She glanced across her shoulder, but his gaze was on the land. And from his bent brow and clenched jaw, he continued to suffer the jar of the horse. Though she had sensed it throughout the ride, the only evidence was an occasional grunt and his perspiration seeping through her mantle and tunic.

She pulled the hood over her head. Having hours earlier abandoned her attempt to hold herself apart from D'Arci, she resettled against his chest.

Silver slashed the sky and met the earth. As evidenced by the crack that followed, this strike was nearer than the last.

"Pray, go to the wood," Beatrix whispered. It was frightening enough to be mounted, but in the midst of a storm...

Silently, Michael vowed they would not pause. Even if all the heavens split open, he would press on, but not only for his injured leg. He had been too near Beatrix Wulfrith too long to keep his mind firm to her sin. True, he had not called to Lavonne's men lest the baron waver in his assurances that justice would be given for Simon's wrongful death, but there was more to it.

Struggle though he did to turn away thoughts of this woman, she slipped through the cracks in him. There was something about her, something innocent, something true. And her voice... Though the words that passed her lips often broke and stumbled, they played him like an instrument strung to the sweetest pitch.

Halting the traitorous turn of his thoughts, Michael reminded himself that Edithe's voice had surely been sweet. If he were not more careful, he would once more fall prey to a woman. Thus, a chamber in the hind tower would be Beatrix's when they reached Soaring—as far from the lord's solar as possible. *Then* he would decide what to do with her. *Then* he would examine the risk of keeping her from his liege, an act of defiance that could cost him all.

Face coursed with rain, Michael searched the graying land. Unless the clouds closed up, there would be flooding, making it all the more urgent they reach Castle Soaring as soon as possible.

Ahead, lightning twice stabbed the earth and thunder rumbled. Then came the unsettling scent of eggs gone foul—sulfur—and more rain. As the latter ran over the collar of his mantle and down his neck, he acknowledged that, if not for the warmth trapped between Beatrix's body and his, a chill would surely set in.

A few minutes later, light shuddered through the clouds and was answered by a resounding crash that caused the woman before him to startle and Sartan to veer.

The lightning was too near. Despite the vow Michael had made to press on, he would have to go to the wood.

Muttering, though normally such curses would have violated the air with as much sting and force as the rain, he turned Sartan.

Lightning rent the air again, thrust its angry heat to the ground a hundred feet in front of them, and passed its violent energy to those in its path. Michael convulsed and, for a moment, feared his heart had stopped, then he heard Beatrix's cry. He tightened his arm around her and his thighs to the saddle in anticipation of Sartan's reaction. As expected, the great destrier reared. If not for the injury to his leg, Michael was certain he could have stayed the saddle. Instead, he and Beatrix pitched to the side.

Though Simon shouted from his cold grave for Michael to release Beatrix and save himself, he could not. He had given his word no harm would befall her upon Sartan—that whatever had happened to her would not happen again.

The impact with the pooled ground was made only slightly worse by the thrust of the small woman atop Michael. Though he had managed to turn and give his good leg the brunt of the fall, the jar to his injured leg worked pain through him.

Breathing hard, lids narrowed against the rain's assault, he watched Sartan rear again ten feet away. When the destrier's hooves returned to earth, it was with a resounding crack—born of the storm, though it seemed of the beast.

For a long moment, all was still, then Beatrix rolled off Michael and onto her knees. The hood fallen away to reveal her luminous eyes, she hovered over him and he saw concern part her fear, followed by realization.

Straining for purchase amid the mud, Michael reached for her, but she hurtled backward and arrested her flight only when she was well out of reach.

Cursing himself, Michael watched her shoulders move with frantic breath. It would be impossible for him to overtake her on foot, but he could do it on Sartan—providing the lady did not immerse herself in the wood before he made it astride.

He glanced to where his destrier trotted a restless circle twenty feet out and quickly returned his gaze to Beatrix. Rain darkening her hair and running off her face, she watched him. Why did she not flee?

Beatrix hardly saw D'Arci past the pieces of memory that had burst upon her when they had fallen from the horse. Slowly, the pieces fit and refit until, at last, remembrance swept through her in one long, unbroken vision—running to Sir Ewen's destrier, Sir Simon trapping her between his horse and the other, his cruel grip on her wrist, being dragged onto his saddle, his hands and mouth on her, raising the dagger, the pommel striking the horse, the horse rearing, falling...

She dropped to her knees and, amid the sodden grass, gripped a hand over her face. Though she now knew why she feared what she did, she was not sure she should be grateful. Still, she had survived Sir Simon's assault, the fall into the ravine, and this other fall broken by Michael D'Arci. Not at all like—

Nay, not at all. D'Arci had assured her that whatever had made her fear horses would not befall her again. To his detriment, he had stayed true. Still, she ought to run, not only from D'Arci but this present danger that marked her for further lightning strikes.

She pulled her hand from her face and saw that D'Arci had made it to his feet. Though she had been granted another chance to escape, here she knelt as if she lacked wits!

She thrust upright, but as she turned away, lightning lit the sky again and revealed the suffering on D'Arci's face.

Telling herself she did not care if he was further injured, she turned halfway around and stilled. She could not leave him now, just as she had been unable to abandon him to the crypt.

Once more wishing she could ignore God's hold on her, she lifted a hand from beneath her mantle, dashed the rain from her face, and considered Sartan. The destrier's gait revealed it was yet agitated.

Beatrix looked to D'Arci who would have her to ground were he sure of foot. The rain plastering his hair to his head, he watched her. Knowing what she must do, she pushed her shoulders back and stepped toward Sartan.

"Curse you, halt!" D'Arci shouted as she skirted him, doubtless expecting her to run.

From the corner of her eye she saw him move to follow her and gauged that at least twenty feet separated them. When Sartan ceased his circling and turned to her, she drew a deep breath.

"Stay back!" D'Arci shouted.

"I am not afeared," she whispered. After all, these past hours she had been astride the beast.

As the destrier jerked its head and snorted, D'Arci issued a shrill whistle and, for a moment, it seemed the horse might answer the summons. However, he held.

"Go no nearer!" D'Arci roared.

Beatrix slowed and offered a hand to the horse. "I shall not harm you."

Rain pouring off its coat, the destrier stared at her with one ear forward, the other back.

"I shall not."

"Move away!" D'Arci persisted.

Did he think she meant to mount his horse and leave him to the storm? Or might he be concerned for her? It *was* bold to approach an overwrought horse—the nearest she had come to her old self. Of course, her old self had sometimes been imprudent.

She touched Sartan's muzzle.

"God's eyes!" D'Arci cursed. "Do not!"

The horse breathed her, then his backward ear came forward.

"See now, I mean you no harm." A fluttering in her chest, she patted its neck and gathered the reins.

The horse snickered and stepped back as if to flee.

"There," Beatrix soothed. "Come." She tugged the reins and turned to where D'Arci had drawn near. Though the dark on his face sought to coax fear from her, she did not falter. Sartan followed, offering only slight resistance when lightning struck in the distance.

Beatrix halted before D'Arci and held out the reins. "I did not murder your brother."

Michael stared at her. Why had she not run? That she might defend herself? Was she so fool? Though he told himself he did not believe her, his anger dwindled.

"Your mount." She held the reins nearer.

Michael looked to Sartan and marveled at how easily the great destrier could trod Beatrix. And she, fearful of horses, had approached him as one would a recalcitrant child.

Anger once more pooled in Michael's blood, and without pondering what it meant, he growled, "You could have been killed."

"Would that not have served your idea of…justice?"

All be cursed, it should! Instead, he had feared for her.

Lightning came again, so bright it made him squint. "We must go to the wood." He eased himself to the animal's right side, and though the destrier was tense, he shifted only slightly when Michael put his foot in the stirrup and hoisted himself atop. Teeth ground against the pain, Michael reached to Beatrix.

She stared at him.

Did she intend to run? If so, he could easily take her to ground.

Michael frowned. She'd had her chance to flee and surrendered it so that she might deny her crime. The only explanation was that which he more and more used to resolve the contradiction between his brother's murderer and the woman said to have done the deed—she had to be witless. But even that was becoming less believable. Perhaps because he wished it so.

He eased his tense jaw. "We must find shelter."

With a slight nod, she slid her wet fingers over his.

For a moment, Michael thought lightning had struck near again, but it was only Beatrix. He pulled her up and settled her between his thighs where she went rigid as she had done this morn when they had first left the abbey ruins.

Hooking an arm around her, he turned Sartan toward the wood. As they entered the trees, lightning split the sky and cast a silver glow over the canopy of leaves that deflected the rain. Knowing if lightning landed to the wood, it would likely strike that which stood tallest, Michael searched out a tree that grew short of the others.

Shortly, he halted Sartan. "We shall pass the remainder of the storm here."

Beatrix gripped the pommel, turned, and slid to the ground.

Grateful for the near absence of pain when he lowered beside her, Michael swatted the destrier's hindquarter and watched him trot away. When he turned back, Beatrix sat at the base of the tree, the hood pulled down over her brow and head bent to her drawn knees. He knew he ought to seek separate shelter, but he drew his own hood on, hobbled forward, and lowered beside her. God willing, the storm would soon pass. They must make Soaring this eve.

Over the next half hour, rain came harder and formed a torrent three feet in front of them, lightning lit the wood and was answered by thunder, and not once did Beatrix come out from beneath her hood.

Did she sleep? Michael leaned near.

She prayed—in Latin.

Something innocent about her, something true...

Could such a woman murder? As he drew back, a crack deep in the wood evidenced a tree had been hit, and he felt the quake when it met the ground.

Beatrix jerked her head up.

Though she allowed Michael only a glimpse of her fear, it stirred him. He moved nearer, not realizing he did so until an ache shot up his leg. "'Twill be over soon," he said.

Suppressing the impulse to scoot away, Beatrix clasped her gaze to his. "I am not frightened."

D'Arci angled his head. "As you are no longer frightened of horses?"

Another lie, but she needed to hear it as much as she needed him to. "As I no longer am. Indeed, I have…decided I am done with fear."

His lids narrowed, causing the moisture on his lashes to glisten. "For this you approached Sartan?"

He did not need to know she had also been concerned for his injury. "Aye, to defeat that which hangs over me like these clouds." She tipped her face up. "And to accept that I may never again be as I was, that my… destiny is lost to me." Tears pricking her eyes, she castigated herself for allowing him to peer into her soul.

"What destiny?"

Was he truly interested? Why? And if she told him, what gain? Might he better understand her? Believe what she told of his brother? A vein of hope opened, and try though she did to close it, it opened wider. "You truly wish to know?"

"I assure you, 'tis only curiosity that makes me ask."

A twinge to the heart caused her to rethink whether to tell him of her hopes and dreams. But what harm? "Four years ago, I was…promised to the Church, and began my t-training to serve the Lord."

"You were to be a nun?" There was no mistaking his disbelief.

"As my m-mother wished." Reviled by her stuttering tongue, she clenched her hands.

"But not as *you* wished?"

"Nay, it was as I…wished," she hastily corrected. It was what she had wanted, was it not? She had a heart for God, did she not?

"You are certain?"

"I am. Though now…" She saw the great emptiness of falling, heard her cry and Sir Simon's shout, felt the pain. Pulling a hand from beneath the mantle, she slid it inside the hood and touched her head where the flesh puckered beneath her hair.

"Now?" D'Arci leaned near.

Did her eyes play her false? Or was that concern on his face?

She averted her gaze. "Who would want me now when there is a bridge between my mind and tongue that is often im-impassable? Nay, unless God works a miracle and...restores me, there will be no place for me within the Church. Nor with any man." Her next thought drew bitter laughter from her. "Of course, even if God works a miracle, 'tis not as if I will be...allowed to enjoy it."

D'Arci frowned. Then, unexpectedly, he slipped a hand inside her hood, pushed her fingers aside, and probed the scar.

Why did he touch her? She swallowed hard, and a tear slipped to her cheek.

He brushed it away. "I am sorry," he said, his hooded face bare inches from hers.

Beatrix caught her breath. Something had happened. Something that should not have. And yet she was glad of it. "Why?"

"I do not know." He came nearer until his hood met hers and cloaked them in darkness.

Beatrix quivered. Surely he would not kiss her. But if he did?

In that moment, she wished he would—this man who had pursued her and sought justice for what she had not done. Deeper than anything she had ever believed she wanted, she longed to feel his mouth upon hers.

"I do not know," he said again, his breath caressing her lips.

She could not draw air, but she did not miss it. For what did one need one's breath when they had another's?

D'Arci pressed closer, and yet their mouths did not touch. But nearly. She knew it from the brush of his nose alongside hers.

As she lowered her lids, he breached the last space between them, the slight movement causing her hood to fall back and let in the rain. She hardly noticed, her senses straining toward the barely perceptible brush of his lips—until breath came between them again.

"You have possessed me," he growled.

She opened her eyes. He was so near she had only to lean in to press her mouth to his. And she would have had his own hood not fallen back to reveal eyes lit with accusation. Too late, he realized what he did. And hated her for it.

Shame and indignation rising, she told herself she detested his breath upon her. "*I* have possessed you?" she demanded. "No more than you have possessed me, brother of Simon D'Arci."

The contempt heaped on his kin's name made his lids narrow.

"Are you finished, Lord D'Arci?" Thankfully, the words did not stumble from her. "I am getting wet."

His nostrils flared, and she sensed his struggle to be the one to hold, but he pulled the hood over his head and settled back against the tree. "Quite finished, Lady Beatrix."

A lump in her throat, she resettled the hood on her head and stared through the rain. She tried not to think about Michael D'Arci, not to remember the whisper of his mouth across hers, not to feel what had nearly been her first real kiss, not to convince herself he was different from Simon. Tried, but did not succeed.

She skimmed a finger across her lips and ached at the loss of something that had never been hers and could never be. She truly was a fool.

11

I do not know. Twice he had said it when she asked the reason he was sorry for the injury done her. But he had known, and for the hundredth time, rebuked himself for speaking such; for the thousandth time, cursed himself for what followed. He had come as near to kissing her as a man could without committing the intimacy. If not that the fall of her hood had let in the chill rain, he would have quenched his thirst, perhaps even had her there on the sodden floor of the wood. Was it only need?

He looked from the flickering night sky to the woman who had sat the saddle between his thighs since the passing of the clouds. Her head rested against his shoulder, pale hair bright against the dark of his mantle. Still she slept? He lowered his head and saw her eyes were closed and lips parted.

Feeling another stir of attraction, he peered up through the blue-black darkness. *Any wench will ease this ache,* he told himself. In fact, regardless of his injury, he would see to it this eve. What was the name of the woman he'd had to bed when Christian Lavonne had summoned him from Soaring? He frowned, wondering how he could hardly recall her face though every day she served at the high table and had more than once filled his bed.

As Sartan approached the crest of the hill, the donjon towers came into sight, the moon behind casting a path through the dark as if to guide him home.

Home. Michael turned the word around. After the lies that had reduced him to knight errant, never had he expected to have a home. Forsooth, never had he expected to want one, especially a demesne where it was the duty of a lord to produce an heir. As the getting of one meant the getting of a wife, that Michael would not do. Not yet. Perhaps never. Because of Edithe.

Letting the old pain feed him that it might shatter his uncertainty about Beatrix, he glanced at her. Aye, the same as Edithe. And yet—

Nay, regardless of his lusting loins, regardless of all she had done to prove otherwise, she had killed his brother. And the blood on her gown was all the proof needed. When Michael had stared at the crimson, knowing it bled out as his brother gasped his last, anger had shaken him as it had done when Edithe's accusations sought to cut his own life short. And it shook him now. Regardless of what it cost to ensure justice, Simon would be satisfied.

Michael halted Sartan atop the hill. Castle Soaring soared. Perched on a crag that rose against the night sky, its towers reached well beyond a man's reach. And as with the first time Michael had ridden upon it, he felt as if it had been raised to point the way to heaven—a sentimental thought that always surprised him. Perhaps he was nearer God than believed. Perhaps there was yet hope for him.

With a shake of his head, he returned his attention to the stronghold. It was formidable, though little more than half the size of his liege's castle; majestic, though in daylight it evidenced neglect and disrepair. As with all things of such scale, it would take years to return it to its former state, but its defenses were worthy. Though visiting lords might scoff at unpainted walls, shabby outbuildings, dank rushes, battered furnishings, threadbare tapestries, and simple drink and viands that arrived at table barely warm, few would dare bring an army against Soaring. Much Michael had learned from Duke Henry's quest for the throne, especially how to keep the enemy out. Indeed, any moment now—

The croak of a frog cleaved the night and was answered by another.

This moment. The first torch appeared on Soaring's walls, followed by a dozen more that lit the dark before the castle. Though the glow did not reach as far as Michael, it need not. The thunder of hooves behind and before him sufficed. Despite his absence, his men adhered to his instruction to turn back wayfarers well before they reached the walls.

As the first of the riders took shape, Beatrix's chin came around and the sparkle of her gaze met his.

Hating his need to reassure her, Michael muttered, "My men." Of course, what assurance was that when it meant she would soon address the walls of her prison?

She looked around. "Castle Soaring."

Though she claimed to be done with fear, he wondered if she trembled inside. Telling himself he did not feel for her, Michael peered at the riders—three at the fore and two at the rear, he guessed from the sound of their advance. Aye, his men, but one should never be too certain of anything. It was a pity he had not remembered that with Beatrix.

"Cover your head," he said, drawing his sword.

As she sat forward and draped the hood over her hair, Sir Robert called across the darkness, "Who goes?"

"Your lord!"

Moonlight running the riders' drawn swords, the three ahead reined in their horses.

"Lord D'Arci?" Sir Robert's gruff voice sounded with disbelief.

"I am returned."

As the knight guided his mount forward, the moonlight turned his pock-marked face familiar. The eyes of the red-bearded knight widened. "'Tis so!" he shouted, though he did so with only a pretense of welcome.

With great murmuring, the others guided their mounts nearer.

Sir Robert halted before Michael. "My lord, 'twas feared—"

"Wrongly so," Michael said as a throb wended his leg.

The man inclined his head. When he lifted his gaze, he paused on Michael's splints, next the hooded figure.

Though Michael felt Sir Robert's questioning, the shrewd, ever-scheming knight would not speak it aloud, which was as Michael wished it. Until he decided how best to assure Simon his justice, he would keep Beatrix's identity to himself—and Sir Canute. Considering his infirmity, Michael would need help with her, and the older knight would be discreet.

His injury reminding him that the sooner he dismounted the sooner he could tend it, he returned his sword to its scabbard. "All is well at Soaring?"

"'Tis," Sir Robert said.

Michael tapped a heel to Sartan and sped past the others. Across the great open, he felt no tremor of fear from Beatrix, and still none when the lowering drawbridge loosed its dreadful creak and groan. As the planks settled to the ground, Michael nodded to the five men who halted their mounts alongside his.

With murmurings of, "My lord," they reined around to return to their posts.

Michael guided Sartan over the drawbridge, beneath the portcullis, and into the outer bailey. With a lifted hand, he acknowledged the men-at-arms who followed his progress.

As Sartan passed from the outer bailey to the inner where the donjon cut the night sky, Michael thought Beatrix shuddered and had to clamp his teeth against further reassurance.

On the donjon steps, a torchlit figure descended, but even lacking light, Michael would know it was Canute. No others were as tall, excepting Baron Lavonne.

"My lord," the knight called as he stepped into the bailey and came alongside. "'Tis good you are returned."

No questions as to Michael's whereabouts, patience and discretion but two of many qualities to recommend him.

Michael laid a hand on the older man's shoulder. "It *is* good, Canute."

Torchlight flickered across the knight's weathered face as he looked to Beatrix. "I should assist the boy in dismounting, my lord?"

Michael would have laughed if his leg did not trouble him so. Canute was too astute to not realize who Michael had brought to Soaring. "Aye, he is to be put in the hind tower."

"Of course, my lord."

As Michael removed his arm from around Beatrix, he felt a sense of loss. *All be cursed!* She *had* possessed him.

Canute lifted his arms to receive her.

As she moved into them, she looked to Michael. "When you wish to know the...truth about his death, you have but to ask."

He warred inside himself and won. "No absolution."

The mouth he had nearly kissed bent softly upwards. "No absolution."

Then if he gave her over to trial she would not claim madness? What other defense, then? That she had not done the deed? That she had merely defended herself against further ravishment?

Michael's gut tightened. She lied. It was absolution she sought, and having foolishly revealed it, she endeavored to undo her mistake.

As Sir Canute set her to her feet, Michael brooded that he had two days, mayhap three, to decide how best to ensure Simon his justice, for once tidings of his return reached his liege, Lavonne would likely descend. And with him would come questions about the hunt for Beatrix and suspicion over who had accompanied Michael to Soaring. That last was unavoidable.

Though the loyalty of most of Michael's men was unquestioned, several had been placed at Soaring to assure Lavonne's hold on the demesne—placed by Aldous whose mind aspired to catch up with the deterioration of his body. The old man believed none were above suspicion, including his own son. Thus, despite his confinement, he was kept apprised of all that happened, not only at Broehne's sister castles, but at Broehne. Though Christian Lavonne was not oblivious to his father's methods, he tolerated it as being the old man's due.

As for the men set at Soaring, Michael knew who they were, one of them the same who had intercepted his ride on the castle. If Sir Robert, the illegitimate issue of Aldous Lavonne, did not send word this night that an injured Michael had returned and not alone, he would do so before dawn. As usual, Robert's squire, who delivered the message, would report all to Michael. Such means Michael did not like, for it put Squire Giffard at risk, but it was how it was done. Sir Robert was oblivious, Aldous Lavonne assuaged, and Michael informed.

Michael watched as Beatrix entered the donjon and went from sight. It was as he wished it. When his course was decided would be soon enough for him to see her again.

Nearly barren. Beatrix halted inside the chamber that had taken a half dozen turns of the winding stair to reach. There was a small bed, a brazier, a basin, and an oilcloth stretched across the narrow window. No rushes on the floor, no chairs, no sheets or blankets on the mattress, no shutters at the window. But it *was* a prison. Even so, it would be more comfortable than the dank, dark crypt where she had lived this past month. Of course, there she'd had herbs to sweeten the night.

But it was not as if she would be long at Soaring. Regardless if D'Arci usurped his lord's privilege or she was allowed to defend herself at trial—a trial she had so feared, but for which she now yearned— she would soon leave. As for absolution, she had spoken true when she agreed there would be none. She was not witless or mad and would not claim such.

"Is there anything you require, lad?" the knight asked.

She turned to where he leaned a shoulder against the door frame. "I am no lad." She dropped the hood to her shoulders.

His grooved brow smoothed slightly. "I did not think you were."

"But you—"

"Lady Beatrix, is it not?"

She nodded. "I am the one your l-lord has searched for."

Up went a silver eyebrow. "The one responsible for the injury done him at Broehne?" Displeasure edged his voice. "And the injury done him now?"

Of course he had noticed the splints.

"The one who put a dagger to his brother?"

As she saw no benefit in arguing the matter of Sir Simon, she crossed her arms over her chest. "I am the one."

The knight took a step forward. With eyes that seemed to peel back the layers of her, he murmured, "You are as expected."

That she did not expect. "I do not understand."

"'Twas not intended that you should." He cleared his throat and looked past her. "I shall bring a blanket, coal for the brazier, and a pitcher of water for you to bathe." His gaze dropped. "And viands to quiet your belly."

She pressed a hand to her midriff.

"Is there anything else you require?"

"Naught that you can afford me."

He inclined his head and turned.

Now she would be alone. If only she had—"Sir Knight!"

"Aye?"

"There is one thing. Could you deliver me a…" The word flew away without a backward glance. She squeezed her lids closed to prevent them from fluttering. Though she conjured a vision of the object, it shied away from her tongue.

"Tell," the knight said.

If not that she needed the comfort of what she sought, she would withdraw her request. "I require…" She swept her tongue over her palate in search of sounds to form the word, but they were not there. Thus, she must go the long way around. She pressed her palms together and opened them. "A book, Sir Knight—the Lord's."

Some of the wrinkles melted from his brow. "A psalter."

"Aye, I am without mine."

"I shall endeavor to secure one for you." He halted in the doorway. "I am Sir Canute. As it seems I am to be your jailer, 'tis as you should address me."

Her reluctant jailer, for it was surely no pleasant task he had been given. "Very well, Sir Canute." Providing his name did not flee her.

He swung the door closed. The key scraped, the lock clicked.

Beatrix stared at the door. Would Michael D'Arci ever come through it? Remembering what had happened between them, she touched her lips. Warm breath sweeping her fingers, she told herself that only a fool would believe the near-intimacy meant anything to Michael D'Arci, but could a man who truly believed such ill of her do what he had nearly done? For all of his threats, her heart told her she need not fear him. And in that moment she knew what beat through her. She felt for this man whose brother had tried to ravish her. Might such flutterings lead to more?

"If I may, my lord, you seem changed."

Michael looked from the flames that spat heat across the hearth to Canute who had yet to take a seat. Other than astride a horse, the man rarely sat. Because of his stiff hip, he told, but Michael knew it was also an issue of vulnerability. In the event of an attack, it was always best to be on one's feet. "What say you?" he asked.

The aged knight straightened from the chair he had leaned against this past hour while he recounted all that had transpired at Soaring in his lord's absence. "Only that you do not seem yourself." His lips twitched. "Else my memory fails me."

Though Michael knew he should not pursue the conversation, he said, "How do you mean?"

"You are thoughtful."

"Surely you do not say I have not been so before?"

"You have, but 'tis as if you do not know your course now that you have what you sought all these weeks—a course you knew well ere we parted at Broehne."

He spoke of Beatrix. But Michael *did* know his course. He turned his hand and considered the pale tress he rubbed between thumb and forefinger. The string binding it evidenced the persistent handling to which he had subjected it during Canute's recounting—frayed and in dire need of replacement. Of course, now that he had Beatrix, he had no need for such a reminder.

"Too," Canute continued, "though you have now been returned to Soaring for two hours, I see no wench on your lap."

He *had* promised himself one, and still he might send for a wench once the affairs of the demesne were settled. But if not this night, then the next.

"The journey was long and, as you can see"—Michael nodded at his resplinted leg—"I am somewhat lamed."

"The workings of Lady Beatrix, I wager."

His pride pinched at being bested by the woman, but it was Canute to whom he spoke, a man who knew him better than his own father. It was Canute who had released Michael's beaten body from the manacles with which Edithe's father had bound him, Canute who had taken him away and taught him the ways of knight errantry, Canute who had fought alongside him during Duke Henry's battles. There was none he trusted better.

"Aye," Michael conceded. "The witch sent me down a hole."

"Pray, tell."

It took only minutes to cover what had happened at Purley Abbey and during the journey to Soaring, but it was enough for Canute to finally seek his backside to a chair. At the end of the telling, he murmured, "I see."

Not all of it, but what had nearly happened between Michael and Beatrix need not be told.

"So for this you are so thoughtful." Canute steepled his hands beneath his chin. "That though 'tis told that Lady Beatrix murdered your brother, and all evidence you have of that, she did not leave you when 'twould have best served her. You are thinking she does not seem one to murder."

Once again wavering over her innocence, though he had vowed he would do so no more, Michael drummed his fingers on the chair arms.

"How does she explain Simon's death?" Canute asked.

Michael met the man's gaze and watched for what he knew would sound from the depths of those old, brown eyes. "She says she but defended herself when he ravished her."

Understanding lit the knight's eyes. "A place you have been before, eh, friend?"

Michael quieted his fingers. "A place to which I did not expect to return."

Canute leaned forward. "Put your mind to this, Michael. The woman *did* murder your brother. There is no other explanation."

Michael returned his gaze to the hearth. The dwindling flames caressed the logs, blackening them and reducing them to ashes, reminding him of Edithe. "'Tis as I tell myself again and again."

"You should." Canute pushed up from the chair. "Heed me as you did not years past. Keep from Lady Beatrix as you should have kept from Edithe."

With the foolishness bred of the young, Michael had ignored the warnings of the household knight who had served Edithe's father. For it, he had lost all. And could lose all again.

"This night, send word to Baron Lavonne of your return, *and* of Lady Beatrix's capture."

"As you know, word of my return has already gone."

"Aye, but not by your hand."

He was right. Regardless of this war waged over Beatrix, Michael was Baron Lavonne's vassal. It would bode ill if he did not himself send tidings. "I give you leave to send word of my return."

"And of Lady Beatrix's capture?"

Though Michael nearly argued that if he surrendered Beatrix she might be granted absolution, he knew the argument would not hold with the older man. Forsooth, it barely held with him. Why did he waver? Because she had not abandoned him to the crypt? That, during the storm, she had forfeited escape that she might restate her innocence? That he had never before felt such need to kiss a woman as he had done there between their hoods?

That last slipped in before he could slam its fingers in the door. The result of abstinence, he told himself. That was all.

"You will send word?" Canute asked again.

Why did he press so hard? In the next instant, Michael castigated himself for questioning his old friend. Canute did it to assure no ill befell Michael's lordship, for it was a terrible risk to refuse the baron tidings of Beatrix's capture. If it was later discovered that Michael held her...

Still, against all he knew was best for him and Soaring, he said, "I shall soon enough inform Baron Lavonne."

"When?"

"When I am ready."

Canute lowered his arms to his sides. "As you would, my lord." Once more putting their friendship behind him and placing himself in service to Michael, he stepped back. "I leave you to your rest." He traversed the rush-strewn floor but came back around when he reached the door. "You have not asked after her."

Affecting nonchalance, though he once more stroked the tress, he said, "Had she escaped, I am certain you would have told me."

Canute was not amused, as evidenced by his lowering brow.

Though Michael knew he should end the conversation, he asked, "She is being difficult? Refusing to eat or some such?"

"Nay, she ate most heartily."

He did not care, and yet he was tugged by a longing to once more see her as she had presented at Broehne—as near an angel as one of fleshly form might take.

"Methinks you would do well to seek a wench," Canute said.

Michael narrowed his gaze on the man. "'Tis good we are friends, Canute."

"It is good, my lord." He opened the door and stepped into the corridor. "Very good."

12

SHE WAS HAD.

Christian knew he ought to be pleased by Lady Beatrix's capture, and yet he was pinched with regret. It would be different if not that he was to wed her sister, but still the king required it. And Christian would not oppose the edict, as he had not done when it was first issued despite his father's rantings. He wearied of the raids against the Wulfrith lands in the name of his slain brother, Geoffrey. The time had come for peace, and marriage between warring families was often the best solution. Thus, he would wed the older sister whose looks were told to be as distant from Lady Beatrix's as the dark of night was from the light of day. Unfortunately, if such a union was made in the after swell of the sister's trial, it could only bode ill. Should Lady Beatrix be found guilty, her lethal punishment would hang between Christian and his wife forever. Unless she, like Christian, cared little for her sibling.

Christian studied the flames that beat against the walls of the great fireplace. It was true he had not cared for his older brother, Geoffrey, who had been self-serving and of such ill bent not even Christian was spared his mockery and cruelty. Many were the days Christian had watched as his brother was groomed to rule the barony. Many were the resentments felt that so great an honor be placed in such unworthy hands. Far too many had been his unspoken longings to be his father's heir.

Though reason told Christian he was not at fault for Geoffrey's death at the hands of the Wulfriths, he felt responsible. The jealous youth he had been—promised to the Church and mostly confined indoors with his tutor—had prayed for something to happen that would allow him to be named heir. Since little short of Geoffrey's death would have made that possible, it had been hopeless, or so Christian had believed until, years later, tidings of his brother's death was delivered to the monastery.

By then, Christian had forsworn his rebellious leanings and accepted his destiny to honor the name his father had given him. Thus, he had been unprepared for Geoffrey's death and so guilt-ridden by his answered prayer that he had nearly refused his father's summons to assume his title.

Though the cost of reclaiming a son who had taken final vows was high, Aldous Lavonne had paid it. In the years since, Christian had watched his embittered father waste away amid an excess of ale and petty vengeance against the Wulfriths—vengeance that Christian had allowed to continue as if it might somehow comfort his ravaged father.

Wondering what had become of Christian Lavonne, a man who had finally yielded all to God, who had bent and beaten the steel of his soul into a shape surely pleasing and useful to the Creator, he blinked at the flames. What irony if this was now his destiny—hell's fire into which he would descend for having so nearly abandoned his faith. Indeed, he whose knees had once been calloused from prayer rarely attended mass now, and then only when the presence of visitors required it.

He shook his head. He had lived both sides of the world—God's and man's—and neither satisfied. Surely, somewhere in the space between he would find the peace and fulfillment for which he yearned. Mayhap once he was wed and his wife swelled with child...

Returning to Gaenor Wulfrith, who had yet to come out of hiding, Christian looked to D'Arci's missive that told that not only was he returned to Soaring, but he had not returned alone. Christian had already been informed of Soaring's mysterious visitor by the earlier missive received from his illegitimate half-brother, Sir Robert, but it was D'Arci's missive that confirmed the hooded figure was Lady Beatrix. His missive also told that, due to an injury, D'Arci was unable to return her to Broehne.

Christian cast his gaze around the hall. Though servants cleared away the nooning meal, a dozen or more knights lingered over their tankards. Then there was the squire who had carried D'Arci's missive. Upon delivering it, the mud-spattered youth had retreated to the edge of the dais.

Christian lowered the parchment. "Squire Percival, tell your lord I am pleased."

The young man inclined his head. "As is your will, my lord."

"Ease your thirst ere you make the return journey to Soaring."

The young man hesitated as if surprised there was not more to be told to his lord. And there was not—for now. "I thank you, my lord." He descended the dais and strode across the hall on legs that would soon support the weight of armor.

Christian almost envied him his training, which he himself had been denied though he had often defied his father by hefting swords, spears, and pikes in an attempt to attain what was refused him. True, now he had all to which he had once aspired and proven himself worthy of lording the barony, but the bestowal of knighthood was merely token—and empty as was so much in the life that should have been Geoffrey's.

Christian gripped the parchment harder as he recalled the raging battle fought alongside Duke Henry shortly after Christian was titled "baron." Though he had not been entirely inept at arms, it was soon apparent to himself and others that he was not a man to whom one should entrust one's life. But not until one of King Stephen's knights had bled him had he accepted what his father had known all along. Despite a yearning for the sword felt as a boy, as a man he did not possess the bloodlust of a true warrior. Indeed, his instinct for survival was all that sustained him through the battles—no lusting after the blood of others, no pride or triumph in the taking of lives.

Remembering how his father had scorned him when he returned home injured, how he had muttered that Geoffrey would not have allowed an enemy near enough to draw blood, Christian tensed further.

Of course, Geoffrey *had* allowed such, and for it he was dead. According to the Wulfriths, it was his due. And Christian was inclined to believe it.

The crackle of parchment returned him to the hall, and he stared at the missive in his fist before settling back in his chair. When Squire Giffard had earlier delivered Sir Robert's missive, Christian had wondered how long it would be before D'Arci deigned to send word of his return. Though the keepers of Christian's other castles would not dare delay, too often the physician did. But it seemed the man remained loyal despite his unease that justice would be denied Simon. He had good reason to fear such.

Self-serving though it was, Christian did not want Lady Beatrix's unfortunate fate entwined with his and his future wife's. But what else was there for it, especially considering his father's obsession with the opportunity to see a Wulfrith punished for his son's death? To see a Wulfrith die.

If not that Aldous was unable to move from his bed, Lady Beatrix might have met her end before regaining consciousness, so changed was Aldous Lavonne by the loss of his beloved Geoffrey. Though once the old baron had revered God, so much that he had promised his youngest to the Church, bitterness had turned him from the Lord. His mind now nearly as ravaged as his body, he lived only for revenge.

Christian lowered the missive to the table. The lady must be brought to trial, though preferably later, rather than sooner as Aldous wished— Aldous who had demanded that Christian attend him after Sir Robert's squire delivered the old man tidings of D'Arci's return to Soaring. Thus, Christian must go and listen to his rantings and plotting for as long as he could tolerate it, which was less and less of late.

If not that time spent with his father kept him apprised of those things Aldous set to motion from the confines of his bed, which could then be controlled, Christian might stop attending him altogether. But despite his father's bent toward madness, Aldous was yet able to think clearly enough to affect the barony of Abingdale. And he did so with the aid of knights who had once served him and Geoffrey. Aldous had placed several at each of Abingdale's castles when Christian had returned home. Though he had said the arrangement was only temporary until Christian settled into his title, still the knights held their posts. In the beginning, their presence had been of benefit when Abingdale's vassals thought to test their "godly" baron, but they were no longer useful to Christian. In Aldous's service, they more often proved a hindrance, if not a danger.

Though Christian could put an end to Aldous's influence, guilt over the answered prayer that had caused his father such pain too often kept him from doing what was best for the barony. Regardless of how his father's actions angered him and sometimes made him feel like a puppet, it was tolerated for memory of the man Aldous had been.

Christian pushed to his feet. A short while later, he opened the door of his father's chamber. The servant who attended Aldous turned where she stood alongside the bed. "Yer lord father is impatient to speak with ye, Baron Lavonne."

Christian stepped into the room. "Leave us."

As she withdrew, Christian stared at the postered bed, much of which lay in deepest shadow. Knowing his father regarded him with but one thought in mind—that he wished it was Geoffrey who came to him—he waited.

"Draw near, boy," Aldous Lavonne slurred past a graveled throat.

No matter that Christian was twenty and six and had many times proven himself a man, he was always "boy" to his father. He stepped to the foot of the bed. "You are pleased by Sir Robert's tidings?"

The old man shifted on his pillows and moved into the flicker of torches that was all the light he allowed the reach of his chamber. "Quite pleased. Robert rarely disappoints."

That last was meant to prick, and it did, for no such kind words did he direct toward Christian. If not for Robert's illegitimate birth—conceived upon a peasant woman and born to Aldous before he wed a noble woman—it was the eldest son who would have been bestowed the title left vacant by Geoffrey's death. For that, Robert resented Christian as Christian had once resented Geoffrey. It would be ironic if the threat was not so real, for though Christian had never sought to harm Geoffrey, Robert was of a different bent.

Eyes shining amid the horribly puckered flesh that was all that remained of his face, Aldous gripped the edge of the coverlet with hands equally scarred by the fire that should have taken his life nearly six years past. Instead, the flames had laid such waste to his body he had been forced to relinquish the barony to Geoffrey.

"You will bring the Wulfrith whore back to Broehne on the morrow," his father said.

It was not a question, but Christian chose to regard it as such. Though he made concessions for the old man's suffering, he no longer took orders from him. "Nay, there is time aplenty to return Lady Beatrix to Broehne."

"Time aplenty!" Aldous thrust forward into the wavering light to reveal the angry red skin in all its horror—from his bald scalp with its few patches of wiry gray hair, to his absent eyebrows, to his deformed ears, to his bent mouth that evidenced the stroke he had suffered upon learning Geoffrey had died. Much of the rest of his body was similarly scarred. No man should have lived through such, but Aldous Lavonne had, and continued to though Michael D'Arci had believed he would not live out a year when first he accepted the position of physician to Christian's father.

Seeing spittle collect in the corner of Aldous's mouth, Christian said, "D'Arci will hold Lady Beatrix until it can be arranged for the sheriff to bring her to trial."

"Arrange it now!"

Though it disturbed Christian to look so near on his father, he did not avert his gaze. "You must be patient. Justice will be done."

With a grunt of disgust, Aldous dropped back against his pillows. "That the Lord should make me suffer such a fool for a son!"

His words roused Christian as was intended, but never would Aldous know it from the face his son presented. "Is there anything you require, Father?"

"Geoffrey," the old man bemoaned. "I require Geoffrey."

Maintaining an impassive face, Christian said, "I shall leave you to your rest."

His hand was on the door when Aldous rasped, "Still you intend to wed that other Wulfrith whore?"

"As the king commands."

Though Aldous fell silent, Christian could almost hear the turning of his mind. Thus, he waited for the plotting that would surely fall from those old lips as Aldous was unable to keep from boasting aloud his plans. However, all Aldous said was, "You are a sore disappointment, boy. Thus, I will do what you have not the heart for—what Geoffrey would have done."

Bitterness digging a deeper hole within him, Christian asked, "And what would Geoffrey have done, Father?"

"His duty, of which you are woefully incapable."

Christian dragged the door open, stepped into the corridor, and closed the door behind him.

"Lord!" he rasped, panting with the effort to contain his seething. He hated to admit it, even to himself, but he yearned for Aldous's approval. Was it worth the cost? Worth going against all he knew to be wrong? And if he did yield, would Aldous give him the respect due a man? Or would the youngest son forever be an unworthy boy in the shadow of the man Geoffrey had become?

Christian dragged a hand down his face. This was not the life he had envisioned when he watched his older brother being groomed toward it.

Lord, what would you have me do? he asked the one he had rarely consulted all these years.

The answer settled immediately upon his heart. *Return to Me.*

But not at the monastery. Not to tonsure and habit. Not to manuscripts painstakingly illuminated by candlelight. Rather, he was to remain at Broehne and seek God upon his knees.

Christian closed his eyes. He was not ready. Not yet.

Through a hall nearly beset by night came Michael's squire. "Tidings, my lord!"

Though Michael knew what such tidings would render, he put aside the missive he had written and returned the quill to the ink pot. Beside

him, Canute clasped his hands atop the journal to which he posted the
demesne's income and expenses, a task that had been given over to him
upon the death of Soaring's steward some months past.

Squire Percival ascended the dais and halted before the lord's table.
Flecked with mud from toe to crown, evidence of his urgent ride across
the rain-soaked country between Broehne and Soaring, he waited.

No missive, then. Michael frowned. It was rare for Lavonne to send
word mouth to mouth. "Deliver the tidings."

"My lord, Baron Lavonne commands me to tell you he is pleased."

"And?"

"Naught else, my lord."

Michael leaned forward. "He did not inquire as to my progress in
locating Lady Beatrix?"

"He did not, my lord."

Lavonne knew, then. But how? Sir Robert could not have known it
was Beatrix who had accompanied him to Soaring. Only—

Torchlight glimmered on Canute's bent head, but though he surely
felt Michael's gaze, he did not look around.

Returning to the night past, Michael heard again his friend's argument that Lavonne be delivered word of Lady Beatrix's capture. Could it
be? Surely not, and yet…

He had entrusted Canute to send tidings to Lavonne of his return to
Soaring. Had he told more? Betrayed?

Canute looked up, and the answer was in his eyes.

If not that Squire Percival shifted his weight, reminding Michael of
his presence, rage would have unfurled. Holding Canute's gaze, Michael
ground his teeth.

As Baron Lavonne knew Michael's infirmity prevented him from
delivering Lady Beatrix, would he venture to Soaring himself to return
her to Broehne Castle or send another to bring her to trial? For a
moment, the thought of Beatrix's fate caused Michael to fear for her, but
he reminded himself of Simon's death and told himself it was probably

best that the baron knew—providing he did not waver from his vow that justice would be given. Even so, Lavonne knew only because of betrayal.

Michael looked around. "You have done well," he told the squire in a voice so tight it nearly snapped.

"I thank you, my lord." The young man strode from the dimming hall.

The moment the great door swung closed, Michael gripped the table's edge and thrust to his feet. "You betrayed me!"

Slowly, Canute rose. "Betrayal was not intended, my friend. Lest you lose all again, it had to be done."

Michael slammed a fist to the table. "By faith! I decide what must needs be done!"

Canute took a step forward. "After Edithe, did you not secure my vow that I not allow you to make so dire a mistake again?"

"I was barely twenty years old!"

"Aye, and for a tumble in the lady's bed you forever tainted the name of D'Arci and set yourself on a road without end."

Remembrance of the woman who had lured him in and named it ravishment, stoked Michael's fire. Leg aching, he turned a hand around the wooden staff that had borne much of his weight this day.

"If you allow your head to lead and not desire," Canute said, "you will agree that I did what had to be done."

Then Canute believed he wished to bed Beatrix? That he felt something for her other than loathing? That—

Hell's fire! Regardless of the betrayal, Canute believed right. Desire had refused him his course. But though he had nearly kissed Beatrix, she was responsible for Simon's death. He must not forget it.

A hand fell to his shoulder. "Name it what you will, I but kept my vow and shall not be sorry for it."

Michael met the knight's gaze. "Leave me."

After a long moment, Canute said, "I shall depart Soaring this eve," and turned and traversed the dais.

As he strode toward the stairs, torchlight bounding about the walls and spinning gold among the rushes crushed underfoot, Michael closed his eyes. Try though he did to forswear the good of the man he had long called friend, he could not. Canute had sacrificed his position of household knight to deliver Michael from the wrath of Edithe's father, had taught Michael how to fight not for show but to win, and had been as a father to him. Concern, not malice, was what had made him send word of Beatrix's capture.

Michael drew a long breath. When the woman no longer poisoned his blood, he would be grateful. He opened his eyes. "Leave, if that is your wish. If 'tis not, still you can be of use to me."

Canute turned. Though he had told he would not be sorry for what he had done, regret was in his eyes. "I shall remain."

Michael inclined his head. "Well met—providing the vow I once extracted no longer stands."

"As you would, my lord."

"I would, and henceforth Squire Percival shall tend Lady Beatrix." Squire Percival who would need to be warned to take care with the lady lest she render him unconscious or lame—a warning he had not needed to issue to Canute.

"Anything else, my lord?"

"That is all."

The knight ascended the stairs.

Michael turned his palms up and stared at their quaking caused by his anger. In all this world, was there no one he could trust? Did all lie? Did all betray? It would serve him well if he but accepted it. And now he had every reason to.

He eyed the journals laid open before the chair where Canute had sat. All appeared to be in order—just as his old friend had appeared to be trustworthy. Michael stepped his staff forward and eased into the chair.

An hour later, surrounded by servants and men-at-arms who had bedded down on benches and scattered pallets, he closed the books. All was accounted for. In that, Canute had not failed him. Only with Beatrix.

Michael looked to the ceiling that the failing torches no longer lit and wondered if she slept. Likely—just as she ate. According to Canute, who had twice recounted it though Michael had not asked, she fared well. Still, Michael was tempted to drag his infirm leg up the stairs to see for himself. But the longer he stayed away, the easier it would be to forget he had spent a long, dark night covering a murderess who pretended to be an angel.

He reached for the staff he had propped against the lord's chair. As he levered to his feet, he caught sight of the missive he had just finished writing when Squire Percival returned from Broehne. It was to his stepmother, informing her that her son's murderer was had.

Would it bring her to Soaring? He prayed not, for the woman's health was not as it should be. Indeed, it had turned worse following Simon's death. For a moment, Michael reconsidered sending the missive, but he had given her his word. Too, even if she made the journey, it would do her good to know justice was at hand.

Michael looked to the stairs where a man-at-arms stood at his post. Though the soldier's face was averted, he surely knew the challenge his lord faced in gaining the solar. But he would not offer aid, for it would not be abided. However, once abovestairs, Michael would give himself over to Percival, for it was the duty of a squire to assist his lord in disrobing. Of course, now it was also his duty to keep Beatrix.

Michael stepped the staff forward and descended the dais. As he started across the hall, a shadow freed itself from the darkness, causing him to sweep a hand to his dagger.

"My lord?" a husky voice caressed the night. "You would like?" The woman stepped into the light, a smile on her face, a hand on her hip.

It was the same wench he had several times promised himself since his return on the day past. "Nay," he said. "Ask again on the morrow."

Footsteps.

Roused from a dream, Beatrix peered across the dark to the door. Why did Sir Canute come at so late an hour? Or was it him?

For a moment her heart beat faster, but her ears told that the stride of the one who approached did not belong to one who was lamed. Not the blackguard, then. Which was well——unless whoever approached did so to deliver her to Baron Lavonne.

Trying to calm her heart with the reminder that she longed to defend herself at trial, she levered up and dragged the homespun blanket around her.

Light shone beneath the door and the footsteps fell silent.

Mayhap Sir Canute had located a psalter? Hope reached tentative roots through her, but she pulled them back. Though thrice the knight had tended her this first full day at Soaring, he had said nothing of her request.

The key scraped and the door opened, causing light to rush in that was so bright she was forced to duck her chin.

"My lady?" asked one whose voice was too callow to be spoken from the lips of the gruff knight.

She gripped the blanket tighter. Who was he? More, was he from Broehne? She peered through narrowed lids at the young man in the doorway.

He raised the torch higher. "My lady, I am Squire Percival."

She did not know the name, nor the sparsely bearded face that shone golden in the torchlight. "What is it you wish?"

"My lord has sent me——"

"Baron Lavonne?"

"Indeed not, my lady. My liege is Lord D'Arci."

Relief wended through her. "And Sir Ca——?" She foundered, but finally recalled the knight's name. "What has become of Sir Canute?"

The squire stepped farther into the room. "Lord D'Arci's man is occupied with other matters, my lady. Henceforth, I am to tend you."

Beatrix tucked her feet deeper beneath her. She could not say she liked the older knight who had brought her food and water, but it was worrisome that his attentions had turned elsewhere. Was it possible he had gained D'Arci's displeasure in attempting to deliver her a psalter?

Aye, though it was also possible her request was forgotten the moment the knight agreed to it.

"For what did your lord send you at...middle night?"

The young man's eyebrows rose. "'Tis past middle night, my lady. An hour hence it will be sunrise."

Could it be? It seemed she had hardly laid down. But then, set apart as she was, and with such constant silence, it was difficult to know the passage of time.

"I should bring viands to break your fast?"

"I would be...grateful."

"Anything else?"

Would he tell? Sir Canute would not have. "I would know how your lord fares."

Could a face be bounded by doors, it would close up as tight as the squire's expression. "I shall bring your meal anon."

Nothing lost in asking, she told herself, and would have begged for a psalter if not that he and his torchlight withdrew from the chamber. As much as she longed to call him back, she did not.

The door closed, dousing her in darkness.

Beatrix stared into nothingness and wondered what the squire would not tell.

Michael D'Arci was well, she assured herself. He would soon enough walk without hitch. Or so she prayed.

13

HE OUGHT TO call her to him. Ought to lay with her and be done with this ache. But as with each time he thought it this past fortnight, he went no further. As with each time she offered, he told her to ask again on the morrow.

Glowering at the wench whose hips swayed as she moved about the solar, Michael rubbed his bearded jaw and told himself it was because of his leg that he did not accept what she offered. Though it was healing well, it still bothered him. More, a quenching of desire was not worth the risk of further injury. Beatrix, attended by Squire Percival these past weeks, had nothing to do with his abstinence. Indeed, she had returned to that place where she belonged—guilty of murder. It was amazing what time had wrought.

Michael leaned back in his chair. All that stood between Simon and justice was Baron Lavonne who had yet to collect the accused.

As often happened when Beatrix came to mind, Michael reached to the purse on his belt but stopped himself from pulling forth the pale tress. Why did he persist in holding onto it as one might a talisman?

Determinedly, he settled his gaze on the wench who gathered his garments from atop the chest at the foot of his bed. Try though he did to summon desire, it eluded him.

A rap on the door sounded.

"Enter!" Michael called.

Squire Percival stepped inside. "My lord——" He snapped his teeth closed when the wench came to notice.

"Leave us," Michael ordered the woman.

She sent him another of her smiles and swayed toward the door.

Squire Percival closed it behind her. "Apologies, my lord. I would not disturb you if not that——"

"What have you for me?"

"A question, my lord."

Beatrix again. It had to be. And from the knit of Percival's brow, her latest request troubled him. First, she had begged soap, next an extra blanket, then hand towels. After those first days, Michael had told the squire to use his own judgment, needing no more of her intrusions on his thoughts than already he endured. So what did she want now? A rope with which to mend an unsprung bed? A dagger with which to poke at viands?

"What does she wish?"

"Writing instruments, my lord. I did not think you——"

"Rightly so." What did she want to write? And who? Surely she did not think to steal a missive to her family who still likely believed her dead? "She did not say what she needed them for?"

"I fear I did not ask. I shall, though." He turned.

"Nay, I will go."

The squire came around. "You, my lord?" He glanced at Michael's splinted leg.

He should not, Michael knew. Far better to remain distant, but whatever Beatrix plotted, he would discover it for himself. He reached for the staff, pushed onto it, and turned to Percival.

"I should accompany you, my lord?"

"Nay." Michael stepped toward him. "I but require the key."

The squire dropped it in his palm.

"I will return anon." And he would, for once he stamped out Beatrix's scheme, there would be nothing to hold him to her. But if that were so, why did he feel as if he approached a pool of fresh water following days of unquenched thirst?

Silently vowing he cared nothing for her, he stepped from the solar. Though he easily negotiated the corridor, the tight, winding stair presented a challenge that had him aching deep when he finally reached the door of Beatrix's prison and fit the key.

Before he stepped inside, he cursed himself. Before he settled his gaze on her, he named himself a fool.

She faced him where she stood at the foot of the bed, blue eyes bright and lips slightly bowed as the daylight pouring through the uncovered window cast a glow around her. No longer did she wear men's garments, but a gown. As his eyes grew accustomed to the lit room, he saw she had plaited her flaxen hair and the strands that had escaped curved becomingly around her face—a face that bore faint resemblance to the gaunt woman who had foraged fish for him at the abbey. An angel once more.

All be cursed! A fortnight of retracing her guilt was nearly undone with one glance. As innocent as she looked, she *had* killed Simon.

Beatrix held the stare of the man before her. If not for the sound of his staff on the stairs, she would have hesitated over him, as he looked different with a full beard. Not at all like Simon D'Arci.

She pushed a stray hair behind an ear. Though she knew she should not care how she looked, a wish slipped in that she had asked for a mirror in addition to the comb. Then another wish that it was a lady's gown she wore and not this rough garment that had seemed a luxury minutes past. And if only she had not lingered near the brazier. Though faint, the smell of smoke permeated her gown.

Michael D'Arci entered. Every footfall allowing a glimpse of his discomfort at having ascended the stairs, he followed his staff's lead across the chamber. Unfortunately, there was no chair on which he might settle. There was only her small bed, and that would not do.

Looking hale in spite of the splint, the staff doing nothing to diminish his presence, he halted three feet in front of her and swept his gaze to her feet and up again. "You are much improved, Lady Beatrix."

She smoothed the skirt of her gown. "You feed me well, my lord."

A dark eyebrow slid up his brow. "And clothe you, it seems."

He had not known. Of course, his squire would not perceive a request for women's garments as threatening as a request for writing instruments.

She moistened her lips. "I had hoped you would come."

Her words unsettled the indifference with which he regarded her, causing his eyebrows to jerk and firm mouth to ease. However, he soon enough tightened his face. "For what do you wish parchment and ink?"

Was she wrong? With each passing day without retaliation for his brother's death, she grew increasingly certain there would be none, that what had happened in the wood had changed what he believed of her. But if she was wrong, why did she remain untouched? He did not need both legs firm beneath him to seek justice.

"I wait," he snapped.

"I wish to write down my...defense."

His nostrils flared. "Defense?"

"If I cannot speak it, I shall read it." For the sake of her uncertain tongue, she would commit to parchment what had happened that day at the ravine.

Pale eyes sharpening, Michael stepped closer. "Why?"

The nearness of him causing chill bumps to rise across her skin, she quelled the urge to rub her arms. "I..."

"Speak, Lady Beatrix."

She looked to his grip on the staff. Excepting the ink that stained his fingers—evidence he had recently applied quill to parchment—his large hand was ashen.

Which was greater? His anger or his suffering? "I wish a trial, Lord D'Arci. Thus, I beseech you to send word of my...capture to Baron Lavonne."

His lids narrowed. "Then still you seek absolution."

"Not absolution by cause of a mind gone m-mad. Absolution only should I prove my...innocence."

Something flickered in his eyes, something that seemed to ease the anger there. "You think you can prove it?"

She had to try, and just maybe God would work a miracle. If not, she would likely be hanged or drowned. Perhaps even burned.

Beatrix lowered her gaze and tried to talk back the tears that threatened. She was past such, and yet the thought of losing all when she was just beginning to find herself again, pained her.

She startled when Michael's calloused fingers grazed the underside of her chin. "Look at me, Beatrix."

Had he truly been so intimate with her name? She tried to blink away the moisture that aspired to her lashes, but it remained. She swept her lids up.

"Why did you not leave me in the crypt?"

Unsettled by his unexpected question, she shook her head. "What?"

"You could have fled but you did not. Why?"

"I could not. God would not allow it."

"God?"

She smiled softly. "Do you know Him, Michael?"

He released her chin. "As much as I care to know Him."

Though she should not be surprised by his irreverence, she was. "You do not mean that."

He shrugged. "Where is God? Tell me where He is now that *you* need Him?"

Though she risked much, she sensed he truly wished to know. She took a step nearer and pressed a hand to her heart. "He is here. Always." She turned her hand and laid it to his chest. "And here if you will allow Him to be."

He lowered his gaze to her hand upon him. When he looked up, there was something in his eyes that might have been desperation. "Did you do it? Did you murder my brother?"

"You know I did not." Feeling his heart beat strong and quick beneath her palm, she said, "Here you know it. You have but to accept it"—she touched his brow—"here."

He stilled as if to heed the beat of his heart, then slid a hand around the back of her neck. "'Tis as I wish to do."

A small sound parted Beatrix's lips and came again when he looked to her mouth. This stir, this churning, this strange ache that she had last felt when they met between their hoods in the wood...

As she watched, his pupils spread until all that remained of the color was a fine ring of gray. With a groan, he pulled her in.

She did not resist when his head lowered. Savoring the feel of his lips and the rasp of his beard across her skin, she leaned in, causing him to slant his head and deepen the kiss. She shuddered. However, when she slid her hands up and gripped his shoulders, he wrenched his mouth from hers.

"Your word!" His breath was harsh on her moist lips.

"What?"

"I want your word that you did not kill him!"

At the realization that Simon was yet between them, her heart jumped. "I...vow I did not kill your brother."

No man's struggle could have been clearer. It convulsed Michael's jaw, flared his nostrils, narrowed his eyes. And then his mouth closed over hers.

The kiss was long and hungry, broken only when he moved to her jaw, next her neck, then the shockingly sweet spot between neck and shoulder.

Beatrix dropped her head back. She did not fully understand what was happening between them, but she wanted more. Whatever more was.

It was the bed's familiar creak and groan that stepped into her consciousness—and her conscience. Looking down, she saw he had eased her to sitting on the edge of the mattress.

"Yield to me, Beatrix." He reached for the hem of her skirts.

Caught between the desire to give him what he wanted and the certainty that it was wrong, she could not move. But then Simon D'Arci slipped in to remind her of the last time she had been so near a man, the memory rousing a fear so deep she nearly choked. But when she blinked, it was Michael before her. A man not his brother. Still, it was wrong.

Michael ground his teeth to keep from moving too quickly with Beatrix. Excepting a moment when she had stiffened, she had shown no fear of intimacy as he had thought she might with her talk of ravishment. Still, he did not want to embrace her as one might a harlot. She was not that. Nor was she a murderer, he acquiesced. Whatever the explanation for Simon's death—and he would have it from her later—she could not have murdered.

He glided a hand up her hosed calves, making her gasp, but when he touched her thigh, she twisted away.

"Nay!" She lunged to standing and hastened to the foot of the bed. "We should not."

He turned to her. "Why?"

"It is wrong. 'Tis fornication. A woman should come to her husband chaste—a virgin."

Michael stepped toward her. "But that you no longer are."

"I am! I have...lain with no man."

He halted. She claimed to be untouched—undefiled. Meaning it was not defense against ravishment by which Simon now lay dead and buried. For something else this woman had given his brother the dagger. She was no different from Edithe.

"God's eyes!" he growled. "Lies!"

Her eyes widened. "Michael?"

"Aye, Michael D'Arci, *brother* to Simon D'Arci." He halted over her. "You remember him, do you not? The same who *ravished* you and, for it, was put through with a Wulfrith dagger?"

Color receding, she shook her head.

"Tell me, Lady Beatrix, how it is a ravished woman remains a virgin?"

"Pray—"

"That you ought to do. 'Tis your only hope, though not much of one."

"I beseech you, allow me to explain what happened. I...remember now."

"Of course you do." He looked to the door he had left agape and was grateful none had come through it to witness his dishonor.

"The day we rode to...Soaring, and I fell from your destrier, I remembered the struggle on your brother's horse when he...touched me as he should not have. His horse reared—"

"Enough!" Michael gripped her shoulder. "You are the same as Edithe, and were you the sweetest honey, still I would spit you out."

Confusion stirred her gaze, but something else displaced it. Had he stabbed her as she had done Simon, the pain could not have shone brighter from her eyes. Tears pooled in their depths, making them sparkle like the brightest star in the darkest night.

"You know not how wrong you are," she choked.

As when he had drawn near her, the faint smell of smoke that clung to her teased his nostrils, somehow made sensual by the act he had nearly committed with her. Disgusted that twice in one life he should fall prey to a faithless woman, he released her, retrieved his staff, and swung away. Canute had been right. For all the older man's wisdom and loyalty, few were the words Michael had spoken to him these past weeks.

"What of my trial?" Beatrix called as he reached the door.

He swept his staff around. "Be assured, as soon as it can be arranged, you shall have it."

"This day you will send word of my...capture?"

He ought to smile, but his mouth was too stiff. "I shall not."

"But—"

"Word was sent a fortnight past."

She caught her breath. "I...did not think you would."

Hating that she had come to know him so well, grateful Canute knew her better, Michael said, "Do not think to know me, Lady Beatrix, for you never shall."

Though her eyes remained bright, anger stirred there. "Why would I wish to know a blackguard like you, Michael D'Arci? As you say that I am the same as this…Edithe, so you are the same as your brother."

He knew there was no reason to be offended, but her words raked him. Setting his staff to the landing, he stepped without.

All of her aching, from her eyes, to her wracked heart, to the soles of her feet, Beatrix stared at the door as it closed. In anticipation of what always followed, she lowered her lids.

Scrape. Click.

She told herself she was not hurt by Michael's revelation, but it was no use. Following their arrival at Castle Soaring, when she had begun to believe she need not fear him and worried she might not convince him to reveal her capture that she could go to trial, he had sent word. And now, this day, he had finally kissed her as if—

A sob escaped her, and she was thankful he was too far descended to hear. For nothing would she have him know the fullness of the pain he had inflicted. She lowered to her knees alongside the bed. Though she knew she was where she ought to be, she could summon no words to pour out her grief to the Lord. She was simply too angry.

Sitting back on her heels, she stared at her white knuckles and silently vowed she would allow no man so near her again.

"Nor shall I weep." Especially for Michael D'Arci who was unworthy of a single tear. Michael D'Arci who had sent word.

14

"MY LORD!"

Michael looked up as the man-at-arms negotiated the tables that were settled by those who partook of the nooning meal. "What tidings?" he asked.

The soldier halted before the dais. As those at the lower tables quieted to witness the news, he said, "Your lady mother is come, my lord."

Maude. Not his mother, though Simon's mother was as near a mother as Michael had. Now, without warning, she came to Soaring. He was not surprised. Despite her uncertain health and any other obstacle in her path, she always came and went at will. Nevertheless, Michael was piqued that she had ignored his urging to stay away from the trial. Though the date was not yet determined, a missive had been delivered to Soaring yesterday advising that the sheriff would come for Beatrix six days hence. It would pain Maude much to hear the lies Beatrix intended to speak of her beloved son.

Michael inclined his head. "Very good."

"She comes unto the donjon now, my lord."

Of course she would not wait so that he might properly greet her. Indeed, it was her voice that ascended the steps outside the great doors. If he did not lengthen his stride, she would be across the hall before he.

Michael gripped the staff and pushed upright. "Return to your meals," he ordered those who had paused over their trenchers.

He was halfway across the great room when Maude appeared. Her small stature making her seem almost a child, she paused inside the doorway and squinted at the occupants. Eyes slow to adjust to the relative dim, she called, "Michael!"

He received her into his arms. She had regained some of the weight lost to her recent illness, he noted as he returned her hug, and her arms about him were not those of one frail and infirm. Too, when she drew back and lifted her face, a sparkle was returned to eyes previously bereft of light. The news of Beatrix's capture had to have heartened her.

She frowned over him. "Pity you are not as pleased to see me as I am to see you."

Why deny it when she would know it for a lie? "Circumstances only, dear Maude." He shifted his weight to the staff. "I had hoped you would allow me to see to this matter for you."

Some of the light faded from her eyes, aging her more than the silver that claimed much of her blond hair. "You knew I would not."

As he released her, the elegant Lady Laura paused inside the great doors. Clothed in green that sparkled with the gold thread woven through it, sleeves lined with ermine, she looked as untouchable ever, even with the dark-haired little girl of three winters perched on her hip.

Unfortunate, Michael mused as he stared at the child whose smile always tugged at his heart. Though her mother had been destined to wed a baron, Lady Laura would likely pass the remainder of her days as a lady's companion. A tryst, while fostered with Maude, had produced the child and caused a scandal that saw the young woman disavowed by her family. Fortunately, Maude's kind heart and sense of responsibility prevailed. Not only had she given Lady Laura a permanent and esteemed place in her household, but she had made room for little Clarice. Lady Laura could not hope for better.

She started across the hall, and behind her came Sir Canute. Michael tensed, as he did each time he looked on the one who had betrayed him. Despite his belated gratitude for what his old friend had done, they rarely spoke.

He released Maude. "Join me at table."

A frown rumpled her brow again, and he followed her gaze to his splinted leg. "What is this?"

He had guessed that in her haste to greet him she had overlooked it. "A break. It heals well."

"It looks serious. Pray, when did it happen?"

Had she been delayed but a few days, she need never have known. Of course, the staff that he would require for a time beyond the splints would have revealed him. "Four weeks past."

Her lids narrowed, and he knew where her thoughts had landed. "Your missive told naught of it."

"Naught needed to be told." He turned. "Come, the viands grow cold."

Her hand fell to his arm. "What befell you?"

"It was only a fall, and one from which I shall fully recover."

"'Twas that woman?" Her gaze slid to his scarred brow that evidenced his first encounter with Beatrix. "The same who——"

"This is not the place to discuss it." Though he knew his words were sharp, all that had to do with Beatrix effected such a response.

"It was, wasn't it?"

"Later," Michael said, aware that though the castle folk pretended otherwise, they strained to piece together the conversation.

"Very well, but I shall know all." She started to precede him but halted and looked around. "Sir Piers! Come, come!"

Michael considered the knight who entered the great hall. Though he was of average stature, he exuded confidence punctuated by long, unbroken strides that Michael begrudged him.

"A knight errant," Maude murmured. "My carriage was lamed along the road this morn when he came upon us and gave aid."

Michael's mind worked the possibilities. Now that there was to be a trial, and the sheriff was set to collect Beatrix, her family would soon enough learn she lived—had they not already. Thus, was it only coincidence that this knight had happened upon Maude?

"He proved most useful in returning us to the road. For it, I extended your hospitality. I did not think you would mind."

He did mind, but the man would be watched.

Michael glanced to Canute and received a nod that assured him all would be provided for.

The knight errant presented a moment later. "My lord." His gaze momentarily swept Michael's staff. "I am Sir Piers Farrimond. Your mother has told that I might beg a night's lodging from you."

Michael knew to heed the unsettling at his center. Harmless though the knight might appear, and harmless though he might prove, only a fool would give him his back. "If that is what she has told, I shall allow it."

Without flicker or falter, the man said, "I thank you, my lord."

Shortly, all gained their seats, including Sir Canute who ever endeavored to secure a place beside Maude. And dear Maude, who pretended to not feel what Canute himself affected to not feel, sparkled again.

On the opposite side of Canute sat Lady Laura. Eyes downcast as she poked about her trencher, she did not see Clarice slip from her bench.

Momentarily forgetting Beatrix above, the suspect Sir Piers below, Michael nearly smiled at the crunch of rushes as the little girl traveled beneath the table. However, when she brushed against his uninjured leg and poked her head out from beneath the tablecloth, he gave in to the smile. "Mayhap you think my trencher holds better morsels than your mother's?"

"Clarice!" Lady Laura gasped.

Michael shook his head to assure her he did not mind her daughter's attentions. As always, the lady offered no further protest, though with less hesitation than usual. Relief lowering her shoulders, she returned to that place within that others could only ponder. What had happened to turn her yet more despondent?

As he had known a similar pain himself, he felt for one whose life was lost for a single indiscretion, but surely she ought to be fairly recovered after the passing of four years?

As you are from Edithe? Eight years, is it? Nine?

He beckoned to Clarice. "Come, little one."

A moment later, she was on his lap. As Michael stared at her dark head where she leaned forward to search out his trencher, he felt an unspeakable urge to father such a child. But his little girl's hair would not be so dark. Indeed, he imagined it spun of palest gold—

Nay, black like mine, he corrected himself. *Darker even.* Nevertheless, the first image persisted.

"I would see her," Maude repeated.

Michael rose over her seated figure. "Again, I say 'tis unwise. Leave it be and all shall come 'round."

She pushed out of her chair and strained her neck to peer up at him. "What is it you fear? For my health? That whatever she tells shall do me mortal harm?"

He slammed the staff's tip to the floor and turned in the chamber he'd had prepared for her. Fortunately, it was of fair size, its length allowing him to gain control of his impatience before he came back around.

Though less and less he depended on the staff, he gave it his weight and met Maude's determined gaze. He should have known she would not be content with his brief telling of what had happened between him and Beatrix at the abbey.

"I would not have you suffer the lady's lies," he said. "They will only pain you."

"There is not much that pains me any longer, Michael. And even should there be, I am not so frail I shall collapse upon hearing what the lady tells."

"I would spare you."

She crossed to him. "And I say I would not be spared. Deliver her to me."

"Very well, but you should be prepared."

"Prepare me, then."

There was no painless way to tell it. "At her trial, Lady Beatrix intends to defend her murder of Simon by charging him with ravishment."

Maude's gaze stuttered away. And when she swallowed, the sound was not without effort. "Ravishment." She reached out as if expecting a chair to come to hand.

Michael gripped her elbow and helped her into the chair in which she had sat throughout the telling of his capture of Beatrix.

"For this I would have spared you," Michael said.

"I had hoped 'twould be other than ravishment. For your sake, of course."

Maude was one of the few in whom he had confided about Edithe. She knew his pain and had shared it as a devoted mother would do.

"Of course, there can be no truth to it, can there?"

It baffled him that she should ask. "None."

"You are certain?"

There again, that unsettling sensation. Awkward though it was with his splinted leg, he lowered to his uninjured knee. "Why do you ask such of one you knew better than any other?"

She pulled a hand down her face. "He was long gone from me."

To her, a lifetime, though it was nothing compared to the loss felt by most noblewomen who relinquished their sons to fostering at the age of seven. Simon had been nearly sixteen. "What has that to do with this?"

"Much can change a man."

Disbelief rushed Michael's gut. "Of what do you speak, Maude?"

She shook her head. "Mayhap he—"

"Lady Beatrix speaks lies!" Were it not so absurd, Michael would think her capable of bewitching from afar—that she had cast a spell over poor Maude.

His stepmother shifted in her chair. "'Twould seem so."

And yet still she sounded uncertain. "Though she cries ravishment, Maude, the woman is untouched."

She blinked. "How do you know that?"

Michael nearly cursed himself.

"I see," his stepmother murmured. "And therein lies your own dilemma."

Michael stood. "No dilemma. Lady Beatrix murdered Simon and, for it, shall be punished. Now do you still wish to see her?"

"Aye. You will be present?"

And risk further bewitching? "I think not, but I shall send Sir Canute to stand at your side."

"Canute," she murmured, and he knew she worried over what the knight might think of the lies Beatrix would level at her son. "Nay, Lady Laura shall suffice."

"I insist, Maude. Beatrix Wulfrith is not to be underestimated."

She opened her mouth to protest but then sighed. "You are right."

Was he? Immediately, Michael thrust aside his pondering. "Too, Lady Laura seems not of a mood to attend you. Surely more ill has not befallen her?"

Yet another pall seemed to descend upon Maude. "It has. Ere we departed for Soaring, word was brought that the one she was to have wed before she was—before her unfortunate tryst—will soon take another to wife."

Only now? Four years after his rejection of Lady Laura? He must be nearly as bitter as Michael.

"'Tis a difficult time for Lady Laura, especially as she loved her betrothed."

"Loved him, yet cuckolded him," Michael said, unable to dampen his derision.

Maude's eyes widened. "Do not speak of that of which you know little!"

"I assure you, Maude, I know well the deception of women."

Regret swept the light from her eyes. "And more so now, hmm?"

He turned toward the door. "I shall have Lady Beatrix delivered to you an hour hence."

Silence followed him across the chamber, but as he pulled open the door, Maude called, "I am sorry, Michael."

No sorrier than he who had known to heed his head over his loins.

"You are to come with me, my lady."

Letting the strands from which she had tugged a half dozen snarls slip through her fingers, Beatrix turned from the window to the young man who had entered her prison. "Now?"

Squire Percival nodded.

"The baron has come?"

"Nay, my lady."

Then why was she summoned? Mayhap the blackguard was sending her to Broehne?

Though fear beckoned, she hardened her emotions. No matter the outcome, anything was better than the past ten days of visiting time and again the touch of a man she had thought she knew—a man she had feared could not be convinced to send word of her capture to Barone Lavonne but *had* sent word, proving she knew nothing of him.

She stepped from the window to which she had returned several times since Castle Soaring had lowered its drawbridge to visitors hours past. Whoever had come, it was likely for them she was summoned.

"Shall I be returning?"

"I was not told, my lady, but I expect so."

Did he speak true? Of course, what did it matter? She had come with nothing and would leave with nothing, whether it was this day or a dozen more. "I am ready."

The squire pushed the door wider and stepped aside.

As Beatrix approached it, she shuddered. As much as she hated her prison, she hated more what lay beyond. Determinedly, she drew herself taller and stepped onto the torch-lit landing.

Strange, she mused, but the air was somehow different here. Only her imagination? Or the smoke of torches? Though it was yet hours before darkness descended, it would be as night upon the windowless stairs ahead if not for the torches lighting the passage.

"I shall follow," Squire Percival said as he closed the door.

He would not give her his back, for it would portend ill for him if he fell victim to a head injury or broken leg the same as his lord.

Beatrix began her descent, silently bemoaning the many chances she had been given that would have assured she never came near Soaring. Unfortunately, each time her God-bent heart had guided her elsewhere.

Halfway down the stairs, she trod on the hem of her gown. If not that she slapped a hand to the wall and Squire Percival's fingers turned around her upper arm, she would have tumbled down the stone steps.

She looked over her shoulder. "Unhand me," she said, surprised by the chill in her voice.

The squire released her. "I but wished to steady you, my lady," he hastened as if for fear she might cry ravishment.

She nearly smiled. "Surely your...lord warned you of me?"

He blushed. "He did, but 'twould be remiss if I did not offer aid."

"Methinks your lord would see it different." She turned forward again. As she continued her descent, she marveled at the words that had passed unfettered from her lips. But then, they were born of anger, her truest ally. For a moment, she was gripped with sorrow that her heart should be so hardened, but it was the only way she might survive.

She stepped to the landing and would have continued down the next turn of the stairs to the hall if not that Squire Percival said, "The second door, my lady."

Was it the lord's solar to which he directed her? Surely Michael would not summon her there—unless he had been laid abed. To counter the concern that rose within her, she reminded herself of what he had done to her and crossed the corridor to the chamber.

Squire Percival stepped alongside. Following what seemed a struggle, he said, "'Tis Lady Maude who summons you, my lady. Our lord's stepmother."

Then it was Sir Simon's mother who had arrived in the carriage, doubtless to confront her son's murderer.

Beatrix nearly allowed herself to be touched by the small kindness the squire did in preparing her for the meeting, but said, instead, "Let us not keep the lady waiting."

He pushed the door inward and stepped back.

Two figures stood before the hearth, neither of whom was Michael. Tension easing, Beatrix looked first to the slight woman who occupied one of two chairs. Still lovely in spite of advancing age, she regarded Beatrix with hard, assessing eyes.

Simon's mother, though her only resemblance to him was blond hair amongst the silver. Behind her stood Sir Canute, his countenance no more welcoming than the woman's, and to the right, alongside the bed, was a young woman whose finery told she was also a lady.

Beatrix looked back at Simon's mother. It was time she knew the truth about her son—providing she would listen to the story Beatrix had rehearsed without benefit of writing. Telling herself she did not care what pain she wrought, she raised her chin.

He knew he should stay away, but Maude's reaction bothered him. She had been too willing to consider her son capable of that which Beatrix accused him.

Michael ascended the last step to the landing and halted at the sight of Beatrix on the threshold of Maude's chamber. Despite her expression-less profile, she looked healthy—even more of an angel with her pale hair loose about her shoulders.

He watched her step inside, then considered Percival who stared after her with rumpled brow. Was he also bewitched?

Michael stepped forward, causing the squire's head to come around and a flush to run up his face. Aye, bewitched, meaning he would likely have to be relieved of his charge.

The ascent having strained Michael's injury, he leaned into the staff as he neared Maude's chamber.

Squire Percival stepped aside.

As Michael entered, he was pleased to see Beatrix's back was turned to him. But she surely knew he had come, her shoulders tense and hands at her sides gripping the material of her gown such that her skirts were hitched, allowing a glimpse of ankles. Doubtless, his staff had alerted her to his arrival.

Past Beatrix, he met Canute's gaze, next Maude's. Ignoring the gratitude that shone from the latter's, he glanced at Lady Laura. Though she could not have missed his entrance, she stared at oft-nibbled nails that contrasted sharply with the splendid gowns in which his stepmother clothed her.

It seemed Maude was determined to have her present though Michael had sent Sir Canute to her. True, Lady Laura was her companion, but a confidant in matters such as this?

Though tempted to dismiss her, Michael knew it was not his place. He closed the door and stepped alongside it.

Maude stared at Beatrix. "So, the woman I see before me is that who murdered my son."

It was some moments before Beatrix spoke, but when she did, there was an edge to her voice as of one forsaken by innocence. "Your son was not murdered, my lady."

"He yet lives?" Maude's sarcasm was pained.

Beatrix splayed her hands amid the folds of her skirts.

"Tell, Lady Beatrix," Maude continued, "why did you drive a dagger through my son?"

"You are certain you wish to know what happened between us?" Beatrix's head listed right. "I ask because that which you would have me tell, a mother would not wish to hear of her child."

Though she spoke without the falter to which Michael had become accustomed, she did so stiffly as if she read the words. As she had been denied writing instruments, he guessed she had rehearsed the tale over and again. It made her sound insincere and would surely go against her at trial. Telling himself he was pleased, he glanced at Maude.

"I knew my son well, Lady Beatrix. 'Tis I who shall judge whether you speak true or false."

"Then I shall tell all as I have not yet been allowed to do."

Lies that Michael did not want to hear. Putting a shoulder to the wall, he gripped the staff harder.

Beatrix returned to that day at the ravine and felt a chill sweep her. She saw again Sir Simon's face, heard his taunting, felt his touch.

Dragging herself back to the present, she hoped Lady Maude had known her son better than Michael had known him for a brother— Michael who was at her back and who had proven how little *she* knew of him when he sent word of her capture.

"Do you or do you not intend to tell all, Lady Beatrix?" Lady Maude prompted.

"Pardon, my lady, I…at times, words elude me."

Lady Maude's lids narrowed.

"As you surely know, I accompanied my sister when she fled marriage to Baron Lavonne. The following day, the king and the baron's men overtook us. Sir Ewen…"

Remembering the knight's sightless eyes, she gave a small shake of her head. "Though Sir Ewen and I attempted to lead our pursuers away from my sister, your son and another knight followed us. Sir Simon pulled me from my horse and as…Sir Ewen fought the second knight, your son…"

You know the tale, Beatrix. Tell it!

"Your son touched me as a man should not touch a lady."

Hearing Michael shift his weight, Beatrix mused at the irony that, after all the time they had spent together, this was how he should learn the truth. Not that he would believe any of it.

"Touched you, Lady Beatrix?"

"Aye. My…" Unable to summon the word, though not because it was unavailable, she laid a hand to her chest. He touched me here and…"

She had not realized how uncomfortable it would be to speak of it. Though this past week she had rehearsed aloud her defense, it was tenfold more difficult spoken in front of others.

Lord, if I cannot do it before these few, how am I to do it at trial?

She replenished her breath. "Your son touched me as if I were a harlot."

Lady Maude's hands on the chair arms whitened. Before Beatrix could ponder her reaction, a movement at the bed drew her gaze. The lady there had stepped back to stand alongside the far bedpost with her head lowered.

Who was she? And why was she here? When Beatrix looked forward again, she saw Sir Canute had laid a hand to Lady Maude's shoulder as if to reassure her.

Beatrix swallowed. Where had she left off with the telling?

"You say Sir Simon touched you in the presence of the other knight?" It was Sir Canute who asked. "Naught was told of that."

Beatrix met his cool gaze. "As the other knight was engaged at swords, he did not see."

"Convenient."

Though anger bade Beatrix to argue, she knew she must stay the course if she was to tell all. "After the other knight put his blade through Sir Ewen, he ordered Sir Simon to release me that I might go to my brother's man. It was from Sir Ewen I gained the Wulfrith dagger. Ere he died, he...bade me to use it if needed."

"And so you did," Lady Maude returned to the conversation.

"Not with intent. When the knight who killed Sir Ewen left me alone with your son that he might rejoin the effort to capture my sister, 'tis true I...threatened Sir Simon with the dagger. I fled, but he caught me at the ravine and again dragged me onto his horse—again sought to v-violate me."

"Astride a horse?" Lady Maude scoffed.

"'Twas only the...beginning. Certes, he intended more."

"So you say."

"'Tis true." Vaguely aware that she was losing the thread of her thoughts, Beatrix stepped forward. "Do not think me so fool and innocent that I do not know what a man wants when he touches a woman so—what he intends when he does it against her will."

"Thus, for having touched you, you killed my son."

"Nay! When he tried to take the dagger from me, our...struggle caused his mount to rear and..."

Beatrix grasped at anger in an attempt to make sense of her tongue, but memories of that day held it out of reach. Hearing her breath, she tried to slow it, but the images were too vivid and she looked down. If only she could speak as she had rehearsed. If only Michael D'Arci had not come within.

"And what, Lady Beatrix?" Lady Maude snapped.

A sliver of anger returned to Beatrix, but it was not enough to lay a straight path for her words to travel. "We fell. When I regained consciousness in the...ravine, Sir Simon was atop me. I pushed him off, and 'twas then I saw the..."

"Dagger?" Michael growled.

She startled and hated herself for it. Though she longed to loose anger on him for feeding her a word she could well enough feed herself, she kept her back to him.

"I saw the blade," she purposely renamed it. "It had found his..."

"Heart?" Michael thrust again.

Cool air up Beatrix's skirts alerting her to the hitch of her gown, she lowered her gaze and saw she gripped handfuls of the material. Continuing to face forward, though she ached to confront the man at her back, she loosened her hold. "It struck center of him. I vow his death was not in-intentional. Though I sought to defend my person, I did not willingly wound him. 'Twas hap—"

"Happenstance?"

She swung around to face the blackguard where he leaned a shoulder to the wall. "Do not speak for me, Sir!"

He raised an eyebrow. Surprisingly, the silent taunt turned his bearded face handsome and momentarily transported her to the day she had nearly allowed him to make love to her. Wishing it did not hurt to feel so much for a man who felt so little for her, Beatrix turned back to his stepmother. "It was happenstance, my lady."

This time it was Lady Maude who looked away, and her next words were long in coming. "My son is dead." A minute passed, then another before she returned her gaze to Beatrix. "You say you have not been allowed to tell your tale before?"

"I tried, but…" Beatrix touched the side of her head. "When I fell into the ravine, I struck my head and could not…remember all that had happened."

"But now, with your trial approaching, you suddenly remember?"

Beatrix took another step toward her. "I have remembered for some weeks now. Unfortunately, there has been no one w-willing to listen."

Lady Maude put her head to the side. "Do you make much of this head injury that you might escape punishment for your crime?"

Though the accusation sounded flat, as if the lady did not believe it, Beatrix's ally in anger returned. "I do not. As for the crime of which you speak, 'tis not my crime but your son's. I know it must make you ache to hear the truth, but all I am guilty of is defending myself against ravishment by a dishonorable man no mother ought to be proud of."

Anger pulsed around the room, manifesting itself in the teeth Sir Canute bared and the growl at her back. But before either man could further express their outrage, Lady Maude stayed them with a raised hand. "How do you intend to prove your innocence when there are none to speak in your defense?"

"By speaking the truth myself. By telling what happened that day as I have told you."

"And you think you will be believed?"

"If God wills it. Though I would have you believe me, all that…matters is that my Father in Heaven knows the truth."

"I see." Lady Maude glanced at the lady alongside the bed. Then, as if suddenly weary, her shoulders slumped. "If what you speak is true, I can but wish you Godspeed at trial."

Beatrix caught her breath, and there was no mistaking Sir Canute and Michael were equally surprised by the concession, slight though it was. Though the former's reaction was seen in eyes stretched wide, the latter's was felt on the air as if shouted.

Lady Maude studied her clenched hands. "I have heard all I wish to hear, Lady Beatrix. You may leave."

Her pained voice shook Beatrix, for it was as if she *did* believe what was told of her son. And suffered for it.

Refusing the apology she longed to speak, Beatrix turned. As she started across the solar, she avoided Michael's gaze. Though the tale was finally told, she knew there was no possibility he would believe her.

I do not care. I am done with him, done with feeling anything for anyone who feels nothing for me—including a mother whose son is dead. No sympathy, no empathy, nothing at all.

Still, the words pried at her as she neared Michael. Hating her weakness, she looked over her shoulder. "I am sorry, my lady."

The woman did not look up, but Sir Canute accommodated. His eyes were hard, though as if only because he set his mind to it.

Ignoring Michael, Beatrix opened the door and stepped into the corridor where Squire Percival waited. "I am to be returned to my prison."

As she stepped past him, she wondered how Lady Maude and Michael could not have known what kind of man one's son and the other's brother had been. Or perhaps they had known.

The one who had taken the name of Sir Piers, knight errant, looked up the donjon and considered the hind tower. Was she there? Something told him she was, though nothing had been spoken of her by those he listened in upon. It was as if she was not here, but word from Broehne and her impending trial told otherwise.

The knight grimaced. The task for which he had volunteered was not an easy one. Fortunately, luck had delivered D'Arci's stepmother to him. When she and her entourage paused at the inn at which he had passed the night and he had overheard that she was bound for Soaring, he had arranged for the laming of her carriage. Two leagues from the inn, her wheel had let go as planned. And now he was within D'Arci's walls.

Aware he had been followed to the stables, he flicked his gaze around the garrisoned walls where men-at-arms stood alert at their posts. Castle Soaring might not present as it had surely done in years past, but the soundness of its defenses were without question. Unfortunately, its lord was no fool. But still D'Arci would give up Lady Beatrix.

The knight scooped up another handful of oats. The great animal huffed and sank its muzzle into its master's hand.

"Soon we shall leave." The knight patted the destrier's jaw. "Soon Lady Beatrix will be where she belongs."

15

HE WEARIED OF waiting. Though he had wanted to speak to Maude following Beatrix's departure, his stepmother had asked him and Canute to leave. Surely an hour was time enough for her to recover from the lies told.

Michael rapped on the door. When it opened, it was Maude's face that filled the crack rather than Lady Laura's. Was she not within?

It was on his tongue to ask Maude why she had unsettled herself rather than call for him to enter when she put a finger to her lips, opened the door wider, and stepped aside.

Curled in the middle of the bed, fist to her mouth and lashes to her cheeks, was Clarice.

"'Twould be best if we spoke later," Maude whispered and started to ease the door closed.

Were he patient, later would suffice, but he was not. He put the staff forward. "Where is the child's mother?"

Maude looked down. "As Lady Laura is not feeling well, I bid her to take fresh air in the garden."

It was not unusual. Though the lady was said to serve as Maude's companion, it was not a role she fit. Indeed, if one served the other, it would be Maude. Often she sat with Clarice while Lady Laura took her misery out of doors. But it seemed a task Maude did not mind, especially since Simon's death.

Michael stepped forward.

"Michael, the child—"

"Will not be disturbed."

"But—"

"My word, Maude, I shall not raise my voice sufficient to awaken her."

Her gaze flickered, and he saw the sorrow pooled in her eyes. A deeper sorrow than that which she had brought with her to Soaring— nearly as deep as when she had learned of Simon's death.

Michael laid a hand on her narrow shoulder. "I am sorry for the lies you were made to suffer. I would have had you spared."

She turned from beneath his hand and crossed to the chair she had occupied during her audience with Lady Beatrix.

Michael closed the door and gained the chair opposite her, but before he could ask about her softening toward Beatrix, she said, "What if they are not lies?"

Then it went deeper than a softening. "What do you mean, Maude?"

"Simon was ever in trouble—you know that—but I did not think it dire. He was, after all, a boy." She drew a deep breath. "Then he was sent to the barony of Moreland."

Which had pained her deeply. Michael's older brother, upon gaining the barony following their father's death, had been unaffected by Maude's pleas that had moved her husband to allow what he should not have.

Maude's eyes teared. "He was abused, Michael, abused for being so old to have had no training toward knighthood other than that which you afforded him."

Michael had known the training would be strenuous for Simon, but abusive? Surely Maude exaggerated with that tender heart of hers that could abide little discipline done her son. True, it was common for knights in training to push one another, sometimes cruelly, as they vied to prove themselves more worthy than the others, but it was that which made them men.

"'Tis so." A tear rolled down Maude's cheek. "Though Simon would not tell all of it, things were done to him that—" Her voice broke. "Things were done that roused in him a terrible anger, a need to strike before struck, to hurt as he was hurt." She shook her head. "'Twas my fault. I should have let him go sooner."

Aye, and Simon had wanted to go, but Michael's father had not been able to deny Maude anything. One of the many dangers of love.

"The son who returned to me a knight was not the same who left."

Struggling to control impatience that tempted him to thump his fingers on the chair arm, Michael said, "Of course not. When he left you, 'twas as a boy. When he returned, 'twas as a man. As you surely witnessed with those fostered at our home, it is no easy task to become a knight. Were it, few would leave the battlefield with heads upon their shoulders."

Moving as he had not seen her move in a long time, Maude thrust out of the chair. "This I know!"

A sound from the bed reminding her of Clarice's presence, she looked to the little girl who had rolled onto her back but still slept.

Maude came to stand before Michael. "I understand a knight's training, but what your brother endured, no boy should be made to endure. No man."

As he stared into eyes that spoke what her lips would not, he grew chilled. Surely *that* had not been done to Simon. "Tell, Maude."

She pivoted toward the hearth, but when she turned back, still no words fell from her lips.

"Maude!"

"As I said, Simon would not tell all, but...'twas not natural what was done to him."

Michael lowered his head into his hands and jammed his fingers through his hair. In that moment, he could have murdered—not merely kill as he had done as a soldier, but take another's life ruthlessly...brutally...send his prey to hell. "I never knew," he rasped. "No evidence did I see."

Maude touched his shoulder. "He hid it well. After all, by the time you returned from King Henry's battles, 'twas done. Too, he was with you but a fortnight ere he was called into Baron Lavonne's service."

And Christian's father had held Simon near to Broehne. No more than thrice had Simon accompanied the baron to Soaring, and those times when Michael was called to tend Aldous had been too brief.

Michael leaned back and met Maude's moist gaze. His conviction wavered and mocked him for that which he had been so certain when she first arrived. "For this you believe Simon capable of what Lady Beatrix accuses." Though his past, cursed by the illusive Edithe, denied it, his present recoiled from the implications. If Simon had done what Beatrix accused...

"For this," Maude confirmed.

Michael frowned. "When first Lady Beatrix stood before you, you seemed nearly as certain of her guilt as I, and yet all this you knew of Simon."

Maude's cheeks flushed. "As she told, there are things a mother does not wish to hear of her child."

"Though I agree that what was done to him might cause a man to do unthinkable things, if it was so, surely there would be others who suffered as much by his hand."

Maude looked away. "One would think so."

"Then you know of none——"

Clarice rolled onto her side again, drew her knees to her chest, and tucked her chin.

"The fire wanes," Maude said and crossed to the bed where she lifted the coverlet and pulled it over the girl.

"You know of none?" Michael pressed.

As she tucked the coverlet around Clarice, she shook her head.

Did she hide something?

Though there was no doubt she was reluctant to return to their conversation, finally she dropped into the chair opposite. "The day was long and I would rest."

As much as he yearned to question her further, she looked nearly ill.

He pushed out of the chair and, giving minimal weight to the staff, crossed to Maude. "Rest well. We shall talk again later."

She inclined her head, then settled it back against the chair. However, when Michael reached the door, she called to him.

He looked around. She seemed so small in the chair. So frail.

"Methinks Lady Beatrix does not belong in the tower, Michael."

The concession surprised him and yet did not. "Still 'tis possible Simon did not do what she tells."

She sighed. "You know the lady far better than I."

Her words were meant to stick, and they did.

"Likely better than ever you knew Simon," she stuck more to him.

"And near as well as I knew Edithe," he reminded her.

"Always it comes 'round to that woman."

"One is enough," Michael growled and stepped into the corridor. Nearly forgetting the splint, he crossed to his chamber and slammed the door closed behind him. He stood there several minutes, denying Maude and all she had told. In the end, he doubted as she had intended he should.

Was he wrong about Beatrix? Had the abuses Simon endured changed him so much? He had been a restless and impetuous youth, but could he become heartless—one who would lust upon a helpless woman? Men *did* change, violently sometimes, as evidenced by many of those who returned from prolonged battle.

Michael rubbed his temples. Had Simon become so foul? He feared so, though not only because of what had caused his brother to be so fouled. He feared because it meant he had made an unpardonable mistake that would turn deadly if Beatrix went to trial. Regardless of whether or not she convinced Maude of her innocence and Maude spoke for her at trial, it would not likely be enough.

Dragging his hand down his face, he once more posed the question that threatened to draw and quarter him: Had Beatrix murdered? Though he was not yet ready to concede otherwise, there was one thing he would do. He would allow her the reach of the donjon providing she was accompanied by Squire Percival.

Michael looked to his splinted leg. Four weeks had passed since his fall at the abbey. And six days from now, the sheriff came for Beatrix. He raised the leg, turned it side to side, and extended his foot. Still there was discomfort, but it was time enough. He began removing the splints.

She was cold. Worse, her knees ached. Tempted though she was to add coals to the brazier and ease her weight from the latter, she prayed harder. Considering Michael had been at her back, she believed she had done well in defending herself. However, she would have to do better at trial.

"Unbind my tongue, Lord. Stand me as a rock before Baron Lavonne. And Michael. Deliver me."

"You think He hears your prayers?"

She gasped. She had been too near the Lord to catch the sound of the intruder's ascent of the stairs or the creak of the door.

Opening her eyes on her steepled hands, she hearkened back to the abbey when Michael had stolen upon her there. Much the same he had asked, though then he had named her a murderess.

She rose from her knees and turned to where he stood on the threshold. Though his staff was to hand, the splints were gone.

The sight of him standing firm momentarily wafted relief through her. True, he gave his uninjured leg more weight, but the unsplinted leg bore a good share. And she was a fool for noticing it, for caring for one who had no care for her. The same who had sent word to Baron Lavonne and thereafter come to lie with her.

As she had answered him at the abbey, she said, "God hears the prayers of all, even those undeserving of His g-grace."

"Then also my brother?" he asked, though this time the question was absent derision.

What did he want? "To be heard, one must first pray, Lord D'Arci."

Brow furrowing, he stepped forward. Though he continued to favor his hale leg, his stride was surprisingly smooth, and only a deeper furrowing of the brow attested to any discomfort.

"Why are you here?"

He halted before her. "Six days hence, the sheriff arrives to return you to Broehne Castle where you will stand trial."

Though fear sought to sink its teeth into her, she stood against it. She had known the day would come—longed for it that, regardless of the outcome, there would be an end to her persecution. Now that the day was set, she would not shrink from it. "I shall be ready."

"Will you?" He took another step toward her.

She lowered her gaze, stumbled around her mind, and found her place. However, when she looked up, the answer would not come off her tongue. Michael was too near. It made her ache, especially the masculine scent of him. It was not offensive. Merely, it reminded her of when he had last come to her.

She looked away. She did not care for Michael D'Arci, she told herself as she had done every day since he was last here. Indeed, if not that it would displease God, she would truly hate him. She lifted her chin. "I would be ready if today was the day."

Something flickered in his eyes. "You would need to be."

And the truth was that she might never be ready though over and again she recounted that day at the ravine. "That is all you came to tell?"

"Also that you will no longer be confined."

Her pretense of indifference nearly puddled out from under her. "What do you mean?"

"Until you depart Soaring, you shall be allowed the reach of the donjon."

Hope fluttered through her. Was it because of her audience with Lady Maude? Had she caused the woman to doubt her son's innocence? Michael to doubt it as well?

Lord, to stretch her legs beyond ten paces! To see and smell and hear and touch things beyond these walls! "Why?"

"Squire Percival shall, of course, attend you at all times when you leave this room," Michael disregarded her question.

Then he thought she might try to escape though she had told him she wished a trial—likely believed she had lied. Assuring herself she did not care what he believed of her, she wondered again why he would allow her to leave her prison.

"Anything else?" she asked.

He seemed to hesitate as if there was something, but turned away.

Beatrix crossed to the window and looked out across the castle walls. She waited, but no creak sounded, nor scrape or click. When she looked around, Michael was on the landing.

"I shall send Squire Percival with garments better fit for a lady," he said.

She swept her gaze over the homespun gown that no longer bothered as it had done those first days. Still, it would be nice to once more wear the finery of a lady. "I thank you."

He opened his hand and considered the key that had let him in. "If you will agree to remain in the tower until Squire Percival comes for you, I shall not lock the door."

"I agree."

He curled his fingers around the key and, leaving the door wide, turned his staff toward the stairs.

Beatrix stared at the empty landing as she listened to the sound of his descent. Telling herself it was not regret she felt when all that was left of him was silence, she turned back to the window. This eve she would not be alone. She would sit among the castle folk, share a trencher—

She was not going amongst people who would welcome her. Rather, she would be surrounded by those who believed ill of her. They would stare, whisper, perhaps speak their disdain aloud.

She momentarily considered remaining in her chamber but refused to be so fearful, especially as the freedom granted her meant she might seek out and avail herself of the chapel.

She set her jaw. Aye, this eve she would go belowstairs.

Blood fluttering through her veins, Beatrix descended the lowermost stairs, all the while telling herself she was prepared. It was not entirely true. Had Squire Percival delivered the lady's gown as Michael had said he would, she could more easily endure what lay ahead, but he had not come.

Fearing Michael had changed his mind about allowing her among the castle folk, she had decided to bring her homespun belowstairs. He would not like it, but she had waited long enough.

From her window she had watched the men-at-arms answer the call to meal and pass their posts to others as twilight shuttered the land. Giving them enough time to reach the hall that she might join them as they entered and draw less attention to herself, she had left her prison for the second time in nearly a month.

With the din of the gathering of Soaring's men ascending the stairs on brazen feet, Beatrix counted her footfalls to the bottom and paused to sweep her gaze around the hall. Unfortunately, more were seated than were not. Fortunately, their heads were turned and bent to conversation. As for the high table, its lord was not present.

Refusing to ponder Michael's absence, Beatrix slid her gaze left and right of the lord's chair. Nor was Lady Maude present, but there was Sir Canute. He did not yet see her, but he would. And when he did?

Hoping he would not call attention to her, she searched the lower tables for a place to take her meal. Though it would be proper for her to sit at the high table, and there was enough bench to do so, she was still a prisoner. Too, the homespun gown fit better with those who sat farthest from the dais.

Deciding on the lowermost table that was occupied by four men, she started forward. Thankfully, few paid her heed, and the reason for it became apparent as she made to step past a table and a thick hand turned around her upper arm.

"Where is your pitcher, wench?" a man-at-arms demanded, three layers of chin quivering beneath dry, fleshy lips.

"I…" She gasped. Of course the abrasive gown made her appear to be a serving woman.

The man pushed her back, releasing his hold on her. "Be about it now!"

She glanced over her shoulder. Pitchers were perched alongside platters of viands on the trestle table against the wall, while coming and going were the servants, pages, and squires who served at table.

"Now!" the thirsty man barked.

Beatrix took a step toward him. "Pardon, but I—"

He thrust up from his bench. "I shall not tell you again, wench!" The last of his words spilled into a hall turned suddenly silent.

Beatrix was surprised that his churlish display had tamed the tumult. As she fell to the regard of all, she raised her chin. But before she could form words to defend herself, another hand turned around her arm. It was a touch she knew even before she looked into pale eyes brimming with displeasure.

Michael shifted his gaze to the heavy man. "Seat yourself!"

"But, my lord, the wench—"

"Is not a wench!"

The man's face pillowing with confusion, he quickly lowered himself.

Michael looked around the hall. Almost instantly, the din resumed, though with less fervor than before. Doubtless, he was more responsible for the earlier settling of the hall than the odious man-at-arms.

Michael led her past the table. "You agreed to remain in the tower until Squire Percival came for you."

Wishing she did not so profoundly feel his hand upon her, she said, "I lied—not unlike Edithe, I am sure." Though she intentionally etched the words in derision, she cringed inwardly. She did not like who she was becoming.

Michael's brow lowered further, but before he could form caustic words, she amended, "I did wait, but the garments were not delivered as you said they would be."

"Had you waited a while longer, you would have had the gown. Even now Squire Percival likely delivers it to your chamber."

She looked down her coarse skirts. "I thought mayhap you...decided against allowing me to leave the tower."

"I should have." He guided her around a table. "You cause too much trouble."

A spark leapt through her, and she halted. If he wished to proceed, he would have to drag her before all who affected to not watch them. "Not as much trouble as I *can* cause, as well you know."

Michael turned to her. "You seek to defy me?"

"There is no seeking about it."

Were anger a thing to be held, she could not have better felt the weight of his. However, before he could unfurl wrathful words, she said in a rush, "Now, Lord D'Arci, as I am quite pained with..."

"Hunger?"

Such impatience! Another moment and she would have had the word. "Aye."

Michael released her and swept a hand toward the high table. "Join me."

He meant for her to sit at the lord's table?

All around, feigned conversations were momentarily suspended over their lord's invitation to a woman clothed as a serving wench.

As if unaware of the attention given them—or was it that he did not care?—he urged her forward and followed her onto the dais.

Jaw clenched, Michael looked to Canute who watched. Though Michael had sensed a lessening of the knight's certainty over Beatrix's guilt when she had told her tale to Maude, the older man continued to embrace the belief that Beatrix was no different from Edithe. And Michael could not fault him.

As Beatrix lowered to a bench three removed from the lord's chair, Michael continued past her. Though he had intended for her to sit at his side, he told himself he was grateful she did not, especially as Sir Robert and the others whom Aldous Lavonne had set at Soaring were intent on them.

He took his seat beside Canute.

"Lady Maude is well?" his friend asked as if what had just transpired in the hall was of no consequence.

"She is but tired." For Maude, Michael had earlier left his place at table to ascertain the nature of her absence. Rest was all she needed, she had said, having sent for viands to share with Lady Laura and Clarice in her chamber. Thus, Michael had left them to their meal and returned to find Beatrix mistaken for a servant.

He knew he should not have gone to her defense, should not have corrected the man-at-arms for thinking her a wench. But when he had seen the knave's gluttonous hand on her, he had forgotten all. Regardless, Beatrix's ill-timed appearance in the hall was his fault. He ought to have kept her locked up.

He lifted his goblet and looked over it to the knight who had first sent word of Beatrix's arrival to Lavonne. Aldous's illegitimate son, Sir Robert, continued to watch her. Doubtless, he pondered the meaning of her presence, and whatever his conclusion, this night his squire would ride to Broehne. And what would Aldous and Christian Lavonne think when they learned Beatrix had been allowed the reach of the donjon?

Michael almost snorted. What did he care? He drank down his drink, set his vessel forward to be refilled, and looked to Beatrix.

Her gaze was on her own goblet, but as she tipped it to her lips, she looked at him over the rim only to slide her gaze opposite. Whatever next fell to her regard caused her eyes to widen and the goblet to lower.

Michael followed her gaze to an upper table where his knights sat. But the one she stared upon was not of his household. It was the knight who had been granted lodging for having aided Maude on the road to

Soaring. Sir Piers, if that was his name, returned Beatrix's regard. With a barely perceptible shake of his head, he looked away.

She knew him?

Michael returned to her, but her head was lowered as if she sought to control the breath moving her shoulders.

Fighting the impulse to challenge Sir Piers, Michael considered the trencher that a serving woman placed before him. Better to wait and watch. Better the enemy he knew.

Beatrix stared at her hands in her lap and prayed no others would see their trembling. He had come. And she knew for what. Such a shock it had been to see him, and equally disconcerting to know there was no way to dissuade him from trying to steal her away. He was under orders and would do all that was required of him to ensure he did not fail his lord.

She turned her hands into fists. Never had she felt so mired. Regardless of where she turned, she would be given no aid. All worked against her.

She raised her gaze and focused on her trencher that wafted the heat of a promising meal. Though it no longer moved her, she reached for her spoon and scooped up a chunk of fatty meat for the benefit of Michael whose gaze she once more felt. Praying she had not allowed him a glimpse of her inner writhing, she passed the spoonful into her mouth.

I shall have my trial.

The knight who had somehow stolen into Soaring would have to disappoint his lord, for none would deny her what she needed. Of course, it was easier thought than accomplished.

As she once more reached to the trencher, a movement across the hall made her pause, and she looked up to see Squire Percival step off the stairs. From his florid cast and purposeful stride, he had come from her empty chamber. Did he think she had escaped? Fear Michael's wrath?

Midway between the upper and lower tables, the young man's gaze found her. He halted, but though his lips parted as if to gape, he quickly drew them taut.

Regretting the distress she had caused him, Beatrix lifted the corners of her mouth and shrugged a shoulder. He blinked, glanced once more at Michael, and withdrew.

It was so lovely, it nearly took her breath. She reached to the gown that had been carelessly tossed onto the bed—no doubt when the squire had discovered her missing—and smoothed a hand over the skirt. What was the name of the rich blue cloth upon which torchlight skipped? She knew it, her mother having possessed a bliaut fashioned of the same, but search though she did, she could not remember what it was called.

She fingered one of a multitude of silver leaves embroidered among the folds. She had rarely given much thought to her attire, especially as she was destined for a nun's habit, but suddenly she longed to fit the gown to her. However, so fine a garment surely did not belong on a prisoner.

She met Squire Percival's rigid gaze where he stood in the doorway. "I do not understand."

"As Lord D'Arci told, you are to dress as is befitting a lady."

"But so fine a gown?"

The displeasure he had carried like a shield since escorting her abovestairs following the meal, wavered. "As there is no lady of Soaring, the gown had to be got from Lady Laura, Lady Maude's companion."

The woman who had been present during Beatrix's audience with Michael's stepmother, then.

"She allowed Lord D'Arci to choose it himself."

Michael had chosen it? Of course, it would not have been fitting for his squire to make such a request of the lady. Did Lady Laura resent relinquishing such a fine gown to a woman believed to have murdered her lady's son?

"As you are not as tall as Lady Laura," Squire Percival continued, "the gown had to be hemmed. For this, I was delayed in delivering it to you."

Michael had said nothing of it. "I pray you will forgive me for not awaiting your…attendance," Beatrix offered. "Lest Lord D'Arci decide against allowing me belowstairs, I c-could not wait."

The squire looked momentarily away. When he looked back, he gave an acceding nod. "I am to stand watch at the landing below. Henceforth, when you leave the tower, you must do so under my escort."

"I understand."

"Good eve, my lady."

"Squire Percival," she blurted for fear she would not get the words out soon enough.

"My lady?"

"I-I would like to go to the Lord's chapel."

He frowned. "I must tell you that Soaring is without a priest."

"No priest?"

"He died this past winter, my lady. He was much aged."

"I see." She had hoped to speak with one of God's men.

"Still you wish to go, my lady?"

"I do."

"Then I shall return shortly to escort you."

She stepped forward. "I am ready now."

He surveyed her homespun. "First you should change garments, my lady."

She rubbed the coarse material between thumb and forefinger. "I assure you, 'twill not…offend God."

"Aye, but Lord D'Arci has said you are not to leave the tower without adequate dress."

And there was no use arguing with one who would not go against his lord. "Then I shall change."

He stepped onto the landing and closed the door.

Beatrix gathered the gown against her. Though it had been hemmed, it was still too long, but if she lifted the skirts when she walked, the length could be overcome. And once more she would look like a lady, even without a veil and—

Perse! That was the name of the rich blue cloth. That she had found the word made her smile, but that it was so long in being found caused her smile to slip.

She would have to do much better on the day of her trial.

16

THROUGHOUT THE BREAKING of her fast, time and again the little girl had drawn Beatrix's regard. Though it became obvious she was Lady Laura's daughter, meaning the lady was likely widowed, it was just as obvious that the child was fond of Michael.

Hardly had the meal begun than she was on his lap, and though he continued to converse with Sir Canute, he broke bread and cut bites of cheese for her—and seemed not at all uncomfortable with the arrangement.

When the little girl caught Beatrix watching, she stuck out her tongue as if offended by the smile offered her. Thus, it was surprising that, when the meal was done and the hall was being cleared, the child approached.

Having stepped off the dais, Beatrix glanced at Squire Percival where he awaited her at the stairs and clasped her hands at the waist of the gown that had stirred so many to murmuring this morning. Obviously, it was a curious thing that the turning from night into day found her elevated from homespun to Perse.

Beatrix looked from the little girl who neared to the castle folk who withdrew from the hall to begin their day. Michael was among them. Though throughout the meal he had ignored her, when she had first come into the hall his gaze had drawn near and he had stared at her as a man did a woman he found pleasing.

Beatrix had averted her gaze and next encountered that of the knight who had come to take her away. He had also stared, then glowered at Michael. What had he seen? What had made his jaw thrust? And where was he now?

Guessing he had preceded the others out of doors, she shifted her regard to Lady Maude and Lady Laura who now sat before the hearth. The former's head was bent to a piece of cloth to which she laid stitches, the latter's gaze stuck to the fire.

The little girl halted before Beatrix and poked the skirts of the borrowed gown. "Momma's," she pronounced.

Beatrix smiled. "It is your mother's, and I am most…grateful that she allowed me to borrow it."

"For what?"

Bending to better address the little one, Beatrix said, "I fear I did not bring so fine a gown with me."

"Why?"

"I did not expect to join your mother and Lady Maude in Lord D'Arci's hall."

"Why?"

Beatrix moistened her lips. "What is your name?"

The girl poked the gown again. "Give back?"

"I shall." Beatrix touched her shoulder. "Wh-what is your name?"

The little girl took a step back. "Clawice."

"Clarice is a lovely name."

She stamped her foot. "'Tis not!"

Beatrix glanced at the girl's mother and Lady Maude who both watched the exchange. Hoping they did not think she did the child ill, Beatrix straightened.

"You name?" Clarice asked.

"I am Lady Beatrix."

"Pwetty name."

Before Beatrix could thank the child, the knight who had last eve warned her against revealing him stepped from an alcove. A mere shake of the head was all he had given, but it had told all. And now he advanced on her.

Surely he would not try to take her now, not with Squire Percival—

Beatrix sidestepped Clarice. Though tempted to take the girl's arm and drag her along, she knew it would frighten the child. "Come, Clarice. I must needs...thank your mother for the use of her gown." Gathering up the skirt, she stepped forward and Clarice followed.

The faces of the two ladies at the hearth reflected little welcome as Beatrix drew near—much the same as when Beatrix had ascended the dais and seated herself two down from Lady Laura. And it was that which pulled her shoulders back and chin up. Regardless of what they believed of her, she was their equal.

"My lady," Beatrix acknowledged Lady Maude, then bestowed the same address on the younger woman.

Michael's stepmother set her needlework in her lap. "Lady Beatrix." Though her voice was not friendly, neither was it hateful.

Feeling the knight at her back, Beatrix stepped nearer Lady Laura and Clarice who had gone to stand at her mother's knee. "I thank you for the use of your gown, my lady. I shall, of course, return it."

Garbed in a splendid garment of yellow silk, the lady said, "'Tis not necessary. I have many."

"But Momma, Lady Maude give it to you."

The lady patted her child's hand. "I do not think she will mind."

Lady Maude shook her head, but before Beatrix could thank her, the woman looked past Beatrix and said, "You are leaving us, Sir Piers?"

Beatrix looked around at the knight. Piers was the name he had taken?

"'Twas my intention, my lady," he said, coming to stand alongside Beatrix, "but my destrier took ill overnight. If Lord D'Arci grants it, I shall beg another night's lodging."

"Of course he shall grant it. He is indebted to you for delivering me safely to Soaring."

How had he done that?

"It was a pleasure, my lady."

Beatrix looked across the hall to Squire Percival. Though his face was expressionless, he watched—as did another knight she had not noticed before. The man who seemed to appear out of nothing stood to the far right of the squire, stance rigid, hand upon his scabbard.

He had been set to watch Sir Piers, Beatrix realized. Michael D'Arci was no fool.

Fearing bloodshed should Lady Maude's guest attempt what he had been sent to do, Beatrix determined that she would avoid the man. "I thank you, Lady Maude"—she inclined her head—"Lady Laura. Good day."

As she neared Squire Percival, he asked, "The chapel again, my lady?"

Of course he would think so. For nearly an hour, he had waited on her last eve while she knelt in the deserted chapel praying for God's hand upon her, then again this morning before she came belowstairs.

"Am I permitted to stroll the garden, Squire?"

"Lord D'Arci has said you may."

It surprised her that he had considered she might wish to. "Then that is where I wish to go."

She followed him to the corridor through which viands were carried for the meals, but as they neared the door that surely let into the garden, a voice called, "Lady Beatrix?"

She turned to Lady Laura.

The woman considered Squire Percival. "I would speak to Lady Beatrix alone."

"I am sorry, my lady, but Lord D'Arci has ordered that Lady Beatrix remain in my sight at all times."

"Then 'twill be sufficient that you watch from the door."

The squire hesitated, then retreated.

There was color in Lady Laura's face, and a bit of light in eyes that had been dull when they had spoken in the hall, but she was nowhere near a smile. Indeed, it looked as if her lips never bent upward, the faint grooves alongside her mouth absent. Had they melted away? Perhaps never been?

The woman drew a breath. "All that you told Lady Maude of Sir Simon," she whispered, "I believe."

Beatrix blinked. "I thank you, but how——"

"Momma!" Clarice had entered the corridor.

"I just know," Lady Laura said and bent to receive the child that hurtled toward her. A moment later, she straightened and settled the little girl on her hip.

Though a dozen questions rolled about Beatrix, she said, "You are... fortunate, Lady Laura, to have such a lovely daughter."

The smile that touched the woman's lips was of a bitter bent, but it did turn up her mouth. "I am, but in some things you are more fortunate than I."

What did she mean? It was not Lady Laura who would soon stand trial for a crime not committed. Not she who had little chance of being cleared of murder.

"'Tis so," the lady said and turned back down the corridor.

What made her believe what Beatrix had told of Sir Simon? And why had she sought to tell her so?

"Still you wish to stroll the gardens?" Squire Percival asked.

"Aye." Hastening down the corridor in search of light, Beatrix found it in the glorious herb garden beyond the door.

17

H E ACHED. THERE was no other word for it. Each time he saw her, he knew a discomfort unlike any he had known. It was not the gown, though it clasped her figure as tunic and braies could not do. It was not her flaxen hair, though it tempted his hands. It was not even the health returned to her face that made her nearly the angel he had first looked upon.

What, then? Her blue eyes that rarely met his? Her determined chin beneath blushing lips? Those same lips that knew no bow save when she looked upon Clarice?

Michael drummed on the journal, the figures of which refused to be summed with his attention so divided. Why did the mere thought of her make him ache? Why could he not be truthful—at least with himself? Why could he not sum these accursed numbers?

He slammed his gaze to the entries set down this day and focused on the date Canute had written. For this, more than anything, he ached— the passing of days that portended the arrival of the sheriff three days hence.

He sat back in his chair. The days had passed too quickly, as would the remaining three. Then Beatrix would leave Soaring and never return.

It matters not. As it is a trial she wishes, a trial she shall have.

Which returned Sir Piers to mind. A sick horse! Though Michael had himself seen the beast would not rise from its stall, he did not believe it. And yet the knight had made no move toward Beatrix other than that warning shake of his head.

Was he awaiting orders? Wulfrith's orders? Lavonne's? It could be either, though the latter worried him the most. If Aldous Lavonne feared absolution as Michael had once feared it, he would seek a way to ensure *this* Wulfrith did not go unpunished. And what of Christian? Would he allow his father his revenge as he had done in the past by silently condoning the raids on Wulfrith lands?

Michael stood. Where was Beatrix? The garden again? Squire Percival reported that two and three times a day she sought his escort to that place where Michael grew medicinal herbs—among them comfrey and tansy that he had used to speed the healing of his leg. Or had she gone to the chapel? It was also told that she spent even more time among the dust and desertion of that place that few visited since the passing of Soaring's priest.

Eschewing his staff that his strengthening leg needed less and less, Michael decided to try the garden and strode to the corridor that granted passage. At the far end, the door stood ajar just enough to let in a ribbon of sunlight—and whatever insects happened by.

He scowled as a fly swept past on its way to the kitchen, its merry drone seeming to mock him. However, the scene that awaited him when he pulled the door wide and crossed the threshold was more grievous than the prospect of sharing a meal with filthy insects.

Squire Percival was on his haunches on the path that cut through the middle of the herb garden. And alongside him was Beatrix, also in profile.

The hem of her borrowed gown laid atop her thighs such that her hosed knees were revealed, she reached past the squire. Her arm brushed his and caused a flush to run up the young man's neck. "And this?" she asked.

The squire peered at the plant she fingered. "I know not the name of that one, my lady."

She shrugged, and Michael knew the face she turned to Percival bore a smile. "I cannot think of it either, though I vow I know it."

Jealousy—there was no other word for it—gripped Michael.

Beatrix sat back on her heels. "Mayhap you could cut a s-sprig for me?"

There were other herbs in her lap—fennel of the tiny yellow flowers and sweet woodruff of the white flowers. What did she do? And why did Percival reach for his dagger to accommodate her request?

Michael descended the steps. "You are relieved of your charge, Squire Percival."

The young man lurched to his feet. "My lord! I did not hear you."

"That is most obvious." Acutely aware of the hitch in his stride, Michael glanced at Beatrix. Though she met his gaze, she did not rise.

"I was assisting Lady Beatrix with—"

"I know what you were doing." Michael halted before him. "You are relieved."

The squire lowered his eyes. "Aye, my lord."

As his footsteps receded, Michael considered Beatrix. She had turned her face forward and appeared to look upon the fuzzy leaves and stems of the herb which neither she, nor Squire Percival, could name.

As the garden door closed, Michael said, "Herbs, Lady Beatrix?"

She nodded, causing her silken hair to ripple in the sunlight.

"For what?" He took a step nearer and braced the bulk of his weight on his uninjured leg.

She reached toward the budding herb that would soon produce clusters of exquisite flowers nearly as blue as her eyes and grasped a narrow stem as if to break it. "This one is for...courage."

That so simple a word could tug so forcefully through him told Michael he should not be here. "You speak of the trial." He wished his voice did not sound so tight.

She tugged at the stem, but it was too green to give without damaging the plant.

Michael went down on his haunches beside her. Though the muscles of his leg spasmed, he ignored the discomfort and pulled his dagger. As he reached forward, Beatrix jerked her hand away as if for fear they might touch, a fear she had not shown when it was Percival who assisted her.

Jealousy ripening such that had it a smell it would be most foul, Michael swept his blade through the stem and dropped the cutting in her lap.

She stared at it. "Each time ere my father…took up arms, he had prepared for him a wine cup with…" For lack of the name, she picked up the cutting. "…this. He told that, in battle, it increased courage." She delivered her gaze to Michael. "Not that he required such."

Michael returned his dagger to its scabbard. "'Tis a claim oft made of Borage."

Her sharp breath and wide eyes revealed that she had not missed the elusive word, and twice she mouthed it as if to place it firm in her mind. "Of course," she finally spoke, "mother would say all one needs for courage is God."

"Myself, I would first try Borage."

She frowned.

Thinking the turning down of her mouth ought to make her less appealing and bothered that it did not, he continued, "It is known to cause the blood to run faster. Though"—he smiled—"that might have more to do with the wine into which Borage is put."

Beatrix stared at him.

"So, 'tis courage you seek," he prompted.

Her eyes snapped. "God is my courage. Thus, I am not afraid, if that is what you ask."

"It is not." He pulled the cutting from between her fingers and eyed the drooping buds. "Even with God on one's side, a person can always use more courage, can they not?" He returned his gaze to her. "And yet, you seem less in need of courage than any woman I have known."

She blinked, unsettling the affront she wore. However, its hard angles soon returned. "How many women have you known who...face death for a crime they did not commit?"

None. *Until now,* the forbidden slipped in. As Michael tossed it out, Beatrix smiled bitterly. "'Tis most...remarkable what the prospect of death can make of a person."

He lowered his gaze. And curled his fingers into his palms when he glimpsed her legs amid her skirts.

She must have seen where his eyes went, for she tugged her gown down. "I did not wish to soil the skirts," she murmured and reached for the other two cuttings that had slid from her lap onto the path between them.

Michael also reached for them, and again she pulled back to avoid touching him. Suppressing the anger that sought tinder, he lifted the herbs between them. "Fennel and sweet woodruff, the same used to scent your pallet at the abbey."

His softly spoken words startled Beatrix. He had noticed the herbs? And remembered? Of course, he *was* a physician. Though she knew it should not disturb her so, it was as if they had shared an intimacy. Fearing he once more trifled with her, she searched for something to turn the conversation. "Squire Percival tells that you are not only versed in h-healing, but warring."

From his lowering brow, she had made a mistake in revealing what she had learned from the squire. "Does he?"

"He...mentioned it."

"Then, it seems, you have also bewitched him."

Though it was true the squire had come around, "bewitched" was not a word she would use to describe their relationship. "'Twas told in passing, that is all. Be assured, your squire is—"The word took to wing, leaving no remnant with which to piece it together.

"Loyal?" Michael interceded.

"Aye, loyal to his lord." Knowing that what she spoke would be less believed if she did not grant him her gaze, she lifted her chin. Such pale eyes he had...

Feeling herself lean toward him, she pushed her shoulders back. "What I do not understand is how a man can, in one breath, heal, and in another—"

Lord, it does not bode well for him to be so near! Now what had she wished to say?

"Kill?" Michael supplied the missing word.

Hating his impatience, she inclined her head.

"It has all to do with conscience, Lady Beatrix. As I—"

"Conscience? You mean the Holy Spirit?"

From the frown that furrowed his brow, she knew he was not comfortable that their conversation had turned to God.

"Just as I have not killed without due reason," he ignored her question, "I have not healed those better served to die."

Remembering his ministering hands, she touched her head where he had laid down stitches. "Excepting those better served to die a more v-violent death?"

His gaze wavered, and for a moment she thought he might gainsay himself. Instead, he stood and thrust the herbs at her.

Beatrix also rose but ignored the herbs. "Naught to say, Lord D'Arci?"

"Naught needs to be said, Lady Beatrix."

She folded her arms over her chest. "Pray, what does your conscience speak of me, my lord?"

"Lady Beatrix—"

"What does it speak?"

"Mother Mary! You—"

"I am sick unto death of your profanity!" she snapped. "And your impatience that steals words from my mouth!"

She snatched the herbs from him. Though his flesh barely brushed hers, the brief contact spilled sensation through her. Fearing it, she lifted her skirts and made to step around him. However, he caught her arm and pulled her so near that the heat of his body was almost as tangible as his hand upon her.

Breath feathering her face, he searched her eyes, searched lower, then slowly raised her to her toes and bent his head. "Do you despair of this as well?" he murmured.

Realizing what else he intended to steal from her mouth, she jerked her head to the side, but not before a brief meeting of their lips.

As suddenly as he had taken hold of her, he released her. "By faith!" He thrust a hand through his dark hair.

Beatrix met his fierce gaze and drew the back of a hand across her mouth. "Aye," she said, surprised at the strength of her voice, "I despair of that as well." She skirted him and hurried over the stone-laid path. At the door, she looked across her shoulder and glimpsed regret on his face before he hid it behind a glower.

Though she longed to press her lips against the words that rose unbidden to them, she said, "Yield to God, Michael, else you will never find the peace you seek."

Without waiting to hear what would surely be a caustic rejoinder, she entered the donjon and narrowly avoided a wench who exited the kitchen with a tray of viands borne high.

It was the nooning meal already? Bidding her breath to turn even, Beatrix smoothed her bodice, next her hair, and brushed her lips that yet felt the fleeting impression of Michael's. Why had he kissed her?

At the sound of his uneven footfalls, she hurried down the corridor to the great hall where the castle folk were beginning to gather and where she would sit down to another meal rife with the silence drawn about Lady Laura and Lady Maude, neither of whom had spoken to her since the morning that she had thanked them for the gown. First, though, she would take her herbs abovestairs.

Pondering how odd it was to not have Squire Percival's escort, she did not see the one who leaned against the wall until she was nearly upon him. She faltered and, for a moment, feared this was the moment he had awaited. However, he did not move from alongside the stairway but merely murmured, "This eve, Lady Beatrix."

Heart seeking to free itself from the cage of her ribs, she managed to keep her feet moving until she ascended to the first landing. There, she paused. The scents of woodruff, fennel, and borage whispering through her, she looked to the limp herbs in her clenched and trembling hand and loosed a small, bitter laugh. And Michael thought her less in need of courage than any woman he had known...

Determined to prove him right, she turned up the winding stair. "I shall have my trial," she told the walls. "My word on that."

"Have you decided?"

Michael straightened from lowering Clarice to the bed. The little girl having nodded off on his lap before meal's end, he had carried her abovestairs for the absent Lady Laura. He met Maude's gaze opposite. "Decided?"

"I speak of Lady Beatrix."

Michael tensed and tried to turn aside the memory of what he had done in the garden. Such a fool he was!

"Michael?"

Not since Maude had told him she did not think Beatrix belonged in the tower had they discussed the one who stood accused of murdering Simon. "I was not aware there was a decision to be made regarding her."

Her mouth tightened. "Do not trifle with me. For one so slight, Lady Beatrix perches heavily upon your mind."

"You do not know my mind, Maude."

She came around the bed. "If your mind follows your eyes—which follow Lady Beatrix—I do know it."

He did not like this conversation, but rather than leave it hung out for her to pick at later, he determined he would put an end to it. "Thrice she has escaped me. 'Twould be foolish if I did not watch her."

Maude momentarily closed her eyes, then curved a hand over his jaw. "You forget I know you as my own son, Michael. The eyes that follow

Lady Beatrix are not those of a man who stalks his prey—at least, not for the killing."

He drew back. "My stalking is done. Now I have but to deliver the lady to trial, and that I shall do. For Simon."

Her son's name causing her eyes to brighten, she said, "Only if you make lies of what you know to be true."

"What do you say? That now you are *certain* she did not murder Simon?"

"I have also watched her."

Then that was all, for Squire Percival told she had spoken no more than half a dozen words to his captive since the telling of Beatrix's tale.

"And what have you seen, Maude?"

"The same that you see—or nearly so." Sorrow haunted her eyes. "Thus, you must decide what to do with her. And soon."

With the passing of this eve's moon, there were only two days remaining before the sheriff came.

Michael clenched his hands and swung away. "I have business to attend to."

"I am pleased you have found your heart again," Maude sent after him.

He did not know of what she spoke, but he knew what he must do. Unfortunately, there was not much time in which to do it. He turned out of the chamber. "Squire Percival!"

The young man, earlier relieved of his watch over Lady Beatrix, met him at the door of the solar. "My lord?"

"Summon Sir Canute and take up his watch that he might attend me."

Surprise leaping off his face, Percival hastened from the room to retrieve the knight who had been passed the guard over Beatrix.

"You are leaving Castle Soaring."

Beatrix stared at the one into whose presence she had been escorted. "The...sheriff has arrived?"

"Nay," Michael said. "'Tis not to Broehne you go."

Then the trial was to be held elsewhere? Why? Hating her fluttering lids, she said, "I do not understand."

He straightened from the table. "I am sending you to Stern Castle— to your brother."

Beatrix startled. "You jest."

"I do not. Indeed, I shall deliver you myself."

He who had revealed her capture to Lavonne? The air too thin to satisfy, she breathed deep and tried to make sense of what he told.

"We leave ere dawn."

Why? After three days, had Lady Maude determined to believe her? But even if she had, Michael would not release her unless he also believed—or at least doubted.

Beatrix moistened her lips. "You would have me beg an explanation?"

He strode to where she stood in the middle of the solar. "Be content that your bid for freedom is won and that you shall soon be reunited with your family who will ensure the Lavonnes never again lay hands to you."

She could not content herself with that. Michael was releasing her and intended to return her to Stern himself—or at least he thought he would. "Then you know I spoke true of your brother, that I am not the same as..."

Though over and over the name of the woman to whom Michael had likened her had gone around her head, it failed her now. Which letter had begun the woman's name? Hoping for Michael's patience long enough to search the dark places of her memory, she started with the letter 'a'. Fortunately, Edithe was not far removed. "Then you know I am not the same as Edithe."

Beneath his beard, his jaw bulged, and she knew he regretted telling her the woman's name. "I do not know that. Merely, I am no longer certain of it."

Doubt, then. But in releasing her, Michael would break his vow of fealty, an unpardonable sin where one's liege was concerned. "What of Baron Lavonne?"

"'Twill be told that you escaped." A slight smile touched his mouth. "You have done that often enough."

To his detriment.

"Ere dawn," he said and stepped around her as if to see her from the solar.

Beatrix was tempted, but if she took what he offered, it would be said she had murdered. She could not live like that, nor with the fear that her family's refusal to hand her over to the sheriff would endanger them. "I will not leave."

Michael turned. "What do you say?"

"I shall remain here."

His nostrils flared. "Do you not understand what I offer? 'Tis what you sought hardly a month past."

"And what I no longer seek as I have told you. I shall have my trial."

"Do not be a fool—"

"I am not!" Beatrix stamped her foot. "Not your brother's fool, not Baron Lavonne's fool, and certainly not yours! I am done running from something I did not do."

Pupils darkening, he looked long upon her. "In less than three days, the sheriff will be here." There was a firm calm to his voice as one might use with a difficult child.

She peered up at him through her lashes. "It is as I wish."

"You cannot hope to win."

"If I can make *you* doubt, mayhap 'tis not so far removed to make others."

"Doubt will not save you, Beatrix." He lifted an arm, hesitated, then laid fingers to her cheek. "You will be found guilty. And you will die."

She longed to reject his gesture, but it felt... Though it should not be this way, his touch was a balm to her tattered soul. Mayhap he did care for her. Mayhap it was not mere lust that had made him seek to lie with her. Mayhap he risked all for *her*, incredible though it seemed.

She drew a deep breath. Aye, incredible, just as when she had convinced herself he would not alert the baron to her presence at Soaring...

when she had been so sure of him only to learn there was nothing about him to be sure. Thus, she must remain true to the vow she had made herself. Only it could wipe clean her past and let her live again.

"Though death may be my end," she said, "the truth shall be told about your brother." As the last word spilled, so did realization, and she lurched back.

He did *not* care for her. Did *not* risk all for her.

Wariness recasting his face, Michael lowered his arm.

"I see clearly, Lord D'Arci, what you would not have me see. 'Tis not for my wellbeing that you would deliver me to my brother, but for your stepmother…your hell-bound brother…you." Anger shuddered through her. "You fear for the D'Arci name, that your brother's depravity shall reflect ill upon you. Though I might die, you have not a care for me."

Michael's eyes lit, but whatever anger gripped him, he contained it. "You are wrong. And therein lies my problem. I do care."

His admission would have staggered her heart if not that she told herself he lied. He did not care for her.

Especially not as you wish him to care for you, a voice whispered through her.

I do not wish him to care for me! And he surely did not. What man would? Unless there was considerable gain, men did not take damaged women to wife. Indeed, Michael would suffer considerable loss if he truly cared for her. If the baron relieved him of Castle Soaring, his life would likely be reduced to no better than knight errant. She could not bear being responsible for his downfall.

"I shall not leave." She skirted him, and he let her go.

Squire Percival, who awaited her in the corridor, followed her up the winding stair and left her upon the landing.

Beatrix stared at the door of what had been her prison. In the dark before dawn, would Michael try to force her from Soaring? He could do it—steal upon her while she slept, bind her, and carry her to Stern Castle. Might he? Unfortunately, as the door locked from the outside and there was no bar to drop over the inside, she could not keep him out.

Might she steal from Soaring as she had stolen from Broehne? Deliver herself to Baron Lavonne? It seemed the solution, but she knew it was better for the sheriff to deliver her.

She pushed the door inward, closed it behind her, and crossed to the bed where she lowered to the edge. Try though she did to not think about Michael and the feelings his presence, words, and touch stirred, it was futile.

He cares naught for you! And yet—

She searched for someplace else to land her thoughts. And land they did, on the one who had warned that he would take her from Soaring this eve.

She stood against two. The only good of it, if it could be said there was any, was that she would not have to resist both at the same time.

Beatrix had not murdered. And long he had known it—his heart, that is. It was his head that had made murder of her attempt to escape persecution, his head that made Edithe's sins hers. At the cost of Beatrix, he had wanted to believe the years could not change Simon so. But he had known it, even an hour past when all he had allowed was that he was no longer certain of her guilt. For that, there could be no forgiveness. He had hunted her to ground, made her his prisoner, nearly claimed her virtue, and repeatedly cast another woman's sins upon her. Unforgivable.

Michael settled deeper in the chair and rubbed between thumb and forefinger the tress he had carried with him all these months. In the end, it would be all he had of her—all any would have of her if he did not take her from Soaring. Thus, though she vowed to resist, he would pass to her brother the burden of keeping her from her foolish quest.

He looked from the hearth to the pale strands between his fingers. Though he had given Beatrix enough reason not to believe him, it *was* for her he wished to see her clear of a trial. Not for Maude, for Simon, or himself.

If only she would leave willingly as she would have before that night in the rain. But she had changed—her voice, her bearing, and especially her eyes when she looked upon him. He had done that to her, trampled her innocence and trust when she had yielded to his hungering mouth. All because of Edithe, whom he had once more given the power to take from him—a woman as far removed from Beatrix as Michael was from any hope of righting the wrong he had done.

And he knew why he cared so much that the wrong be righted. Of course, he dared not allow the truth to settle too long, for therein lay weakness and vulnerability, neither of which a man could afford, especially without prospect of gain. Beatrix would not welcome him to her again, unless...

Yield to God, she had said, *else you will never find the peace you seek.*

Might he change his course by yielding to the Lord? Might he know the peace absent from his life? Might that peace include Beatrix? It was asking much—more than anything of which he was worthy.

He stood. There was no time to waste on useless pondering or bent knees. Not when there was so much to be done before dawn.

As Aldous Lavonne's men were not inept, it had proven bothersome to secure everything needed for the journey without alerting those who had passed on the wine this eve, but it was done. Three hours hence, before the sun warmed the land, Michael would take Beatrix east.

Leg throbbing for lack of the staff he had left behind to more inconspicuously negotiate the inner and outer bailey, Michael eased the door closed that accessed the gardens. In turn, the gardens accessed an entrance into the inner bailey that was known to few. Through it, he had returned from the stables.

Wincing at the burn in his calf, he traversed the corridor. The hall ahead was dim, torchlight having hours past cast its light upon the dark. He halted at the end of the corridor and searched out Lavonne's man. As hoped—and expected of the draught that had sweetened the wine at supper—the man-at-arms had fallen asleep where he leaned against the wall to the right. That left only one other who ought to be awake amongst those who made their beds in the hall.

Michael considered the alcove where Sir Justin watched over Lavonne's man—as well as Maude's knight errant, Sir Piers. The impenetrable dark revealed nothing, which was as it should be.

Though tempted to go abovestairs and rest before the journey, Michael crossed to the alcove, but when the breath of acknowledgment he should have received as he passed near was not heard, he turned back. A moment later, his searching hands found Sir Justin where he had slid down the wall onto his knees.

Silently cursing himself for being so arrogant to believe his defenses were impenetrable, Michael dragged the knight from the alcove into the torchlight and pressed fingers to his neck. Sir Justin's veins yet coursed and he had his breath. Someone had landed a blow to his forehead.

Michael jerked around and picked out the pallet on which Sir Piers had stretched an hour past. Though the blanket was turned up, no form was beneath.

18

THE KNIGHT WHO had taken the name of Sir Piers stepped back and released Squire Percival to the landing. No harm done, he determined as he looked upon the young man's slack features—at least, not as much harm as what had been done to the man D'Arci had set in the hall to watch over his unwelcome guest.

By the waning light of torches, the knight returned his dagger to its sheathe and looked up the winding stair over which the squire had stood watch. She was up there, and before middle night was half past, he would have her away from here.

He drew his sword. Watchful lest another stood outside her chamber, he took the steps two at a time. The dim stairs were empty, as was the landing before her door. He returned his sword to its scabbard.

Counting it a boon that the door was unlocked, he stepped inside the chamber.

The coals in the brazier cast a weak glow, spreading light as far as the bed. A bed that did not sleep Lady Beatrix.

He turned his hand around his dagger hilt and peered into the darkened corners that refused to betray what lurked there.

One did not fuel the brazier of an unoccupied room, and yet, despite the door's creak, its betrayal had not provided adequate time for anyone within to seek cover. And surely only Lady Beatrix expected him?

Perchance D'Arci had taken her from Soaring, even now rode to Lavonne? He frowned over that and remembered the night she had been mistaken for a servant. What had happened between her and D'Arci had presented as peculiar, and from D'Arci's reaction and the castle folk's, it was obvious Beatrix's presence in the hall had been unfamiliar until that eve.

He had thought, perhaps, she had escaped her prison, but it made no sense she would come to the hall that brimmed with folk, nor that the man whose brother she was said to have murdered would invite her to join him at table. Of course, these past days of watching one watch the other had presented the unforeseen and unwelcome possibility that something had happened between D'Arci and Lady Beatrix. And he had told his lord as much in a missive dispatched on the day past. So *had* something happened? Beatrix was a beautiful woman, and she surely stirred *him*—

"I thank you that you would r-risk so much to aid me," her voice came out of the dark, "but I shall not go with you, Sir Durand." In the corner beyond the bed, she rose from where she had sat watching him. Waiting for him.

"Beatrix," he murmured, only after speaking her name realizing he did so without title, something he had no right to do. Especially now.

"Pray, deliver...tidings of my family, then leave ere you are discovered."

He eased his hand from the dagger. "The first I can do. The last, I cannot."

She stepped into the brazier's glow. "My sister?" She held her hands at the waist of a homespun garment that had replaced the fine gown she wore belowstairs.

The mere thought of Gaenor unsettled Durand as it had done every day since he had escorted her to Wulfen. Turning memories of her away, he looked to the sister for whom he felt so much and whom he had believed lost to him that night in the wood when Gaenor had wept on his shoulder.

As when Durand had first seen Beatrix again in D'Arci's hall, he was struck by how lovely she was. And yet how different she seemed from the young woman with whom he had fled Stern Castle. And it was not merely her faltering speech. There was a hard light in her eyes, and when she spoke, her voice was forceful and resonated with purpose. Then there was her stiff bearing that contrasted with the carefree figure he had known.

As often happened with those who survived great adversity, she had aged such that the memory held of her all these weeks found little nourishment in the woman whose face did not light and who did not rush to accept his deliverance.

"My sister?" she asked again.

"I delivered her safely to your brother, Sir Everard, at Wulfen."

Relief lowered Beatrix's shoulders. "And where is she now?"

"She is yet at Wulfen, my lady."

Beatrix frowned. "As women are not allowed within W-Wulfen's walls, I expected my brother would seek to secure her elsewhere."

It was a reasonable expectation since the only woman to ever fully penetrate Wulfen Castle was Annyn Bretanne, now Baron Wulfrith's wife, when she had sought revenge against his family in the disguise of a squire.

"Your family has determined it is the surest place to prevent King Henry from laying hold of Lady Gaenor, not only due to its fortifications but because few at Wulfen are aware of her presence."

After a long moment, Beatrix nodded. "Tell me of my eldest brother."

"Baron Wulfrith fares better now that 'tis known you live."

"I am surprised he did not come for me himself."

"He wished to, as did your other brothers. Unfortunately, they have trained far too many boys into knights to go unrecognized."

"I had not c-considered that. What of my mother and sister-in-law?"

"They are well, my lady. The news you had survived the fall lifted the great pall beneath which all have been laboring. Now there is only the trial to deal with, and for that I am here."

She momentarily lowered her lids. "How does Squire Percival fare?"

He was not surprised that she concerned herself over the young man who had stood watch over the stairs. "He shall be sore when he awakens. That is all."

"I thank you, Sir Durand. And now I ask you to return to Stern Castle and tell my brother that I go to...trial willingly that I might defend my innocence."

Willingly? After all she had endured to escape Baron Lavonne? Durand stared at the woman before him. Mayhap the head injury had done more damage than thought. "I fear I cannot do as you ask, Lady Beatrix," he consciously returned her title to her. "I have a promise to keep, and it requires that you come with me."

She shook her head. "Go."

"Lady Beatrix—"

"I am staying!"

God's tooth! In relieving Squire Percival and the knight of consciousness, he had thought the greatest obstacles overcome, but now this small woman loomed just as large. Unfortunately, as much as he preferred to reason with her, there was not the time to do so.

He strode around the bed.

She stepped back. "Upon my word, I shall scream, Sir Durand!"

"And reveal me? Nay, you will not." At least, the Beatrix he had known would not. Hoping some of her remained, he reached for her.

She lunged, lit upon the mattress, and clambered toward the other side.

Landing his knees on the bed, he caught a handful of her homespun gown.

She shrieked, flailed as he dragged her back from the edge, and nearly unmanned him.

Durand tossed her onto her back and clamped a hand over her mouth. Praying her shriek had not made it around too many turns of the winding stairs, he pushed his gaze to hers.

Her eyes were wild, and he knew that were his legs not pinning hers, she would try again for his manhood.

"Hear me, Lady——"

He felt the scrape of her teeth. Fortunately, his palm was too calloused for her to catch hold of.

"Enough!" Struggling to control his frustration, he said, "Listen to me. I am taking you from here——"

The sound of footsteps made him snap his head around. A moment later, a sword hewed the doorway, followed by Michael D'Arci.

Durand cursed. Had he not been distracted by Beatrix's struggle, he would sooner have heard D'Arci's advance and had his sword to hand.

Even as Durand rolled to the side and reached for his hilt, he knew it was too late.

Michael paused only long enough to assess the situation, but it was enough to boil his blood and render his sword arm a taste for killing. He lunged toward the one who had pinned Beatrix to the bed and would have severed the knave's head if not that Beatrix lurched after him.

"Nay!" She threw herself on the knight.

Staying his blade, Michael groped for an explanation of her shielding of the man. And nearly lost the advantage when Sir Piers reached for his dagger.

Michael grabbed Beatrix's arm, thrust her aside, and swept his blade to the knight's neck.

The man's hand paused above his dagger. Then, with grudging surrender, he splayed his fingers. "Come, Lord D'Arci, let us take to arms and decide this now."

"'Tis decided. You die."

Beatrix reached to Michael. "He is not——"

"Stay back!" He knocked her hand aside.

The momentary distraction was all Sir Piers needed. He rolled and gained his feet—and sword—on the opposite side of the bed.

If not for Michael's laming, he could have been upon the knight before the sword hissed from its scabbard.

"Now we decide," Sir Piers said and started around the bed.

Remembering the miscreant pinning Beatrix to the bed, eager to begin the letting, Michael stepped forward. "Come, then."

Beatrix leapt off the mattress. "Hear me! 'Tis Sir Durand——"

The brazier's glow streaked the blade of Sir Piers—now Sir Durand—and Michael answered by deflecting the blow.

Steel upon steel resounded around the room, the force of the meeting causing both men to stagger. They pushed off each others' sword, circled, and like starving dogs warring over a bone, met at the center of the room.

Michael turned his wrist and thrust his blade high, forcing his opponent's blade to follow. The man disengaged and fell back, then came again.

Grunting at the weight he was forced to give his healing leg, Michael fended off the man's attack. Though there was not enough light in the dim room to trace a sword's path, he met each thrust and turned aside blow after blow as the walls of the room rang with battle.

Above the din, he heard Beatrix's protests, though the roar in his ears was too loud to know what she said. Once…twice…he glimpsed her fearful face as he sought to give his full attention to the skilled knight who meant to take what Michael would not give.

Sir Durand—did he know the name?—swept his sword low to deflect Michael's attempt to cut his feet out from under him, then advanced and swung upward.

Michael turned hard on his injured leg and knocked aside the knight's blade. As intended, the move opened a path to Sir Durand's sword arm.

"Cease!" Beatrix cried and lunged between them.

Michael jerked, slowing his swing, but it was not enough to stop it. The tip of his sword caught the sleeve of her gown and found the flesh beneath.

"Nay!" he shouted. But it was so, as evidenced by the blood that rimmed his blade.

Beatrix stumbled back against Sir Durand.

"My lady!" The knight clasped her shoulder.

She looked to the crimson that seeped through her sleeve, clapped a hand over it, and swung her stricken gaze to Michael.

He stepped toward her. "Beatrix, I—"

"Whoreson!" Sir Durand yelled. Lips curling, eyes seeking to impale, he swept his sword to the ready. "Get behind me, my lady," he said and thrust Beatrix to the side.

Michael ground his teeth. If it took the knight's death to gain Beatrix, so be it. However, before their swords could cleave the air, Beatrix closed her blood-smeared hand around the hilt of Sir Durand's dagger.

"No more!" She swept the weapon from its scabbard and waved it between the two men. "I shall return to Stern Castle with neither of you."

Michael stilled. Surely this knight did not also intend to deliver her to Stern?

Sir Durand looked from Beatrix to Michael and, a moment later, his dark fury was displaced by disbelief.

It was then the name came to Michael—Sir Durand, the knight who was said to have escaped with Beatrix's sister.

The irony that Michael had fought a man whose purpose he shared—to deliver Beatrix to her brother—would have made him laugh if not that Beatrix bled. And from the glint in Sir Durand's eyes, he also saw the irony.

But if the Wulfrith knight had come to take her to Stern Castle, why had he spread himself upon Beatrix? And why had she sought to protect him?

There, in her seething gaze, was the answer. Sir Durand had done what Michael would have had to do to take her from here. He had tried to force her.

"I shall not go," she said, pressing her injured arm tight to her side. "Do you hear me?"

"I hear," Michael said and beckoned for her to relinquish the dagger.

She stepped back. "I shall only leave…Soaring in the company of the Sheriff."

Sir Durand reached out his own hand. "Give me the dagger, my lady."

For some reason, Michael was relieved when she also refused him.

"I shall give over to the sheriff." She retreated further. "I trust neither of you."

"You bleed," Michael said. "Allow me—"

"Do not touch me!" She swept the dagger forward. "I have bled before and survived. I shall do so again. *And* have my trial."

"Not if you bleed out your life!"

"And you care when such an end would spare your family's name? That is what you want, is it not?"

With a glance at Sir Durand who continued to heft his sword, Michael took another step forward.

Beatrix retreated to the foot of the bed.

"You know 'tis not what I want," Michael said. "I would aid you, and that I cannot do beneath threat of your dagger."

"You fear I shall put it to you as I did your brother?"

Holding to his awareness of Sir Durand lest it be determined the lord of Soaring remained a threat to Beatrix, Michael continued forward. "You did not put the dagger to Simon," he finally voiced what he knew to be true. "It was not you who killed him."

Her gaze wavered. "You seek to deceive me."

Still Sir Durand held. Watched.

Michael halted before her. "Though 'tis true I would force you from here ere dawn, it is as true that I no longer believe you murdered Simon."

Her eyes delved his, but she would not find a lie in them. Revealing himself beyond what he had revealed to any woman since the betrayal that had lost him all, he dragged from his depths words he had thought never to speak. "You are not Edithe."

That which struck Beatrix was not unlike the lightning on a night that seemed so long ago, a night that she and Michael had come together between their hoods and he had given his breath to her. When something—this Edithe?—had spilled accusations from the same mouth that had nearly kissed her.

Not the same as Edithe. Did she dare believe he did not speak such for his own gain?

Arm throbbing, she lowered the dagger to her waist. "Even so, and 'tis not to say I believe you, I will not flee."

Sir Durand stirred, causing Michael's hand to convulse on his sword hilt.

"And if you never again see your family?" the knight demanded. "If for the remainder of her life, Lady Gaenor bears the blame for your death?"

Beatrix gasped. "It is not for her to bear!"

"But she shall—for the sacrifice you made for her. You know it."

She nearly argued, but he was right. Still, it was better for one to be burdened by undeserved blame than for Beatrix's entire family to suffer King Henry's displeasure. "I am wanted for m-murder. If I do not appear at trial, my family will suffer. I will not take that risk." She held Sir Durand's glower a moment before returning to Michael. "I must do this."

His jaw convulsed. "I know."

Was he merely placating her in hopes of disarming her?

"The bleeding must be stopped," he enjoined.

Though her sleeve was flushed red, the pain had abated. Shock? "First, I would have your word."

"You would believe it?"

Could she trust that he would not force her from Soaring? She glanced at Sir Durand whose mouth drew a flat line that told he also knew what she asked. She looked back at Michael. "I have no choice but to believe it."

Her words were a jab to his integrity, but he inclined his head. "I give my word."

"I do not give mine!" Sir Durand stepped toward them.

"She does not need it," Michael shot back. He lifted his sword from where he had settled its tip to the floor.

For a moment, Beatrix thought jealousy stirred the air, but that was ridiculous. Fearing the two might meet at swords again, she said, "Pray, Sir Durand, do not delay in…giving me your word. I bleed."

His eyes were riled, and a rumble sounded from him, but he grudgingly nodded.

She looked to Michael. "Tend me, if you will."

Once more, he held out his hand.

She gripped the dagger tighter. "I shall keep it."

"Why do you ask for my word if you do not intend to honor it?"

"That I might hear it." She almost smiled. "But *my* word I give that if you do not...deceive me, I will not use the dagger on you."

"Generous," Michael grumbled. "Sit down."

As she lowered to the mattress, the sound of boots on the stairs caused Michael and Sir Durand to raise their swords.

When the trespasser appeared in the doorway, sword at the ready, the sight of Squire Percival breathed relief around the room. However, the moment the young man picked out Sir Durand, he came across the room.

"Hold!" Michael shouted.

The squire's boots skittered over the floor. Shoulders heaving, he arced his sword before Sir Durand. "My lord, 'twas this miscreant who rendered the blow that laid me down."

"I know who bested you." Michael glanced at Sir Durand whose stance told that if the squire overstepped his sword skill, he would suffer. Michael returned his sword to its scabbard. "A misunderstanding only, Squire."

"Misunderstanding?" Percival exclaimed, then again when he caught sight of Beatrix's crimson sleeve.

"Do not question me, Squire. Fetch a torch."

Percival thrust his sword into its scabbard, strode from the room, and quickly returned to set a flickering torch in a wall sconce.

"Now escort Sir Piers to my solar," Michael directed, "and bring my physician's bag."

"Your solar?" Sir Durand asked with suspicious brow.

"Await me there. We must needs talk."

Sir Durand looked to Beatrix. Then, keeping his sword to hand, he followed Squire Percival out.

"When you have done that, Squire Percival," Michael called, "see if you can rouse Sir Justin who was also visited by Sir Durand this eve. He is in the hall."

Beatrix frowned. However, when Sir Durand glanced over his shoulder, the glint in his eyes was explanation enough. He had been busy belowstairs.

Michael turned back to Beatrix. "May I?"

She lowered the dagger. As he bent over her and folded back her sleeve, she stared at his dark head and was disturbed by a longing to push her fingers through his hair.

Foul! There was naught she wanted from this man, no matter what he—

His hand slid across her forearm and upper arm, tripping sensation across her skin, and when he probed the pained flesh around her injury, her awareness of him hardly diminished.

He sent word of your capture, she reminded herself, but it was futile. Changing her grip on the dagger, she attempted to send her mind wandering so it would not settle too long on Michael.

"It is not deep," he said. "If it requires a half dozen stitches, it will be much." He looked up. "I am sorry, Beatrix. I would not have seen you harmed like this."

He sounded so sincere—

For his own end, she countered, dragging to mind the hurtful things he had said. "How *would* you see me harmed, Lord D'Arci?"

"I would not," he growled.

"Why?"

"Because I was wrong."

With her own eyes, she saw the words come off his lips, with her own heart, she felt relief that she knew she ought to reject. "You meant it—that I am not the same as…Edithe?"

Did she only imagine it, or did he draw nearer? "You are unlike any woman I have known." The hand he lifted to her face was not imagined, nor the thrill when his calloused fingers caressed her skin. And Beatrix nearly let him kiss her, nearly met his mouth.

She pushed his hand aside. "I want no more of you, Michael D'Arci. Tend my wound if you will, then be gone."

Only when his face hardened did she realize his features had softened during their exchange. Could she call that softening back to more closely look upon it, her gullible self would do so. Fortunately, each new hurt he visited on her made her more prudent. She would not fall his way again.

He released her arm, straightened, and stepped back.

Beatrix clasped a hand over her injury, and neither spoke again until Squire Percival's return.

"What of Sir Justin?" Michael asked as he accepted his physician's bag.

"He was just returning to consciousness when I found him, my lord. By note of his wrath, he shall recover sufficiently."

Michael looked up from spreading his instruments and medicinals on the coverlet. "Where does Sir Justin await me?"

"The kitchen, my lord. I did not think it wise for him and Sir Piers to share the solar."

"Well thought, Squire. And of those in the hall?"

"Quiet, my lord."

"Good. Leave us."

As Squire Percival's footsteps receded, Beatrix looked to the vial that Michael chose, then the needle he lifted for threading.

"It will hurt some," he murmured.

With a curt laugh, she said, "Hurt is something to which I seem to have grown...accustomed."

He met her gaze past the needle, and when he spoke, there was regret in his voice. "So you have."

He lowered to his knees before her, lifted her arm, and began to minister as he had done when she had sustained her head injury. This time, though, she was conscious. This time, she felt every brush of his blunt fingers, breathed the masculine scent of him, and gazed upon his bowed head. And time and again she had to remind herself of the ills he had cast on her no matter what he now believed—or, at least, professed to believe.

Though the pungent salve he applied made the pain tolerable, for those endless minutes she was grateful for his presence that diverted her thoughts from the needle's tug and tuck.

"'Tis done," he finally said.

She eased her hand on the dagger and looked from his face that was level with hers to the linen wound around her arm. The bleeding was staunched, no crimson penetrating the weave.

"I thank you," she breathed.

He nodded. "Now I would examine your head injury."

"For what?"

"A good physician keeps himself apprised of his patient's progress."

A laugh parted her lips. "And now you wish to be a good physician? After all these weeks?"

"Will you allow it?"

"I assure you, 'tis…well-healed. Only a scar remains to remind me of its getting."

"Will you allow it, Beatrix?"

Something in his eyes slipped through a soft place in her hardened heart, and she said, "I will."

He pushed his fingers through her hair and lifted it away.

Beatrix stared at the wall as he traced the ridge with a calloused finger.

"It seems a long time ago," he murmured.

Years. Many years. Indeed, it was as if this life and that had not even crossed paths. All had changed.

"I know you cannot forgive me now," Michael said, "but I pray that one day you will."

Though she longed to believe his sincerity, in that direction lay a fool's quest—one already visited in believing he would not reveal her to Baron Lavonne. "If you knew how to pray, Lord D'Arci, I might... believe you. Now, are you done?"

His eyes shuttered. "I am." He stepped back and swept his instruments into his bag.

Aching deeper than her injury, Beatrix watched him stride across the room with a hitch that bespoke the strain of his clash with Sir Durand. "You will keep your word?" she called as he reached the threshold.

He turned and looked to the dagger in her fist. "You will honor it?"

And yield up her best defense should he or Sir Durand speak false? "As best I can."

From the flare of his nostrils, he understood she would not give up the dagger. "I cannot fault you," he said and pulled the door closed.

Beatrix listened to his tread on the stairs. Too soon, silence fell, bestowing a gift she did not wish to open. But open it she did, rendering up the quiet that was necessary for reflection.

Though she shook her head, it all rushed back—every moment, every word, every expression and emotion. Such sincerity Michael had shown, and how she wished to clasp it to her. How she wished to believe he believed, to care that he cared. But the pinprick of doubt pricked deep, warning of untold pain if she went the way she had gone before.

"I shall not," she told herself. She would have a trial, regardless that Michael and Sir Durand wished otherwise.

She stood and crossed to the corner where she had lain in wait when her brother's man first came within. Unfortunately, her throbbing arm weighted less heavily upon her than fatigue and, though she struggled against sleep, she began to dream dreams she should not.

19

"You love her."

Abruptly, as if run through with Sir Durand's sword that had yet to be sheathed, Michael halted his progress across the solar.

With his back to the fire, legs spread, Sir Durand raised an eyebrow. Though the expression smoothed the hard edges of his face, it remained humorless—almost bitter—and Michael realized there was much beneath the surface of the knight's words. But though Sir Durand might have such feelings for Beatrix, Michael did not. It was guilt that rode him. And desire. Naught to do with the heart, though Canute had also suggested it a quarter hour past.

Before returning to the solar, Michael had sought the stables where his old friend awaited his lord and Beatrix for the ride east. The change of plans and news that Baron Wulfrith's man had come for Beatrix had chafed Canute, but there was no mistaking his relief, for Canute knew as well as Michael that if they took Beatrix from Soaring, they would not likely return—could not return. Thus, he had encouraged Michael to allow Sir Durand to fulfill the task set him by Baron Wulfrith. And been disheartened when Michael refused.

Silently cursing his uneven gait, Michael continued to the foot of the bed, dropped his physician's bag atop the chest, and retrieved the staff he had earlier set against the bedpost.

He turned. "You trespass in believing you know me, Sir Durand, just as you trespassed in deceiving my stepmother in order to steal into my home."

"A necessity that requires no apology."

A grim smiled tugged at Michael's mouth. "Forsooth, I did not expect one."

The knight smiled his own tight smile. "'Tis good we are of a mind."

"Hardly, for I shall not allow you to take Beatrix from Soaring."

The man's brow rippled. "'Tis the answer you seek. If I carry her away, no suspicion will be cast upon you. Thus, your lordship will remain secure."

If not for the rub in his chest that would have been of interest to Sir Durand with regards to Michael's feelings for Beatrix, Michael would not have faulted him for suggesting such. After all, a month past it *would* have been the answer to the question of Beatrix.

Michael stepped his staff forward. At a distance that would grant him space in which to draw his sword, he halted. "I gave Beatrix my word. I shall keep it."

The knight's hand turned restless on his sword hilt. "There are some things for which a man can be forgiven for breaking his word."

"Not this. As I shall keep my word, so shall you keep yours."

"Then you wish her to go to trial? To meet her death?"

"'Tis not what I wish, but what she needs——"

"Needs!" The tip of Sir Durand's sword came up off the floor.

Michael pulled several inches of cold steel from his sheath. "I may yet be somewhat infirm, but if blood is to be shed, yours will flow as readily as mine."

"I will not allow her to die."

"As I will not. Though I shall keep my word that I will not obstruct her trial, if she is found guilty, there my word ends."

"What say you?"

Though Michael's plan was not fully formed, the end result was all that needed to be told—for now. "With your aid, if necessary, I shall deliver Beatrix to Soaring. Or out of England to France, if needs be."

The man's sword tip lowered. "'Tis easier done now."

"If she were willing."

"And if still she is not willing when she stands before the noose?"

Michael set his shoulders back. "That is what a gag is for, Sir Durand."

The knight nearly smiled. "Ah."

"Are we agreed?"

"I will aid you, D'Arci, but this I vow—with you or nay, I shall allow no harm to befall *Beatrix*."

The knight's emphasis on her Christian name, coupled with an easy lack of her title, bode a familiarity that first pricked, then jabbed, an emotion with which Michael was becoming grudgingly acquainted. What man eschewed a lady's title in speaking of her unless she were dear to him? Even he——

It was then he realized he had also dropped the title of "lady" and could not remember when last his thoughts had dwelt upon her as anything other than Beatrix. And there was another thing: Sir Durand had been deliberate in his familiar use of her name, meaning he wished to return to that which he had spoken of when Michael first entered the solar. But love was a place Michael had never been and would not now go.

He returned the inches of blade to its scabbard. "You shall remain Sir Piers."

The knight sheathed his own sword. "So I shall." After a long moment, he said. "If she loved me as she appears to love you, I would take her to wife."

Beatrix loved him? Impossible. Obviously, Sir Durand knew little of women, especially those wrongly scorned and falsely accused. No woman could love so great to forgive such ill. "This time you trespass upon Lady Beatrix," Michael growled. "She feels naught for me but contempt."

"I fear not." Sir Durand pivoted toward the door. "And that is most unfortunate."

Michael bit back the rejoinder that should not be spoken to a man's back. "Cur," he growled as the door closed behind the knight. He crossed to a chair, dropped into it, and thrummed his fingers on the arms.

Wise though Sir Durand affected to be, he was wrong about Beatrix's feelings. Michael would make amends, and that was all. Once Beatrix was gone from his life, all would be well. And lost. But for what did a man need a home when he was a man alone?

Still, as he swept his gaze around the solar, he missed what he had never thought to miss, and now, what would likely never be: a true-hearted wife to share his bed and children to mark the passing of days. Indeed, unless he beget an illegitimate child, the name of D'Arci would never be sown from his loins.

He stared disbelievingly at her barren bed, but then her breath came to him and he followed it to a corner where she sat with her chin on her chest. Fair hair touched by torchlight from the landing outside the room, the hand that held the dagger lax in her lap, she slept—as Michael had been unable to do these past hours.

How long had she clung to wakefulness before losing the opposite battle he had waged?

He glanced at the window that dawn had yet to light and reconsidered his vow to allow her to go to trial. She was vulnerable enough for him to make a lie of it, and he wished to, but his word was all she asked—and wanted—of him. If he took that from her, there would be nothing to hold her to him, and she would hate him all the more.

He bent, eased the hilt from her chill fingers, and slid the dagger beneath his belt. A hand behind Beatrix's back, one under her knees, he lifted her slight figure. Careful not to jostle her injury, he turned and, in one surprisingly smooth stride, reached the mattress. But rather than set her from him, he stared at her. It was not the first time he had considered how much he liked the feel of her, but this time he did so willingly. As if she belonged in his arms, she fit perfectly, and he realized that what he held in that moment he would not likely hold again.

Eager to distance himself from his inner unrest, he lowered Beatrix to the mattress. After confirming her bandage remained dry, he turned the coverlet over her and pulled the dagger from his belt. He would leave it as proof of his vow. Setting it on the squat bedside table, he looked one last time at Beatrix.

He thought her lashes fluttered and frowned at the momentary cessation of her breath. "It is upon the table do you require it," he murmured and walked around the bed.

As the door groaned closed, Beatrix lifted her lids and caught sight of the dagger before the light from the landing swept from the room.

He had kept his word. Thus far.

Having awakened to find her hand emptied of salvation, she had barely had time to close her eyes before Michael turned from the table to the bed. Panic had thrummed through her, born of certainty that he intended to use her lapse to take back his word.

Not this eve, though. The next? With the arrival of the new day, only two nights remained before the sheriff arrived to deliver her to Lavonne.

She shivered. It was as she wished, but the prospect of standing at trial twisted her into a tighter knot. Clenching her teeth against chattering, she dragged the coverlet nearer and tried to think elsewhere.

Numb to all but the heat wafting across the chamber, Aldous Lavonne stared at the brazier's glow and remembered. How many years ago? Six? Seven? Regardless, it seemed much nearer. So near he heard his shouts, then screams. And the pain!

That was not mere remembrance. Providing he remained completely still, it was tolerable. But something so slight as a deep breath could leave him panting for relief from the fire within that no amount of water could quench.

Hearing mutterings somewhere near, he looked around. They did not come from the chamber woman who slept on a pallet alongside his bed. It was his own voice. The voice of a madman? It was not the first time he had put the question to himself.

He clenched his hands. What a fool he had been to enter the burning mill. What a fool to try to save men and women of common birth. After thrice bringing the ungrateful wretches out of the inferno, God's reward was to place a wall of fire before him. There had been no way out but through the flames. No other way to save himself—if one could call "saved" a body almost completely consumed by fire. Still, despite his bitterness, he had clawed his way back to God. Until Geoffrey was murdered. Until this ravaged body was further besieged by a stroke. But the Wulfriths were as much at fault as pitiless God who sat on His throne without a care for his loyal servants.

Vaguely aware that his thoughts were not following a straight path, Aldous reflected on Eve who had been the downfall of all mankind. And for her greed and treachery, men paid the price, honorable men like Geoffrey who had died for Wulfrith's whore, Annyn Bretanne; men like Sir Simon who had died for Wulfrith's whore sister, Lady Beatrix.

Thoughts stumbling out of the dark corridor down which they had wandered, Aldous coughed and moaned at the strain upon his body. When he finally settled, he lifted an edge of the coverlet and dragged it across his spittle-flecked mouth, then returned to that dark corridor where Lady Annyn and Lady Beatrix slithered.

He seethed in the knowledge that the sisters of Eve who embraced the serpent and led men to their deaths had yet to pay a price for their sins. But even if Wulfrith's wife—who should have been Geoffrey's!—escaped retribution, his sister would not.

Harking back to the tidings that Michael D'Arci had released Lady Beatrix from the tower and provided her with lady's garments, Aldous spat across the bed. When Robert's squire, Giffard, had told of it, it had enraged Aldous, but it had hardly compared to his rage over Robert's speculation that D'Arci had fallen under the spell of the Wulfrith whore.

Though it was hard to believe any man would look the way of such a witless creature as Lady Beatrix was said to be, it seemed D'Arci had fallen prey.

"Pity," Aldous breathed. Pity that so fine a physician would likely pay the same price that Geoffrey and Simon had paid. Of course, once Lady Beatrix met her deserved end, Aldous would have no further need of D'Arci's services, for then he could finally release his hold on this accursed life.

Aldous curled his scarred lips and easily justified what he had set into motion by placing the blame on Lady Beatrix who was the same as all women—disloyal, perfidious, deceitful.

Aye, punishment would be given where punishment was due. And royal justice be spat upon! The king's man, recently arrived at Broehne to oversee the trial, had stood at the end of Aldous's bed and arrogantly advised that the best end to Sir Simon's murderer was absolution.

Often the best way to deal with defendants whose minds are not whole, the justice had said.

Aldous had rejected that Lady Beatrix be allowed such a defense, but the man's only response was to smile tolerantly and restate that it was for the best.

It had taken all the will Aldous possessed to not throw his goblet of ale at the man. Christian—that whelp!—knowing the emotions that held together his father's ruined body, had stood at the window throughout the justice's visit, eyes boring into his father, searching for what Aldous intended. Searching, but not finding. And he would not, for this time all would be done without his aid or knowledge.

Though Aldous knew the turning of his lips was only token, the fire having burned away all semblance of a smile, he allowed himself the indulgence afforded by the knowledge that he still had Robert.

Twinged by the affection with which he had once regarded his eldest son, a conniving, self-serving spawn for whom he had provided all despite his illegitimacy, Aldous cast aside the emotion.

Robert had proven time and again that he was undeserving. Still, he had his uses, among them a jealous longing to undermine Aldous's legitimate heir. Thus, when Christian failed to honor his father's wishes, as he did more and more of late, Robert could be counted on to assure that Aldous continued to exercise a measure of control over the barony. Unfortunately, his loyalty did not come without risks, for always the eldest son aspired to prove he was the worthiest of the three. If not for Aldous's warning that not even the deaths of Geoffrey and Christian would see Robert named heir, the eldest would likely have arranged their demise. The possibility had once so frightened Aldous that, upon Geoffrey's ascension to "baron," he had sent Robert to serve at a neighboring barony. And there he would have remained if not for Christian's woeful inexperience. Aldous had called Robert home and had yet to regret the decision, for his eager son did what was asked of him—a perfect fit for Aldous's latest plan. Not that Robert wouldn't need help, but that had been taken care of.

Aldous chuckled as he pondered what a few well-placed coins could buy. Greed shining bright from her eyes, his chamber maid had scurried off to do his bidding—as quietly as possible lest Christian turn suspicious and attempt to undo all that must be done.

"Christian!" Aldous hissed.

In the next instant, a memory of his youngest son opened a path in the middle of his seething—the six-year-old running toward him across the bailey with arms flung wide, leaning out of the saddle to sweep the boy astride, the boy's flushed face and hot breath on Aldous's face, his hopeful smile as he turned a hand around his father's sword hilt, the chastening, followed by gentle teasing intended to draw a smile from downturned lips, their joined laughter...

"Christian," Aldous bemoaned. "Christian." Had he known what lay ahead, he would have allowed his son his heart's desire—would have fit a sword to his small hand and taught him the ways of men who fight. Instead, Christian was taught the ways of men who pray and, in his heart, still believed all the Church had taught him—all his father had insisted he learn, and for which the boy had years later professed to hate his sire.

A sigh slipped from Aldous. Surely there was time yet to remedy his son's shortcomings. Surely he would come around. Though he would never be Geoffrey, still he was a Lavonne. And there was hope in that. There had to be.

20

Two days.

Wishing she had a scabbard, though the linen in which she had wrapped the blade sufficed, Beatrix slid the dagger into the top of her hose and dropped her raised skirts.

Two days, which was the reason she was late to break her fast. Not until the sun had fully warmed her window had she emerged from beneath the coverlet. As she had not been able to sleep since awakening to find Michael over her, she had belabored the memory of Sir Simon's attack—put questions to herself that might be asked at trial. She would be ready. *Must* be ready.

She sighed. It was probably good that Michael had denied her quill and parchment, for the monotonous rehearsal sharpened the telling such that when she spoke aloud her defense, it sounded less stilted. But for all of her practice, it would not be easy. An audience of none was far less intimidating than the many she would soon face.

She turned to the door, lifted a hand to tuck her hair behind her ears, and winced at the pain that shot through her arm. Though the bandage remained dry, Michael would likely wish to examine the injury, forcing her near him again. And that she did not want.

Because you do want it, the whisperer taunted.

Shortly, she entered the hall. It was quiet there, the voices of Lady Maude and Lady Laura the only ones to fill the space where the women lingered over their meal.

As Beatrix neared the dais, Lady Maude looked up. "Lady Beatrix, we did not expect you this morn."

Did she and Lady Laura know what had transpired on the night past? The glances they exchanged told so, but Beatrix doubted many others knew.

She ascended the dais. "I apologize that I am late."

Lady Maude gained her feet. "I would bid you to join us, but already we have lingered too long. Lady Laura?"

Beatrix was disappointed, for she would have liked to speak further with Lady Laura about what she had said in the kitchen corridor days past. It was as if she avoided Beatrix. Or was Lady Maude responsible? Since that day, always Michael's stepmother was quick to her feet when Beatrix came near—quicker yet to take Lady Laura with her. Why? What did she fear?

"You are coming?" Lady Maude prompted when her companion remained seated.

"I shall soon join you and Clarice abovestairs, my lady."

Beatrix looked from Lady Maude, who seemed to hang over the other woman, to Clarice who peered at her from where she stood alongside her mother.

"Then we shall wait upon you." Lady Maude moved to resume her seat.

"'Tis not necessary." Lady Laura shifted her gaze to her daughter. "Clarice has been patient long enough. Have you not, my sweet?"

The little girl nodded and grasped Lady Maude's hand. "I'm tired of here."

A stricken look flashed in the older woman's eyes, but she said, "Then we shall go elsewhere."

Clarice tugged the woman forward. However, when the two drew alongside Beatrix, Clarice paused and once more jabbed a finger at the skirts of her mother's gown. "When you give back?"

Lady Laura gasped.

Beatrix smiled. "Soon." She glanced at Lady Maude who avoided her gaze. "Methinks I shall not...need it much longer."

"Good." The little girl stepped past.

Moving slowly, as if aged another twenty years, Lady Maude allowed Clarice to pull her across the hall and up the stairs.

Lady Laura waved at the platter of viands. "Break your fast, Lady Beatrix."

Beatrix slid onto the bench beside her. Though her appetite had suddenly dwindled, she reached her uninjured arm forward and chose a piece of crusty bread and a thick slice of cheese.

Here was the opportunity she had awaited. However, as she sought to address Lady Laura, her thoughts cluttered and she could not set her tongue to words that ought to be easy to form.

"How does your arm fare?" Lady Laura asked.

"Well, I think."

The lady lifted her goblet. "Lord D'Arci is a fine physician."

Seeking her way back to the path forsaken, Beatrix inclined her head. Now for the answers only Lady Laura could give.

"Be it wine or ale, my lady?" a tart voice intruded.

And Beatrix's thoughts scattered again. She looked to the serving woman. "W-wine, please."

The woman set a goblet on the table, poured, and turned back toward the kitchen.

As Beatrix sipped the wine, she met Lady Laura's gaze over the rim. She lowered the goblet. "I have wanted to speak to you."

"This I know."

"What you said—"

"What I should not have, but I did, and I regret it only for Lady Maude's sake."

"I do not understand."

The sorrow in the woman's eyes doubled. "Only because you have not looked near enough upon my daughter—as Lord D'Arci has never done, though Clarice has given him many opportunities." She sighed. "Of course, one does not see what one does not wish to see."

"You speak in riddles, my lady."

"I speak most plain for any who listen, whose minds are not closed, who——" She gasped. "Forgive me. I forgot that you…"

Beatrix folded her hands in her lap. "Though 'tis true I am oft slow to speak, and sometimes my thoughts…crowd that I cannot speak them at all, my mind is not closed."

"Forgive me," the lady said again. "Too long I have held to me what should be obvious to those nearest." Momentarily, she closed her eyes. "I fear I am burdened by what I cannot tell without doing more harm to one who has done me kindnesses I can never repay."

Lady Maude? But what had Clarice to do with it? And what of Lady Laura's belief in Beatrix's innocence?

"Lady Beatrix——"

Beatrix held up a hand. "A moment, please."

How does it all fit? Think! As her thoughts turned over, Lady Laura bit her lip as if in anticipation of what Beatrix could not quite touch.

…because you have not looked near enough upon my daughter.

If she did, what would she see?

…just as Lord D'Arci has never done, though Clarice has given him many opportunities.

What did Michael not see?

Beatrix lifted her gaze to Lady Laura. For Lady Maude's sake, she should not have told Beatrix that she believed her tale of what Simon had tried to do.

Clarice, Michael, Lady Maude, Simon…

Understanding dawned, and as if Lady Laura saw it on Beatrix's face, the woman nodded.

Beatrix's breath caught. How could she not have seen it? It was all there, every piece joining one with the other, and yet she had been unable to make the fit.

Lord! The Beatrix of old would not have been so slow of wit. Unfortunately, as she was not likely to fully recover, she would have to make do with what she had gained back. And try to be content.

"It happened in the storeroom," Lady Laura whispered.

Where Sir Simon had got her with child. "I am sorry."

Lady Laura looked to her lap. "When I heard Simon was murdered by a lady, I knew the reason." She dashed moisture from her cheeks. "Though Lady Maude did not wish to believe it, methinks she also knew."

"Then she knows what...happened to you?" The moment Beatrix posed the question, the answer struck, returning her to the day she was summoned that Lady Maude might look upon her son's murderer. Lady Laura had been silently present where she stood alongside the bed.

"'Twas she who found me ravaged."

Beatrix saw the torment in Lady Laura's eyes. "And...Sir Simon?"

"He did not deny he had lain with me, but told I wanted it—begged for it though my bliaut was torn and I was bruised near everywhere." A sob punctuated the words. "I was betrothed to a man I loved. Never would I have..."

"I know."

"As did Lady Maude. Still, she bade me to tell no one—to wait upon my menses. They did not come."

But Clarice had. Pretty little Clarice who could not know from what violence she had been sown.

"Your...betrothal was broken?"

"Aye, no man wants a wife who has given herself to another."

"But you did not give yourself."

"Tryst or ravishment, the end is the same: a woman tainted, no lie to hide her swollen belly."

Beatrix understood, though she did not wish to. For Lady Maude, Laura had not raised the hue and cry. Indeed, she seemed to have taken the blame for Simon's cruel act.

"None but you and Lady Maude know the truth?" Beatrix asked.

"None. An unfortunate tryst with a visiting knight, it was told, and for it, Lady Maude vowed she would provide for me and my child." Her weary lids lowered. "My family denies me—refuses to acknowledge that Clarice is of their blood. Hence, Lady Maude is all we have. And she has been so kind."

So indebted.

Lady Laura rose abruptly. "What shall you do with what I have told?"

What could she do? Might she present at trial—

"Whatever you decide, Lady Beatrix, I cannot serve as a witness for you. Though I ache for what you have suffered and what you must face, I will not reveal to all the world what kind of man my lady's son was—especially what kind of man my daughter's father was."

Beatrix's emotions twisted, though she understood the lady's reasons. If Lady Laura *was* believed after so many years of silence, dire damage would be done to those she loved. "I would not ask it of you. I shall hold your secret close."

But the man who had slipped behind a tapestry when Beatrix entered the hall was not certain *he* could hold it so near. Canute clenched his hands and ground his teeth.

This morning, when Michael bid him to watch over Lady Beatrix, he had grudgingly acceded, as yet unconvinced she was innocent of the crime for which she would be brought to trial. Now...

Had he ever made so dire a mistake? What Edithe had done to Michael had made him certain that no word that passed a woman's lips was to be believed, especially when the words cried ravishment. In his mind, all women were guilty of something. But perhaps not. Especially where Maude was concerned. With her, he had come as near to loving a woman as ever he had done. She, whom he respected more than any female, stood back as Lady Beatrix presented herself for certain death. Not that he did not understand why she did it. Were it known what her son had done, the humiliation might kill her. And he must not forget Clarice. Surely it was better she was believed to have been born of a tryst than ravishment.

He listened to the receding footfalls that told only one lady remained at table. Beatrix? The bench creaked, followed by a prayer spoken in Latin. Aye, Lady Beatrix.

A curse upon Sir Durand for interfering on the night past! May he rot——

Canute bit back bitter laughter. A curse on himself for having prayed something——anything!——might turn Michael from his quest to deliver Lady Beatrix to her family. For what he had done in sending word of her capture, he ought to be flogged. Worse! Had he not...

He shook his head. Two days, then Lady Beatrix was Lavonne's.

None tried to stop her, even when she stepped off the bottom step into the inner bailey.

Staggered by Lady Laura's revelation, Beatrix halted. There was nothing she could do with what had been revealed to her. Nothing that would free her of a sin she had not committed. Nothing had changed. She would have to defend herself as planned and pray God was with her.

She looked to the men-at-arms on the walls, then the castle folk who bustled about the bailey to fulfill their service to their lord. They watched her, most firmly Sir Durand who stood alongside the fence that enclosed the inner stables——until the destrier at his back nibbled his shoulder.

The knight turned and extended a hand, from which the horse greedily accepted his offering.

Beatrix put her chin up, her skirts as well, and stepped around a cart. Though she knew Sir Durand remained Sir Piers to all but a few, she crossed to his side.

He frowned heavily, and she knew he did not think it wise for her to approach him. "You should leave Soaring, Sir Durand. There is naught I...require of you."

Ignoring his destrier's nudge, he said, "Naught but my absence?"

Hating that she must seem ungrateful for what he had tried to do, she said, "I am sorry, but it must be as it is. Tell my brother——"

"Methinks it best *you* tell him."

She laid a hand on the top rail of the fence and squeezed. "Pray, Sir Durand—"

"How is your arm?"

"It heals."

"And my dagger?"

Conscious of its press against her leg, she said, "It serves."

He grinned, causing grooves to appear alongside his mouth.

He was handsome, and for a moment she forgot her bid to see him gone from Soaring and remembered all the times he had sought her gaze. Strange that she had never felt the flutterings for him that she felt when Michael—

Rejecting such thoughts, she stepped nearer Sir Durand. "You know you cannot accompany me to Broehne, do you not?"

He patted his destrier's muzzle. "If you go, so shall I."

"I am going, Sir Durand, and if you go, you may be recognized."

"I may be as a spider slung from a beam, Lady Beatrix, but I shall be there—*if* you go."

Then he might not honor his vow.

He leaned in. "Others may not, but I make a distinction between a vow freely given and one stolen."

"Sir Durand—"

"I see your destrier is of a better mind today, Sir Piers," Michael's voice came across the corral.

Beatrix saw he stood in the stable doorway. Wiping his hands on a cloth, he held Sir Durand's gaze.

Though it would be fitting for the knight to draw back, he did not relinquish the narrow space that separated him from Beatrix. "He is of a much better mind today, Lord D'Arci, though I fear it might be another day—mayhap two—ere he sees fit to release me from your hospitality."

"Two days ought to suffice." Michael looked to Beatrix. "There is something you require, my lady?"

"Naught of you, my lord." Across the distance, she saw his jaw tighten.

"He looks to be jealous," Sir Durand murmured.

He was wrong. Surely he was.

"But mayhap I err, my lady."

"You do."

"But not in telling that *you* feel for him."

Feeling as if cut wide and spread for all to look upon, Beatrix glared at him, "Aye, you err. And trespass."

A corner of his mouth tugged. "'Tis as Lord D'Arci said to me last eve."

He had discussed her with Michael? When she looked around, Michael was gone. Had he returned to the stables?

"I would escort you to the donjon," Sir Durand said, "but it does not appear that you require an escort."

She followed his gaze to the landing before the donjon doors where Sir Canute stood. Though his hands were behind his back and his attention appeared to be elsewhere, she knew Sir Durand was correct.

"I wager he has watch over you—to ensure I keep my vow, of course." He sighed. "It seems Lord D'Arci is most determined to keep his own vow."

He was? Beatrix had only begun to ponder it when realization returned her to Sir Canute. Had he been near when she broke her fast? Might he have overheard what Lady Laura told?

Sir Durand jutted his chin toward the donjon. "Go."

She did, but in a different direction. Shortly, she traded daylight for the dim of the stables that housed Soaring's mounts.

A lad, lugging a bucket in one hand, toting a shovel in the other, halted in the aisle between the stalls. "My lady?"

She nearly retreated, but when a snort sounded from a stall at the far end, she knew it was Sartan. And Michael was with him.

She shook her head at the lad, inched up her skirts, and stepped forward.

The boy edged aside to allow her past and continued toward the stable door with his pungent burden.

Of the dozen stalls Beatrix passed, all but four were occupied, and nearly every one by a horse of remarkable color and stature. Sartan was in the end stall.

His great eyes rolled over her as she halted before the door, then he snorted and tossed his head as if in welcome.

Michael did not accord the same, though he had to know he was no longer alone. He kept his back to her where he stood at the destrier's shoulder, his dark head bent to whatever task he tended.

"You should not be here," he bit.

Jealousy? Nay, Sir Durand erred.

"With the injury done you last eve, you should be at rest."

"Sartan is well?"

Michael reached to a pot at his feet. Before he straightened, she caught sight of the gash in the destrier's neck. It was packed in salve, to which Michael added more.

"What happened?"

"The mare was not of a mind to be mounted by Sartan and gave back some of what she got."

Heat rose to Beatrix's cheeks, and she averted her gaze to the earthen floor.

She did not hear Michael move until the stall door opened. "Forgive me, I should not have said what I did."

Seeing the urgency in his eyes, she realized he mistook her discomfort for something else. Fear?

Michael stared into Beatrix's upturned face. What had he been thinking to speak of Sartan's mating with the mare? He had *not* been thinking, so tightly wound by the sight of her with Sir Durand that his tongue had strayed. As soon as the words were out, he had known his mistake and needed no confirmation of it, but confirmation was given when he had looked around.

"Do not fear me, Beatrix. Simon's sins are not mine."

"This I know," she surprised him. "I have…known it for some time."

He stepped nearer and was relieved when she did not retreat. "I ache for you, Beatrix—to hold you and feel your mouth against mine."

Her breath caught. "You desire me? How can that be?"

Denying himself the temptation of her lips, he asked, "How can you doubt it?"

She touched the side of her head. "I am not as other women, not as I once was. Though I have…regained much, what I am is not what a man wants or needs."

He urged her chin up. "If you will allow me, I will show you how wrong you are."

A sad smile scored her mouth. "Desire is not enough."

Whence came the words he next spoke, he did not know, but they slid from him as if there was no question they could not answer. "I did not say it was." He lowered his head.

When his beard brushed her smooth skin, she did not pull away, when the first taste of her met his lips, she did not deny him a second. Such sweetness she was, twisting his desire, recasting it, making something of it he had not known it could be. Always before, desire had resided in his loins only. This was different. Just to touch her, to lay his mouth to hers, to breathe her…

Lids fluttering closed, Beatrix pressed against him and parted her lips.

Michael deepened the kiss, but when he felt his body bind tighter, he drew back. "You lack for naught, Beatrix," he murmured.

Cheeks flushed beneath the sweep of her lashes, she opened her eyes.

As he stared into her vulnerability, urgency gripped him—and fear that the Lavonnes would content themselves with nothing short of her death. "Let me take you from here. Now. This very moment."

She frowned, and he felt her pull away even before she stepped back. "For this you kissed me? To make of me a p-puppet?"

He should have known she would think as much. "Beatrix—"

"Once is enough to be very wrong about a person." She crossed her arms over her chest. "I will not let you do that to me again."

When had she thought different of him? In the rain when she had surrendered to his kiss? When she had nearly staggered to learn word of her capture had been sent to Lavonne? It had to be.

"I give you my word, Beatrix, I will remedy what I have wrought."

"You are saying you would...carry me away without cover of night?" She retreated another step and slid a hand up over her injured arm. "...without tale that I escaped?"

Michael lowered his arms to his sides. "It is as I would do."

Her chin dimpled with emotion. "I am to believe you would give all for me, Michael D'Arci?"

Strange how "all" no longer sounded much. "'Tis true I would not return to Soaring."

She searched his face. "Then you love me?"

The word, small though it was, startled him. Sir Durand had suggested the same and Michael had felt as if struck, but to hear Beatrix speak it pierced him straight through. Why? Because, perhaps, the asking of it meant *she* loved *him*?

Smile as tight as a bowstring near release, she raised an eyebrow. "I did not think so. Desire only, then, Lord D'Arci, and what a fool you would be to...yield all for the mere ease of it."

She was wrong, of course, but love?

She turned away. "*That* I would not ask of you."

Michael stared after her as she traversed the aisle between the stalls, and he too soon found himself alone with a mire of emotions. But that was remedied when the horses turned restless in their stalls and Sartan snorted loud in answer to the appearance of young Giffard.

Michael castigated himself, not only for what the squire might have come upon had Beatrix not retreated, but that Beatrix had made him forget what had summoned him to the stables. Sartan's wound had required further packing, but that had merely occupied Michael while he waited for Sir Robert's squire to deliver news from Broehne.

Michael nodded the young man forward.

With a stride that spoke of self-possession, Squire Giffard followed Michael into the vacant stable opposite Sartan's. Here it was safe to speak, for even if a cat wandered into the stables, the horses would alert Michael.

"What tidings, Squire?"

"Most worthy, my lord." Looking the knight he would be when his training was complete two months hence, Giffard drew himself up to his full height. "The baron's father has directed Sir Robert to accompany the sheriff when he delivers Lady Beatrix to Broehne."

That did not surprise.

"And in doing so, to be of good heed."

A threat to Beatrix? Feeling a vice about his chest, Michael said, "Continue."

"Brigands, my lord—hired to ensure the lady does not reach Broehne."

Had Aldous Lavonne so little confidence in securing Beatrix's death sentence? Why?

"It seems the justice who has come from London is not amenable to the baron's desire," the squire answered Michael's unspoken question. "He seeks absolution for the lady."

Absolution. The word that had angered Michael when Beatrix had spoken it in the darkness of the crypt, momentarily beget the opposite emotion, but no absolution could there be if she was killed en route to Broehne.

"When? And where?"

The squire grimaced. "I fear 'twas not told, my lord."

That would make it difficult to defend against, especially as the men Michael would need to assemble would have to follow at a distance unbeknownst to the sheriff or Aldous Lavonne's men.

Had the missive told more than what Sir Robert had revealed in Giffard's presence? Unfortunately, the old baron was sound enough of mind to seal the missives carried by the squire, ensuring the contents were viewed only by the one for whom they were intended.

Still, Michael was grateful for what he did know. It was fortunate Sir Robert did not suspect his squire's loyalty—a loyalty gifted to Michael for the personal interest he took in the boy's training.

"You have done well, Squire," Michael said. "I thank you."

Squire Giffard pivoted and opened the stable door.

As the horses roused with Giffard's passing, Michael looked to his hands. Regardless that these past years of lording had rarely put a weapon to them other than for practice, his palms and fingers were hardened and calloused from years of knight errantry. What had once maimed and killed, now more often healed, but he would be ready for Lavonne's brigands.

To their grave misfortune, *they* would not be ready for him.

21

QUILL, INK, PARCHMENT. All that she had asked for and been denied. And there was more. She stepped to the chair and small table that had also appeared in her chamber.

Biting her lower lip that too well remembered the kiss pressed upon it a quarter hour past, Beatrix picked the speckled quill from the ink pot.

Had she been wrong to reject Michael? Might all he had done been for love, though he reacted as if repelled by the word? Did a man do this for desire only when there were women aplenty to bed? What did Michael feel for her? And what did she feel for him? True, he had offended when she had asked if he loved her, but her own insides had twisted to hear the words come off her lips. Did she love him? Was that what this ache was? She prayed not, for nothing could come of a woman like her loving a man like him.

Ink ran down the quill's shaft and formed a bead that hung from the tip long enough for Beatrix to sweep the quill back to the ink pot.

"He wished you to have it," Sir Canute said at her back.

She turned to where he stood in the doorway and noted he looked less imposing than usual. "You are following me."

"A charge I have been given."

"One you do not like." She was pleased with her crisp delivery. Wondering what he wanted with her, wishing he would let it be known that she might ask about Lady Laura, she said, "Honesty is a virtue, Sir

Knight." But how honest would he be if she inquired into his whereabouts when Lady Laura had revealed her secret pain? And if he had been lurking, would he honor the lady's bid to keep the tale from other tongues? "Were you near this morn when I came b-belowstairs to break fast?"

His mouth soured at the corners. "I was—and near enough to learn a truth I would not have guessed."

She nearly groaned. "You should have shown yourself."

"I was to remain as unobtrusive as possible that you would not feel like a prisoner."

A prisoner when *she* refused to escape. "Considerate," Beatrix clipped. "What do you intend, Sir Canute?"

"It is not my tale, and yet Lord D'Arci ought to know."

Know that the little girl who adored him was his niece? Though Beatrix agreed that Michael should be told, it was not for Sir Canute to do.

She crossed the room to where he stood at the threshold. "As Lady Laura's confession was not meant for you, I pray you will...affect to have not heard it."

He looked down from his lofty height. "Then you will not use the tale for your defense?"

Though she felt small in his shadow, she did not step back. "As I told Lady Laura, I will not."

"But without it, you have little with which to defend yourself."

"The truth and God shall serve as my defense." The words poured from her without slop or drip, and she was heartened that she continued to progress even without benefit of anger.

She glanced over her shoulder. "And now, also, I have a means of writing it down lest my tongue turns wrong."

The knight considered her, then nodded. "I think you will prevail, my lady. Indeed, it shall be my prayer."

Dare she believe his sincerity? "I thank you."

Though she expected him to withdraw, he said, "An apology is due you, my lady—one, methinks, that will explain much I am certain my lord did not tell."

"What is it?"

"I betrayed my lord, and for it was relieved of my guard over you the day following your arrival at Soaring." His jaw convulsed. "Michael rejected my urging to send word of your capture to the baron. Thus, I kept a vow he had demanded of me years ago and sent word myself."

She blinked. "You?"

Color smudged his cheeks. "Though my lord would not admit it, I could see he doubted your guilt—that whatever had happened between the two of you had begun to turn him to a man who thinks first with his loins. And I feared that if he went that way, he would lose all."

Beginning to tremble, Beatrix reached for the wall alongside the door and braced a hand to it as the mortar with which she had built walls around herself began to dissolve. Michael had not sent word.

Canute touched her shoulder. "You should sit down."

She looked up. "I did not believe he would tell of my capture, and when he said he had..."

"I am sorry. In trying to protect a man no longer in need of my protection, I erred grievously."

Michael had wanted her to believe he was so unaffected by her that he had not hesitated to send word to Lavonne, had wanted her to think she did not know him, had accused her of being no different from—

"Pray, Sir Canute, who is Edithe?"

As if Beatrix had turned leprous, he dropped his hand from her and stepped back.

She followed. "I beseech you, tell me."

His teeth clenched, but finally he said, "Edithe is the reason I did what I did, and that is all I can tell, my lady."

"But he accused me of being the same as she."

"He may have said it, but he knows you are not."

And had said so on the night past. What had Edithe done that Sir Canute would not tell? What great ill weighted Michael?

The knight turned away. "If you require me, I shall be on the landing below."

"Sir Canute!"

He looked around. "My lady?"

"Thank you."

His lids briefly lowered. "You are more generous than I would be."

"I understand why you did it."

"Nay, you do not, but methinks one day Lord D'Arci will tell you all." He strode onto the landing and halted. This time when he came around, it was not at her urging. "'Twas that woman who gave my lord reason to believe that of which you are accused," he said.

Then Edithe had killed someone dear to Michael? Beatrix opened her mouth to ask, but the knight began his descent of the stairs. When he went from sight, she crossed her chamber and sank onto the chair.

Michael had not sent word. She lifted fingers to her lips in remembrance of his kiss. It had felt so real. For a moment it had made her think—

What? That she and Michael...

"Impossible." But were it possible, Michael would lose all as Sir Canute feared, for the baron would not suffer his vassal to have any relation with her. And regardless of what Michael wanted, she could not ask him to give up Soaring. She did not know how she knew, but it was very real to him—something he would miss to his end days.

He had not sent word.

She lowered her head to the table and gave in to the longing to know, even for a short time, what she had thought to never know—what she had never truly wanted before Michael.

He had not sent word.

She looked to the writing instruments.

He *did* care for her.

She pushed to her feet only to pause. It was a mistake to seek him out after what had happened in the stables and tempt what should not be tempted. But naught would happen, she told herself. She simply needed to speak with him.

Treading her conscience, she hurried from her chamber and descended the stairs to where Sir Canute turned a furrowed brow upon her.

"My lady?"

"I seek your lord's solar."

"He is not yet returned to the donjon. Indeed he may not return for some time."

She had not expected he would, as it seemed he spent much of his days out of doors between the workings of the inner and outer baileys. "I shall await him in the solar."

Sir Canute sidestepped, barring her advance. "My lady, I am certain Lord D'Arci would prefer that you remain in your chamber."

Ignoring the voice that told her to heed the knight, she said, "Will you escort me, or do I go alone?"

Grudgingly, he led her down the corridor.

The solar was empty as expected. What was not expected was the starkness of the chamber that had escaped her notice when Michael had summoned her here to tell her she was leaving Soaring. It was he who had filled her gaze, turning all else to shadow that now had form, minimal though it was.

Though fairly large, the room was furnished with the bare necessities, as if it belonged to one of lesser nobility rather than the lord of the castle. The only luxury was the scent of woodruff wafting from the rushes. No covering upon the long table against the wall, and set around it, two worn chairs. No curtains around the bed that boasted only a simple coverlet. No gilded, carved chest, but a plain iron-banded box. And the walls...

Though flecks and patches of paint were visible, it was many years since the scene that spanned the chamber had known form.

"Soaring has been thirty years without a lady," Sir Canute said.

"You are…perceptive, Sir Knight."

"Not always, it seems."

She allowed a sympathetic smile. "Thirty years," she murmured and stepped farther into the solar. "Why so long?"

She heard the rushes rustle as he followed her within. "Ere Lord D'Arci was named lord of Soaring, it was held by Lord Chavelle. After his wife died birthing their first child, and with her their babe, he did not wed again."

Love? It seemed every nobleman wished an heir to pass his possessions to. Had Lord Chavelle's wife been more to him than proof of his prowess?

Beatrix glanced at the bed. And what of Michael? Because of Edithe he also denied himself an heir? Or might he be betrothed?

The possibility drew a line of ache through her.

"Is there anything you require, my lady?"

Wishing he would be perceptive again and answer her unspoken question, Beatrix shook her head. "Naught but your word that you shall not…violate the confidence with which Lady Laura gifted me."

"I will think on it."

Beatrix watched him pull the door closed, then once more considered the furnishings. She swallowed hard when the bed fell to her regard. "Nothing will happen," she whispered. "Nothing I do not wish to happen."

And therein lies the problem, does it not?

She turned her mind to what she might do with what could be hours before Michael's return and hit upon the answer. Though by now she ought to be able to present her tale of what had happened at the ravine all those months past, she would pass the time preparing her defense.

She was in his bed.

Michael closed the door and, amid the flicker of torchlight, crossed the solar. As he neared the bed, the dagger atop the clothes chest drew his regard—the same Beatrix had taken from Sir Durand. Dare he believe its presence there indicated she trusted him? If so, why?

He looked at where she curled on the opposite side of the mattress. She slept, at once provocative and innocent in the shifting light that fingered her silken hair, chased across her features, and sighed over her gowned legs and hips.

When he had come abovestairs following a day of preparing his men for the ride to Broehne, he had been unsettled by Canute's warning that Beatrix awaited him within—that she had done so through the nooning and past the supper hour, taking her meals abovestairs. And now, to see her in his bed after she had spurned him in the stables...

Nay, it was for something else she had come. For a moment, he entertained she had changed her mind about allowing him to steal her from Lavonne's revenge, but it was not so. Later, after the trial, he would himself deliver her to her family, regardless of whether she was freed or the sentence of death was pronounced. *That* she could not turn him from.

Though he knew he ought to rouse her, he was stopped by the sight of her. Though he knew he ought to seek the farthest corner, he lowered to the mattress edge.

Lips parted, lashes shadowing her cheekbones, eyes moving beneath her lids, Beatrix continued to sleep.

He did not know how long he sat staring at her, but sometime later he used the excuse of fatigue to lie down. The three feet that was all that separated them was a mistake, making him ache to hold her. How could he have ever believed ill of her? One had but to gaze upon her and hear her voice...

Though it seemed hours before sleep took him, Michael fell into dreams of the brigands who would try to take from him what did not belong to him.

When had he come within? Hour after hour had crawled by until Beatrix had so tired of defending herself to the walls that she had fallen asleep in a chair before the hearth. Sometime later, she had awakened, cramped and aching. She had resisted the bed, knowing it was inappropriate but had finally succumbed. What had Michael thought when he found her here?

Though her cheeks warmed, she did not retreat but watched him sleep in the gray before dawn. The hard angles of his face had softened, causing him to look more approachable than she had seen him. Once again ignoring her inner voice, though it spoke louder than ever she had heard it, she scooted across the mattress and leaned over him.

Dark hair fell across his brow, his straight nose flared with breath, and his usually grim mouth relaxed amid a stiffly whiskered jaw. Remembering his lips on hers, she closed her eyes.

"What is it you want?" he rumbled.

She opened her eyes and found him watching her.

"What, Beatrix?"

She drew back. "I should not have…"

He turned a hand around her arm.

The injury done her two nights past protesting the pressure of his fingers, she startled.

"I am sorry." Michael released her.

Across the slow light of coming morn, Beatrix met his gaze and knew there was concern there. "My arm is fine."

"I should examine it."

"I must needs go."

"Why?" His question was so softly spoken she wondered if it was merely the breeze come through the windows.

"It is wrong for me to be here."

"I do not think so. But tell me why you made it clear on the day past that you want naught to do with me, and now you are in my bed."

"I did not intend to lie down. I…" She shook her head and blurted, "You did not send word."

He frowned.

"Of my capture. You did not send word to Lavonne."

"Canute," he muttered, then said, "In my anger, I let you believe 'twas me who sent word. I thought you had deceived me, that I had deceived myself into believing you were different from..."

"Edithe."

"Aye, Edithe."

The name came off his lips so raw and bitter Beatrix felt his pain. She lowered to her side to face him. "Though Sir Canute...confessed to sending word to Lavonne, he would not tell what Edithe did to you. Will you tell me?"

With a scornful sound, he curved a hand around her jaw. "Speak of a woman like that when I have a woman like you in my bed?"

She laid a hand over his. "A woman who should not be here. But I shall stay if you will tell me of her."

He glowered.

"For her, you believed ill of me. Am I not to know whose sins I have borne?"

"It was a long time past."

"But not so long that you have forgotten it."

That he could not argue, and Beatrix deserved to know why he had retaliated against her. Too, perhaps the tale would help her to forgive him for his treatment of her.

"I have forgotten none of it," he said, "for it would have been the end of me had Canute not released me from my chains."

"Chains?"

Even now Michael could hear their rattle, feel their weight about his ankles and wrists, the manacles abrading his flesh as he strained against them with an anger so profound he felt as if it was another he watched from across the dark, dank cell.

"Her name was Edithe Warbole, and she was the daughter of the baron with whom I fostered during my knighthood training. She was fair of face and beginning to curve where a woman ought to curve, but I had little interest in one promised to another. Still, she sought my side, and more frequently once I was knighted."

The image of the cunning woman he conjured made him tense further. "Though I scoffed at Canute when he warned me that she sought a way out of her betrothal to a man three times her years and would use me to that end, I listened to him—well I did, even when she attempted to rouse my jealousy by trysting with household knights too fool and too tight in the loins to leave her be."

"One eve, after I had partaken of too much drink, I did not turn her away when she caught me upon the stairs." He remembered her pretty face and pouting lips, tasted the deception of her mouth. "She led me to her chamber, and we…" A bit more light crept through the windows to reveal Beatrix's drawn face. "I took what she gave, Beatrix, and I have ever lived to regret it."

"What happened?"

"Her father came upon us and she accused me of ravishment."

The disbelief of Beatrix's expression told that she grasped what had made him believe Simon's attempt to ravish her was a lie.

"She beat at me, bit and kicked as her father dragged me off the bed—and did not cease with her lies even when the men-at-arms battered me bloody. I was thrown into a cell and remained there for days."

The dank scent struck his senses, and he closed his eyes to invoke the cell again. "The door opened, and there was the baron. I thought it was death come for me, but he offered something he was certain I would accept—marriage to Edithe, and with it, lands of my own."

"You did not…?"

"Accept?" he spoke for her, only to regret his impatience. "I did not. No man would wish his daughter to wed a man who ravishes. I knew he had discovered the truth of her—had he not already known of her many trysts. In my anger, I named Edithe a whore and vowed I would never fetter myself to one so deceitful. Not even for land."

Michael saw again the baron's florid face and felt the man's spit on his brow, then his fists. "I was beaten again and left to die." Hatred washed over him as it had done that day.

Beatrix slid a hand over his bearded jaw. "I am sorry."

He knew she was—that she was as far from Edithe as the earth was the sun. Suppressing the need to pull her to him, he laid tense fingers to her lips. "I thought you were the same, that you falsely accused Simon of ravishment as she had accused me."

"I know. And now I understand."

But could she forgive him?

She pressed a kiss to his fingers. "How did you escape?"

Gripped with the memory of the cell door swinging open, peering at the light past swollen lids, Michael pulled his hand from Beatrix. "Canute sacrificed his fealty to the baron to free me. During my years of training, he had been as a father to me. As if I were a son to him, he came for me. 'Twas then I demanded his vow to never again allow me to fall prey to a woman. And his vow he kept in sending word of your capture."

"Did Edithe's father give chase?"

"Token only, though he made it known across the land that I was a ravisher of maidens. As I was welcome nowhere, I was forced to become a knight errant to make my way."

"What of your family?"

"Had I asked, my brother would have aided me as best he could, but I did not. It was enough that I paused from time to time to be with them—and young Simon." Remembrance of the boy aroused Michael's grief. "I thought I knew him, but there are things we do not always see in those with whom we are nearest."

"You could not have known."

"Perhaps."

"Did Edithe wed her be—"

Michael clamped his teeth to keep from supplying the word she sought.

"Betrothed?" she finally said.

He almost smiled. "Another knight was convinced to take her to wife. Six months following our tryst, she birthed a large, healthy boy child. 'Twas told the babe had hair of darkest red, unlike mine or his mother's."

Beatrix pushed up on an elbow. "Then you were absolved."

"It is not so easy, that. It was evidence enough that I had not stolen her virtue, but not enough to wipe the lies from the minds of those who feared for their daughters."

Beginning to seethe again, Michael forced himself to focus on the woman before him rather than the one far behind. With each passing moment, Beatrix became clearer, pushing Edithe into the shadows— deeper and deeper until he had hope she would remain there.

He brushed the hair back from Beatrix's eyes. "I ask for your forgiveness. Will you grant it?"

Her mouth curved, stinging him with the need to fit his lips to hers. "I shall."

As much as Michael longed to lose himself in her, he wanted—nay, needed—to hear what she had yet to voice.

"Why did you come, Beatrix?"

Her smile wavered and she lowered back to the pillow beside him. "When we arrived at Soaring, I...was certain that, though I asked it of you, you would not send word of my capture to Baron Lavonne. So sure was I that your heart knew I could not have done what was said of me. Then you told otherwise and I realized I could not tr—"

"Trust?" Michael picked the word for her and nearly groaned. *Lord, to be a patient man!*

"Aye. I thought I could not trust myself to know you or anyone. Then Sir Canute told 'twas he who sent word, and I realized I do know you, Michael—*have* known you. That I can trust myself."

"What is it you know of me, Beatrix?"

She looked down. "That you care for me."

He did, and more. Did she know that as well? "For this you came? To tell me this?"

"Aye."

"Why?"

"Because of what is in here." She slid a hand to her chest.

Michael felt as if he held his breath. "What is that?"

"Something without end. Something that both pains and…
pleasures."

He would describe it so himself. How ironic that Beatrix, with her
difficulty in speaking, could voice what he could not.

She met his gaze. "Methinks it is love."

The word sank into him, and he wondered how long he had waited
to hear it.

"And yet," she continued, "is it possible to love one who does not
return that love?"

Now she asked of him what he had asked of her. And he knew the
answer, but to speak it…"It surprises that you could feel such for me,"
he said, only to castigate himself for denying her. Though the solar was
yet too dim to see the color of her eyes, he imagined something flickered
in their depths.

"You could not have known about your brother," she defended him
despite her disappointment over his lack of words. "And after what
Edithe did…"

Michael slid his fingers up her jaw and across her smooth cheek.
"She shall touch my life no longer, nor yours." If only he could say the
same of Aldous Lavonne.

Pulling her nearer, Michael savored her warm breath that fanned his
face. "If you would allow it"—he angled his head and brushed his mouth
across hers—"I would make love to you, Beatrix."

Her silence weighted the spaces between them, but then she pressed
nearer and touched her lips to his. "As it may be all we ever have of each
other, I yield."

Need rolled through Michael. The stored impatience of all these
weeks spilling from him, he pushed up, turned her onto her back, and
claimed her mouth. But as he tasted her, her words returned to him—
words he had chosen to let pass in order to meet the needs of his flesh.

As it may be all we ever have of each other, I yield.

Though not so long ago, she had entreated him to yield to God, here
he was as far from yielding as he had ever been, allowing base desires to

corrupt and tempt her to do something she knew was wrong. All because she did not trust that they would be together after her trial. Though she claimed she did not fear the outcome—was certain God would be with her—she did not go so far as to trust in her deliverance.

"Michael?"

He met her questioning gaze and realized he had pulled back.

"What is it?"

He fell to the mattress beside her. In the utter still, he knew she believed he had rejected her. Then he heard her breath release and felt the mattress give as she turned from him. He looked to where she curled on her side.

Was he destined to hurt her at every turn? He leaned over her. "Beatrix, look at me."

She turned her head and her sorrowful gaze met this.

"Not like this," he said and brushed his lips across hers. *Patience,* he counseled as the brief contact made him ache deeper. If there was to be anything beyond this day for them, he must become what he was not—a patient man. Or as near to one as he could come. "I do not want to regret our joining, and I especially do not want you to regret it."

Beatrix rolled onto her back. "I do not understand."

In the dawning of day, he rose from the bed. "Aye, you do. You understand better than I."

She stared at him, then all of her seemed to recede into the mattress. Averting her gaze, she said, "Too well I know."

Michael started to turn away, but her pain pried at him, and he knew that what she needed he could finally give her. "When you come to me, it shall be as a chaste bride—as God wills."

Her lids sprang back, revealing eyes that sang with disbelief.

"'Tis so. I love you, Beatrix."

Her gaze wavered amid tears. "But I am not…may never be…" She swallowed. "You are sure you do not mistake d-desire for something it is not?"

"I am well acquainted with desire, and though I desire you, this is far more."

His sincerity gripped Beatrix's heart, but still it was hard to believe he felt so much for her.

"I shall have you to wife, Beatrix, this I vow."

To wife when tomorrow she would be given into the hands of the sheriff? When her path lay crooked, narrow, and abounding with uncertainty? When it meant Michael would lose all?

"Unless," he said, "you choose the Church instead."

The Church, which she had once longed for and which might still be possible providing her speech continued to improve. Would she choose it over Michael? Or was it a matter of should she choose it? She stared into his beloved face and knew.

She sat up. "I want you, Michael, but on the morrow, when the sheriff—"

He laid a hand to her cheek. "Though I have never been a man of God, I have found my faith. Share it with me, Beatrix. Aid me in yielding to God."

She relinquished the argument and settled a hand over his upon her face. "I shall."

He bent to kiss her.

Knuckles rapped at the door. "My lord!" Squire Percival's voice came through the wooden planks. "The sheriff has come!"

22

"You do not need those."

Beatrix turned to where Michael stood in the doorway of her chamber and caught her breath at the sight of his beardless jaw. *He is not Simon.* Still, the resemblance made her heart stutter. *He loves you.*

"I vow you shall not," he said softly.

She looked to the square of linen into which she had folded the herbs picked from his garden—courage in the palm of her hand. Courage he did not believe she needed. He was right, especially now that she had his love. She lifted her chin. "I shall hold you to your word."

With a slight smile, he slid his gaze down her mantle—the same one she had taken from him at Broehne.

She bit her lip and fingered the bit of red visible past the dark lining she had once more turned to the outside.

"Nor do you need that," he said. "I shall have Squire Percival fetch a mantle better fit for a lady."

"I do not wish another."

"It looks like it belongs to a beggar, Beatrix."

How it looked did not matter. What mattered was that it yet carried his scent, impossible though it seemed. "Still I shall wear it."

After a long moment, he nodded and strode into the tower room, the ring of metal drawing her gaze to the chain mail he wore. Though it was not uncommon to don armor for a journey, she was bothered that he had done so. When he had come to Broehne and then followed her to the abbey he had not.

He halted before her.

Beatrix searched his smooth face above hers and once more ached over the absence of beard that had this morning teased her cheek. Did he not realize how much he resembled his brother, dark of hair though he was?

Forcing herself to see Michael beyond Simon, she said, "You shaved."

"The better to present at trial when I stand at your side."

At her side...She folded the herbs into the cloth and handed them to him.

He ignored the packet. "It disturbs you, Beatrix?"

"Even if you and...Simon shared only a father, you have much the look of one another."

He dragged a hand across his jaw. "I did not consider that, but had I"—he lowered his arm—"still I would not wish to hide behind a beard."

As much as she might want it, she could not ask it of him. She looked to the folded linen with its promise of courage. "It is something of a shock, 'tis all. I had forgotten how much—"

He lifted her chin and set his face so near hers she had only to lean in to meet his mouth. "I am Michael, and I vow never again will you know sorrow at the hands of a D'Arci."

Strange that his resemblance to Simon diminished the nearer he drew. Because of what was in his eyes that could never have shone from his brother's?

When he bent his head, Beatrix closed her eyes.

"Look at me," he said low.

She did.

"See 'tis me who kisses you..." He caressed his mouth across hers, then pulled her nearer. "...who holds you..." He lifted her hand from her side and pressed it to his mailed chest. "...who loves you."

Michael. How could she mistake him for any other?

"Who do you see, Beatrix?"

"Only you."

"As I see only you," he said, and she realized he referred to the shadow thrown by Edithe that no longer fell upon her.

He stepped back and opened the purse on his belt. "Now I have something to show you—something I no longer need." He drew forth a lock of flaxen hair.

Beatrix blinked. "That is mine?"

"In tending your wound at Broehne, I had to cut away some of your hair. Though I kept a lock as a reminder of the one who had taken my brother's life, the more I came to know you the less I remembered my reason for carrying it. It simply reminded me of Beatrix Wulfrith, a woman I could never hope to have."

She smiled. "In that you were wrong."

"For which I thank God."

She touched the lock of hair. "I also thank God that you no longer need this."

"Aye. For what do I require a part of you when I have the whole and ever shall?"

Daring to believe it, she laid a hand on his chest to feel the beat of his heart. However, it was not detectable through the chain mail. "I have not seen you in armor before."

Michael stiffened. "It is a long ride to Broehne."

"No longer than when last you rode there." When, wearing his mantle, she had brushed past him on the drawbridge.

"A mistake."

More than a mistake, but she knew he would tell no more. She laid her head to his chest. "If only we could have had one more day."

"There shall be many more."

He could not know that. Still, she was heartened to hear him say it.

He released her. "You are ready?"

"Nearly so." She stepped to her bed, lifted the pillow, and returned the herbs to the place she had earlier secreted them. "Now I would pray. Will you pray with me?"

Discomfort grooved Michael's face, and she was certain he would refuse, but he crossed to her side. They knelt and, to her surprise, it was Michael who yielded up the words. Though they were stilted and broken as of an uncertain child at his father's knee, he asked for guidance and protection during the journey and, lastly, Beatrix's deliverance at trial.

"Amen." He met her gaze. "Now you are ready?"

She accepted the hand he offered and rose. "I am."

As were his men, Michael reflected, though another day would have better prepared them for what was meant to assure Beatrix did not reach Broehne.

With that thought, he nearly cursed Aldous Lavonne who had surely arranged for the sheriff to arrive early—Aldous who had either learned his plan for revenge was compromised or feared it might be. However, Michael would not commit the sacrilege of uttering vile curses so soon after beseeching God's blessings. God willing, Sir Durand would not disappoint. But if he did...

Quelling the impulse to renew his offer to steal Beatrix away, Michael said, "Let us not keep the sheriff waiting any longer."

At the threshold, Beatrix looked over her shoulder at what she left behind. Not much, really, excepting the quill and ink that told all that Michael had been unable to tell until this morning.

"I did not thank you." She looked to him. "I do."

"I should have sent them sooner."

She shrugged. "Though I believed I needed them, I have found my way."

"As have I."

Her heart convulsed. How strange that he should love her, and yet how obvious it should have been. The Michael D'Arci of these past weeks was not the same man who had stood over her at Broehne and demanded justice. Love had changed him. But was it a love destined for nothing?

Fervently wishing to return to his arms to deeper impress upon herself the memory of him, she looked at his hand on hers. And nearly smiled at the bare glimpse afforded of her own.

"If you truly wish to do this, Beatrix, we must leave now."

Another offer to steal her away. "It is as I wish."

He stepped aside for her to precede him.

At the first landing below, Squire Percival awaited them. "Sir Canute tells that all is in readiness, my lord."

Though Beatrix knew she should not make anything of Michael's hesitation, it unsettled her. What if he—

"I am pleased," he said with what sounded like false ease.

She turned, but before she could voice her fear, he said, "I have given you my word, Beatrix."

Was she so easily read? Could *she* so easily read *him*? Though tension remained about him, his eyes seemed true. They *were* going to Broehne.

"I trust you," she said and turned to resume her descent, but before she set foot on the first step, a door down the corridor opened.

"Lady Beatrix," Lady Laura called. With Clarice gripping her skirts, she hastened from Lady Maude's chamber. "This is for you." She thrust a bundle into Beatrix's arms. "A gown, a veil, a circlet—"

"And Momma's slippas," Clarice chirped, her face turned up like a flower to the sun, "but methinks you feet not big enough."

Beatrix nearly laughed. "Then I must needs stuff the toes?"

The little girl nodded.

Beatrix touched her shoulder. "I shall miss you, Clarice."

"When you come back?"

"I…"

"Worry not," Michael interjected. "You shall see Lady Beatrix again."

Such promises he should not make. And were they alone, she would tell him so.

As if satisfied with Michael's assurance, Clarice hugged an arm around her mother's legs.

Beatrix met Lady Laura's gaze. "I thank you."

Though the lady did not speak another word, her eyes told that she wished Beatrix well.

Next, Lady Maude stepped into the corridor. Clasping her hands at her waist, she met Beatrix's gaze, inclined her head, and turned back into her chamber.

"Come," Michael urged.

Gripping the bundle, Beatrix began her descent. Halfway down, she asked over her shoulder, "They shall not attend the trial?"

"Maude is most indignant, but I am sending them home."

Of course. If he stood at her side, Soaring would not be his to return to. Not his to protect—or its inhabitants. Thus, he would not leave those he loved in Lavonne's vengeful hands.

She halted and turned to where he stood above her. Grateful Squire Percival did not follow closely, she implored, "Love me though you do, I beseech that you affect otherwise, that you do not—"

"The only way I want Soaring is with you, Beatrix. Without you it means naught."

Then he would lose all.

"Now go."

Aching, she took the remaining steps to the hall and was grateful when Michael drew alongside her. Out of the corner of her eye, she saw Squire Percival step past and cross to the doors.

She looked around the great room. Seated at the lord's table was the man whom she guessed was the sheriff. At first, he did not notice her, intent as he was on a conversation with one of Michael's knights—Sir Robert?—but the others seated around him soon called his attention to her.

The sheriff shoved back, causing his bench to screech. "At last!" He traversed the dais, and the knight with whom he had been speaking followed.

"Fear not," Michael spoke low.

The sheriff halted before Beatrix. "Lady Beatrix of Stern?" he said with steely formality that sent hushed silence around the hall.

"I am."

"I am the sheriff, Baron Tyrell. By order of the justice of the royal court, I am charged with delivering you to Broehne, the seat of the barony of Abingdale, that you be handed up for trial for the murder of Sir Simon D'Arci, brother of Michael D'Arci, son of Lady Maude D'Arci. How say you?"

She foundered, but when her lids threatened to flutter, she put her chin higher. "I am not guilty of the crime you have…cited, though I shall willingly answer my accusers."

Merciful Lord, only one slight hitch to my speech! Now if the trial would go so smooth.

"Willingly!" scoffed the red-bearded knight who stood alongside the sheriff.

Feeling Michael tense, Beatrix shifted her gaze to the taunting eyes of the man she had glimpsed from beneath her hood the night of her arrival at Soaring. Though she had seen little of him since, when he fell to her regard, she sensed he watched her.

"And what other keen insight have you to add to the good sheriff's summons, Sir Robert?" Michael asked.

Color rose up the man's neck. "I was merely—"

"Aye, you were," Michael dismissed. "If your men are ready, Sheriff, Lady Beatrix is eager to proceed to Broehne."

"Of course they are ready," the sheriff snapped.

"Then let us ride." Without regard to what any might think, Michael gripped Beatrix's elbow and led her forward.

"You should not," she whispered, hoping her words would rise past his hard jaw to his ear.

He did not loosen his grip.

"Where is Sir Durand?" she asked low as they stepped into the sunshine.

"Gone ahead," he said with a look that told her to ask no more.

Why? Unfortunately, she would simply have to trust that Michael knew what was best. She looked to the horses. There, held by Squire

Percival and standing more glorious than any destrier, was Sartan, a berth of space around him that no other horse boasted.

"Sartan is sufficiently healed for the ride?" Beatrix asked.

"Well enough to carry two," Michael said as they entered the inner bailey.

For all the admiration due the noble beast, apprehension stole up Beatrix's spine. Attempting to quiet her fear with reasoning—telling herself it was better astride Sartan with Michael than astride a milder horse alone as she had braced for—she pressed her shoulders back.

Michael led her forward. However, for all her show of surety, she trembled when he gripped her about the waist to hoist her into the saddle.

He paused, pulled her left hand from the bundle she carried, and laid it on Sartan's muscled neck. "He knows you, Beatrix, and I shall be with you." At her nod, he fit his hands to her waist again.

"D'Arci!" the sheriff exclaimed. "A horse has been provided for the lady."

Michael settled her into the saddle and took the bundle from her. "She rides with me, Baron Tyrell." He fit Lady Laura's gift into a saddle bag.

The sheriff stepped alongside Michael. "This is unseemly."

Though the man ranked well above him, Michael fit a foot in the stirrup and swung up behind Beatrix. "My apologies, Sheriff, but I will not argue the matter." He accepted the reins that Squire Percival reached to him.

Baron Tyrell sighed. "As you will."

Sir Robert, however, was immensely displeased. Upper lip curling to reveal discolored teeth, he stood at the base of the steps and stared at Michael and Beatrix.

She did not yield to his gaze, ardently vowing she would be the last to look away. And she was. Sneering, Sir Robert strode to his mount.

"Dear Lord," Beatrix whispered, "enemies all around."

But what of Sir Canute? She searched the dozen who took to their mounts and recognized an aged knight among them. It was Sir Hector who had fought Sir Ewen to the death. The same who, eager to resume his search for Gaenor, had not heeded Beatrix's protest against leaving her alone with Sir Simon though the knight's eyes and words had told he knew it was a risk. Still, he likely believed her to be a murderess. Had Lavonne ordered his man to be among her escort? Or had the knight volunteered? If the latter, did he seek retribution for Sir Simon's death?

Sir Hector met her gaze. Though the encounter was brief, she glimpsed none of Sir Robert's malice. Shortly, he and the others urged their mounts forward.

As Michael turned Sartan to follow, Sir Canute came into view where he sat astride his destrier before the inner drawbridge. He also wore armor. Despite the certainty that something was afoot, relief swept Beatrix to know Michael was not alone.

Passing over the drawbridge, he slid an arm around her and pulled her back against him. Though the hard links of his mail made for an uncomfortable seat, it felt more right than anything in the world. In Michael's arms was where she belonged.

Distracted time and again from the watch he kept for Lavonne's brigands, Michael silently cursed his arm around Beatrix's waist that made him keenly aware of the first cradle their children would know. Now was not the time to be distracted, not with brigands awaiting their chance in the woods. Such a fool love made him!

He considered the stream they approached. Unfortunately, it was necessary for the horses to take water. Fortunately, Michael had thwarted Sir Robert's earlier call to enter the wood by announcing they would rest further on where the stream ran deeper and clearer out of the wood, knowing it would be easier to defend against an attack in the open rather than amid the trees. Sir Robert had been most unhappy.

Beatrix looked over her shoulder. "Must we stop?"

Having sensed her growing trepidation during the long ride, Michael was momentarily surprised by her eagerness to reach Broehne. But perhaps she also sensed that they were followed.

"What bothers you, Beatrix?"

"What lies ahead. I wish the b-burden lifted from me."

"It shall be."

"When I think of all I have gained that I might now lose…"

Michael ached for her. "I shall not allow you to go to your death."

No sooner did she ease against him than she stiffened. "What do you intend?"

He ground his teeth. "A trial I have promised, but there my word ends. Do you understand?"

Her nostrils flared, and he knew she feared that what he intended would bring him ill. He pressed his lips to her forehead. "I will suffer no argument."

"You should not show such affection!"

"Nor will I fear Lavonne." Still, he looked over his shoulder to be sure there was no movement in the wood behind. Nothing of Lavonne's brigands, nor of Michael's men who rode watch there. God willing, the latter would overtake the former and Beatrix would be spared the knowledge of what they intended.

He looked back around and caught the gaze of several of their escort who were not quick enough to look away.

"They watch us," Beatrix murmured.

"You think I care?"

"You ought to."

"All will come 'round. You shall be my wife and the mother of our children."

Beatrix searched Michael's pale eyes and turned more determined that *she* would secure her release. Never again would she run from anyone, and certainly she would not suffer Michael to do so. She turned forward as the horses were reined in before the stream and tried to appreciate the sunlight that appeared between gathering clouds.

Though it took little time to water the horses, from the tension Michael exuded, it was as if he were being made to wait hours. Even Sir Canute and Squire Percival appeared eager to resume the journey. Not so for Sir Robert and several others. Leaving their destriers at the stream, they gathered a distance away and talked among themselves.

"To your mounts!" Michael called.

A protest rose from Sir Robert's group.

"Not even a quarter hour is gone, D'Arci," the sheriff said between chews of dried meat. "Another quarter hour will do no harm."

Michael lifted Beatrix back into the saddle. "You may linger if you are so inclined."

The sheriff hastened to his mount, as did the others.

"Something is amiss?" Beatrix asked as Michael fit a foot in the stirrup.

He settled behind her. "If we arrive late, it will bode ill to interrupt the baron's supper."

Nay, it was more than that.

As Michael turned Sartan from the stream, Beatrix looked to Sir Canute who held his back so straight it was as if it had been put through with a pole. And Michael was no less rigid. He put his arm around her, but before he turned his hand about her waist, he touched his sword hilt.

As he spurred Sartan forward, Beatrix considered the wood. What was there?

It would be nearly three hours before an answer was forthcoming.

23

THROUGH THE SOFT rain and gray of twilight that slowed their party to a trot, Beatrix peered from beneath her hood as the crumbling walls of Purley Abbey came into view. Though her escort likely paid little attention to the ruins, she could not look away. It was there she had begun to learn Michael. There he had first touched her. Did he remember?

When she looked around, his gaze told that he did.

"We shall pause there," he said.

"For what?"

"For what I denied you." He considered the beaten road, and she knew he touched his sword again as he urged Sartan to a gallop that carried them past their muddied entourage.

"Lord D'Arci!" the sheriff called.

With Sartan kicking up sodden earth that sprayed those behind, Michael guided the destrier off the road and up the incline.

"You are certain, my lord?" Sir Canute spoke above the rain as he and two other knights drew alongside.

"The better of two evils," Michael said, continuing toward the abbey. "Be prepared."

"Evils?" Beatrix asked. "Prepared for what, Michael?"

He halted Sartan before the nave and swung out of the saddle. Hood fallen back, rain flecking his hair, he said, "I shall return anon."

"I will accompany you."

He laid a hand on her knee and glanced at his knights where they halted to the left. "I would have you remain with Sir Canute."

"D'Arci!" the sheriff called again as he and the others neared. "What do you?"

Michael adjusted his belt to bring the hilt of his sword nearer to hand, then stepped to Sartan's head and clapped the destrier's jaw. "I leave her in your care, my friend," he murmured, then strode toward a portion of outer wall reduced to a height of less than three feet.

Beatrix watched him scale the crumbling wall and continue toward the breach in the ceiling of the crypt. Did he intend to go down into it? What was there that he believed he had denied her? However, he did not pause at the breach, though he did glance down as he passed.

Then she knew. He sought the psalter she had left in the chapel when he had forced her from the abbey. But there was something else to which he aspired: the better of two evils, and the reason he had so often touched his hilt throughout the ride.

When a rumble struck across the land, Beatrix thought it was thunder, but thunder did not rise to war cries, nor take the form of a score of riders who surged out of the wood behind the abbey.

Brandishing death beat of steel and honed to slaughter, the brigands swept toward them, and not even the absence of sunlight off blades could detract from the terrible sight. And Michael was at the center of it.

The fear Beatrix had refused to feel at Soaring gathered and panic struck at the realization that all she had gained these past weeks might now desert her...cripple her...once more make her a fool who could not turn her tongue around words. But then came anger. "Michael!"

Sword to hand, he lunged back the way he had gone. However, there was too much distance separating him from his destrier, and he was forced to come around amid the ruins to fend off the first rider who leapt the opposite wall.

Though fear urged Beatrix to dismount when Sartan hooved the ground, sense made her abandon her sidesaddle pose. Yanking up her skirts, she tossed a leg over Sartan and straddled him.

"Canute!" Michael shouted. "Get her away from here!"

As the knight reached for Sartan's reins, Beatrix searched out the remainder of the entourage. The sheriff wielded his sword, as did several others, including Squire Percival, but Sir Robert and his group were slow to react. Indeed, the knight appeared more intent on her than the brigands.

Sir Canute dragged on Sartan's reins to turn him. With a snort and a toss of its massive head, the big horse sidled away.

A moment later, the crash of swords defiled the murmur of rain. As Beatrix watched Michael turn his blade off the sword of a man who swung steel from atop a horse, another brigand spurred toward him, while a dozen others set themselves at Beatrix and her escort. And more riders came out of the wood. It seemed hopeless until she realized that the newest arrivals were not brigands. They were Michael's men, surely set to follow at a distance in the event of an attack.

Feeling Sartan strain against Sir Canute's urging, then shift his weight backward, Beatrix gripped the pommel and tightened her thighs.

Sartan reared, causing her hood to fall back and the reins to tear free of Sir Canute's hand. Upon his return to the ground, the great destrier pulled right and lunged away.

Beatrix held on as the beast gathered its legs beneath him, but then she saw Michael. Whereas moments earlier he had faced two brigands, now there was one. Though she had never wished death on anyone, she prayed he would drive down another to the dark abyss from which such evil was bred.

"My lady!" Sir Canute shouted as he attempted to overtake Sartan. "The reins!"

The muddied ground rushing below her, she raised her head as the destrier rounded a mighty oak that grew between it and the road—the road that would take her away from Michael.

She caught the reins and threw her weight back, causing Sartan to halt and jerk his head side to side. As she attempted to turn him back toward the abbey, Sir Canute neared. And behind him came brigands.

The knight dragged his mount around and swept his sword up to fend off the first attacker. Though his swordsmanship was apparent with the first blow, the brigand seemed a fair match.

Beatrix looked to the others who came for her and caught a glimpse of a rider who sought to overtake her pursuers—Sir Hector, the aged knight who had abandoned her to Sir Simon's vile attentions. He was also setting himself at her? No sooner did the dread thought strike than he landed a death blow to one of the brigands.

"Beatrix!" Michael's shout rose above the grind and clatter of steel.

She saw him leap the fallen wall. Rain-purified sword showing no evidence of the men it had put through, he ran toward her. It was then more riders came out of the wood.

Mother Mary! Surely Michael and her escort could not—

A brigand came alongside her. Decayed teeth filling his mouth, he swung his sword high.

Beatrix turned Sartan aside, but she was not to know whether she reacted quickly enough, for Sir Hector once more came to her aid. As blade met blade bare feet from her, a whistle split the air that she recognized as Michael's means of summoning Sartan.

"Away, my lady!" Sir Hector shouted.

Even before she gave the destrier her heels, it set its course. Intent on answering its master's call, it lunged past Sir Hector, then Sir Canute who had taken his own struggle with a brigand to the ground.

Beatrix searched out Michael and saw him step over a man he had surely laid down. But there were yet others who came for him. He deflected another sword, causing the rider to veer, but when the attacker came back around, Michael's healing leg made him lurch.

Merciful Lord, do not allow him to sacrifice all for me!

Beatrix urged Sartan onward, but as she neared, an extraordinary thing happened. One of those riding toward Michael slew one of their own. At least, she thought they were of the same bent, but when she looked nearer on the man who had let blood, she saw past the rain and gathering dark that it was Sir Durand.

Had he come with Michael's men who had followed from cover of the wood? She swept her gaze over the battling warriors, and her heart nearly bolted when she lit on a face dear to her.

Her oldest brother, Garr, was there, and to his left fought her younger brother, Abel. They had come for her. And the men who next surged around her were Garr's household knights.

The great destrier's flight arrested, Sartan danced about in search of an opening.

"Hold, my lady," a knight called as he edged his mount nearer.

She pulled the reins, but Sartan was too agitated to obey, and became more so when Michael shouted again. Beatrix craned her neck and saw another brigand was fast upon him. "Nay!" she cried.

Michael sent thanks heavenward that Sir Durand had succeeded in the task set him to reach Garr Wulfrith and his men who, en route to Soaring, had surely been forced to ride hard to compensate for the day stolen from them by Aldous Lavonne's conniving. And more thanks he gave that Beatrix was now under the protection of her brother's men. Between sword strokes, he had seen the brigand raise his sword to her and had tried to reach her, but it was not only Beatrix's death that was sought. For defying Aldous Lavonne by loving a woman marked for revenge, the brigands also came for Michael, as evidenced by the number who set themselves at him.

It had come as no surprise that they had attacked at Purley Abbey. As the assault had not been a question of "if," but "when," they had met at the place of Michael's choosing. And he had been the bait to tempt them out of the wood.

Still, despite all that had gone in Michael's favor—above all, Sir Hector going to Beatrix's aid—it was no guarantee that his men and Wulfrith's would prevail.

Lord, Michael prayed, *if naught else, keep Beatrix safe.* A moment later, the brigand before him exposed the vulnerability of his neck and Michael swung. The man toppled face down in the mud.

Rain running into his eyes, Michael surveyed the ruins he had chosen for his battleground. The sheriff was engaged, as was Canute. As for Aldous Lavonne's men, they offered only enough resistance to assure they did not meet the fate intended for Beatrix and Michael. Fortunately, Michael's and Wulfrith's men were felling those in whom Lavonne's men took little interest.

It would be over soon and, God willing, he would still be standing.

As he searched out his next opponent, he caught sight of a formidable warrior who had set himself at three brigands. It had to be Garr Wulfrith. Though Michael had only heard of him, he had met several of those whom Wulfrith had trained into knights while fighting for Duke Henry. All worthy. All deadly—as would have proved the next brigand if Michael had not glimpsed his approach.

Putting a two-handed grip to his sword, he swung around to meet the one who came on foot. Their blades clashed, the force of their meeting clearing the miscreant's grin. With a roar and a spray of spittle, the brigand swung again and caught Michael's sword arm.

Almighty! Though his chain mail did not fail him, the blow shot pain fingertip to shoulder. Turning away the next blow, Michael grunted as spasms shook his forearm. He needed space, and he knew where to find it.

Putting his back into his next swing, he sank his blade into the flesh of his pursuer's upper arm. It disabled the man long enough for Michael to make for the wall of the nave. As anticipated, the brigand followed him over.

Mud sucking at his boots, the dimming of day cloaking the ruins in lengthening shadows, Michael took the path traveled once before when Beatrix was the prey. Thrice he came about and hefted his sword to widen the space between him and the brigand, twice more he drew blood, and with each step he led the man the way he had once gone. This time Michael cleared the breach.

A shout...a resounding crack...silence.

Michael swung around, straddled the sodden ground, and put his sword before him as a mounted brigand swept forward.

Lord, I yield to you. Guide my sword and ever shall I endeavor to be worthy of Beatrix. My tongue I will curb and my impatience.

At the last moment, he sidestepped, swept up his sword, and nearly gained the man's head.

Issuing vile curses not unlike those Michael had spouted when he had landed in the crypt, the brigand turned his horse before the small chapel. It was the last time he would charge; however, when he rose from the mud, he was sword ready. Though not as big a man as the one who lay at the bottom of the crypt, he was agile, responding to Michael's swings as if the sword were an extension of his arm. Blow for blow he gave, push for push, his only weakness a recklessness likely borne of having nothing for which to live. A weakness Michael no longer shared.

Measuring each sweep of the sword, knowing where his blade would strike before it landed, Michael forced the man toward the chapel where Beatrix had slept while he occupied her crypt. The brigand stumbled on the threshold but righted himself before Michael could do more than leave a mark on his face. He would not live long enough for it to scar.

Into the dim chapel they went and, shortly, a tormented cry spilled into the nave.

Beatrix peered through the rain at the chapel and prayed it was not Michael who had shouted, while all around the remaining brigands gathered their horses beneath them and flew back to the wood, leaving behind more than a dozen who had bled out their lives for a purse of silver they would never spend.

"'Tis done," a household knight said at her back.

For Michael as well?

"My lady, are you harmed?" Sir Durand drew alongside.

Staring at the chapel, Beatrix shook her head. *Come out, Michael. Pray, come out.*

It seemed a lifetime before a figure appeared in the doorway, but by the width of his shoulders, the dark of his hair, and the flutter of her heart, she knew who it was. Before any could gainsay her, she slid from Sartan's back.

"Beatrix!"

Vaguely aware it was Garr who called, she lifted her skirts and ran. The rain, continuing to pour from the sky as if from a pitcher, ran off her hair and down the neck of her mantle, but she hardly noticed. There was only Michael.

She knew when he saw her, for his stride lengthened in spite of his uneven gait, and his grim face lit amid the gathering darkness.

"Beatrix!" If not that her brother caught her shoulders, she would have collided with him.

She peered up at him where he had lunged into her path. "Garr."

He searched her face with such intensity, it was as if he did not quite believe it was her. Then he enfolded her in his thick arms. "God has answered my prayers."

Despite her longing for Michael, she clung to the big man whose love for her she had never felt more strongly.

It was Abel who pulled them apart with a derisive snort. "You are not the only one to have worried over our sister, Mighty Wulfrith."

Garr relinquished her. Though their youngest brother's arms did not enfold her as tightly, he laid a kiss to her brow. "At last, our little sister is returned to us."

Beatrix afforded Abel a fond smile before searching past him to where Michael stood twenty feet back. His brow troubled, he watched. Waited.

"Michael," she breathed and pulled her arm from Abel's grasp. But as she stepped past, Garr once more set himself in her path.

"Beatrix, he is Lavonne's man."

"No longer." She shook her head. "He renounces all—"

"Beatrix—"

"I love him!" And she did not care if those who had drawn near heard.

Garr's jaw tightened. "'Tis as Sir Durand tells, but—"

"He loves me."

Garr looked down his long nose at her. "Loves you when 'tis told you killed his brother?"

"He knows different now—that I but defended myself, that it was a...an accident."

"And you are certain he believes this to be true?" It was not really a question, but scorn for a heart he believed to have made a fool of her.

Beatrix took a beseeching step toward him. "Surely you saw how he...fought for me."

"Aye, but it could be trickery—devised to draw the Wulfriths out that Lavonne might work greater revenge for the death of Sir Geoffrey."

"You are wrong."

"You are going home, Beatrix."

She stumbled back. "Nay—"

"Baron Wulfrith!" Michael called.

Garr turned, and only then did it occur to Beatrix that her brother had exposed his back to a man of whom he believed such ill. But a moment later, she saw the reason for his confidence. As her brother's men had been trained to do, they had taken control of the gathering of knights and men-at-arms. Though their numbers were fewer than Michael's and the sheriff's men combined, the circle they drew around the others ensured greater numbers were not needed to defeat those trapped within their net.

"Lord D'Arci?" Garr continued to deny himself his sword despite the one Michael yet gripped.

"Your sister wishes a trial," Michael said, seemingly undaunted by the Wulfrith show of strength.

"This Sir Durand has told."

"Then you also know she shall have her trial as I have promised her."

"As is required by law," the sheriff announced. As he urged his mount forward, a barely perceptible signal from Garr caused one of his knights to check the sheriff's approach. Though Beatrix expected the same when Michael strode forward, Garr allowed his advance, the only move he made being to settle a hand to his sword hilt. And that told more than any sweep of the blade could.

"Garr, I beseech——"

With one swift move, he set her back from him. "Abel!"

Seeing her younger brother advance, Beatrix lunged forward and placed herself between Garr and Michael.

With three strides separating him from Wulfrith, Michael halted. Remembering the last time Beatrix had erected herself as a defense between two men, he growled, "I will not allow you to come between me and my opponent again, Beatrix."

"My brother is not your...opponent." She looked back. "Are you, Garr?"

Wulfrith turned his hand around his hilt. "Any man who sets himself against me is my opponent."

"Aye, but not any woman, as was taught to you by your own wife, Annyn. It is *I* who opposes you, Garr. *I* who wishes a trial. *I* who extracted Michael's vow that I be allowed to prove my innocence."

"Stand aside, Beatrix!" Michael thundered.

She threw up her hands. "Do you not see? You want the same thing— to keep me from Lavonne's retribution. But I will not live out the... remainder of my life in hiding." Her blue eyes blazed. "It is not what God intends for me. And so I yield to Him who knows well His plans for me. I will go to trial. I will trust in Him."

To Michael's surprise, her words caused the fire in her brother's eyes to dim, his jaw to loosen, and his hand on his hilt to ease. "Beatrix," he rumbled, "what you ask——"

"Not ask, but require. You must trust my decision, and Michael as well." She took a step toward her brother. "As your heart knew Annyn, so my heart knows Michael."

Wulfrith stared at her and Michael knew he struggled against his warrior self that demanded he deliver his sister. Finally, Wulfrith settled his gaze on Michael.

Michael did not waver, but returned the renowned warrior's scrutiny. Aye, a big man—broad of shoulder, deep of chest, and long of leg. Massive, and yet more agile of foot than a smaller man, as evidenced by the brigands he had effortlessly laid down. If needs be, Michael would give him a good fight, but it was doubtful he would be standing at the end of such a match. Still, he would cross blades with him if Wulfrith determined to place himself between Beatrix and the vow Michael had made her. Unfortunately, Beatrix knew it as well, continuing to defy him by standing as a defense between him and Wulfrith.

She took another step toward her brother. "Faith, Garr. Surely you can grant me this."

Hand flexing on his hilt, he said, "I can, but only for so long. I do have other vows to keep, Beatrix."

"Garr!" the younger brother protested.

Wulfrith lifted a staying hand. "It is done, Abel. Now let us be of good care that I not regret it."

Beatrix ran into Michael's arms. When he did not enfold her as he longed to do, she lifted her face to his.

"Michael?" She winced as her gaze swept the broken flesh that ran from his brow to his hairline. "You are hurt." She reached to his face.

He caught her hand. "I am well." His voice was tight with the anger he fought to suppress.

"If my in-interference has wounded your man's pride, I am sorry, but you asked of me what I could not do. I will not stand meekly aside while...bloodlust grows between two men I love."

He searched her face, agonized over the fear he had felt that he might lose her, wondered how he had ever come to care so deeply for another, questioned why someone like him should be gifted with the love of a woman like her.

Was it God at work—opening a door to which Michael was hardly worthy, making him yearn to be worthy regardless of what might be required of him? He closed his eyes and, as he found himself doing of late, turned his thoughts heavenward. *Lord, fill me as You fill Beatrix. I am Yours.*

"Michael?"

"I understand," he said, and there, before all, he tipped up her face and closed his mouth over hers. As she leaned in, it was as if there was no rain, no ruins, no others.

"Night is nearly upon us!" the sheriff intruded. "It bodes ill to remain without castle walls while brigands run the wood."

Michael released Beatrix. "I have something for you." He pulled the small, black object from beneath his chain mail.

She stared at it. "My psalter."

Gotten from the chapel into which he had driven the brigand. "I am sorry for having denied you its comfort."

She smiled. Then, seeing her treasure was in danger of becoming a sodden mess, she hurried it beneath her mantle.

Michael sheathed his sword and turned her toward her brothers who waited alongside their destriers.

"D'Arci," Wulfrith said as they neared.

Michael halted before him, while beside him Beatrix tensed. "Wulfrith."

The warrior stepped forward and, in a voice that would not carry, said, "Sir Durand tells me you received word to expect such an attack."

"I did."

"From whom?"

Michael drew an arm across his drenched face. "A friend."

"You will not tell who this friend is?"

Time aplenty to learn to trust Wulfrith. "I will not, though I will say that the tidings that Beatrix was not to reach Broehne was intended for one of Soaring's knights—Sir Robert, who is among our escort and who sought to facilitate his liege's yearn for revenge."

"His liege being Baron Lavonne," Wulfrith growled.

"Nay, not the baron."

Wulfrith's brow furrowed. "Make yourself clear, D'Arci."

"This is not something Christian Lavonne would do——"

"Ha!" Abel guffawed.

"He is not such a man," Michael said, "but his father is, and though Aldous Lavonne is infirm, he yet commands much of what happens upon the barony."

"How is that possible?" Wulfrith demanded.

"By way of men who remain loyal to him——men like Sir Robert, Aldous Lavonne's eldest, albeit illegitimate, son."

A glimmer of surprise was all Wulfrith allowed. "I see. And what of Christian Lavonne's place in all this?"

"Unfortunately, for reasons to which none are privy, he allows his father his mischief."

"The little monk is a coward, then," Abel muttered.

Michael nearly laughed to hear Christian described so. The baron was a bigger man than either of the Wulfriths, which was saying much, and though Christian had yet to find his stride as lord of all he possessed, none who knew him would name him a coward.

"Continue," Wulfrith prompted.

"Though 'tis true Christian knew of the raids on your lands, and in the beginning may have condoned them, it is his father who ordered them. Christian simply..." Michael shook his head. "...allowed his father to work revenge for the death of his son." No coward, but a man torn.

"And what of the brigands who set upon us? You are saying Christian Lavonne had naught to do with them?"

Michael was struck with the realization that though Christian may have been privy to his father's plans, he had sought to subvert them by sending Sir Hector and other loyal knights with the sheriff. This time, he was not allowing his father what was no longer his to command. There was comfort in that.

"That is what I am saying. Though he surely suspected what his father intended, he did not condone or hire the brigands."

Wulfrith's eyes locked on his, and Michael felt as if the man delved far beyond his dilated pupils. "So once more, the baron of Abingdale simply stood back."

"Nay, he sent knights loyal to him to escort your sister to Broehne—among them, Sir Hector, who saved her life."

"It was Sir Hector who laid down the brigands? The same who slew my man, Sir Ewen?"

"The same."

Wulfrith looked to where the older knight sat his horse, and Michael knew he struggled to reconcile the one who had slain one of his knights with the one who had delivered Beatrix. "I see. Then Aldous Lavonne fears my sister will not meet her end at trial."

"Aye, the justice who has come to Broehne seeks absolution for her."

Beatrix gasped. "You did this, Michael?"

"I did not, though I would not oppose it were you granted a privilege often afforded those who are noble."

"But I do not want absolu—"

"This I know, Beatrix." To fight the impatience endeavoring to undo him, he clenched his hands. "But Aldous Lavonne does not. For this, he sent the brigands."

"And shall be surprised when my sister and you arrive alive and whole," Wulfrith said.

Then, despite his distrust of Michael, he had been aware that Beatrix was not the only one who should have met her death among the abbey ruins.

"Let us not make him await his disappointment longer than necessary," Wulfrith said. "Mount up!"

Drawing Beatrix nearer his side, Michael stepped past the Wulfrith brothers. Though fury tempted his hand to his sword as he neared Sir Robert and those who conspired with him, he did not pull it. There would come a better time. The ache in his calf turning his uneven gait to a limp, he was grateful when Squire Percival led Sartan forward.

"Lord D'Arci," Sir Robert called, "by measure of your limp, it appears you have further injured yourself."

Though Michael could not prevent his hand from gripping his hilt, he did not unsheathe the sword but met the eyes of the knight who gazed out of heavily creased lids. "And it appears you are none the worse, Sir Robert." He looked to the man's companions who contrasted sharply with the others who wore the sure marks of battle.

Though none were near the years of their youth, neither were their bodies broken such that they could not wield a weapon—especially Sir Robert whose sinewed bulk defied his weathered face.

"Indeed," Michael added, "one might question whether you, or Sir Charles, or Sir Philip raised a sword."

The knight's face colored.

Michael looked to the sheriff whose tunic was splattered with blood. "What do you think, Sheriff?"

"Most curious."

It was good he had seen to their protection himself, Michael brooded, and looked to those he had caused to ride the wood. But not all were present. Nor were they expected to be, for the brigands had known their swords well. Still, Michael's anger stirred. Every one of his men he knew, especially those he had convinced to abandon the mercenary life of knight errantry by promising them better at Soaring. Hopefully, Michael's dead were not among the few who had taken wives and sown children.

Michael looked to Squire Percival. "How many lost?"

The young man's mouth grimmed amid a cut and abraded face. "Of Soaring's men, my lord, three."

Three who would have lived if not for the venomous Aldous Lavonne. Three who might have lived if not for the perfidious knights set to watch over Soaring.

Though Michael knew now was not the time to determine which of his men had fallen, he swept his gaze over those the night attempted to conceal from him. Sir Dominic was absent—unwed. Sir Martin was absent—unwed as well. Sir Thomas—widowed, his wife having died birthing a girl child who would now be two summers old.

Michael tried to cap his anger, but habits too far from being called 'old' surfaced. "Curse Aldous Lavonne!" He released Beatrix and swept his sword from its scabbard.

"Michael!" She caught his arm. "Do not!"

Though he longed to shake her off that he might feed this yawning ache to avenge his men and a little girl who was left with naught, he met Beatrix's beseeching gaze.

"Not here. Not now," she pleaded. "Wait on Him, Michael."

"I wager they do not bear so much as a scratch!" he seethed.

"Even so, trust in Him who delivered you from the brigands and sent Sir Hector to my side."

Michael followed her gaze to the aged knight who sat upon his mount to the left of Sir Robert—a man to whom he owed more than he could repay. A man who had once served Aldous Lavonne. A man who, though he spoke not a word against his former liege, had transferred his fealty to the youngest son. And for it, Beatrix lived.

Michael thrust his sword into its scabbard, then lifted Beatrix into the saddle and settled behind her. As he turned Sartan toward the road, he caught Sir Hector's gaze and nodded him forward.

The knight drew alongside.

"I owe you much, Sir Hector."

"In that you are wrong, Lord D'Arci. Not only was it my charge to watch over the lady, but I had a debt to repay."

"What debt?"

"The lady knows of what I speak." Sir Hector spurred his horse and became a shadow in the night.

"Of what does he speak, Beatrix?"

She looked up at him from beneath her hood. "That day at the ravine, I...beseeched him to not leave me alone with Sir Simon. Though Sir Hector"—

Her next words escaped Michael as a memory returned of the day he had answered the summons to Broehne Castle and found Simon laid out in the hall. Sir Hector had been there. Sir Hector who had said little. Sir Hector whose regret had slipped away each time he glanced at Simon.

—"to fear," Beatrix finished.

"What was that last you said?"

"Though Sir Hector assured me I w-would be safe, 'twas as if he knew that I had reason to fear."

Michael clenched his hands. Though he had finally accepted what Beatrix accused his brother of having tried to do, the possibility it might not have been the first time Simon had trespassed upon a woman made him ache deeper.

Pieces. Always more pieces. But would there be enough to construct an adequate defense to free Beatrix? Was there something to which Sir Hector might testify that would aid her?

Those questions and others would have to wait, for it was growing darker and Broehne Castle was yet distant.

24

BEATRIX HALTED JUST inside the doors and looked around the hall that had been shadow-fallen the night of her escape from Broehne. Even now there was not much light, their arrival having been delayed well past the supper hour when the castle folk bedded down for the night. However, the three torches lit upon their arrival allowed her to pick out the benches and pallets on which many made their beds.

"Lady Beatrix," a familiar voice called from across the hall, and two figures rose from the lord's table.

Michael squeezed her elbow. "I stand at your side."

She looked up at him. "This I know."

Baron Lavonne, accompanied by the sheriff, stepped from the dais into the dim light. "I pray you will forgive my state of dress," he said as he advanced, a robe belted about his tall figure. "I had just retired to my chamber when word was brought of your arrival."

Word that had been delivered more than a quarter hour past when first the sheriff and Sir Hector, then Sir Robert, entered the donjon and Beatrix and her escort had been made to wait outside. Feeling the presence of her brothers at her back, knowing they would not be content to remain there, she stepped forward. A few moments later, she and the baron faced each other at the center of the hall.

Christian Lavonne looked down at her from his lofty height, and in his gaze was anger. However, a moment later he turned it on Michael. "D'Arci."

"My lord."

Not for much longer, for surely the baron would not tolerate his vassal's support of her. It made her ache.

"I am told you were waylaid by brigands." The anger in his voice deepened.

Beatrix did not have to look at Michael to know contempt curled his mouth. "It could not have been Sir Robert who told you so, as I would have wagered my life he was largely unaware of the attack."

Garr stepped forward, drawing so near Beatrix that his shoulder brushed hers. "Agonize not, Baron Lavonne, for I vow the brigands will plague your barony no more."

As if only then noticing Beatrix's brothers, though that was impossible considering their weighty presence, Lavonne shifted his gaze to Garr. "And I suppose I have you to thank for that, Baron Wulfrith."

"Among others."

"A show of force, hmm?" Christian Lavonne shrugged his shoulders back. "So, the Wulfriths once more honor Broehne Castle with their presence." He shifted his gaze to Abel who stood over her shoulder. "It has been many years. Welcome."

Silence tensing in the spaces between them, the sheriff stepped forward. "It appears all is in readiness for a trial on the morrow, Baron Lavonne."

Christian Lavonne looked at him, and Beatrix sensed he was not pleased. Why? Though she would have liked to believe it was, indeed, because he was unlike his father who sought her death—that he wanted no part of it—she did not venture hope there.

"Then a trial we shall have," he said, tightly.

"Of course"—the sheriff glanced at Beatrix—"if you wish to hold a day or more—"

"Nay," the baron said. "Not only am I certain Lady Beatrix would have the matter done with, but the justice has waited long enough to continue his circuit. Tomorrow it shall be."

"Then already a jury is chosen." Danger darkened Garr's voice.

Lavonne looked to him. "It has been determined that the accusing jury shall also stand as the trying jury."

As Garr tensed further, Beatrix knew he struggled to keep his word that she would be allowed a trial.

"'Tis late." Lavonne looked behind. "Sir Hector will see you to your chambers abovestairs."

As the knight stepped from the shadows surrounding the dais, the sheriff cleared his throat. "Pardon, Baron Lavonne, but the justice has ordered that the lady be delivered to the corner tower in the inner bailey."

Though Beatrix knew tower rooms were often used to accommodate noble prisoners, affording them much of that to which they were accustomed, it was still a prison. And from Michael's stiffening, he liked the idea less than she.

"Then the justice ordered wrong, Sheriff," Lavonne surprised them all. "Even if only for this night, the Wulfriths are my guests and shall be accorded the hospitality due them."

If only for this night. Meaning tomorrow night she might be a condemned prisoner.

The sheriff looked as if he might argue, and he had the power to do so, but he shrugged as if weary of the whole matter. "Very well."

Sir Hector halted before Beatrix and Michael. "I will show you to your chambers." He looked to her brothers.

Though she knew Garr exercised enough control to not set upon the knight for the death of Sir Ewen, she was not so sure about Abel who had been Sir Ewen's friend. True, it was now known Sir Hector had saved her life, but Abel might forget that long enough to exact retribution.

From Sir Hector's unwavering gaze, he also seemed aware of the potential for peril, but he pivoted toward the stairway.

As Beatrix and Michael followed, Lavonne said, "I would speak with you, D'Arci."

Though Beatrix felt Michael's reluctance to leave her side, he said, "Of course." He turned to her, drew his hand up the back of her arm and down again. "Certes, I shall be a while, as I must needs also tend those injuries sustained by your brother's men and mine."

During their wait outside the donjon, he had seen to the more serious injuries, but there were others that required his physician's skill.

"Until I join you," he said, looking past her to Garr and Abel, "I am sure you will not lack for company."

"She will not," Garr said.

As her brothers led her across the hall behind Sir Hector, Beatrix ached over Michael's absence, and on the first stair looked over her shoulder.

He met her gaze, nodded, and turned to Baron Lavonne.

It had been hard to watch her walk away, but necessary. Now, standing before Christian Lavonne in the lord's solar, impatience gnawed at Michael as he wondered how long before he could return to her. The only good of it was that he could not have left Beatrix better protected. For certain, Wulfrith and his younger brother would allow no ill to befall her.

"I am pleased you survived the attack," the baron rent the silence.

"Some did not."

"So I am told. Unfortunately, it could not be prevented."

"Could it not?" Michael demanded, uncaring that such a tone one did not use with one's liege. But Christian Lavonne was no longer his liege, was he?

The baron's jaw shifted. "Nay, it could not."

Michael took a step toward him. "Because you allow your father to usurp your role, to act in your name, to reduce you to a mere figurehead."

Eyes biting like the snow of deepest winter, Christian Lavonne said, "Unless it is your intent that we meet at swords, D'Arci, do not further presume to know my father, and especially not me."

"It takes no presumption to know who sent those brigands and who stood by and allowed it."

The shadow that fell across the baron's face was as much borne of anger as the waning torchlight. His right hand flexed, and Michael knew he imagined a sword there. But though the blade had replaced his monk's psalter, he had yet to truly master it despite intense daily practice.

Would his skill ever match his longing? Or was longing the problem—that too much of his life had been spent upon the Church to allow him to ease his grip sufficiently to eschew the class that prayed for the class that warred?

Michael drew a deep breath. "And yet," he allowed, "it is most curious that you sent Sir Hector lest your father attempt what he did—and for which I do thank you."

Christian Lavonne considered him a long moment, then narrowed his lids. "Are you still my man, D'Arci?"

Unsettled by the question he had not expected, and which suggested the matter was not decided, Michael hesitated. In the end, the only answer was, "When Lady Beatrix is done with this trial, we shall wed."

Without flicker of surprise, the baron said, "I did not expect you would ever take a woman to wife, you who likes women less and enjoys their variety better than any man I have known. Truly, I thought you ruined by the lady, Edithe."

Of course he knew of the woman's accusation of ravishment. Despite having come late to his title, Christian Lavonne was well-versed in matters pertaining to his vassals and the administration of his lands.

"I had also thought myself ruined." Michael noted the subject did not chafe as much as it had once done. "Lady Beatrix proved me wrong."

"Then you profess to love this woman who is said to have murdered your brother."

"I do." As always when he thought upon Simon, he had to step back from memories of the young man he had known. "As I also profess it was not murder that befell Simon."

The baron's gaze drifted to the rush-covered floor. "So it seems."

Michael was jolted. "What do you know?"

"That there will be an alliance between the Lavonnes and the Wulfriths," he said with spare emotion, "and henceforth, there shall be peace between our families."

"Peace only if the Wulfriths' sister is not falsely convicted of murder."

"Aye, which is as I would propose to Wulfrith."

Impatient, Michael said, "Tell."

Christian Lavonne's eyes brightened, the intensity of which Michael had only seen when, in swordplay, he gained an advantage over those who had mastered the sweep and thrust of a blade that yet eluded him. "If Wulfrith agrees to hand up Lady Gaenor for marriage without further delay, Lady Beatrix will have the witness she requires to prove her innocence."

Between the spaces of what the baron said and did not, Michael glimpsed the aged knight who had come to Beatrix's aid. "You speak of Sir Hector."

Michael did not think he had ever seen Christian Lavonne smile, but something suspiciously near that deepened the corners of his mouth. "You are perceptive, D'Arci."

"And you are more ruthless than imagined."

"A man bargains with what he has."

And what he had was Beatrix's life, providing she was unable to save herself as she was determined to do. If she failed...

"And if Wulfrith does not agree to hand up Lady Gaenor?"

For a moment, Michael glimpsed wavering in the baron's eyes. "Though it is yet to be seen whether you remain my man, D'Arci, there is no question that Sir Hector is loyal to me."

And would not testify unless directed to do so. Michael knew he went too far with his next words, but his ire would not be curbed. "It seems you may yet make your father proud, Baron Lavonne."

Aye, too far. Were a sword at hand, his liege would surely have turned it on him. Not that Michael wouldn't soon enough remind him of the skill he yet lacked.

The flickering torchlight recasting Christian Lavonne's face time and again, one moment making him appear human, the next bestial, he said, "Tell Wulfrith I require his answer by dawn."

Knuckles sounded on the door.

"Enter," the baron called.

Michael turned and all of him tightened when Sir Robert stepped inside. "My lord," he grudgingly acknowledged the baron.

Though Michael was well aware the knight was far from Christian Lavonne's favor, he had never so deeply sensed the anger that accompanied the baron's dislike of his half-brother. "What is it you require, Sir Robert?"

"The physician." The knight's gaze landed hard on Michael. "Our father asks after him."

Christian Lavonne looked to Michael. "You will attend him?"

Could he trust himself? Or would the sword at his side prove too much temptation when he stood over the one who sought Beatrix's death?

Telling himself he would do nothing to lose the ground gained in his quest to draw nearer God and prove himself worthy of Beatrix, Michael said, "I will, but first I shall see to the injuries sustained by Baron Wulfrith's men and my own."

Though he expected his liege to object, he said, "As you will." He looked to Aldous's misbegotten son. "Tell our father the physician will tend him shortly."

From the thrust of Sir Robert's bearded jaw, it was far from the response he desired, but he withdrew.

Michael also turned to go, but when he reached the door, the baron called to him, "I would have you know that the justice seeks absolution for the lady if she will but accept it."

"She will not."

Christian Lavonne inclined his head. "So I am told. Thus, it falls to the jury to determine her fate—a jury chosen by the justice himself."

That Michael had not known. Refusing to embrace relief, as it might prove a weakness when there was still so much that could go wrong, he said, "To your father's utmost displeasure, I am sure."

"Which is mine to deal with. And I shall."

Then perhaps Christian Lavonne would eventually shrug out from beneath the mantle of Aldous's influence. God willing, it would not be too late by the time he fully emerged as the sole and unquestioned baron of Abingdale.

"We were told you had sustained a head injury."

Beatrix looked up at Garr from the chair he had placed before the hearth for her. "Evidence of which you have already noted, I am sure." She glanced at Abel who sat in the chair opposite hers.

"Aye," Garr said, "though the injury seems not as severe as feared."

She could not help but smile at the welcome observation and sent up a silent prayer that she would present as well on the morrow. "I am much recovered. God willing, I shall con-continue to improve." *Only one error, and a small one at that.* "Mother is well?"

"She is."

"And Gaenor?"

Garr's gaze shifted. "Better since she was told you live."

"And before it was told?"

Abel cleared his throat. "She has long borne pain and guilt over the loss of her little sister. But she fares better now and shall surely continue to do so."

"She is not ill, is she?"

Abel shrugged. "Sick of heart, is all."

"Worry not over her," Garr said. "She shall recover fully." Then, as if uncomfortable with further talk of Gaenor, he said, "What of the Church, Beatrix?"

Knowing he would not be budged to speak further on their sister, Beatrix said, "Though it is what you and mother wish for me, and what I once wished for myself, I choose Michael. To w-worship and love our Savior, I do not have to…commit my life to the Church. He lives in me as He will live in the children Michael and I make."

"From what I have heard, this D'Arci is hardly a godly man."

And the curse that had broken from his lips when he learned his men had died only reinforced those tales.

"Especially where women are concerned," Abel muttered, earning himself Garr's barbed gaze.

Then they did not think she knew of the false accusation of ravishment against Michael. Before Beatrix could tell otherwise, Abel snorted. "I only repeat what was told to us and confirmed many times over, Garr."

"I know of what you speak," Beatrix said. "Michael has told me all, and I believe him to be as wronged as I am in being accused of murdering Sir Simon."

"And if it is deceit he works upon you?" Abel asked.

"He does not. He loves me."

"Perhaps," Garr said, "but will love be enough?"

She met his gaze and knew he had returned to the matter of godliness. "God grows in Michael. That is enough."

Abel sighed, sank deeper into the chair, and thrust his legs out before him. "Let us pray you are right."

Of Beatrix's three brothers, he was the most curious of all, one moment a reflection of Garr, the next of Everard, then their father, and sometimes their mother. Somewhere behind all those reflections, resided Abel himself, but he showed himself too rarely to be truly known. And, strangely, he seemed content with the arrangement, as if it was a game he quite enjoyed.

"You are prepared for the morrow, Beatrix?" Garr asked.

"I am."

He dropped to his haunches beside her. "If you are found guilty, I shall deliver you free of Broehne."

"As Michael himself has vowed, but 'twill not be necessary, for I will deliver myself." She had to believe she could or she would falter when she stood at trial.

Garr's nostrils flared. "Already a jury is chosen. A jury likely disposed toward Aldous Lavonne."

"Then I must needs dispose them...otherwise."

He rose and turned toward the bed. "You need sleep for the morrow. Abel and I will stand watch."

"I would like to wait on Michael."

"It could be hours ere he returns. Sleep, Beatrix."

Her lids *were* heavy. But though she did not believe she would gain much rest, she agreed. However, she was still awake an hour later. And Michael had yet to return.

Curse King Henry! Curse the Wulfriths! Curse D'Arci! Curse them all!

The shaking of the bed evidencing how hard he trembled, Aldous pulled himself back from the silent rantings that filled his head to screaming pitch. If he was not careful, this writhing would crack open his heart and he would be denied what he most needed—to leave this world knowing the Wulfriths felt the loss and pain he had long suffered.

If those accursed brigands had not failed him, if D'Arci had not known what was intended and set men to the woods, if the traitorous physician had not conspired with the Wulfriths to outnumber those who were to have seen the Wulfrith whore dead...

He lifted a hand to drag it down his face only to pause on his disfigured fingers that had once been straight and tapered, that had gripped a sword strong and true, that had clasped the hand of the woman who had grown to love him as it was good for a wife to do.

He squeezed his eyes closed, but the memories followed him to the backs of his lids. With panting breath, he opened his eyes and stared at the door that had yet to admit D'Arci.

How he longed to suffer life no more. If not for the greater need to give back what the Wulfriths had dealt him, he would not. But now that they were within his walls, they would not emerge unscathed, nor that perfidious scum, D'Arci. That vile, loathsome, godforsaken—

Aldous saw a flash of white, felt something in the confines of his skull stretch taut, then heard—would swear he heard—something snap.

Shuddering, he focused on his bent and burned fingers. And smiled as the last vestiges of the man who had sacrificed his very skin to save ungrateful wretches slid away. It did not matter that his soul also slipped away. After all, souls were burdensome, ever holding a man back. Inducing him to compromise. Fabricating excuses for those who were lacking. Disposing him toward honor and civility when the edge of a sword was far more effective. Turning him from justice where justice was due. It did not matter. What mattered was a life for a life—more, if possible.

By the time the door admitted the physician, Aldous was strangely calm. "Ah, D'Arci." He let his voice smile where his lips could not. "Come."

Never had Michael been received by Aldous in such a manner. Indeed, the old baron had only ever been morosely mute or abrasively demanding. Michael redoubled the vigilance with which he had entered and swept the shadowed room for any who might be lurking. Determining that he and the old man were alone, he approached the bed.

"Nearer." Aldous beckoned.

Reminding himself of his dagger that could be brought to hand in a moment, Michael halted alongside the bed and looked down on the one who would continue to seek Beatrix's death. And was tempted to yield to this fire that would have him free the world of such wickedness— wickedness that became more evident when Michael looked into eyes that would have held the devil in awe.

Despite Aldous's strangely calm exterior, he fomented over his failed brigands. And yet there remained something in his depths that had once been in greater evidence—torment. A bare flicker, but still present.

As always, Michael felt a pang for the old man's suffering, though this time it was against his will.

Aldous waved him nearer. "Surely you do not fear a withered old man near death," he grunted out so low that Michael had to strain to catch the words.

As Aldous intended he should do, he bent low.

The words Aldous's moist lips delivered to his ear revealed the truth of him. "My revenge begins with your whore." He sniffed loudly. "Indeed, the smell of her burning flesh is upon the very air we breathe."

Michael's sympathy fled, and he knew he would never again be in danger of its return. Anger again tempting his hand to the blade, he curled his fingers into his palms and put his mouth near Aldous's ear. "Nay, 'tis the death of your brigands you smell. And, God willing, your own." That last he could not contain. Straightening, he looked down upon the old man.

A corner of his mouth convulsing, Aldous stared at Michael. "Unless you intend to murder me as the Wulfriths murdered my son—and your brother—I will never yield up this life until justice is done."

"Justice," Michael scoffed. "Cling to your justice as long as you will, old man, but never will your evil touch Lady Beatrix. On the morrow she goes free."

Aldous's lashless lids spasmed, but he recovered. With a smile that was little more than a flat line warped at the corners, he said, "Free from this world but not hell."

Knowing that if he remained, his conviction to keep from putting Aldous through would fail, Michael turned away. "On the morrow," he said as he crossed to the door.

When he stood in the corridor with the door at his back, he drew a deep breath and several more before deeming himself calm enough to approach Wulfrith with Christian's proposal.

Would the baron's terms be acceptable or wanting? Michael wondered as he advanced on the chamber where Beatrix's brothers watched over her. Though she was determined to free herself, he prayed Wulfrith would hand over one sister to better the other's chance of gaining a verdict of innocence. And no guilt would Michael feel for his desire to improve Beatrix's chances, for still she would be allowed to defend herself as promised.

He paused before the door behind which he had several times passed a night at Broehne and frowned. Beatrix could not be told that her sister was the price paid for Sir Hector's witness, for she would oppose the bargain, regardless that King Henry would eventually force the Wulfriths to surrender Lady Gaenor, regardless that marriage to Christian would not be such an ill union as feared. The baron had shown a stripe of ruthlessness that had threatened to undo Michael, but it was not yet as deep and wide as his father's. As the wife of Christian Lavonne, Lady Gaenor might never be loved, but neither would she be ill-treated. There was consolation in that. Now if the Wulfriths could be convinced.

25

A QUARTER HOUR into dawn and still no word from Wulfrith.

Christian stared at the empty space between him and the door and silently cursed the thwarting of his plan. He had been certain his offer would be accepted, albeit grudgingly, but the Wulfriths did not even deign to send word of their rejection. Arrogant knaves!

"I do not think they are coming, my lord," Sir Hector said from the opposite side of the table that claimed nearly a quarter of the lord's solar.

"So it appears."

"Then?"

Christian knew what he asked, just as he had known on the night past what he would answer. "As Lady Gaenor will eventually be my wife, still you will bear witness for her sister."

No surprise rose on the aged knight's face, for he knew his lord better than Michael D'Arci. And Christian resented him for it.

When a rap sounded on the door, he called, "Enter!"

His squire stepped inside. "My lord, Baron Wulfrith—"

—"calls," Wulfrith growled, pushing the young man aside, as did the Wulfrith knight who followed.

As Sir Hector stepped forward, sword to hand, Christian rose and gripped his own sword hilt, but when Wulfrith's sheathed sword remained at his side, Christian also left his blade sheathed. With a slight shake of his head intended to restrain Hector, he asked, "There is something you require, Baron Wulfrith?"

The man halted before him. "A discussion of your proposal." Wulfrith acknowledged Sir Hector with a glance—Hector whose guard was divided between Wulfrith and the knight who took up a position near the door.

Accustomed as Christian was to looking down on other men from his ample height, there was something exhilarating about meeting this man eye to eye. Indeed, though Wulfrith's reputation as a warrior was well known, Christian almost wished the man would set upon him.

He looked to the uncovered windows. "It is past dawn, Baron Wulfrith."

Wulfrith's grey-green eyes revealing his anger, the red-veined whites witness to his sleepless night, he said, "Dawn enough."

Christian raised an eyebrow. "I do not see what discussion there is to be had. Either you accept or you do not."

"I have my own terms."

Christian looked to his squire who stood inside the doorway glowering between the two men who had pushed past him. With a thrust of the chin to indicate the young man should withdraw, Christian returned to Wulfrith. "Speak."

"Ere I accept your proposal, I would know to what Sir Hector intends to testify in my sister's defense."

"That will be revealed at trial."

"You think me so fool to agree to hand over my sister based on your word that this knight's witness will be of use?"

"As King Henry has commanded that your sister and I wed, I do not require your agreement to deliver her. Be it a sennight hence, be it a year, she *will* come to Broehne."

Something drew Christian's gaze to Wulfrith's knight, and he saw the man's face was flushed and teeth nearly bared. Indeed, he seemed to seethe as much as his lord. Interesting.

Christian looked back at Wulfrith. "I but wish to avoid further delay and strain between our families that will reflect poorly on the Wulfrith's loyalty to King Henry."

The baron's nostrils flared, and Christian knew he struggled with things beyond his control, just as Christian had done much of his life. "Do you accept or do you not?"

"Not as the proposal stands. I will deliver Gaenor only if I deem Sir Hector's witness is of use at trial. Now, do *you* accept, or do you not, Lavonne?"

Though Aldous Lavonne would have rejected such terms, it was near enough what Christian wanted. He would have to have faith, were faith yet possible for him, that Wulfrith was honorable as was told. Fortunately for them both, Christian knew what kind of man Geoffrey had been such that he would not allow his brother's death to sway him in the direction their father had gone.

"I accept," Christian said, though it chafed that he should be the one to accept the proposal he had set in motion.

Wulfrith leaned forward and surprised Christian with a brief kiss on the cheek. "*That*," he said low, "is to remind you that whatever you do to my sister, Gaenor, I shall do to you."

Hands aching from the ferocity with which he closed them into fists, Christian met Wulfrith's gaze as the man stepped back. "Providing you are honorable enough to abide by our bargain," he said, "your sister has nothing to fear from me, nor you, nor any others of your family, nor your people."

The arrogant man smiled. "Then we understand each other." He strode to the door where his knight remained unmoving, the man's wrathful gaze upon Christian.

"Sir Durand," Wulfrith clipped, the name causing Christian to frown and the knight to jerk as if surprised to find his lord so near.

As the knight followed Wulfrith from the chamber, Christian realized this was the one said to have used the name "Sir Piers" to gain entrance to Soaring—and who had then led Wulfrith to the abbey to avert the attack. But there was something else about the name—

"Sir Durand seems as displeased as his lord," Sir Hector said, stepping before Christian.

"Curious," Christian murmured, only to recall the other reason the name was familiar. Sir Durand was the knight who had escaped with Lady Gaenor. Was the death of his fellow knight at Sir Hector's hands responsible for his animosity? Or something else?

"It seems there will soon be a wedding at Broehne," Sir Hector mused.

God willing.

"You are a fool, Lady Beatrix."

It seemed always the answer to those who did not understand what she did. Though she now realized that the man before her was only trying to aid her, she snapped, "What I am is innocent, and that I shall prove."

From where he stood inside the doorway of the chamber, arms over his chest, the king's justice glanced at Michael and Abel before returning to Beatrix. "My lady, absolution would—"

"But justify my murder of Sir Simon. I did not murder him, and I shall not...admit to having done so."

"She will have her trial." Michael stepped past her and halted before the justice. "A trial that delivers a verdict, be it of innocence or guilt."

The man's mouth pinched. "There can be no guarantee that Lady Beatrix will be found innocent, though I have chosen the jury to ensure it is not tainted."

Beatrix closed her eyes. Upon awakening this morn, Michael had revealed to her that Aldous Lavonne had not chosen the jury. However, she was once more relieved to hear the justice confirm it—such relief that she thought perhaps a breeze had come through the window.

She looked to the justice. "Then I shall have a fair trial, which is all I ask."

"As you would, my lady." He lowered his arms to his sides. "It is time."

Already the jury was convened? But the sun was barely risen...

Beatrix looked to Michael. Though his face might appear impassive to others, she knew his foreboding.

"We require a few minutes," he said.

As the justice exited the room, the personal guard who had escorted the man abovestairs placed themselves one in front of him and one behind.

Michael closed the door. When he turned back, Beatrix saw his lower jaw was forward. Though she did not doubt he believed he and her brothers could steal her from Broehne Castle if the trial went wrong, he was grim for fear of what she would soon face.

"'Tis as you wished it," he growled.

She clasped her hands at the waist of the green gown given to her by Lady Laura. "As it must be."

"Lord!" Abel flopped back in the chair from which he had unfolded when the justice entered. "'Twould be more expedient to gag and steal you away, sister."

"Then I am grateful you are the younger brother and not Garr," Beatrix said and wondered again where Garr had gone. Though he had been here when she awakened, he had mostly stood at the window and brooded over the bailey below. Shortly after dawn, he had exchanged glances with Michael and Abel and stalked from the chamber. Surely he should have returned by now?

Before she could ask after him, the eldest Wulfrith entered. As Michael turned to him, Abel looked up from his chair and something once more passed between the three men.

"What have you done, Garr?" she demanded.

He halted and set his hands on her shoulders. "My word stands, Beatrix. Rest in it."

Still, something—

"Let us pray," he said.

She expected Abel to grumble all the way to her side, but he spoke not a word as he rose from the chair. Seeking out Michael, she saw he hesitated to join them and felt his discomfort at what Garr proposed. However, when she smiled at him, he strode forward and slid his hand into hers. They bowed their heads.

Though Beatrix had always been in awe of Garr's faith, she had never been more grateful for his guidance. For those who thought belief in God made one weak and vulnerable, they had but to hear the words her eldest brother spoke above their heads to be convicted otherwise. Regardless of what happened today, God was with her always.

"How say you, Lady Beatrix?"

Struggling with a mix of fury over Aldous Lavonne's presence in the hall, the old man having been carried down by Sir Robert, and ache over Beatrix who stood alone on the dais before the justice, Michael stared at her.

Again and again, he lived the fear in her eyes when she had looked on the scarred old man and realized who he was, but he had contained his emotions. He would not allow Aldous the satisfaction he sought in presenting himself at trial—Aldous who no longer seemed to care that others gaze upon the devastation wrought by fire.

"Lady Beatrix?" the justice prompted.

She looked to the jury that shared the lord's table with him. "I did not do what is said of me," her voice rose clear across a hall crowded with knights, men-at-arms, and castle folk. "Thus, I do not seek…absolution, which is best reserved for those ill of mind. That I am not."

"You understand, Lady Beatrix, that if you are found guilty you shall hang?"

"You understand, Lord Justice, it would be an innocent woman you hang?"

Michael almost smiled. Though it would be best if she did not test the man's patience, she was to be admired. For all she had suffered and now faced, she was strong.

"So say you 'nay'." The justice lowered his gaze to the parchment before him. "Resume your seat."

Beatrix stiffened. "I would speak in my defense."

The man began to tap the tabletop as Michael often did when his own patience was drawn thin. "Do I allow you to speak further, Lady Beatrix, 'twill be in my time, not yours. Return to your seat."

Although twenty feet separated Michael from Aldous Lavonne who sat to the right, Michael heard the other man chortle. Fury rose in him as he looked around, poured through him when he met Aldous's gaze that held a glimmer of merriment amid an otherwise gaping void.

As for Christian, he sat stiffly beside his father, the darkness that had risen on his face with Aldous's appearance still evident. Doubtless, he did not condone his father's presence. Providing his anger held, both Aldous and Sir Robert would soon discover that the barony had truly changed hands.

When Beatrix lowered to the chair between Michael and her older brother, it took all of Michael's reserve to not put an arm around her.

"Am I not to be allowed to tell my tale?" she whispered.

Though a defendant was not always given leave to speak, especially a female, Michael did not believe the justice would deny her. He slid a hand across the table and covered her fingers. Knowing Aldous Lavonne watched, he smiled. "Patience," he murmured. Ironic that *he* should counsel such...

As the justice set the parchment aside, movement sounded from the doors behind and a muttering rose among those in the hall.

Michael nearly groaned as, past the press of heated bodies from which a cloying scent rose, he glimpsed a familiar figure. He ought to have known Maude would follow. But at least it appeared she had not dragged Clarice and Lady Laura with her.

Silently cursing her will that would make it more difficult to take Beatrix from Broehne, if necessary, he snatched her gaze to his as she stepped down the path that her rank as a lady caused to open ahead of her.

A sad smile aging her drawn face, she looked from Michael's displeasure to Beatrix.

"Who interrupts these proceedings?" the justice demanded.

Maude made him wait until she reached the dais. Regal as a queen, she inclined her head. "Lady Maude D'Arci, mother of Sir Simon D'Arci."

The justice rubbed the space between his eyebrows, then flicked his hand toward the tables before the dais. "You may remain."

So gripped by his own reaction to Maude's appearance that he had not noted Beatrix's, Michael was struck by her pale face and the tension in her hand beneath his.

As Maude gained a seat behind them, Beatrix drew her hand free of Michael's.

He bent his head to her. "She will not speak against you."

Beatrix nodded. She knew that. But why had the lady come? To tell Lady Laura's secret? Surely not. Merely to observe?

"Sheriff," the justice called, "present the evidence."

Baron Tyrell strode from where he stood at the far end of the lord's table and lifted the dagger that lay before the justice. "As Baron Lavonne's men will bear witness, this dagger was wrested from Lady Beatrix Wulfrith when she and Sir Simon were found on the ledge in the ravine." He turned it for all to see, set it back on the table, and lifted Beatrix's bloodied gown. "This is the bliaut the lady wore, and it is Sir Simon's blood upon the bodice."

The brows of the men of the jury crumpled as they considered the proof of Beatrix's guilt, and several began to talk amongst themselves.

"Call forth your witnesses," the justice ordered.

The sheriff returned the bliaut to the table and beckoned toward the back of the hall. Shortly, two men approached the dais.

"Sir Kearse, my Lord Justice," the sheriff indicated the short, rotund man, "and Thomas Mason. These men found Lady Beatrix holding the dagger over the body of Sir Simon."

Michael glanced at Beatrix.

She shook her head and whispered, "I do not remember them."

Considering her head injury, that did not surprise him.

"You attest this to be true, Sir Kearse and Thomas Mason?" the justice asked.

"Aye, my lord," both spoke as one.

"Yet you did not see Lady Beatrix use this dagger against Sir Simon."

"Nay, my lord."

"So 'tis an assumption that evil intent caused the wound that killed Sir Simon."

The men exchanged glances, and it was the knight who said, "What else was there to conclude, Lord Justice?"

The king's man sighed. "For this reason, 'tis I who preside over this trial."

Michael did not need to look around to know Aldous's seething, for it spilled on the air like poison.

"Is there anything else you would tell?" the justice asked.

"Only that we nearly had to break the lady's hand to wrest the dagger from her," Thomas Mason said.

"She attempted to turn it on you?"

"Nay. 'Tis just that she would not release it."

"No crime in that," the justice muttered and turned his attention to the sheriff. "Have you any other witnesses?"

"I fear there are none who saw the deed, Lord Justice."

The king's man inclined his head and waved at the two men. "You are dismissed."

As they filed past the table where Beatrix sat, the justice settled his gaze on her. "Lady Beatrix, ere your guilt or innocence is determined, have you something brief to say?"

She blinked. Already her trial was near its end? And he would allow her to speak but "something brief"? After weeks of turning her tale, untangling her thoughts and tongue that she might defend herself? All for nothing?

"Lady Beatrix?"

"You can do this," Michael breathed.

"I know." She glanced at Garr and Abel who returned her gaze. Either they were confident of the testimony thus far or confident that they could steal her away.

She gained her feet. "I have something to say, Lord Justice."

"Come forward."

She ascended the dais and, praying her voice would not waver, said, "Sir Simon's death was un…"

Lord, unbind my tongue!

She looked to the jury. "His death was as unintentional as it was unfortunate."

"This does not sound brief, Lady Beatrix."

"Pray, have patience, Lord Justice, and I shall prove my innocence."

He nodded for her to proceed.

"As you know, I accompanied my sister when she fled our home to escape marriage."

Imagining Christian Lavonne's eyes on her—worse, those of his horribly disfigured father whom Michael was certain was responsible for the brigands—she suppressed a shudder. "Sir Simon overtook me at the ravine and…"

Calm, Beatrix. You know what to tell.

"…he touched me as a lady should not to be touched."

The justice's eyebrows rose. "You say he ravished you?"

"Nay. Baron Lavonne's knight, Sir Hector, was there. After he laid down my escort, Sir Ewen"—she forced the image aside lest it trip her tongue—"he ordered Sir Simon to release me that I might go to my brother's knight. It was from Sir Ewen I gained the dagger ere he died. As Sir Hector was eager to continue his pursuit of my sister, he gave me into Sir Simon's charge." She almost sighed to have the words flow unhindered from her.

"And you did not protest?"

"I did, but he...methinks Sir Hector knew my reason for protest, for he gave Sir Simon warning ere he departed."

"What manner of warning?"

"It was...more a look than words."

"A look. Hmm."

He made it sound silly. "After Sir Hector departed, Sir Simon taunted me. Fearful of what he intended, I pulled the dagger and warned him to come no nearer. But he did, so I ran to Sir Ewen's mount beside the...ravine. Sir Simon gave chase and caught me between his horse and the other."

She glanced at the jury, uncertain whether or not to be heartened by their rapt countenances. "He pulled me onto his saddle and taunted me for having no one to defend my virtue. Though I would not relinquish the dagger, he...touched me again...ravished my mouth..."

The memory caused bumps to rise across her limbs. "I feigned a swoon and nearly freed myself, but when he caught my arm and wrenched it down, the handle of the dagger struck his destrier and it... reared. We fell." She filled her lungs deeply. "All I remember is the pain, and when I awakened Sir Simon was stretched atop me. Somehow, the dagger had...found his heart."

The justice considered her. "Anything else, Lady Beatrix?"

Was there? Something that might further prove her innocence? That might help the jury see beyond the bliaut with its blood-stained bodice? She looked to where it lay on the table and winced in remembrance of the sticky moisture that had bled through the material. However, in the next instant her mind cleared and the lies told about her unraveled further.

Thank You, lord.

She touched the psalter on her belt, stepped to the dagger, and touched its hilt. "'Tis true I wielded this at the ravine." She looked to the jury. "And as this dagger drew blood, so too is the blood on my bodice that of Sir Simon. I do not deny it. But by defense it was got, not murder."

"As you have already told, Lady Beatrix," the justice spilled impatience. "Now you are finished?"

"Nearly finished, Lord Justice."

He grumbled but waved for her to continue.

She lifted the bliaut and looked to the jury. Was there one among them who would believe? If not, they were blind—else corrupt.

"Why has none questioned Sir Simon's blood upon me?"

They frowned.

"Though I am accused of setting upon him and putting my dagger to him, how is it his…blood covers my bodice?"

The men frowned deeper. Did they understand? She glanced at the justice and was somewhat heartened by his risen brow.

"Sir Simon's blood does not merely fleck my gown, which it would have done had I intentionally driven the dagger into him. As all can see from the great amount on the bodice, there was no distance between us when the wound was made. When we fell into the ravine, he landed atop both the dagger and me."

Some of the mens' eyes lit, and she prayed it was understanding that did it.

"The whore lies!" a graveled voice rent the silence.

Beatrix jerked her head around. The old man beside Christian Lavonne had been frightening to look upon before, but the hatred staining his face and the spittle frothing his lips turned him hideous.

"Though you would have it be otherwise that my family be as pained as yours," she addressed Aldous Lavonne, "I speak the truth."

As the old man's scarred face flushed deeper and the muttering in the hall swelled, Christian Lavonne rose from his chair. Face grim, he beckoned two men-at-arms forward. "Return my father to his chamber."

Aldous looked at the men who stepped forward, then lurched out of the chair only to crumple at his son's feet.

Christian Lavonne hastened to his haunches. However, as he reached to Aldous, the old man struck out and raked his son's cheek.

"Traitor!" This time, Aldous's flailing fist caught his son's arm, an ineffectual blow only in that it hardly moved the young baron. Emotionally, though, the old man found his mark, for anguish lit his son's face before he once more hardened it.

Waving the men-at-arms back, Christian Lavonne reached again. "Father—"

"I am not your father!" Aldous twisted away. "You are unknown to me! Dead to me! More dead than Geoffrey!"

As all watched and murmured, Christian caught hold of Aldous's arms.

"Do not touch me, accursed spawn!"

If Christian had not been such a large man, he could not have overpowered his thrashing sire, but he swung him up into his arms and strode past those who opened a path for him as they had done Lady Maude.

"Robert!" Aldous Lavonne called.

But the eldest son did not need to be summoned, for he had already detached from the onlookers and made to follow. As he drew near, Christian halted. Though what he said to his half-brother could not be heard above the roused onlookers, the words he put through clenched teeth caused the knight to falter and the old man to wail. Then father and son mounted the stairs and disappeared around the first turn.

"Order!" The justice shouted. When the din dwindled to hushed voices and whispers, he asked, "You are finished, Lady Beatrix?"

"There is naught else to tell of that day."

He looked past her. "Are there any others who would speak to the accusation against Lady Beatrix?"

A voice traveled strong and sure across the hall. "I would."

It was Sir Hector. Heart pounding so hard it felt as if it might break free of her chest, Beatrix stared at him. Surely he did not intend to bear witness for her. Baron Lavonne had left the hall, but the knight's liege would soon enough learn what happened in his absence.

He ascended the dais. "I am Sir Hector. For twenty and five years I have served as a knight to the Lavonnes."

Clearly, the justice had not expected any others to step forward. And from his scowl, he was not pleased. "Speak, Sir Hector."

"Though 'twould seem the lady does not require my witness, I testify that what she told is true. She did protest when I left her in Sir Simon's charge, and I did warn Sir Simon against laying hands to her."

"Why would you believe it necessary to issue such a warning, Sir Hector?"

The knight hesitated. "Previous to that day at the ravine, such an accusation was made against Sir Simon by a serving woman."

As murmurs once more rose, Beatrix felt Michael's tension assail the air. If not that it was surely difficult for him and his mother to bear witness to such testimony, she would have reveled in relief for the credence Sir Hector added to her testimony.

With a slice of the hand, the justice silenced the din.

"However," Sir Hector continued, "as the woman was wanton and had previously accused another knight of the same when he did not pay her the coin promised, the baron determined the accusation was false."

"And you, Sir Hector? What did you think?"

"I . . ." He glanced at Beatrix. "The serving woman had been beaten—not badly, but bruised. Thus, I did doubt it was merely a matter of payment. But 'twas not enough doubt to punish a man for something he might not have done."

The justice tapped a finger to his lips. "Where is this serving woman?"

"Therein lies the reason for my warning to Sir Simon, Lord Justice. The serving woman disappeared some weeks later and was not seen again. Of course"—he looked again to Beatrix—"I truly did not expect Sir Simon would harm a noblewoman and thought my warning was sufficient should he consider such."

Unfortunately, he had not known about Lady Laura whose ravishment had resulted in a child.

"I am sorry, my lady. Had I known, I would have remained behind."

Beatrix stared at the man who had killed Sir Ewen, who had found no satisfaction in doing so, and who had saved her life.

"Then you believe the lady's tale, Sir Hector?"

"I do not believe her accusation against Sir Simon is false."

"You may step down." The justice looked to Beatrix. "Now you are finished, Lady Beatrix?"

She looked to Michael.

He inclined his head and she knew that though he yet feared for her, all had gone well.

"There is no more to tell, Lord Justice."

"Then, as all witnesses have spoken—"

"I have not spoken." Maude stepped forward. Though she halted alongside Michael, she did not meet his gaze.

"Lady Maude," the justice said, "pray have your speak and let us conclude this matter."

"As my stepson and Sir Hector stand with Lady Beatrix, so do I, though it pains me deeply."

"Explain, Lady Maude."

"Though the blood spilled upon Lady Beatrix's bliaut was sprung from my own veins, I believe my son did that of which the lady accuses him."

The justice sat forward. "Why?"

"The serving woman's accusation against my son was, in fact, not the first such accusation leveled at him. And that is all I shall say."

Amid the resulting din, Michael stared at Maude's profile. Simon had ravished one before the serving woman—at least, attempted to? And she had held the knowledge to her? Why? And Who?

A face rushed at him—lovely, tormented, lonely. Then another— pretty, uncertain, lost. Lady Laura. Clarice.

Michael could not contain his groan. All the truths he had held close turned to lies!

When Maude met his gaze, there were tears in her eyes. "Forgive me, Michael. I did what I thought needed to be done. Now I make amends."

Could he forgive her? She had known but had thought it sufficient to reveal the ill done Simon that had made him such a man. And not for Lady Laura. Nay, for herself. Her shame. And now Beatrix—

He looked to where she stood with her hands at her waist, pity and regret lining her face. And somehow he knew she had known what Maude revealed. By the saints! Why would she not—

Because she is true. Because no fiber of her resembles Edithe. And he, who had once sought to see her hang for Simon's murder, had been gifted with her love. Was there a man more undeserving?

"You are certain you will say no more?" the justice asked.

"I cannot."

"Then these proceedings shall break. In one hour I will deliver the determination of Lady Beatrix's guilt or innocence." He motioned to the men-at-arms. "Escort Lady Beatrix to her chamber."

Michael met Maude's gaze. "We shall speak on this later." He stepped past her and reached Beatrix ahead of the men-at-arms.

She looked up at him, and though he longed to ask about Maude's revelation, he knew it was not the time. He clasped her hand and led her from the dais. Wulfrith and Abel followed.

"Lady Beatrix," a voice met their backs.

They turned to Sir Hector. "Fear not, my lady," he said. "Ere I spoke, already you had won the day."

"How do you know you that?" Michael asked. Though no more proof was needed and it appeared the jury was not tainted, it was still no guarantee she would be found innocent.

"Had you looked near upon the old baron, you would have seen it in his eyes."

Just as he would have seen had he looked near upon Simon... Maude...Lady Laura...Clarice. Clarice, his niece.

"But have a care, Lord D'Arci and Lady Beatrix," the knight added. "Aldous Lavonne is not the honorable lord I once served. Until he gains what he is determined to take from the Wulfriths, methinks he will linger. And wait—along with those who are yet loyal to him."

Michael knew that, and for it would have Beatrix gone from here as soon as the verdict was rendered, even if Sir Hector erred in believing she had won. "I thank you, Sir Hector."

The knight looked to Wulfrith. "You know I killed your man, Sir Ewen."

"I do."

"It was not what I wished, but there was no other way."

"Was there not?"

"As you surely know, Sir Ewen was not only a worthy opponent, but loyal to your family. Though twice I wounded him, neither wound was enough to keep his sword from severing my own life. He was too determined to die, if necessary, to prevent Lady Beatrix from being taken. And so he did."

Michael watched the man who would be his brother-in-law, wondered what turmoil brewed beneath the warrior's hard-faced countenance.

"Sir Ewen *was* worthy," he concurred, "and loyal. Thus, he knew what was required of him, just as you know what is required of you, Sir Hector. As only one could prevail in such a contest, no further explanation is required."

The knight nodded. "There is one other thing you should know. Though my lord, Christian Lavonne, was not trained up to rule this barony, he is worthy and will prove a good husband for Lady Gaenor."

Whom Wulfrith would be expected to hand up if Beatrix was found innocent. Of course, considering how well Beatrix had done, along with Maude's support, he might deem the knight's testimony useless. Would he?

"I will consider that, Sir Hector."

"I pray you do." The knight turned away.

"Do you think he is right?" Beatrix asked, lifting her face to Michael.

About the verdict? Or Christian Lavonne? Both? He squeezed her hand. "Soon we shall know."

26

HE WAS THRUMMING his fingers again, just as impatience had caused him to do when last she was at Broehne Castle and had feigned sleep in hopes he would abandon his vigil.

Strangely, this time there was something almost comforting in the sound he beat on the window sill. Aye, Michael D'Arci was yet an impatient man, but this time he was impatient to deliver her from punishment.

Staring at his back from the chest she sat upon, Beatrix started to smile. However, no sooner did she allow the corners of her mouth to lift than he said, "You knew about Clarice."

How did he know? Had her face betrayed her? More, why had he not asked until this moment? Although it seemed hardly an hour had passed, two had passed though the justice had decreed otherwise. And before now, Michael had not come anywhere near mentioning Maude's revelation. Of course, until a few minutes past, her brothers had also occupied the chamber. Now they had departed—Abel to ascertain the reason for the delay, and Garr...

Though he had offered no explanation, she guessed he sought to further his plan of stealing her away if the verdict went wrong.

Michael looked around.

Grateful he did not appear angry, she crossed to the window. "I knew."

"Maude told you?"

Beatrix laid her palms to his chest. "'Twas Lady Laura who revealed the manner in which Clarice was got."

A muscle jerked in his jaw. "When?"

Mayhap a *bit* angry. "The morn after Sir Durand tried to take me from...Soaring."

Michael's chest expanded with a taut breath. *More* than a bit angry? "Ere you came to me in the stables?"

"Aye. You wish to know why I did not tell you."

His eyebrows nearly touched. For certain angry. "I *know* why you did not tell me." Long seconds passed before he released a breath of frustration. "You are honorable—much to your detriment." Brow easing, he drew a hand up her back and pulled it around to cup her jaw. "You are unlike any woman I have known. And I do not understand how ever I could have believed ill of you."

She smiled. "A brother's love. Though Simon surely...changed from that who you knew, you knew him ere you knew me."

"Have you no guile, Beatrix?"

"When necessary—as when a man who makes himself my enemy chases me through abbey ruins."

He remembered as well, and for it rubbed his leg. Though, for a moment, it looked as if he might smile, his face turned troubled. "The D'Arcis have caused you much pain, and yet you stand with me as if my armor bears no tarnish."

"A woman's love, Michael—a love that knows the truth of you."

He kissed her, but no sooner did she lean in to him than he drew back and gripped his sword hilt.

A moment later, Abel and Garr entered. At the sight of Beatrix and Michael standing near, they hesitated, then Garr said, "The verdict has been rendered."

Though Beatrix felt a jolt of fear, she said, "I am ready."

"Come forth, Lady Beatrix."

Hearing every draw of her breath, Michael looked to the woman beside him. No words did she speak, for it was all in her eyes. She nodded and stood.

Sending up a prayer that Maude was well beyond the castle walls as he had arranged should the verdict go wrong, Michael watched as Beatrix touched her psalter and stepped around him.

He let her go, though a harder thing he had not done. But his men and her brother's men were ready—all armed, all in place. He braced his legs apart, the better to rush to standing with his sword in hand.

As Beatrix ascended the dais, the justice stood. "May all know by these proceedings," he poured his voice across the hall, "the verdict given this day shall stand for all days and that any who deem otherwise shall, by their acts, suffer the charge of treason."

Michael felt the impression of his sword hilt though it was not yet to hand. To whom did the justice speak? God willing, it was Aldous Lavonne who festered in his chamber abovestairs.

The justice looked to the accused. "After much scrutiny, the charge that Lady Beatrix did murder Sir Simon D'Arci"—

Beatrix stared at the man, fearful she would be unable to hear him over the sound of her heart in her ears.

—"is found lacking. Therefore, Lady Beatrix Wulfrith is innocent. So says the royal court."

Amid the rousing of the castle folk, Beatrix could not move, and when finally she did, she nearly went limp. All she had prayed and prepared for...

God had provided. Now a wife she would be to Michael and one day a mother to their children.

"Thank you," she whispered, though the justice could not possibly hear her above the din.

With a voice that ascended the others, he said, "'Twas you who won your freedom, Lady Beatrix."

"Thank you," she said again and swung around to meet Michael's smile across the distance.

Though the din in the hall suddenly changed, her heart was too filled with joy for her to seek out the cause. Thus, the alarm that transformed Michael's face reached her first, next the drawing of his sword, then his shout as he and her brothers lunged toward her.

She snapped her head to the right. Dagger aloft, bearded face mottled, Sir Robert hurtled his great bulk toward her.

"Run, Beatrix!" Michael shouted again.

She jumped back but came up against the table. Knowing she was only bare seconds from the vengeance that ascended the dais a stride ahead of Michael, she turned to flee and belatedly realized she had given Sir Robert her back.

She did not know if the heat of the knight's body was real or imagined, but she felt it. And knew she would soon feel his dagger.

"Lord!" Michael shouted, realizing he and her brothers could not reach Beatrix ahead of Sir Robert. An instant later, his anguished plea was answered by an animal cry of pain.

Protruding from the shoulder of the one who sought Beatrix's back was a dagger. An instant later, Sir Robert crashed to the dais with such force the cloth on the lord's table flapped.

Clearing the writhing knight who clasped his shoulder and grunted with pain, Michael caught Beatrix's arm as she bounded from the dais. She cried out when he pulled her around and gasped when she saw it was him.

He dropped his sword and crushed her to him.

Merciful Lord, you spared her! By the hand of the one whose dagger protruded from the knight's shoulder, God had given her back to him.

"Order!" the justice roared.

Pressing Beatrix's head to his chest, Michael looked over his shoulder at her brothers. Hands gripping hilts, faces flushed, the Wulfriths stood over Sir Robert who had pulled the dagger free and was attempting to stem the flow of blood. Could they contain the bloodlust that surely swelled their veins, or would they render immediate judgment on one who had attempted to carry out the task surely given him by his depraved father?

As the justice continued to call for order, Michael searched the yammering faces for the one who had sent the dagger flying, but it wasn't until his gaze met Christian Lavonne's that he found who he sought. Once again, the baron had thwarted his father—had known Aldous would not accept defeat and been prepared for this.

Christian turned toward the stairs.

A glance at the Wulfrith brothers showed that they had also searched out their sister's savior, a man who had proven himself though still they might object to their sister wedding him. Would they make good the bargain struck for Sir Hector's witness?

"He is...dead?" Beatrix asked.

Michael looked into her upturned face. "Though the baron but wounded him, he can harm you no more."

"Christian Lavonne? He threw the dagger?"

"Aye." He cupped her face. "It is over, Beatrix."

She stared at him until, finally, confusion gave way to a smile. "Aye, it is." She rose to her toes and kissed him.

Michael reveled in the taste of her, basked in the knowledge that none could part them, and sent up a prayer of thanks for the gift of her love.

"D'Arci!"

Michael eased his hands from Beatrix's waist where he had lifted her into the saddle and turned with her brothers to watch Christian Lavonne cross the outer bailey.

The big man halted before them. "You will remain keeper of Castle Soaring?"

After what had happened at trial, Michael had thought the baron would reconsider. "You wish it so?"

"I do."

"What of your father?"

Emotion flickered across Christian's gaze. "His mind is gone."

Which was the only reason he did not pay the price that his illegitimate son would pay—imprisonment in London for treason, just as the justice had warned would befall any who acted against the verdict. "Still he will conspire against you."

"He may try, but he will fail, for I have determined to release those vassals who remain loyal to him."

"Those you *know* are loyal to him."

"That is true, but I have not been blind these past years and I know well those who serve him."

"What of the men he has set at Soaring and the other castles?"

"They will also be released. Henceforth, I will tolerate no further interference in the administration of this barony."

Michael knew he meant it, but the problem of his father remained. His mind might be gone, but that did not make him any less dangerous. Indeed, it likely made him more so. However, providing Christian was able to root out all of those who might offer aid to Aldous, surely the old man would be unable to work any more ill.

"Your answer, D'Arci?" Christian prompted.

Michael was tempted, especially as it would secure his future with Beatrix by providing a worthy home for her and their children. "You know I cannot remain as your father's physician."

"I do. Should he require anything, I shall send for the healer from the village of Tippet."

He spoke of the widow, Helene, a young woman who not only delivered babes with ease but was proficient with needle and thread and well-versed in the use of medicinal herbs. Michael's only regret was that she would be made to suffer Aldous's company. Of course, given her spirited disposition, she would not likely tolerate the old man's ill treatment.

Michael laid a hand on Beatrix's knee. "What say you?"

A gentle breeze lifting her flaxen hair, she said, "If 'tis your desire, I would return to Castle Soaring with you and become your wife."

"But is it what *you* want?"

"It is."

"It seems a good offer," Wulfrith said, surprising them both.

Michael looked around. "Though I do not seek your approval, Baron Wulfrith, I am glad to have it."

The big man inclined his head. However, Sir Abel offered up little himself. Though one side of his mouth edged upward, his face remained mostly impassive. And over his shoulder stood Sir Durand who had not been there minutes earlier.

Before the knight shuttered his face, Michael caught a glimpse of his longing for the woman he had thought to rescue. Though Michael could not fault the man for his feelings, neither could he suppress a stab of jealousy that another felt for Beatrix. But it was Michael she loved, and that reminder redeemed him.

Michael turned back to his liege. "I shall remain keeper of Castle Soaring."

Christian inclined his head and looked to Baron Wulfrith. The question of the bargain they had struck rose between them.

It was Wulfrith who spoke first. "You are most proficient with a dagger, Baron Lavonne."

Likely a surprise, for Wulfrith would surely have heard of Christian's attempt to master the sword.

With a wry turn of the mouth, Christian said, "Distance often proves my best ally, Baron Wulfrith. It assures that I do not lose sight of my goal as can happen when one draws too near."

"As with a sword."

Christian's jaw hardened. Doubtless, it pinched his pride that Wulfrith knew his sword skill was wanting. Of course, it was not only the sword to which Christian referred. More, perhaps, he referred to the back he had turned on God that he might prove himself worthy of this barony, as well as the ever-increasing distance he placed between his revenge-hungry father and himself.

"What of our agreement, Baron Wulfrith?" Christian asked. "You will honor it?"

"I will."

Though his capitulation surprised Christian, as evidenced by his narrowed lids, he quickly recovered. "Then you will deliver Lady Gaenor to Broehne Castle without further delay."

Guessing it was Sir Durand who drew a sharp breath, Michael did not look around. Doubtless, the knight who had delivered Lady Gaenor free of the king's decree did not approve of the Lavonne and Wulfrith alliance.

And from Wulfrith's lowering brow, he knew it as well. Still, he held Christian's gaze. "Only enough delay to assure my sister has time to become accustomed to the idea of marriage."

"How much will she require?"

This time, Wulfrith did hesitate. "Let us be done with one wedding first"—he glanced from Michael to Beatrix—"then we shall talk."

"Providing we do more than talk, Baron Wulfrith."

"The agreement will be honored." Wulfrith strode to his horse.

"My lord," Michael acknowledged the man who was to remain his liege.

"D'Arci." As Christian started back across the bailey, Michael put his foot in the stirrup and swung up behind Beatrix.

Trying not to worry over Gaenor, telling herself Christian would be a good husband to her sister, Beatrix shifted around and met Michael's gaze.

Such gray eyes he had, and in their depths was something she knew would shine for no other.

"Now we shall make a life together," he said, bending near. "I love you, Beatrix."

"As I love you." She kept her eyes open as his mouth covered hers. And nearly shook her head. How could she have ever believed he resembled Simon? Michael. Only Michael.

Epilogue

Stern Castle, July 1157

"YOU ARE HAPPY."

Reflecting on her wedding day that had made her one with Michael, Beatrix smiled at her sister. "I am very happy."

Though the smile Gaenor returned was small, it seemed genuine. "Then I rejoice with you." She looked out across the hall and sighed. "Married..."

As she herself would soon be, though they did not discuss that.

"Michael seems"—Gaenor shrugged her too-thin shoulders—"a good man."

Searching him out, Beatrix looked across the great hall and instead found her mother engaged in a conversation with Lady Maude. Her heart swelled for the woman who had been so set upon her youngest daughter becoming a bride of Christ, yet who had spoken no word against Beatrix's decision to wed. Though it surely made Lady Isobel ache to not see her dream fulfilled, she accepted it, just as she accepted Michael.

A beloved laugh drew Beatrix's gaze, and she found her new husband amid the din of celebration that surely knew every crack and corner of her brother's home. Beside him was her second brother, Everard, a laugh prying at his curled lips until it bounded forth over something Garr said. Then they were all laughing, including Annyn who cradled her infant son, and the grave Sir Canute who somehow found his host's three-year-old daughter perched on his hip.

Beatrix sighed. "Aye, Michael is a good man." And once the wedding guests were enjoined to take their leave—be it on the morrow or several days hence—they would begin their life together. Husband and wife.

Gaenor laid a hand over Beatrix's. "You are blessed, little sister."

"As you shall be."

Somber silence was followed by Gaenor's attempt at laughter. "You have to say that to me."

"Aye, but it is also true. Christian Lavonne—"

"Did not come." Gaenor shrugged as if it did not matter, but it did. Though it had been expected that, on the occasion of Beatrix and Michael's wedding, she would finally meet the man whom King Henry intended her to wed, the baron had sent word that he was delayed. Unfortunately, he had given no reason for his absence. Thus, as they would not meet until the morrow—or perhaps later—Gaenor's effort to immerse herself in Beatrix's joy had begun to thin.

Thinking it best to speak of something else, Beatrix said, "Tell me of your stay at Wulfen Castle."

As she and Gaenor had always suffered exceeding curiosity over their family's stronghold that was forbidden to women, it seemed the best choice. However, Gaenor merely shrugged again as she had done often since her return from Wulfen four days past. "As I have already told, our brother, Everard, mostly kept me confined to a tower room in the donjon."

Of course it would have been necessary, not only to maintain Wulfen's integrity as a castle dedicated to training boys into men but to suppress word of Gaenor's presence should King Henry grow impatient with the continued delay in carrying out his decree.

"Then you saw no men other than our brother and the knights a-assigned to see to your needs?" Beatrix hoped the stammer she endeavored to keep from her speech, especially in Gaenor's presence, went unnoticed.

Her sister averted her gaze. "From my window, I sometimes watched the young men train."

Beatrix knew her sister well enough to realize she was holding something close to her. With an expectant grin and a raised eyebrow, she teased, "Methinks you are not telling all."

Gaenor considered Beatrix as if weighing the risk of revealing something of great import, then looked to the lavishly laid table before her. "'Tis true, but naught can come of what I do not tell."

"Mayhap I can help."

"You cannot. Regardless of my own wishes, I shall soon wed Baron Lavonne."

It was only a suspicion that settled on Beatrix, but she said, "Is there someone else, Gaenor? Another you would rather wed?"

Her sister startled, then shrugged yet again. "I did meet a knight at Wulfen, but I hardly know him well enough to wish marriage."

One of those whom Everard had chosen to provide for her stay? Though it seemed the most likely answer, Beatrix was surprised that her brother would not choose aged and experienced knights for the task.

"How well *do* you know him?" she asked, though she knew her question might cause Gaenor to once more shrug away a response.

"We...talked. In the chapel. That is where I met him."

"Surely you were not allowed to attend mass with the men?"

"Of course not. I went only after they were done that I might have the chapel to myself."

"Then how——"

"He was there one day when I thought I was alone."

"When he should have been training pages and squires?"

Gaenor shook her head. "He was not one of our brother's men, but a visiting knight."

That explained one thing, but not another, for Wulfen rarely accepted visitors. In fact, those who escorted pages and squires to Wulfen for training did not tarry.

"Truly? How long did he visit?"

Gaenor drew her bottom lip between her teeth. "More than a month, though I did not meet him until a fortnight past."

Though Beatrix sensed she delved too deep, she pressed on. "For what purpose was he at Wulfen?"

"Abel and Everard were training him."

"A knight? A man who has already earned his spurs?"

Though it did not come as a surprise when Gaenor pressed her lips to deny further response, it disappointed, and Beatrix chastised herself for pressing so hard. Whatever else had happened between her sister and the knight, no more would be told this day.

"Of course, you are surely relieved to be returned to Stern Castle," Beatrix tried to salvage the conversation.

Gaenor sipped her wine.

"Wulfen must have been t-t-" Thoughts running too far ahead of her tongue to keep pace, Beatrix clenched her teeth and dragged the elusive word back to her. "It must have been tedious."

This time Gaenor could not help but notice Beatrix's faltering speech, and as with each time she did so, she winced. However, unlike on past occasions, she did not withdraw.

A flush warming her hollow cheeks, nearly attaining the depth of the color of her bliaut, she said with urgency, "Do you forgive me, Beatrix?"

"For what?"

"For the ill words I spoke the day King Henry delivered his decree that a Wulfrith wed a Lavonne. More, for what happened to you—what would not have happened had you and Sir Ewen not drawn the king's men away from me and Sir Durand."

"Gaenor—"

She shook her head, stirring the troubled air around her. "I thought I would die when I saw you in the ravine and realized the sacrifice you had made to save me."

Beatrix gripped her sister's hand. "There is naught to forgive. You were hurting when you said what you did and never would I fault you for it. As for what happened to me, had I to do it again, I would, for it brought me Michael."

Gaenor scrutinized Beatrix's face, and her shoulders began to ease. "God favors you, Beatrix. You must please Him mightily." She smiled softly. "If only I knew Him as you do, perhaps I might better face what lies in wait for me."

Christian Lavonne, who she feared would pounce on her as if she was prey. As much as Beatrix wished to dissuade her sister of what she believed of the baron, it would be futile. However, as Gaenor had thrown wide the door to God who, alone, could provide what she needed, Beatrix grasped the opportunity. "You can know God as I do. You have but to let Him in."

"It is not so simple."

"It is far from simple, but still a-attainable."

Gaenor looked across the hall as if searching someone out.

Beatrix followed her gaze to their mother, then Michael and their brothers whose gathering now included a brooding Sir Durand. As always, Beatrix felt regret for the pain she had caused him in not returning his feelings. She could only hope he would find someone worthier of his affection.

Gaenor sighed. "Attainable even when one has sinned greatly?" she asked so softly it was as if she did not intend to speak it aloud.

Beatrix looked around. Should she let Gaenor's words pass as if unheard? Determining it was another opportunity to assure her sister of God's love, she said, "Whatever you have done, Gaenor, you have but to ask for forgiveness and it will be granted."

A flush crept her sister's face. However, as the musicians once more took up their instruments to play for the wedding guests, Gaenor recovered sufficiently to quip, "And if I ask Him to deliver me free of marriage to Baron Lavonne, will that also be granted?"

"If it is in His will."

With a smile that turned her exceedingly pretty despite its wry turn, Gaenor mused, "Always His will, which means I shall wed

Lavonne—unless the baron determines he does not want me. Which is possible." Gaenor pressed her palms to the table and rose.

Forcing down the questions she wished to ask that her sister was surely unprepared to answer, Beatrix looked up.

With another glance at the gathering of men, Gaenor bent and kissed Beatrix's brow. "God willing, I shall one day see through the eyes of love as you do, little sister."

Beatrix had to believe she would—that the man she had glimpsed in Christian Lavonne would grow to love her sister as she deserved to be loved. "You shall."

Gaenor sighed. "Now I am going to dance at my sister's wedding." She strode the length of the dais and partnered with a household knight who, though not as tall as she, turned her about the floor with ease.

"Will you dance with me, Wife?"

Despite her worries over Gaenor, Beatrix beamed up at her husband. "I will."

He drew her to her feet and gazed into her upturned face. "I like the way you look upon me, Beatrix D'Arci."

"Do you?" Remembering Gaenor's words, she said, "That is because I look upon you through the eyes of love."

"As I look upon you." Michael kissed her.

Sighing into the man who had yielded all for her, Beatrix thanked God that He had willed that she and Michael become one—He who had always known well His plans for her. As He knew well His plans for Gaenor.

Excerpt

THE REDEEMING

Age of Faith: Book Three

Wulfen Castle, England, June 1157

To the death.

Perspiration running into his eyes, the blood of a half dozen wounds seeping through the weave of his tunic, Christian Lavonne reminded himself of what was required to best his opponent.

Think death.

Drawing back his sword, he eyed the vulnerability of the knight's neck that glistened with the efforts of the past half hour.

Feel death.

Lunging forward, he shifted his grip on the hilt.

Breathe death.

Smelling his opponent's bloodlust, he arced the blade toward the exposed flesh that would assure victory.

Embrace death.

Putting from him all he had been taught of mercy and forgiveness, he slashed the blade down. And met steel.

"Surely you can do better!" the knight spat.

Christian growled, swept his blade up off the other man's, and swung again—only to yield up the blood of his forearm.

"Ho!" The knight grinned. "Do I unnerve you, Lavonne? Make your heart beat faster? Blood run colder?"

Christian knew it was anger the other man sought. And he would have it.

Heart pounding as if upon the stoutest door, he swung again. Missed. Again. Missed. Again. And finally set his blade to the knight's lower thigh. However, he was allowed but a moment of satisfaction before his opponent leapt at him.

Christian jumped back from the thirsty blade and came up against the fence. If not for the thrust of his weight that caused the wood to crack, the knight would have had what he sought—blood for blood. Christian plummeted backward and landed hard on the splintered fence rail.

"You are had, Lavonne." His opponent settled the crimson tip of his blade to the great vein in Christian's neck. "Beg for mercy."

Throat raw with exertion, Christian flexed his hand on his sword hilt. "Never, knave!"

Fire leapt in the man's grey-green gaze and the stench of death rose to Christian's nostrils. Blessedly, it retreated on the knight's great sigh. "Well, then"—he turned his blade down, set its tip to the ground, and leaned on the hilt—"at least humor me with a recitation of the lesson that applies to the dire situation in which you find yourself."

Grinding his teeth, Christian rolled to the side and gained his feet. "That would be lesson one."

"One?" With a forearm, the knight brushed back the damp brown hair clinging to his brow. "Pray, enlighten me as to how that applies to your sound defeat."

Christian glared. "I do not refer to *your* lesson, Sir Abel, but mine— one in which I fear you are in true need of instruction."

A suspicious light entered the knight's eyes. "Aye?"

"Address one's better as befits their station."

Sir Abel's gaze narrowed, but just as it seemed the tension might once more see them at swords, he made a sweeping bow. "Most esteemed *Baron* Lavonne, pray honor this lowly knight by reciting the appropriate lesson." He straightened. "I humbly await your good grace."

Insufferable! And only a sharp reminder of the reason he was at Wulfen Castle made it possible for Christian to give the knight what he asked. "Lesson Three, neglect not one's back."

"Correct. Of course, considering you were already dead, 'tis hardly relevant."

"*I* was dead? You were dead first."

Sir Abel snorted. "You flatter yourself, Lavonne——er, *Baron* Lavonne."

Christian looked from the bloodied and rent fabric behind which the knight's heart beat to the torn fabric centered on his bowels. "Were we not merely practicing at swords, Sir Abel, twice I would have done more than score your flesh. Indeed, your very life would be forfeit."

"Had you a sword arm." The knight swung up his blade and pointed at the bloodied tear in Christian's sleeve.

"Which would have been entirely possible with a leg cut out from beneath you." Christian jutted his chin at where the fabric was split above the knight's knee.

And so they might continue until every crimson tear was accounted for, as they had done each day these past three.

Though when they had first faced one another on the training field a month ago and Sir Abel's skill at sword had made Christian's appear sorely inadequate, Christian had improved greatly. Despite the knight's disdain for his pupil, he was an excellent instructor. Given more time, it was possible Christian would attain a level of mastery similar to that enjoyed by his warrior-bred opponent who would soon be his unwilling brother-in-law. And that possibility had to be as surprising to Sir Abel as it was to Christian who had not only been born to the Church but had attained tonsure and habit before gaining an inheritance of which he had only ever dreamed. Unfortunately, the cost of the coveted inheritance had been the death of his older brother, something for which he had yet to forgive himself.

"The lesson is done." Sir Abel thrust his sword into its scabbard and pivoted.

Christian glanced at the sun that had yet to touch the treetops of the distant wood. "Done?"

As if he did not hear the dissension in his pupil's voice, Sir Abel continued toward the walls of Wulfen Castle.

"Methinks 'tis *I* who unnerves *you*, Sir Abel," Christian called.

The knight swung around.

Christian almost smiled. "I who makes your heart beat faster, your blood run colder."

"Flatter yourself if it so pleases, Lavonne," Sir Abel once more dropped Christian's title. "As for me, I remain content in the knowledge that, as long as mastery of the sword eludes you, I am in no danger of forfeiting my life."

"Your blood tells otherwise."

"Ha! Mere scratches."

Why he felt impelled to argue with the insufferable man, Christian did not understand, especially as their mutual animosity had lessened considerably since his arrival at Wulfen. But before he could advance the argument, Sir Abel said, "Do you wish to know the reason you have yet to truly master the sword, Baron?"

With half a dozen strides, he retraced his path across the parched grass and halted before Christian. "Regardless of how angered you become when we meet at swords, regardless of how many times I mark your flesh, you cannot wholly commit to the taking of life."

A retort sprang to Christian's lips, but he did not loose it, for what Sir Abel said was true. Though the knight took every opportunity to remind his pupil what was required to defeat an opponent—to think, feel, breathe, and embrace death—and several times Christian had nearly succeeded in reaching such a place within himself, he could not fully accept that death should be the end result of all clashes between men. As for attaining that place while at practice, that was the most bewildering of all, for how could one truly seek another's death without actually committing the act?

Sir Abel took another step toward him. "The reason you cannot defeat me, Lavonne, is that you do not wish me dead."

Suppressing the urge to repay aggression with aggression, Christian said, "Need I remind you that we are not truly at battle?"

The knight shrugged. "Whether that is so or not, a warrior must believe that all that stands between him and death is the taking of his opponent's life. Even when merely at practice."

Christian stared at the man who stood nearly as tall as he. "If what you say is so, it follows that few squires would attain the rank of knight, for all would lie dead."

"Those who train at Wulfen—"

"—learn to control the moment between life and death. Aye, this you have told many times."

The knight's face, flushed with the exertion of their contest, darkened further. "When you and I are at swords, all I think of is your death."

"And when we are not at swords?"

When Sir Abel finally answered, the anger that had spat words from him was nearly wiped clean. "It is true I am opposed to my sister wedding you, and that your death would resolve the matter, but do I truly wish it? Nay, Baron Lavonne"—titled again—"outside of practice, I do not wish you dead."

Not for the first time amazed at how quickly the knight cooled his emotions, Christian drew a deep breath in an attempt to tamp down his own. "I shall take comfort in that."

Sir Abel started to turn away, but halted. "Heed me well. Though you have much improved since your arrival, when next you face a true enemy—and you shall—you must wish his death. Can you do that?"

Though Christian had taken lives in battle following the attainment of his title, he had never done so with a desire to see an opponent dead.

It was not bloodlust that drove him, but the mere—and potent—need to survive. And survive he had barely done.

"If you cannot, you will make a widow of my sister. Now tell me, can you or can you not do it?"

It was not the first time the knight had issued the challenge, and would not be the first time Christian was unable to assure him.

Sir Abel broke the silence. "Born to the Church you may have been, but it is no longer who you are. Indeed, as evidenced by your refusal to bow your head at prayer or enter the chapel, it is most obvious you have given God your back."

His words jolted, not only because the conclusion drawn was so near the truth, but that Christian's absence from mass and his inability to show proper respect at the blessing of meals had not gone unnoticed— and by this seemingly ungodly man who told that a knight must seek death to prevail.

"Do not make God your reason for not doing what is required of you, Baron Lavonne. If you cannot protect my sister, your people, and your lands, that title for which you demand respect will be lost." He swung away.

Feeling every beaten ridge and furrow of his sword hilt, Christian watched the man disappear around the castle's northern wall.

Deny it though he longed to do, it was good he had trod his pride and accepted the invitation to train at Wulfen Castle. If it was necessary to seek another's death to prevail, he might eventually fail, but with the skills acquired beneath Sir Abel's grudging instruction, there was less chance than before. He *would* protect his people and lands, as well as the woman with whom King Henry had commanded him to speak vows— Gaenor Wulfrith who had fled with her sister nearly five months past to escape marriage to him.

Easing his grip on the sword, Christian scanned the walls of Wulfen Castle that had been the Wulfrith sisters' destination all those months ago. Though it was believed that Lady Gaenor had made it here to her family's stronghold, a castle exclusive to men and dedicated to the training of boys into knights, her younger sister had not. While being pursued by the king's and Christian's men, Beatrix Wulfrith had met with ill. Thus, if not for Christian's physician, a man with a powerful reason to hate her, she would be dead. Instead, a fortnight hence she would wed Michael D'Arci, the man who had saved her life. And at that wedding, Christian would finally meet Gaenor who was told to bear little resemblance to her petite and comely sister.

Christian grimaced. Not that he cared what the woman looked like. Rather, he resented being made to wait so long to meet her. Though he had thought he might encounter her during his training here, it seemed she had been removed to one of the family's other castles. As for talk of her ever having been present here, a woman among so many men, there was none—as if she had never come. And perhaps she had not, though it seemed the surest place to secrete her.

He eyed the men-at-arms visible between the battlements of the stronghold, next the immense donjon that rose at the center of the enclosure. Ominous. No surprise that King Henry had not brought an army against his vassal to sooner bring about the alliance required of the warring Wulfriths and Lavonnes. Indeed, if not for the bargain Christian had struck with the oldest brother, the Wulfriths might yet defy the king's edict. But Christian had delivered what he had promised and, providing the Wulfriths delivered what they promised, soon he would wed.

Resolved to meeting his betrothed at her sister's wedding in July, Christian wiped his blade on the hem of his tunic and returned his sword to its scabbard. Only a fortnight longer, he reminded himself, and the darkness of these past years might begin to recede. Except for that cast by his father, of course—the aged and ailing Aldous Lavonne who vowed he would not seek his grave until the death of his beloved son, Geoffrey, was avenged. Geoffrey, whose passing had made Christian heir to all of Abingdale.

Once more stabbed with guilt, Christian set off toward the castle with a heavy tread intended to grind all thoughts of his brother underfoot. It worked. For a while.

"Accursed cur!"

Everard looked over his shoulder at his younger brother whose arrival on the training field was evident well in advance of his appearance. Noting the numerous rips in his brother's clothing, Everard attempted to suppress the smile begging at his mouth.

Abel ground to a halt. "You think it funny?"

Trying to gain control of the larger smile that sought to crack his face wide, Everard turned back to the squires who had paused in their hand-to-hand combat to await further instruction.

He nodded for them to continue and returned his attention to Abel. "I do think it funny, little brother. Though, in the interest of brotherhood, I would prefer that I not win our wager, it seems I have done so yet again." He tracked his gaze down Abel, tallying the number of times Christian Lavonne had found his mark. "At least a dozen strikes, and your instruction lasted half as long as it should have." He held out a hand. "I have won."

Abel glared at his outstretched palm. "Ill gotten gain," he grumbled, then dug into the purse on his belt and slapped two pieces of silver in his brother's palm.

"'Twas your wager." Everard rubbed the coins together. "I but accepted, and reluctantly, if you recall."

"Reluctant as a groom on his wedding night," Abel scorned.

Though Everard was not one to make free with his emotions, he nearly laughed, for it was true he liked to wager, especially this brother who was determined to best him at every turn. Indeed, any moment now—

"A new wager!" Abel propped his hands on his hips.

"Methinks you ought to sleep off this one ere wagering more coin than you can afford to lose."

Abel gave his purse a shake. Satisfied with the jangle, he said, "On the morrow, Lavonne will land less than a dozen marks."

"A mere dozen when this day he proved capable of such—and in half the time?" Everard shook his head. "A fool's wager to make against a man who is progressing as well as the baron."

Abel considered him, considered him some more, then grudgingly conceded, "Aye, a fool's wager." He blew a breath up his face that caused the dark hair on his brow to lift. "The knave *is* progressing better than expected. If he would but set his mind to the taking of life, he might prove quite dangerous."

Abel and his talk of death. If not that Everard shaved his head, he might drag a handful of hair from his scalp. "You know that Garr does not approve of such means, Abel."

"Godly Garr whose knees are surely worn out from the amount of time spent kneeling at prayer." Abel glanced heavenward. "Not that I do not believe in showing the respect due God. It just seems unproductive to expend so much time conferring with the Lord who is more inclined to listen than respond."

Everard narrowed his lids. "You think?"

"No more than you." Abel looked pointedly at Everard's knees, the material of which was far from worn. "I suppose I should be grateful you do not seem to mind the manner in which I train those given into my charge—at least, the end result."

Though Everard longed to deny it as he knew Garr would have him do, he could not, for there was a fierceness about the squires that Abel trained into knights—one that made it difficult for other squires to best them. But Everard would never admit it.

Knowing it was best to leave the subject be, he returned to the matter of the man whom the king was determined to make their brother-in-law. "What word would you have me send to Garr?" he asked for the dozenth time since Lavonne's acceptance of the invitation to better his sword skill—a self-serving invitation to allow the Wulfriths to more closely observe the baron and determine whether or not to defy the king's order to hand over Gaenor.

"Send word that, with much loathing, I concur that Christian Lavonne does not appear to be the same as his father or brother."

It was as Everard had concluded from his own observations this past month. "You are surprised?"

Abel shrugged. "As you know, I *was* present when Baron Lavonne came to Beatrix's aid."

Mention of the attempt on the life of their youngest sister caused Everard's insides to coil. Though it was true he had not been present, charged as he was with overseeing the training at Wulfen Castle since Garr had wed four years past, he knew all that had transpired.

The worst of it was that Christian Lavonne's illegitimate brother, Sir Robert, had done their father's bidding to work revenge on a Wulfrith. If not for the dagger Christian had thrown, Beatrix would lie dead. Instead, it was Sir Robert who had fallen. But just as Christian could not seek death now, neither could he then. Thus, the wounded Sir Robert languished in a London prison and would likely remain there until the end of his days.

The only pity of it was that Christian's father, Aldous Lavonne, was too infirm to suffer the same punishment. For that, Everard and his family feared for Gaenor. The old man might be laid abed, but when their sister went to live at Broehne Castle as Christian's wife, Aldous would surely take every opportunity to work ill on her. Meaning something would have to be done about the old man. Given a say in the matter, Everard would have him removed to one of the barony's sister castles.

"It seems Gaenor is to wed," Abel spoke across his brother's thoughts.

Everard slid a hand over his shaved pate. "At least her groom is better able to defend himself at swords."

"Well enough, I suppose. Of course, if there was some way to make him forget all that was poured into that monk's head of his, he might do better than merely defend himself."

Everard clapped a hand on his brother's shoulder. "Then it is good, little brother, that you have a fortnight in which to remedy what ails your pupil." Providing Lavonne remained at Wulfen Castle until the journey to Stern Castle to meet Gaenor at Beatrix's wedding.

Abel responded as expected. Lids narrowing, teeth baring, he said, "A month I have given him that should have been used for the betterment of my squires. I am done. If Lavonne requires further training, it falls to you."

Though Abel surely expected an argument—indeed, was looking for one—Everard had already decided to relieve his brother of the task. "As you would have it." He strode toward the squires whose hand-to-hand combat had progressed to the far side of the enclosure, and his brother's surprised silence followed him.

"Everard!" Abel shouted.

Everard looked around.

"You"—Abel jabbed a finger in his direction—"are worse than Garr."

"Aye. Anything else?"

Abel pivoted, causing a cloud of dust to rise in his wake.

Everard glanced at the donjon visible above the castle walls. Wondering if today's contest between Abel and Baron Lavonne had boasted an audience beyond those who patrolled the castle walls, he returned to his squires.

About The Author

TAMARA LEIGH HOLDS a Master's Degree in Speech and Language Pathology. In 1993, she signed a 4-book contract with Bantam Books. Her first medieval romance, *Warrior Bride*, was released in 1994. Continuing to write for the general market, three more novels were published with HarperCollins and Dorchester and earned awards and spots on national bestseller lists.

In 2006, Tamara's first inspirational contemporary romance, *Stealing Adda*, was released. In 2008, *Perfecting Kate* was optioned for a movie and *Splitting Harriet* won an ACFW "Book of the Year" award. The following year, *Faking Grace* was nominated for a RITA award. In 2011, Tamara wrapped up her "Southern Discomfort" series with the release of *Restless in Carolina*.

When not in the middle of being a wife, mother, and cookbook fiend, Tamara buries her nose in a good book—and her writer's pen in ink. In 2012, she returned to the historical romance genre with *Dreamspell*, a medieval time travel romance. Shortly thereafter, she once more invited readers to join her in the middle ages with the *Age of Faith* series: *The Unveiling, The Yielding, The Redeeming, The Kindling,* and *The Longing.* Tamara's #1 Bestsellers—*Lady at Arms, Lady Of Eve, Lady Of Fire,* and *Lady Of Conquest*—are the first of her medieval romances to be rewritten as "clean reads." Look for *Baron Of Blackwood,* the third book in *The Feud* series, in 2016.

Tamara lives near Nashville with her husband, sons, a Doberman that bares its teeth not only to threaten the UPS man but to smile, and a feisty Morkie that keeps her company during long writing stints.

Connect with Tamara at her website www.tamaraleigh.com, her blog The Kitchen Novelist, her email tamaraleightenn@gmail.com, Facebook, and Twitter.

For new releases and special promotions, subscribe to Tamara Leigh's mailing list: www.tamaraleigh.com

Made in the USA
Columbia, SC
01 December 2017